GLAMOROUS POWERS

GLAMOROUS
POWERS

Susan Howatch

ALFRED A. KNOPF

NEW YORK 1 9 8 8

THIS IS A BORZOI BOOK
PUBLISHED BY ALFRED A. KNOPF, INC.

Library of Congress Cataloging-in-Publication Data
Howatch, Susan.
    Glamorous powers.
    Sequel to: Glittering images.
    I. Title.
PS3558.0884G47   1988   813'.54   88-45347
ISBN 0-394-57145-2

Manufactured in the United States of America
First American Edition

Contents

PART ONE

THE
VISION

"*Ecstasy or vision begins when thought ceases, to our consciousness, to proceed from ourselves. It differs from dreaming, because the subject is awake. It differs from hallucination, because there is no organic disturbance: it is, or claims to be, a temporary enhancement, not a partial disintegration, of the mental faculties. Lastly, it differs from poetical inspiration, because the imagination is passive. That perfectly sane people often experience such visions there is no manner of doubt.*"

W. R. INGE
Dean of St. Paul's Cathedral, London, 1911–1934
CHRISTIAN MYSTICISM

I

"The apparent suddenness of the mystical revelation is quite normal; Plato in his undoubtedly genuine Seventh Letter speaks of the 'leaping spark' by which divine inspiration flashes on him."

W. R. INGE
MYSTICISM IN RELIGION

I

THE vision began at a quarter to six; around me the room was suffused with light, not the pellucid light of a fine midsummer morning but the dim light of a wet dawn in May. I was sitting on the edge of my bed when without warning the gold lettering on the cover of the Bible began to glow.

I stood up as the bedside table deepened in hue, and the next moment the floorboards pulsed with light while in the corner the taps of the basin coruscated like silver in the sun. Backing around the edge of the bed I pressed my back against the wall before any further alteration of consciousness occurred. Firm contact with a solid object lessens the instinctive fear which must always accompany such a radical transcendence of time and space.

However after the initial fear comes the equally instinctive acceptance. I had closed my eyes to lessen the terror of disorientation but now I forced myself to open them. The cell was still glittering, but as I watched the glitter faded to a shimmer until the scene resembled a view seen through the wrong end of a telescope, and I could perceive my body, remote and abandoned, pressed against the wall by the bed as if impaled there by invisible nails. I looked aside—I could see my body turning its head—and immediately the darkness, moving from right to left, began to erase the telescopic view. My eyes closed, again warding off the fear of disorientation, and this time when I reopened them I found I was once more moving in a normal world.

I was myself, inhabiting my body as usual and walking along a path through a wood of beech trees. Insofar as I was conscious of any emotion I was aware of being at ease with my verdant, tranquil surroundings, although I felt irritated by the persistent call of a wood-pigeon. Eventually the pigeon fell silent and as the path began to slope downhill, I glanced to my left at the chapel in the dell below.

The chapel was small but exquisite in its classical symmetry; I was reminded of the work of Inigo Jones. In the dull green light of the surrounding woods the yellow stone glowed a dark gold, a voluptuous contrast to the grey medieval ruins which lay behind it. The ruins were in part hidden by ivy, but as I moved closer I could see the slits in the wall of the tower.

Reaching the floor of the dell I faced the chapel, now only fifty yards away across the sward, and it was then that I noticed the suitcase. Standing at the edge of the trees it was sprinkled with labels, the largest being a triangle of red, blue and black design; I was too far away to read the lettering. Afterwards I remembered that I had regarded this suitcase without either curiosity or surprise. Certainly I never slackened my pace as I headed for the chapel, and I believe I knew even then that the suitcase was a mere image on the retina of my mind, a symbol which at that point I had no interest in interpreting.

Hurrying up the steps of the porch I lifted the latch, pushed the right-hand half of the double-doors wide open and paused to survey the interior beyond.

There was no transept. A central aisle stretched to the altar at the east end. The altar-table was stark in its austerity, the only adornment consisting of a plain wooden cross, but again I felt neither surprise nor curiosity. Evidently I was as accustomed to this sight as I was accustomed to the fact that the nave was only three-quarters full of pews. Walking across the empty space which separated the doors from the back pew, I could smell the lilies which were blooming in a vase beneath the brass memorial plaque on my right. I gave them no more than a brief glance but when I looked back at the altar I saw that the light had changed.

The sun was penetrating the window which was set high in the wall to the left of the altar, and as the ray began to slant densely upon the cross I stopped dead. Unless I stood south of the Equator I was witnessing the impossible, for the sun could never shine from the north. I stared at the light until my eyes began to burn. Then sinking to my knees I covered my face with my hands, and as the vision at last dissolved, the knowledge was branded upon my mind that I had to abandon the work which suited me so well and begin my life anew in the world I had no wish to rejoin.

OPENING my eyes I found myself back in my cell. I was no longer pressing against the wall but kneeling by the bed. Sweat prickled my forehead. My hands were trembling. There were also other physical manifestations which I prefer not to describe. Indeed I felt quite unfit to begin my daily work but so profound was my state of shock that I automatically embarked on my morning routine, and minutes later I was leaving my cell.

Perhaps I have erred in starting this narrative with an account of my vision. Perhaps I should instead have offered some essential biographical details, for the repeated mention of the word "cell" has almost certainly conveyed the impression that I am an inmate of one of His Majesty's prisons. Let me now correct this mistake. For the past seventeen years I have been a member of the Anglican brotherhood of monks known as the Fordite Order of St. Benedict and St. Bernard. I may still be judged eccentric, anti-social and possibly (after this account of my vision) deranged. But I am not a criminal.

In order that such an abnormal experience can be put in its proper context and judged fairly, I must attempt a thumbnail sketch of my past so let me state at once that in many ways my life has been exceedingly normal. I was brought up in a quiet, respectable home, educated at various appropriate establishments and ordained as a clergyman of the Church of England not long after my twenty-third birthday. I then married a young woman who possessed what in my young day was described as "allure" and which a later generation, debased by the War—the First War, as I suppose we must now call it—described as "It." For some years after my marriage I worked as a chaplain to the Naval base at Starmouth, and later I volunteered for duty at sea with the result that much of my ministry was spent away from home. In fact I was absent when my wife died in 1912. For another seven years I continued my career in the Navy, but I judge it unnecessary to recount my war experiences. Suffice it to say that after the Battle of Jutland I never felt quite the same about the sea again.

Accordingly in 1919 I left the Navy and became the chaplain at Starmouth Prison. The advantage of this change was that I was able to see more of my children, now adolescent, but the disadvantage was that I became aligned with an authority empowered to administer capital and corporal punishment, two practices which are entirely contrary to my conception of the Christian way to treat human beings. However I endured this harrowing ministry as best as I could until finally in 1923 the hour of my liberation dawned: with both my children launched on their adult lives I was able to retire to the Cambridgeshire village of Grantchester, where the Fordites had a house, and embark on my career as a monk. I had known the Abbot, James Reid, since my undergraduate days at the University two miles away, and although I had lost touch with him some years earlier it never occurred to me not to seek his help when I was at last free to join the Order.

I shall gloss over the disastrous beginning of my new life and simply state that after three months at Grantchester I was transferred to the Fordites' farm at Ruydale, a remote corner of the North Yorkshire moors where the monks lived more in the austere style of Cistercians than Benedictines. Here I embarked on a successful cenobitic career which reached its apex in 1937 when I was transferred back to Grantchester to succeed James Reid as Abbot.

This brief autobiographical recital—remarkable more for what I have omitted than for what I have deigned to reveal—is all I intend to disclose at present about my past. No further disclosures are needed, I think, to show that my ministry has always demanded a strong constitution, absolute sanity and considerable reserves of spiritual strength. In short, although I write as a monk who has visions, I am neither a hysteric nor a schizophrenic. I am a normal man with abnormal aspects—and having abnormal aspects, as Abbot James had assured me when I was a troubled young ordinand, was what being normal was all about.

"But beware of those glamorous powers, Jon!" he had urged after we had discussed my gifts as a psychic. "Beware of those powers which come from God but which can so easily be purloined by the Devil!" This had proved a prophetic warning. For the next twenty years, while I remained in the world, my life was one long struggle to achieve the correct balance between the psychic and the spiritual so that I could develop properly as a priest, but it was a struggle I failed to win. There was little development. I did become a competent priest in the limited sense that the world judged my ministry to be effective, but my spiritual progress suffered from inadequate guidance and an undisciplined psyche. As Father Darcy told me later, I was like a brilliant child who had learnt the alphabet but had never been trained to read and write. However this situation changed when I became a monk, and it changed because for the first time I found the man who had the spiritual range and the sheer brute force of personality required to train me.

I have reached the subject of Father Darcy. Father Darcy is relevant to my vision because he made me the man I am today. I must describe him, but how does one describe a brilliant Christian monster? Father Darcy was unlike any other monk I have ever met. No doubt he was also unlike any monk St. Benedict and St. Bernard ever envisioned. Both intensely worldly and intensely spiritual (a rare and often bizarre combination), this modern cenobitic dictator was not only devout, gifted and wise but brutal, ruthless and power-mad.

As soon as he became the Abbot-General in 1910 he embarked on the task of waking up each of the four houses which had been slumbering on their comfortable endowments for decades. Having dusted down each monk, he reorganised the finances and courted not only both Archbishops but the entire episcopal bench of the House of Lords in an effort to increase the Order's worldly importance. As a private organisation it was not directly connected to the Church of England, even though since its birth in the 1840s it had received the somewhat condescending blessings of successive Archbishops of Canterbury, but Father Darcy's diplomatic ventures ensured that he and his abbots were treated with a new respect by the ecclesiastical hierarchy. Meanwhile the spiritual tone of the Order had been markedly raised, and by the time I became a monk in 1923 the Fordites were well known for the guidance and counselling given to those who sought their help. The restored tradition of Benedictine scholarship was also being noticed with approval.

It will be obvious from this description that Father Darcy had the charism of leadership, but in fact he possessed all the major charisms and these gifts from God were buttressed and enhanced by a perfectly trained, immaculately disciplined psychic power which he had dedicated entirely to God's service. He was a formidable priest, a formidable monk, a formidable man. But he was not likable. However Father Darcy cared nothing for being liked. He would have considered such a desire petty and self-centered, indicative of a disturbed psyche which required a spiritual spring-cleaning. Father Darcy cared only about being respected by those outside the Order and obeyed by those within; such respect and obedience were necessary so that he might work more efficiently for God, and Father Darcy, like all successful dictators, put a high value on efficiency.

My habit of calling him Father Darcy is new. Only people outside the Order call us monks by our surnames preceded by the title "Father," if the monk be a priest, or "Brother," if the monk be a layman. For the last thirty years Father Darcy had been addressed by his monks as "Father Abbot-General," but after his death a month ago it had become necessary to adopt another designation in order to distinguish him from his successor, and to me "Father Cuthbert" had merely conjured up a picture of a cosy old confessor unable to say boo to a goose. In accordance with the constitution of the Order, which decreed that all monks were equal in death, he had been referred to throughout the burial service as "Cuthbert," but whenever this word had been uttered something akin to a shudder of horror had rippled through the congregation as if Father Darcy were still alive to be enraged by the familiarity.

All the abbots attended the funeral. Cyril came from Starwater Abbey, where the Fordites ran a public school; Aidan, my former superior, came from Ruydale, and I came from Grantchester. Francis Ingram, Father Darcy's right-hand man, organised the funeral and offered us all a lavish hospitality at the Order's London headquarters, but he did not conduct the service. That task fell to Aidan as the senior surviving Abbot.

"It's hard to believe the old boy's gone," said Francis Ingram after-wards, as he helped himself to a very large glass of port from the decanter which was normally reserved for visiting bishops. "What a wonderful capacity he had for making us all shit bricks! It's going to be uncommonly dull without him."

Monks are, of course, supposed to refrain from using coarse language but sometimes the effort of keeping one's speech free of casual blasphemy is so intense that a lapse into vulgarity is seen as the only alternative to committing a sin. It is a notorious fact of monastic life that without the softening influence of women, men tend to sink into coarse speech and even coarser humour; when I returned to Grantchester in 1937 as Abbot, I found a community so lax that their conversation during the weekly recreation hour recalled not the cloister but the barracks of the Naval ratings at Starmouth.

My promotion in 1937 was unorthodox, not only because monks who follow the Benedictine Rule are supposed to remain in the same commu-nity for life but because the monks themselves normally elect an abbot from among their own number. However Father Darcy had decided I could be of more use to the Order at Grantchester than at Ruydale, and Father Darcy had no hesitation in riding rough-shod over tradition when the welfare of the Order was at stake.

"Many congratulations!" said Francis Ingram when I arrived at the London headquarters to be briefed for my new post. "I couldn't be more pleased!" Of course we both knew he was furious that I was to be an abbot while he remained a mere prior, but we both knew too that we had no choice but to go through the motions of displaying brotherly love. Monks are indeed supposed to regard all men with brotherly love, but since most monks are sinners not saints, such exemplary Christian charity tends to resemble Utopia, a dream much admired but perpetually unat-tainable.

It was not until the April of 1940 when Father Darcy died that Francis and I saw our meticulously manifested brotherly love exposed as the fraud which it was. I have no intention of describing Father Darcy's unedifying last hours in detail; such a description would be better confined to the pages—preferably the uncut pages—of a garish Victorian novel. Suffice it to say that for two days he knew he was dying and resolved to enjoy what little life remained to him by keeping us all on tenterhooks about the succession.

It is laid down in the constitution of the Order that although abbots are in normal circumstances to be elected, the Abbot-General must choose his own successor. The reasoning which lies behind this most undemocratic rule is that only the Abbot-General is in a position to judge which man might follow most ably in his footsteps, and the correct procedure is that his written choice should be committed to a sealed envelope which is only to be opened after his death. This move has the advantage of circumventing any last-minute dubious oral declarations and also, supposedly, removing from a dying Abbot-General any obligation to deal with worldly matters when his thoughts ought to be directed elsewhere. However Father Darcy could not bear to think he would be unable to witness our expressions when the appointment was announced, and eventually he succumbed to the temptation to embark on an illicit dénouement.

There were four of us present at his bedside, the three abbots and Francis Ingram.

"Of course you're all wondering how I've chosen my successor," said the old tyrant, revelling in his power, "so I'll tell you: I've done it by process of elimination. You're a good man, Aidan, but after so many years in a Yorkshire backwater you'd never survive in London. And you're a good man too, Cyril—no one could run that school better than you—but the Order's not a school and besides, like Aidan, you're too old, too set in your ways."

He paused to enjoy the emotions of his audience. Aidan was looking relieved; he would indeed have hated to leave Ruydale. Cyril was inscrutable, but I was aware of his aura of desolation and I knew Father Darcy would be aware of it too. Meanwhile Francis was so white with tension that his face had assumed a greenish cast. That pleased Father Darcy. Aidan had been a disappointment, Cyril had been a pleasure and Francis had been a delight. That left me. Father Darcy looked at me and I looked at him and our minds locked. I tried to blot out his psychic invasion by silently reciting the Lord's Prayer but when I broke down halfway through, he smiled. He was a terrible old man but he did so enjoy being alive, and in the knowledge that his enjoyment could only be fleeting I resolved to be charitable; I smiled back.

Immediately he was furious. I was supposed to be writhing on the rack with Francis, not radiating charity, and as I sensed his anger I realised that in his extreme physical sickness his psychic control was slipping and his spiritual strength was severely impaired.

He said to me: "And now, I suppose, you've no doubt whatsoever that you'll step into my shoes! Proud, arrogant Jonathan—too proud to admit his burning curiosity about the succession and too arrogant to believe I could ever seriously consider another candidate for the post! But I did consider it. I considered Francis very seriously indeed." He sighed, his rheumy old eyes glittering with ecstasy as he recalled the next step in his process of elimination. "How hard it was to choose between the two of you!" he whispered. "Francis has the first-class brain and the skill of the born administrator, but Jonathan has . . . well, we all know what Jonathan has, don't we? Jonathan has the powers—those 'glamorous powers,' as poor old James used to call them—and they made Jonathan the most exciting novice I ever encountered, so gifted yet so undisciplined. Yes, you have all those gifts which Francis lacks, Jonathan, but it's those gifts which make you vulnerable as you continue to wage your lifelong battle against your pride and your arrogance. Francis may be less gifted but that makes him less vulnerable, and besides," he added to Cyril and Aidan, "Francis has the breeding. Jonathan's just the product of a schoolmaster's mésalliance with a parlour-maid. He'd serve cheap port and young claret to all the important visitors, and that wouldn't do, wouldn't do at all—we must maintain the right style here, we're a great Order, the greatest Order in the Church of England, and the Abbot-General must live in the manner of the Archbishop of Canterbury at Lambeth. So all things considered," said the old despot, battling on towards the climax of his dénouement, "and following the process of elimination to its inevitable conclusion, I really think that the next Abbot-General should be a man who can distinguish vintage claret from a French peasant's *vin ordinaire*."

He had lived long enough to see the expressions on our faces. Sinking blissfully into a coma he drifted on towards death until an hour later, to my rage and horror, the Abbot-General of the Fordite monks became none other than my enemy Francis Ingram.

It would have been hard to imagine a superior less capable of dealing with my vision.

3

MY antipathy to Francis was undoubtedly the main reason why I did not confide in him as soon as I had received my vision, but possibly I would have been almost as hesitant to confide in Cyril or Aidan. For twenty-four hours after the vision I was in shock. I believed I had received a call from God to leave the Order, and this belief at first triggered a purely emotional response: I felt an elated gratitude that God should have revealed His will to me in such a miraculous manner, and as I offered up my thanks with as much humility as I could muster, I could only pray that I would be granted the grace to respond wholeheartedly to my new call.

However eventually this earthquake of emotion subsided and my intellect awoke. Reason tried to walk hand in hand with revelation and the result was disturbing. My first cold clear thought was that the vision was connected with my failure to become Abbot-General; it could be argued that since the Order, personified by Father Darcy, had rejected me I was now rejecting the Order, a rejection which, because it had been suppressed by my conscious mind, had manifested itself in a psychic disturbance.

This most unsavoury possibility suggested that I might have fallen into a state of spiritual debility, and as soon as I started to worry about my spiritual health I remembered that I was due to make my weekly confession on the morrow.

My confessor was Timothy, the oldest monk in the house, a devout man of eighty-two who possessed an innocent happiness which made him much loved in the community. After my installation as Abbot I had picked him to be my confessor not merely because he was the senior monk but because I knew he would never demand to know more than I was prepared to reveal. This statement may sound distressingly cynical, but I had been brought to Grantchester to bring a lax community to order, and since in the circumstances it would have been inadvisable for me to display weakness to anyone, even the holiest of confessors, I had decided that the temptation to set down in the confessional the burden of my isolation should be resisted.

As I now contemplated my duty to set down the burden represented by my vision, I knew that the most sensible solution was to circumvent Timothy by journeying to London to lay the problem before my superior. But still I balked at facing Francis. Could I make confession without mentioning the vision? Possibly. It was the easiest solution. But easy solutions so often came from the Devil. I decided to pray for guidance but as soon as I sank to my knees I remembered my mentor and knew what I should do. Father Darcy would have warned me against spiritual arrogance, and with profound reluctance I resigned myself to being at least partially frank with my confessor.

"... AND this powerful light shone through the north window. As the light increased in brilliance I knelt down, covering my face with my hands, and at that moment I knew—" I broke off.

Timothy waited, creased old face enrapt, faded eyes moist with excitement.

"—I knew the vision was ending," I said abruptly. "Opening my eyes I found myself back in my cell."

Timothy looked disappointed but he said in a hushed voice, much as a layman might have murmured after some peculiarly rewarding visit to the cinema: "That was beautiful, Father. Beautiful."

Mastering my guilt that I had failed to be honest with him, I forced myself to say: "It's hard to venture an opinion, I know, but I was wondering if there could be some connection between the vision and the death of Father Abbot-General last month."

Since he knew nothing of Father Darcy's deathbed drama I fully expected a nonplussed reaction, but to my surprise Timothy behaved as if I had shown a brilliant intuitive insight. "That hadn't occurred to me, Father," he confessed, "but yes, that makes perfect sense. Father Abbot-General—Father Cuthbert, as I suppose we must now call him—was so good to you always, taking such a special interest in your spiritual welfare, and therefore it's only natural that you should have been severely affected by his death. But now God's sent you this vision to help you overcome your bereavement and continue with renewed faith along your spiritual way."

"Ah." I was still wondering how I could best extricate myself from this morass of deception when Timothy again surprised me, this time by embarking on an interpretation which was both intriguing and complex.

"The chapel was a symbol, Father," he said. "It represents your life in the Order, while the mysterious bag beneath the trees represents your past life in the world, packed up and left behind. And your journey through the chapel was an allegory. You opened the door; that represents your admittance to the Order as a postulant. You crossed the bleak empty space where there were no pews; that signifies those difficult early months when you began your monastic life here in Grantchester." Timothy, of course, could remember me clearly as a troubled postulant; one of the most difficult aspects of my return to Grantchester had been that there were other monks less charitable than Timothy who took a dim view of being ruled by a man whom they could remember only as a cenobitic disaster.

"But you crossed the empty space," Timothy was saying tranquilly, "and you reached the pews; they represent our house in Yorkshire where you found contentment at last, and the lilies placed beneath the memorial tablet symbolise the flowering of your vocation. Your walk down the central aisle must represent your progress as you rose to become Master of Novices, and the bright light at the end must symbolise the bolt from the blue—your call to be the Abbot here at Grantchester. But of course the light was also the light of God, sanctifying your vision, blessing your present work and reassuring you that even without Father Cuthbert's guidance you'll be granted the grace to serve God devoutly in the future." And Timothy crossed himself with reverence.

It was a plausible theory. The only trouble was I had no doubt it was quite wrong.

5

HAVING revealed my most urgent problem in this disgracefully inadequate fashion, I then embarked on the task of confessing my sins. "Number one: anger," I said briskly. My confessions to Timothy often tended to resemble a list dictated by a businessman to his secretary. "I was too severe with Augustine when he fell asleep in choir again, and I was also too severe with Denys for raiding the larder after the night office. I should have been more patient, more forgiving."

"It's very difficult for an abbot when he doesn't receive the proper support from all members of his community," said Timothy. He was such a good, kind old man, not only in sympathising with me but in refraining to add that our community had more than its fair share of drones like Augustine and Denys. My predecessor Abbot James had suffered from a chronic inability to say no, with the result that he had admitted to the Order men who should never have become professed. The majority of these had departed when they discovered that the monastic life was far from being the sinecure of their dreams, but a hard core had lingered on to become increasingly useless, and it was this hard core which was currently, in my disturbed state, driving me to distraction.

Having mentally ticked "anger" off my list, I confessed to the sin of sloth. "I find my work a great effort at the moment," I said, "and I'm often tempted to remain in my cell—not to pray but to be idle."

"Your life's very difficult at present," said Timothy, gentleness unremitting. "You have to deal with the young men who knock on our door in the hope that they can evade military service by becoming monks, and then—worse still—you have to deal with our promising young monks who feel called to return to the world to fight."

"I admit I was upset to lose Barnabas, but I must accept the loss, mustn't I? If a monk wishes to leave the Order," I said, "and if his superior decides the wish is in response to a genuine call, that superior has no right either to stop him or to feel depressed afterwards."

"True, Father, but what a strain the superior has to endure! It's not surprising that you should be feeling a little dejected and weary at present, particularly in view of Father Cuthbert's recent death, and in consequence you must now be careful not to drive yourself too hard. You have a religious duty to conserve your energy, Father. Otherwise if you continue to exhaust yourself you may make some unwise decisions."

I recognised the presence of the Spirit. I was being told my vision needed further meditation and that I was on no account to make a hasty move. Feeling greatly relieved, I crossed "sloth" off my list and rattled off a number of minor sins before declaring my confession to be complete; but unfortunately this declaration represented yet another evasion, for the two most disturbing errors of the past week had been omitted from my list. The first error consisted of my uncharitable behaviour during a disastrous quarrel with my son Martin, and the second error consisted of my unmentionable response to the unwelcome attentions of a certain Mrs. Ashworth.

6

AFTER making this far from satisfactory confession to Timothy, I retired to the chapel to complete my confession before God. Later as I knelt praying I became aware of Martin's unhappiness, a darkness soaked in pain, and as I realised he was thinking of me I withdrew to my cell to write to him.

"My dear Martin," I began after a prolonged hesitation,

I trust that by now you've received the letter which I wrote immediately after our quarrel last Thursday. Now that four days have elapsed I can see what a muddled inadequate letter it was, full of what *I* wanted (your forgiveness for my lack of compassion) and not enough about your own needs which are so much more important than mine. Let me repeat how ashamed I am that I responded so poorly to the compliment you paid me when you took me into your confidence, and let me now beg you to reply to this letter even if this means you must tell me how angry and hurt you were by my lack of understanding. I know you wouldn't want me to "talk religion" to you, but of course you're very much in my thoughts at present and I pray daily that we may soon be reconciled. I remain as always your devoted father, J.D.

Having delivered myself of this attempt to demonstrate my repentance, I was for some hours diverted from my private thoughts by community matters, but late that night I again sat down at the table in my cell and embarked on the difficult task of writing to Mrs. Ashworth.

"My dear Lyle," I began after three false starts. I had been accustomed to address her by her first name ever since I had once counselled her in an emergency, but now I found the informality grated on me.

Thank you so much for bringing the cake last Thursday afternoon. In these days of increasing shortages it was very well received in the refectory.

Now a word about your worries. Is it possible, do you think, that your present melancholy is associated in some way with Michael's birth? I seem to remember that you suffered a similar lowering of the spirits after Charley was born in 1938, and indeed I believe such post-natal difficulties are not uncommon. Do go to your doctor and ask if there's anything he can do to improve your physical health. The mind and the body are so closely linked that any physical impairment, however small, can have a draining effect on one's psyche.

I'm afraid it's useless to ask me to heal you, as if I were a magician who could wave a magic wand and achieve a miracle. The charism of healing is one which for various reasons I avoid exercising except occasionally during my work as a spiritual counsellor, and as you know, I never counsel women except in emergencies. This is not because I wish to be uncharitable but because a difference in sex raises certain difficulties, as any modern psychiatrist will tell you, and these difficulties often create more problems than they solve. May I urge you again to consult Dame Veronica at the convent in Dunton? I know your aversion to nuns, but let me repeat that Dame Veronica is the best kind of counsellor, mature, sympathetic, intuitive and wise, and I'm sure she would listen with understanding to your problems.

Meanwhile please never doubt that I shall be praying regularly for you, for Charles and for the children in the hope that God will bless you and keep you safe in these difficult times which at present engulf us all.

Having thus extricated myself (or so I hoped) from Mrs. Ashworth's far from welcome attentions, I then wasted several minutes trying to decide how I should sign the letter. The Fordites, though following a Benedictine way of life, are Anglo-Catholics anxious to draw a firm line between themselves and their Roman brethren, so the use of the traditional title "Dom" is not encouraged. Usually I avoided any pretentious signature involving the word "Abbot" and a string of initials that represented the name of the Order, but sometimes it was politic to be formal and I had a strong inclination to be formal now. However the danger of a formal signature was that Lyle Ashworth might consider it as evidence that I was rejecting her, and I was most anxious that in her disturbed state I should do nothing which might upset her further. An informal signature, on the other hand, might well be even more dangerous; if I had been writing to her husband I would have signed myself JON DARROW without a second thought, but I could not help feeling that a woman like Lyle might find an abbreviated Christian name delectably intimate.

I continued to hesitate as I reflected on my name. Before entering the Order I had chosen to be Jon, but abbreviated names were not permitted to novices so I found I had become Jonathan. Yet so strong was my antipathy to this name that later, as I approached my final vows, I had requested permission to assume the name John—the cenobitic tradition of choosing a new name to mark the beginning of a new life was popular though not compulsory among the Fordites—and I had been greatly disappointed when this request was refused. I suspected Father Darcy had decided that any pampering, no matter how mild, would have been bad for me. It was not until some years later when I became Ruydale's Master of Novices that I was able to take advantage of the fact that shortened names were not forbidden in private among the officers, and a select group of my friends was then invited to use the abbreviation.

As time went on I also dropped the name Jonathan when introducing myself to those outside the Order who sought my spiritual direction, and now I had reached the point where I considered the name part of a formal "persona," like the title "Abbot," which had been grafted onto my true identity as a priest. I thought of Lyle Ashworth again, and the more I thought of her the more convinced I became that this was a case where Jon the priest should disappear behind Jonathan the Abbot, even though I had no wish to upset her by appearing too formal. I sighed. Then shifting uneasily in my chair I at last terminated this most troublesome epistolary exercise by omitting the trappings of my title but nevertheless signing myself austerely JONATHAN DARROW.

7

NEITHER Lyle nor Martin replied to my letters, but when Dame Veronica wrote to say that Lyle had visited her I realised with relief that my counsel had not been ineffective. However I continued to hear nothing from Martin and soon my anguish, blunting my psyche, was casting a stifling hand over my life of prayer.

By this time I had exhaustively analysed my vision and reached an impasse. I still believed I had received a communication from God but

I knew that any superior would have been justifiably sceptical while Francis Ingram would have been downright contemptuous. It is the policy of the religious orders of both the Roman and the Anglican Churches to treat any so-called vision from God as a delusion until proved otherwise, and although I was a genuine psychic, this fact was now a disadvantage. A "normal" man who had a vision out of the blue would have been more convincing to the authorities than a psychic who might be subconsciously manipulating his gift to reflect the hidden desires of his own ego.

I wrote yet again to Martin and this time, when he failed to reply, I felt so bitter that I knew I had to have help. I could no longer disguise from myself the fact that I was in an emotional and spiritual muddle and suddenly I longed for Aidan, the Abbot of Ruydale, who had looked after me with such wily spiritual dexterity in the past. As soon as I recognised this longing, I knew I had to see him face to face; I was beyond mere epistolary counselling, but no Fordite monk, not even an abbot, can leave his cloister without the permission of his superior, and that brought me face to face again with Francis Ingram.

Pulling myself together I fixed my mind on how comforting it would be to confide in Aidan, and embarked on the letter I could no longer avoid.

"My dear Father," I wrote, and paused. I was thinking how peculiarly repellant it was to be obliged to address an exact contemporary as "Father" and how absolutely repellent it was to be obliged to address Francis as a superior. However such thoughts were unprofitable. Remembering Aidan again, I made a new effort to concentrate. "Forgive me for troubling you," I continued rapidly, "but I wonder if you'd be kind enough to grant me leave to make a brief visit to Ruydale. I'm currently worried about my son, and since Aidan's met him I feel his advice would be useful. Of course I wouldn't dream of bothering you with what I'm sure you would rank as a very minor matter, but if you could possibly sanction a couple of days' absence I'd be most grateful." I concluded with the appropriate formula of blessings and signed myself JONATHAN.

He replied by return of post. My heart sank as I saw his flamboyant handwriting on the envelope, and I knew in a moment of foreknowledge that my request had been refused. Tearing open the letter I read:

My dear Jonathan,
Thank you so much for your courteous and considerate letter. But I wonder if—out of sheer goodness of heart, of course—you're being just a little too courteous and a little too considerate? If you have the kind of problem which would drive you to abandon your brethren and travel nearly two hundred

miles to seek help, I suggest you journey not to Ruydale but to London to see me. I shall expect you next week on Monday, the seventeenth of June. Assuring you, my dear Jonathan, of my regular and earnest prayers . . .

I crumpled the letter into a ball and sat looking at it. Then gradually as my anger triggered the gunfire of memory the present receded and I began to journey through the past to my first meeting with Francis Ingram.

8

I FIRST saw Francis when we were freshmen at Cambridge. He was leading a greyhound on a leash and smoking a Turkish cigarette. He was also slightly drunk. During that far-off decade which concluded the nineteenth century Francis looked like a degenerate in a Beardsley drawing and talked like a character in a Wilde play. In response to my fascinated inquiry, the college porter told me that this exotic incarnation of the spirit of the age was the younger son of the Marquis of Hindhead. The porter spoke reverently. Even in those early days of our Varsity career Francis was acclaimed as "a character."

I wanted to be "a character" myself, but I was up at Cambridge on a scholarship, my allowance was meagre and I knew none of the right people. Francis, I heard, gave smart little luncheon-parties in his rooms and offered his guests caviar and champagne. Barely able to afford even the occasional pint of ale, I nursed my jealousy in solitude and spent the whole of my first term wondering how I could "get on."

"If you get on as you should," my mother had said to me long ago, "then no one will look down on you because I was once in service."

I was just thinking in despair that I was doomed to remain a social outcast in that bewitching but cruelly privileged environment when Francis noticed me. I heard him say to the porter as I drew back out of sight on the stairs: "Who's that excessively tall article who looks like a bespectacled lamp-post and wears those perfectly ghastly cheap suits?" And later he said to me with a benign condescension: "The porter mentioned that you told his fortune better than any old fraud in a fair-ground, and it occurred to me that you might be rather amusing."

I received an invitation to his next smart little luncheon-party and put myself severely in debt by buying a new suit. The fortune-telling was a success. More invitations followed. Soon I became an object of curiosity, then of respect and finally of fascination; I had discovered that by devoting my psychic gifts to the furtherance of my ambition, the closed door were opening and I had become "a character" at last.

"Darrow's the most amazing chap," said Francis to his latest *chère amie.* "He reads palms, stops watches without touching them and makes the table waltz around the room during a séance—and now he's taken to healing! He makes his hands tingle, strokes you in the right place and the next moment you're resurrected from the dead! He's got this droll idea that he should be a clergyman, but personally I think he was born to be a Harley Street quack—he'd soon have all society beating a path to his door."

By that time we were in our final year and I was more ambitious than ever. It was true that I was reading theology out of a genuine interest to learn what the best minds of the past had thought about the God I already considered I knew intimately, but I was also possessed by the desire to "get on" in the Church and I saw an ecclesiastical career as my best chance of self-aggrandisement; I used to dream of an episcopal palace, a seat in the House of Lords and invitations to Windsor Castle. Naturally I had enough sense to keep these worldly thoughts to myself, but an ambitious man exudes an unmistakable aura and no doubt those responsible for my moral welfare were concerned about me. Various members of the divinity faculty endeavoured to give me the necessary spiritual direction, but I was uninterested in being directed because I was fully confident that I could direct myself. I felt I could communicate with God merely by flicking the right switches in my psyche, but it was a regrettable fact that my interest in God faded as my self-esteem, fuelled by my social success, burgeoned to intoxicating new dimensions.

"How divinely wonderful to see you—I'm in desperate need of a magic healer!" said Francis's new *chère amie* when I arrived to "dine and sleep" one weekend at her very grand country house. A widowed twenty-year-old, she had already acquired a *fin de siècle* desire to celebrate her new freedom with as much energy as discretion permitted. "Dear Mr. Darrow, I have this simply too, too tiresome pain in this simply too, too awkward place . . . "

I was punting idly with the lady on the Cam two days later when Francis approached me in another punt with two henchmen and tried to ram me. I managed to deflect the full force of the assault, but when he tried to use the punting pole as a bayonet I lost my temper. Abandoning the lady, who was feigning hysterics and enjoying herself immensely, I leapt aboard Francis's punt and tried to wrest the pole from him with the result that we both plunged into the river.

"You charlatan!" he yelled at me as we emerged dripping on the bank. "You *common* swinish rotter! You ought to be castrated like Peter Abelard and then burnt at the stake for bloody sorcery!"

I told him it was hardly my fault if he was too effete to satisfy the opposite sex, and after that it took five men to separate us. I remember being startled by his pugnacity. Perhaps it was then that I first realised there was very much more to Francis Ingram than was allowed to meet the eye.

In the end his henchmen dragged him away and I was left to laugh at the incident, but I only laughed because at that moment my psychic faculty was dormant and I never foresaw the future. A month later the lady, who had been telling everyone I had miraculously cured her abdominal pain, became violently ill, and in hospital it was discovered that her appendix had ruptured. She died twenty-four hours later.

I knew that because I had temporarily removed the pain she had refrained from seeking medical advice until it was too late, and as the enormity of the catastrophe overwhelmed me I perceived for the first time the danger in which I stood. Contrary to what I had supposed my psychic powers made me not strong and impregnable but weak and vulnerable, a prey to any passing demonic force. I had used my powers to serve myself and the result had been tragedy. I now realised I had to use my powers to serve God, not merely in order to be a good man but in order to survive as a sane rational being, and as I finally recognised a genuine call to the priesthood I stumbled through the meadows which separated Cambridge from Grantchester and knocked on the door of the Fordite monks.

9

AT that stage of my life I had no thought of being a monk. I was merely desperate to obtain absolution from someone who, unlike the stern authorities at Laud's College, might hear my confession with compassion, and if anyone had told me that one day I would myself enter the Order I would have laughed in scorn.

It would be edifying to record that my spiritual problems were solved once I came under the Abbot of Grantchester's direction, but although James Reid was the holiest of men he was quite the wrong director for me. I liked him because he was fascinated by my psychic gifts and this, I regret to say, enhanced my pride by making me feel special. The result was that I fell into the habit of using my powers to manipulate him until we had both fooled ourselves into believing that we had achieved a successful rapport. In retrospect the truth seems obvious: I was still so spiritually immature that I could only tolerate a director who cocooned me in indulgence, and beyond my genuine desire to devote my life to God's service, my psyche was as disruptive and undisciplined as ever. The years of my troubled priesthood had begun.

I saw no more of Francis after we came down from Cambridge, and for a time I was so absorbed by my preparations for ordination that I never thought of him, but five years later when I was a married Naval chaplain I heard the astonishing news that he had entered the Order. He began his monastic career at the Starwater house, some forty miles from where I worked at the Naval base in Starmouth, but I had lost touch with the Fordites by that time and I saw no reason why I should ever meet Francis again.

However word of his progress continued to reach me as he rose with lightning speed to the office of Bursar, no mean post in a place like Starwater Abbey where there was a large school to run and complex accounts to be kept. He was still at Starwater when I myself entered the Order in 1923, but as my career was unfolding at Ruydale we never met. Nor did we correspond. He represented a past which I could remember only with shame, and I suspected that I represented a similar burden of guilt to him. But then in 1930 he was transferred to the London headquarters in order to assist its ailing bursar, and in a flash of foreknowledge I knew that our lives were drawing together again after completing some enigmatic circle in time.

Our reunion came sooner than I had anticipated. I underwent a period of crisis which I have no intention of describing so I shall only record that it concerned the house-cat, Whitby, and nearly terminated my career as a monk; Father Darcy had to be summoned to Yorkshire to set me back on the spiritual rails. I recovered from my crisis, but six months later Father Darcy decided to reassure himself that I had fully surmounted the disaster which was now known as "the Whitby Affair," and I was summoned to London for an inspection.

The summons was most unusual. No one ever visited London from Ruydale except Aidan, who was obliged to travel there once a year for the Abbots' Conference, and although I was apprehensive at the prospect of being inspected by Father Darcy, I was also flattered that I was to receive special attention. However when I arrived in London in a state of wary but not unpleasant anticipation, it was a rude shock when I found myself welcomed not by the Guest-Master but by the new bursar, Francis Ingram.

"So you're still as lean as a lamp-post!" he exclaimed. "But what happened to those owlish spectacles?"

"My sight improved with age. What happened to the greyhound?"

"He died of a surfeit of champagne."

We laughed, shaking hands as if we were the oldest of friends, but I was unnerved by his aura of hostility. It lay like a ball of ice beneath the warmth of his welcome; to my psychic eye it was unmistakable, and immediately I heard myself say: "Perhaps we should agree to draw a veil over the past."

"Should we? Personally I think it's more honest to face one's disasters and chalk the whole lot up to experience. After all," said Francis, suddenly fusing his middle-aged self with the undergraduate of long ago, "Wilde did say that experience was the name men give to their mistakes."

I said with as much good humour as I could muster: "Still quoting Wilde? I'm surprised our superior permits it!"

"Then perhaps now's the moment to make it clear to you that I'm the favourite with a license to be entertaining," said Francis at once, and as he smiled, making a joke of the response, I recognised the demon jealousy and knew our old rivalry was about to be revived in a new form.

I said abruptly: "You've told him about the past?"

"How could I avoid it? As soon as the rumour reached London that you'd got up to something thoroughly nasty with a cat I said: 'That reminds me of my salad-days.' And then before I knew where I was—"

"He'd prised the whole story out of you."

"But didn't he know most of it anyway?"

"I admit I told him about the Cambridge catastrophe, but I never mentioned you by name. And now, of course, he's decided it would be amusing as well as edifying to batter us into brotherly love—he's summoned me here not just to put my soul under the microscope but to purge us of our ancient antipathy!"

This deduction proved to be all too correct. Every evening after supper Father Darcy would summon us to his room and order a debate on a subject of theological interest. The debates lasted an hour and were throroughly exhausting as Francis and I struggled to keep our tempers and maintain an acceptable level of fraternal harmony. Afterwards Father Darcy would pronounce the winner, dispatch Francis and embark on a fresh examination of my spiritual health. By the end of the week I was so worn out that I could hardly drag myself back to Yorkshire.

Before my departure I said in private to Francis: "I hope the old man doesn't intend to make a habit of this. All I want is a quiet life at Ruydale."

"Dear old chap!" said Francis. "You don't seriously expect me to believe that, do you? After a few years of living on the Yorkshire moors a man of your ambition would feel like Napoleon marooned on St. Helena!"

"I don't think that's funny, Francis."

"I'm hardly delirious with amusement myself."

"Obviously you see me as a rival, but I assure you—"

"Don't bother. I'm not in the mood for hypocrisy."

"What's this—a nursery tantrum? I've never seen such an unedifying exhibition of jealousy in all my life!"

"And I've never seen such a plausible performance of a holy man devoid of ambition, but my dear Jonathan, just answer me this: has it never occurred to you that for a holy man devoid of ambition you seem to be carving out a quite remarkably successful career?"

I turned my back on him and walked away.

10

IT is a relief to record that this disgraceful scene was not repeated; no doubt Francis was afterwards as ashamed of our hostile exchange as I was, and when we met again he even took the initiative in apologising for the incident.

I paid six more visits to London before I was transferred to Grantchester, and each time Father Darcy pitted us against each other in debate, dragged our antipathy into the open and, in a metaphorical sense, rubbed our noses in the mess to discourage us from further antagonism. I was reminded of how one house-trains a cat. In the end Francis and I were so chastened by this remorseless spiritual purging that we almost became friends, but I never felt I knew him well. My psychic faculty, blunted by the antipathy which we both learnt to master but not erase, was dead in his presence. I received no insights which would have offered me the key to his character, nor could I perceive the texture of his spiritual life. Our debates had revealed his powerful intellect, but I came to the conclusion that although he was intellectually able he was spiritually limited and that this fact lay at the root of his jealousy. He was quite intelligent enough to know his limitations, more than intelligent enough to conceal them whenever possible and certainly human enough to resent a man who displayed the gifts he secretly coveted but knew he would never attain. He was also, I soon realised, deeply envious of the effortless psychic understanding which existed between Father Darcy and myself, and when I realised how much he depended on our mentor's approbation I found myself driven to question the propriety of their relationship.

Father-son relationships are as forbidden in the cloister as the notorious "particular friendships" which prurient laymen find so titillating, but I thought that Father Darcy, in characteristic fashion, might be riding rough-shod over the rules in order to give Francis some form of psychological security which could prove beneficial to his character. I was not jealous. I had no desire whatsoever that Father Darcy should treat me as a son; I had a tough enough time surviving his attentions as a spiritual director. But I did wonder if Father Darcy was taking an unwise risk, and I wondered too, as time passed, if he was using Francis to gratify some immaculately concealed emotional need.

I knew I was of intense interest to Father Darcy, but the interest was essentially detached; I was just the parlour-maid's son who had presented him with the challenge of a monastic lifetime but who could nonetheless be kept at arm's length in Yorkshire. But Francis was the man from his own class with whom he could feel at ease, the man who had to be transferred to London not merely to supervise the Order's financial affairs but to keep the Abbot-General company in his old age. Such a situation was all very comfortable for Father Darcy, but was it good for Francis? I often considered this question but could never answer it with any degree of confidence. Perhaps Francis needed this special attention in order to make the most of those limited spiritual gifts. It was possible. With Father Darcy any bizarre monastic situation was possible—as I realised all too clearly when he lay on his deathbed and declared that his successor must be a man who could tell vintage claret from *vin ordinaire.*

Francis took care to say to me afterwards: "I'd like to think that despite the old man's appalling final antics we can somehow contrive to be friends."

"Of course. Why not?" I said equably before retreating to my cell to seethe with rage.

"I fear I shall still worry in the future about you and Francis," confessed Aidan to me after the funeral, but I only answered with all my most fatal arrogance: "I can't imagine any difficulty arising which can't be easily resolved."

Less than two months later I received my summons to London and I travelled there in the knowledge that I was deep in difficulties which were incapable of an easy resolution. Moreover after years of rivalry Francis now had me where he wanted me: in a position which was utterly subject to his will.

It was a bitter pill to swallow.

II

JOURNEYING beyond the walls of one's cloister was always a disturbing experience—I shall never forget my first journey from Ruydale to London when I encountered the amazingly exposed legs of two flappers on the train—and now I found myself more disturbed than ever. But this time I barely noticed the female passengers. I was too busy reading *The Times.* It seemed the French had collapsed. Pétain had ordered a cessation of the fighting and was in touch with the Nazi command. For weeks the countries of Europe had been falling to the Nazis and now after the collapse of Denmark, Norway, The Netherlands and Belgium, it appeared that France too had been conquered. Without the French we would be quite alone. More than fifteen hundred years of Christian culture hung by a thread and the Devil's breath was hot upon our necks.

I found myself thinking that the chaos in the world mirrored the chaos in my psyche. I saw my career as a monk hanging by a thread, and as I forced myself to acknowledge that my vision could have been a delusion I was aware of the demonic menace which always had the power to annihilate me. A second later I was trying to recover my equilibrium by telling myself I should put my trust in God, but the trouble was, as I well knew, I was quite unable to put my trust in Francis Ingram.

Unless I wanted to be judged an apostate I could not leave the Order without his permission, and that meant my entire future rested on his ability to exercise the charism of the discernment of spirits, the gift from God which enabled a man to perceive whether a situation was divinely or diabolically inspired. Francis, as I had long since decided, was spiritually limited. This did not mean he was incapable of exercising the charism of discernment, for with God's grace even the most unlikely people can display charismatic powers, but it did mean that I had ample opportunity to worry about how far he was capable of placing himself in God's hands so that he might act as a channel for the Holy Spirit. Francis was a clever, cunning, efficient, ambitious, jealous, charming and outwardly devout monk. But was he a good one? I found I could derive no reassurance from reflecting that Father Darcy would hardly have willed the Order to a monk who was merely a first-class administrator. Sickness had undermined Father Darcy's powers at the end of his life, and it was more than possible that in a moment of weakness he had given way to the temptation to leave the Order not to the best monk he ever trained but to the best son he never had.

These lowering thoughts occupied me throughout my journey on the Underground railway from Liverpool Street Station to Marble Arch. Then I pulled myself together as best I could, gathered up a few scattered shreds of faith and trudged north through the brilliant June sunshine to the townhouse which had once belonged to the Order's founder, Mr. Horatio Ford.

I 2

"MY dear Jonathan, how wan you look!" said Francis in his most theatrical voice as I entered the room where he conducted his daily business. "But then the news in this morning's *Times* is enough to make anyone blanch.

I confess I'm seriously tempted to buy a wireless in order to hear Mr. Churchill's broadcast tonight—only the thought of Father Darcy turning in his grave deters me."

"If Father Darcy were alive he would already have discovered what kind of wireless the Archbishop keeps at Lambeth Palace and he'd be busy ordering a better one from Harrods!"

We laughed. The interview seemed to have begun in a promising spirit of amity, but I was acutely aware that the amity was no more than skin-deep.

When I had first met Francis in his gilded youth I had been reminded of that famous acid description of Julius Caesar: "He was every man's woman and every woman's man." But despite this appearance of ambivalence he had paid carnal attention only to the opposite sex and it was not until years later, when I became enamoured of modern psychological theories, that I suspected he was a homosexual who had indulged in heterosexual affairs to conceal his true inclinations not only from the world but from himself. Later still, when I had become far more cautious in applying modern psychology to complex characters, I became less confident of this facile diagnosis and wondered if the effete airs of Francis's youth had merely been part of a mask he had assumed in order to draw attention to himself; I even wondered if the mask had been his way of damping down strong heterosexual inclinations which he believed might disrupt his life disastrously. But whatever the truth was about his sexuality, the fact remained that in his maturity no one could have called him effete. He was a tall man, though not as tall as I was, and the passing years, stripping aside the air of decadence, had substituted a flamboyant air of distinction. He had fine dark eyes, expressive dark eyebrows and a remarkable head of silver hair which he wore longer than a monk should, no doubt out of vanity. I was surprised Father Darcy had permitted it. The Fordites may have dispensed with the medieval custom of the tonsure, but they are still expected to keep their hair decently short.

As I entered the room and we embarked on our friendly opening remarks, he moved gracefully around the corner of his large, handsome desk to meet me. The room too was large and handsome, littered with the antiques old Ford had left behind, and, as Father Darcy had once boasted smugly: "More than a match for any of the Archbishop's private chambers at Lambeth." Father Darcy had been dangerously bold in his belief that to attract worldly respect the Order should present a worldly facade, and personally I deplored such a policy. The Abbot-General's office in which I now stood was in the enclosed part of the house, which meant that no one outside the Order ever saw it, but nevertheless it was furnished as lavishly as the Abbot-General's Parlour where important visitors were received. There was even, I regret to record, a peculiarly gross chandelier hanging from the centre of the ceiling.

After we had laughed with studied heartiness at the thought of Father Darcy ordering the latest wireless from Harrods, we moved swiftly through the formula of cenobitic greeting like actors in a well-rehearsed play. As Francis paused by the desk I knelt, touched his Abbot's ring with my lips and then rose to shake his hand. A moment later we were both seated facing each other across his desk.

"I'm sorry to hear you have a difficulty with your son," said Francis, idly picking up my letter in which I had requested his permission to visit Yorkshire. "What's the trouble?"

"As it happens I've now decided that Martin isn't my main worry at present." I had to will myself to add: "My major difficulty lies elsewhere."

Francis, who had been rereading the letter, at once glanced up. "Oh?" he said. "And what, may I ask, is your major difficulty?"

I said: "I want to leave the Order," and at that moment the die was cast.

II

*"When Tertullian, who was not a mystic, says that most men apprehend God by
means of visions, we realise how natural it seemed to the ancients to believe that
these experiences were a genuine and by no means unusual revelation."*

W . R . I N G E
MYSTICISM IN RELIGION

I

I HAD expected a theatrical reaction but none came. Not a muscle moved
in Francis's face; his fine eyes were unreadable. Finally he dropped the
letter on his desk, donned a pair of spectacles and produced from a drawer
a clean sheet of foolscap. Then after dipping his pen in the ink he wrote
at the top of the page: "JONATHAN DARROW: 17th June, 1940," and said
casually: "I assume that when you say you want to leave the Order this
isn't a mere whim that's tickled your fancy?"

"I'm sorry, I expressed myself badly. What I want is of course quite
irrelevant. But I believe this is what God wants."

Francis underlined his heading and asked: "When were you first aware
of this call?"

"May the seventeenth."

Francis raised an eyebrow, ostentatiously examined his desk-calendar
and allowed a pregnant pause to develop. But eventually all he said was:
"How did you become aware of the call?"

"I had a vision."

A second pause ensued and was allowed to reach a far more advanced
stage of pregnancy. Francis took off his spectacles, dangled them between
his thumb and forefinger and glanced at the chandelier as if each crystal
had demanded a careful inspection. Then, replacing his glasses, he pushed
them down to the tip of his nose and looked at me over the frames.
Francis had a whole series of such mannerisms; I always found them
excessively irritating.

"You had a vision."

"Yes."

"You had a vision of profound importance on the seventeenth of May and yet it's only now that you deign to confide in your superior?"

"I felt I needed time for reflection."

"How arrogant! You have what can only be described as a disruptive experience which must inevitably have affected your spiritual life, and yet you coolly decide you're in a position to reflect on the experience at leisure!"

I said at once: "I was in error. I'm sorry."

"So you should be." Pushing back his glasses to the bridge of his nose he wrote: "Reflects for a month but now admits the arrogance of his failure to confide in me immediately." On completing this sentence he added in his most acid voice: "And now I suppose you'll tell me that you've failed to confide in your confessor! Incidentally, who is he?"

"Timothy." Remembering that Francis had not yet visited the house at Grantchester I offered the most fundamental description I could devise. "He's our senior monk, a very good, holy old man."

"Cosy for you," said Francis. "I'm only surprised Father Darcy sanctioned someone so pliable, but then I suppose he thought you couldn't go too far astray so long as he was alive to keep an eye on you."

I said nothing.

"Very well," said Francis, writing the word "VISION" on a fresh line, "you'd better tell me what happened," and I began my account of the abnormal in the most normal voice I could muster.

2

WHEN I had finished, Francis drew a line under his last note and stared in silence at the written page. "Is that all?" he said abruptly at last. "There weren't, for example, six naked women dancing merrily in the glade?"

"Absolutely not!"

Unexpectedly Francis smiled. "I was only thinking that apart from the ending, which I admit is spectacular, it's a dull sort of vision, isn't it? No naked ladies, no heavenly choirs, no disembodied voices exhorting you to great spiritual feats."

"I'm sorry, I'll try to have a more entertaining vision next time."

He laughed. I was tempted to relax but sensed that he wanted to lure me off my guard. "Tell me," he was saying idly, "how often do you have these visions?"

"On average about once every four years. A far more common experience is foreknowledge, a flash in the consciousness which lasts no more than a couple of seconds."

"How accurate are these flashes?"

"There's a high margin of error. But the correct predictions can be striking."

"But you admit you're often wrong."

"Certainly. I believe the future is foreknown to God but not foreordained—or, in other words, I believe there are many futures but the future which actually happens in finite time is one which can be shaped by the exercise of man's free will. I think my failures occur when man steps in and alters the pattern."

"Quite. But I really must resist the temptation to be diverted," said Francis, "by an enthralling discussion of determinism and free will. Now if we may return to your visions"—Francis sighed as if he found the word a heavy cross to bear—"do they always relate to the future?"

"Not necessarily. They may represent the present or past seen from another angle. Or if they do relate to the future, the past may be present as well. It's as if I'm moving in a dimension of reality which exists beyond time as we understand it."

"How do you classify this present vision as far as time's concerned?"

"I think I've seen the future. There was nothing of the past or present in it at all."

"And maybe nothing of the future either. But before we get bogged down in scepticism," said Francis, allowing me no chance to comment, "give me an example of a vision which was rather less enigmatic than this one. I feel I need some yardstick of comparison."

After a pause I said: "In my last vision—not this present one, but a vision I had in 1937—I found myself back in the prison where I worked before I entered the Order. I was walking down one of the main halls, but then I turned out of the past into an unfamiliar corridor and entered a large room which was certainly like no cell that exists in the prison service. About a dozen prisoners were confined there but they didn't see me, so I knew that in this particular dimension of reality I wasn't physically present. At the same time I felt deeply involved; perhaps I was psychically present in my prayers. Then as I drew closer, I realised the prisoners were grouped around a man who lay dying and that this dying man was being tended by a priest whom I recognised. It was Charles Ashworth, the Canon of Cambridge Cathedral and the Tutor in Theology at Laud's. I act as his spiritual director. Then I felt the evil emanating from the walls and as I automatically began to recite the Lord's Prayer, the vision ended." I paused before adding: "Over the years I've become increasingly certain that I saw a scene in a future prisoner-of-war camp."

"Where's Ashworth at the moment?"

"Still safe in England. But he's become an Army chaplain." Before I could stop myself I was prejudicing my case by voicing the opinion I so much wanted to believe. "However there's a good chance that the vision won't come true; I think it may have been a psychic aberration brought on by the strain of my translation to Grantchester."

Francis immediately pounced. "What makes you so sure that this latest vision isn't a mere psychic aberration?"

I kept calm. "The light shining through the north window was the light of God. The knowledge imprinted on my consciousness formed a divine revelation. Unlike the Ashworth vision I felt no doubt afterwards, no confusion."

Francis said sharply: "What did Timothy think?"

"He saw the vision as an allegory, but he was handicapped by the fact that I concealed the revelation at the end." I recounted Timothy's interpretation.

"And do you dismiss this allegorical approach entirely?"

"I'm sure I was in a real place—but I concede there may have been symbolism present. I don't believe the suitcase existed on the same level of reality as the chapel. I suspect it represented travel, or possibly change."

"Tell me why you're so convinced that you were moving in a landscape which actually existed."

I said without hesitation: "The quality of the detail. It was unusually distinct. In the chapel I even smelt the scent of the lilies, and such an experience is most unusual in a vision. The sense of smell is nearly always dormant."

Francis made a long note before extracting a fresh sheet of foolscap from his desk. Then he said: "After the vision had ended, what sort of state were you in?"

"I was trembling and sweating. The amount of psychic energy required to generate a vision always produces a powerful physical reaction."

"Were you sexually excited?"

Silence. I was acutely aware that the longer I took to reply the more questionable my hesitation would seem, but several seconds elapsed before I could say: "Yes, but that doesn't mean anything."

"That's not for you to decide." Francis wrote on his fresh sheet of foolscap: "Possible evidence of sexual trouble," before he glanced up in time to catch me reading his writing. "Jonathan, would you kindly desist from flaunting the perfect sight you've been fortunate enough to acquire in middle age and abstain from any attempt to decipher my notes? That's an order."

"I'm sorry."

"The correct response to an order from your superior," said Francis, "is 'Yes, Father.' And by the way, are you aware that since this interview commenced you haven't once addressed me in an appropriate manner?"

"I'm sorry, Father. Please forgive me."

There was a pause. Having flexed the muscles of his new power and found them in good order, Francis allowed himself a discreet sigh of satisfaction before he picked up his pen again. "Very well, let's continue with the subject of sexual intimacy—or, to use the coarse abbreviation of the younger generation, 'sex.' How many women are there in your life at present?"

"There's my daughter—"

"Let's leave Freud out of this, shall we?"

"There's the Abbess at Dunton. She's a splendid old lady of seventy-eight whom I see when I pay the Abbot's traditional call on the nuns once a year."

"And let's leave out the old-age pensioners, too. Is there any woman under forty whom you've been seeing regularly?"

"Only Mrs. Charles Ashworth, the wife of the theologian I mentioned just now."

"Is she attractive?"

"Not to me. In fact I rather dislike her. May I stress at this point that my vision has absolutely nothing to do with women and sex?"

"Why are you getting so ruffled on the subject of women and sex?"

"I'm not getting ruffled! I'm simply impatient because—"

"When did you last see Mrs. Ashworth?"

Silence.

"Jonathan?"

"I last saw Mrs. Ashworth," I said, "on the sixteenth of May."

"The day before your vision."

"Yes." Now it was my turn to gaze up at the chandelier as if every crystal had demanded a meticulous inspection.

"And apart from the visit of Mrs. Ashworth," said Francis as the nib of his pen whispered across the page, "what else happened on the sixteenth of May?"

"Nothing much. There were the usual minor irritations—Augustine, one of my drones, fell asleep in choir and another drone, Denys, had to be reprimanded for raiding the larder."

"Just another dreary monastic day—but outside in the world it wasn't dreary at all, was it? It was painfully exciting. Chamberlain had just fallen, Churchill had taken over as Prime Minister, the British Army in France was heading for the ordeal of Dunkirk—"

"In such circumstances it was a relief to be diverted by my drones."

"Your drones and Mrs. Ashworth. Was she your only visitor that day?"

"No." I hesitated before adding neutrally: "My son came to see me."

"Ah yes," said Francis. "Martin. Obviously now is the moment when you should tell me about your current difficulty with him."

I glanced down at my hands and to my horror I saw their outline begin to blur. Willing my Abbot's ring to remain distinct, I managed to say: "It was nothing. We had a disagreement but that's irrelevant to the subject under discussion."

"That's not for you to judge." As my vision cleared I saw him write "MARTIN" and underline the name twice. "Has anything else happened to upset you lately—apart, of course, from Father Darcy's death and your failure to become Abbot-General?"

By this time I had myself so tightly in control that I never even flinched. "No, Father."

Francis removed his spectacles and to my profound relief I realised the interview was drawing to a close. "Well, Jonathan," he said dryly, "you've certainly given me food for thought. I trust you've made adequate arrangements for your prior to hold the fort in your absence?"

"I did tell him that I'd almost certainly have to stay overnight—"

"Overnight?" Francis regarded me incredulously. "Did you really think this matter could be settled in a few hours?"

"No, of course not, but I thought that after you'd cross-examined me you'd merely suggest various avenues of prayer and meditation before sending me back to Grantchester to reflect further on the problem."

"I see. That's what you'd do, would you, if you were the Abbot-General?"

After a pause I said: "Yes, Father."

"But you're not the Abbot-General, are you?"

"No, Father."

Francis pushed his telephone across the desk towards me. "Ring your prior and tell him you're going to be away for a week."

3

I HAD to cancel not only a number of counselling appointments but an important retreat for theological students. I felt sorry for my prior, burdened with the necessity of making numerous awkward telephone calls, but he brushed aside with admirable alacrity the apology I felt he deserved.

While I was speaking to Bernard, Francis was engaged in writing a letter. "Take this to the infirmary," he said when he had finished. "The first thing to do with any monk who has visions is to give him a thorough medical examination. I've told Ambrose you're a psychic so he won't immediately jump to the conclusion that you're off your head, but I've forbidden him to ask you about the contents of your vision and I forbid you to reveal them."

"Yes, Father."

"When Ambrose has finished his examination, you'll probably be in time to make an appearance in choir. I shall expect to see you in the chapel and also afterwards in the refectory. As for the afternoon, you must spend it in prayer. I suggest you meditate on the subject of truth and pray for the courage to be entirely honest with me during the ordeal which lies ahead for us both. Then at four o'clock you'll return to this room and I shall inform you how I intend to proceed."

"Yes, Father."

He made a gesture of dismissal and at once I departed for the infirmary.

4

I HAD first met Ambrose the Infirmarian in 1923 during the turbulent opening year of my monastic life; when Father Darcy removed me from Grantchester I had spent the night at the London headquarters before being dispatched to Ruydale. After an indescribable scene in the punishment cell and another equally harrowing ordeal in which I had been obliged to kneel in a humiliated state in front of the Abbot-General's table in the refectory while the brethren ate their supper, I had been dumped in the infirmary to be repaired and Ambrose had given me the welcome reassurance that the Christian spirit was not entirely absent in that rich, repulsive house.

Later I had met him on my unorthodox visits to London after the Whitby Affair. He had sought my company during the Saturday recreation hour, and I suspected he was interested in me because he had heard I possessed the charism of healing. He was in correspondence with Wilfred, the Infirmarian at Ruydale, a man who unlike Ambrose had had no formal medical training but who nonetheless possessed considerable gifts as a healer, and Wilfred had probably let slip a detail or two which had stimulated Ambrose's curiosity. However since I was forbidden to discuss my ill-fated career as a healer, this curiosity had remained unassuaged.

"Good morning, Father!" he said, meticulous in respecting my office even though before my final preferment he had been one of the brethren invited to call me Jon. "I heard you were visiting us today but I didn't realise I was going to have the pleasure of talking to you." And when he had read Francis's letter he said with an admirable serenity: "Do you normally enjoy good health?"

"Very good health," I said, and at once wondered if I sounded too firm. Psychics are sensitive on the subject and never more so than when their powers are being critically examined.

Ambrose asked a number of mundane questions about my bowels, bladder, heart, eyes and teeth before enquiring if I were prone to suffer from headaches. Immediately I knew he was toying with the idea of a brain tumour.

"I never have headaches," I said.

"Never?" said Ambrose mildly.

Realising that I was sounding thoroughly implausible, I changed course and admitted to the occasional headache.

"Have you ever suffered from epilepsy?"

"Absolutely not!"

"Quite so, quite so," said Ambrose, very soothing. "But I'm sure you understand that the question has to be asked. I must say, it certainly sounds as if you're unusually fit for a man of your age—and what age would that be exactly, Father, if you'll forgive my asking?"

I was caught unprepared. To my surprise I found the question annoyed me, and my surprise was followed by an emotion which I can only describe as a rebellious embarrassment. I said abruptly: "One's as old as one feels and I feel no more than forty-five."

When Ambrose looked astonished, I saw the stupidity of my evasion and regretted it. Flatly I said: "I've just had my sixtieth birthday."

"Congratulations! I trust the milestone didn't go unmarked?"

"No, my daughter wrote and my grandchildren sent cards."

"What about your son?" said Ambrose, and at once I knew he had been briefed to make an inquiry about Martin.

"He came to see me."

"How nice!" Ambrose began to take my blood pressure. "What's he doing nowadays? I suppose he's too old to be called up." At that time compulsory enlistment only encompassed men up to the age of twenty-seven.

"No doubt he'll eventually be assigned to some non-combatant task. He's a pacifist."

"I admire those young men for having the courage of their convictions," said Ambrose generously. I knew his favourite nephew was in the Air Force. "What terrible times we live in! I feel I know now exactly how St. Augustine felt when he witnessed the civilised world collapsing and saw the barbarians at the gates of his city. Indeed sometimes," said

Ambrose, listening to my chest with his stethoscope, "no matter how deep one's faith, it's impossible not to feel depressed."

We had reached the subject of depression. After Ambrose had completed his tour with the stethoscope, peered down my throat and congratulated me on having kept all my teeth, I said firmly: "Before you ask the question you've already framed in your mind, may I assure you that I'm not in the least depressed?"

Ambrose gave me a quizzical look. "I was actually going to ask if you'd been aware of overworking lately."

I opened my mouth to say no but instead forced myself to admit: "Perhaps."

"Overwork can lead to exhaustion and then depression becomes a danger, even with people who aren't normally depressed. Any trouble getting to sleep?"

"Not usually."

"And getting up? I was wondering if, when this vision began, you were lying in bed and wishing you could stay there all day."

After a pause I said: "I wasn't lying in bed when the vision began. I was sitting on the edge."

"Ah. And what exactly happened? I'm not asking for details of the vision, I hasten to add, but merely for a description of the signs which preceded it."

"My visual perceptions altered. Colours became very bright."

"Did you at any time lose consciousness?" said Ambrose, still surreptitiously clinging to the notion of epilepsy.

"No. My visions are always one continuous experience, the abnormal consciousness flowing directly out of the normal consciousness and back again."

"Is it at any time an out-of-the-body experience?"

"Yes, in the transitional period between the normal and the abnormal I can look down on my body from above."

"Well, that's all very orthodox for a psychic, I suppose," said Ambrose, compensating for his obsession with epilepsy by accepting my descriptions calmly. "When did you start having these experiences?"

"I've always been psychic in the sense of being able to receive flashes of foreknowledge. But the psychic energy required to generate the visions didn't develop until I was fourteen."

"The age of puberty? By the way, that reminds me—I'd better examine you for possible prostate trouble."

We had reached the subject of sex. I kept quiet and waited.

"No sign of disease," said Ambrose presently. "Good. But I wonder if you have any more mundane problems in that area? For instance, I had a man in here the other day who was plagued by early-morning erections. Of course nothing could be more common than an early-morning erection, but this man suffered such discomfort that he found he could only obtain relief by masturbating, and as he was a priest this put him in a difficult spiritual position."

"Self-abuse hardly results in an easy spiritual position for a layman either, Ambrose."

We both laughed.

"Of course a lot of monks would give their back teeth to have such problems," remarked Ambrose, washing his hands. "It's curious, isn't it, how a man likes his equipment to be in working order even though he's taken a vow not to use it? I find that psychologically interesting."

I made no comment.

"I'm told that this vision of yours was accompanied by certain sexual manifestations," said Ambrose, forced by my silence to abandon his discreet approach. "I presume this means you had an erection."

By this time I was getting dressed. Buckling the belt of my habit I said: "It's unhelpful, Ambrose, to press the connection between the sexual force in the body and the psychic force in the mind. There may indeed be some sort of link, but exactly what that link is can only be a matter of speculation and in my opinion any sexual manifestations which occur are essentially irrelevant."

"They're not indicative of sexual frustration?"

"One of my most striking visions," I said, "occurred during my marriage when I was regularly enjoying my marital rights."

"Then I'd certainly agree sexual frustration couldn't have been involved on that occasion, but what about this present incident? Has celibacy been uncomfortable for you lately?"

"Certainly not, and personally I'd have taken a very sceptical view of that monk who could only solve his physical problem by masturbating! I hope you had the good sense to tell him to apply cold water more liberally and work harder."

"So with regard to your present vision—"

"It had nothing to do with sex, Ambrose."

"But nevertheless it was accompanied by—"

"Why are you laying such stress on this trivial physical phenomenon? Sexuality should be accepted without fuss, not turned into an object of morbid speculation!"

"Yes, Father. Did you ejaculate?"

"Ambrose, I know you're asking these ridiculous questions with the best will in the world, but I really think—"

"I'm sorry, I didn't mean to upset you—"

"I'm not upset!"

"—but I'm merely anxious to get everything quite clear in my mind. Now, if these sexual manifestations are irrelevant, am I right in thinking that the visions have nothing to do with any event, sexual or otherwise, which may be taking place in your life at the time?"

I willed myself to be calm and recalled my duty to be honest. "No, that's not right," I said with reluctance. "There's usually an event which seems to act as a trigger." I hesitated before adding: "In 1937 I had a vision about a young priest whom I'd just helped through a grave spiritual crisis. It seemed clear afterwards that this crisis, which had absorbed me deeply, had acted as a stimulant, triggering this psychic glimpse of one of his possible futures."

"And may I ask if you've identified the trigger of this latest vision?"

I said flatly: "There was no trigger. The vision came from God."

We sat in silence for a moment. I sensed that Ambrose was anxious to signal not only his respect for me but his reverence for any gift from God, and because I was aware of his sympathy I managed to control my anger when he eventually asked: "Have you felt persecuted lately?"

"No. And I haven't been hearing voices either. I'm not a paranoid schizophrenic."

"The most difficult patients, as any doctor will tell you," said Ambrose, smiling at me, "are always the ones who like to run their own interviews and dictate the results to their unfortunate physicians." He stood up before adding: "However I have to admit that in my opinion you're physically very fit for a man of sixty, and I'm not surprised you feel no older than forty-five."

At last I was able to relax. "Thank you, Ambrose!" I said, smiling back at him, but after I had left the infirmary I realised he had ventured no opinion on my mental health at all.

5

"*I'VE* been reading your file," said Francis when I returned to his room at four o'clock that afternoon. "Of course I'd read it before—I plucked it from the safe as soon as the old man had breathed his last—but in the light of the present situation I find it doubly fascinating."

Father Darcy, like all efficient dictators, had kept files on those subject to his authority so that he always knew who was likely to cause trouble. The information had been acquired not only from the regular reports of his abbots but from his annual visitations to their houses.

I said dryly: "I doubt if a fascinating file should be a source of pride."

"That shows a promising spirit of humility." Francis, entrenched behind his theatrical mannerisms, began to flick idly through the assorted papers in the bulging cardboard folder, and suddenly I wondered if he were feeling insecure, playing for time while he steadied his nerves. "The part I enjoyed most," he was saying amused, "was the section about Whitby the cat. Whitby! Was he named about the Synod?"

"Of course."

"You'll be surprised to hear Father Darcy gives him a favourable mention. 'A very superior animal,' he writes, 'much admired by the community.'"

I said nothing, but the mention of Father Darcy seemed to give Francis the confidence he needed and he embarked on the necessary speech. "This is how I intend to proceed," he said briskly. "Every afternoon at this time you'll come here and we'll discuss certain aspects of your situation. Let me hasten to reassure you that at this stage I've no intention of behaving like either a prosecuting counsel or a member of the Spanish Inquisition; I merely want to shine a torch, as it were, into various obscure areas to try to widen your perspective on what I suspect is a very difficult and complex reality. Then I'll send you back to Grantchester for further reflection."

"Yes, Father."

"After a month of further reflection," said Francis, soothed by my immaculate docility and steadily gaining in confidence, "if you still feel called to leave the Order, you must return here so that I can wheel on the rack, take you apart and poke around among the pieces. It'll be very unpleasant but I've no choice; I'm responsible as your superior for the care of your soul, and I can't possibly release you from your vows until I'm absolutely certain that this call comes from God and not from—but no, we won't talk of the Devil. Father Darcy would, but I'm not Father Darcy, and to be honest I think he was a great deal too obsessed with demonic infiltration and very much too fond of exorcism."

This confession intrigued me. It was the first time I had ever heard Francis disagree with our mentor or hint at his own private spiritual attitudes. Cautiously I said: "Father Darcy was a psychic and it's easier for psychics, I think, to talk symbolically of forces which they can perceive so clearly but which normal people find opaque."

"Oh, don't misunderstand!" said Francis at once. "I'm not one of those liberal theologians who cheerfully write off the Devil as passé! Obviously demonic infiltration exists—look at Hitler. But you're not Hitler, Jonathan, and I think that any corruption of your call is going to come from the dark side of your personality within you, not from the dark forces of the Devil without."

"Father Darcy would say—"

"Father Darcy would say the Devil could be at work in your psyche, but that would just be his old-fashioned Victorian shorthand for what you and I know to be the disruptive force of the subconscious mind." Francis, who had discarded his theatrical mannerisms as his confidence increased, now leant forward across the desk to hammer his point home. "So let me repeat: it's not the Devil we have to fear here but a dislocation of your personality, possibly brought on by emotional strain or overwork or some cause which is at present hidden from us."

There was a pause while I debated whether it would be wiser to make no comment, but finally I was unable to resist saying: "A dislocation of the personality is by no means always incompatible with a genuine call. Indeed in some cases a call can't be heard until some dislocation occurs to open the spiritual ears."

Francis immediately felt intimidated. "I trust you're not intending to carp and snipe at everything I say."

"No, Father, I'm sorry."

"It may indeed be the case that God is calling you by putting you under psychological pressure," said Francis irritably, "but how can we tell that until we uncover the exact state of your psyche and see whether the pattern reveals the hand of God or the self-centred desires of your disturbed ego?"

"Quite." As I assumed my meekest expression, Francis suddenly realised that if he persisted in his ill-temper I could outflank him by taking a saintly stance which would make him look both petulant and foolish. His innate cunning triumphed over his insecurity; at once he altered course.

"Once I believe your vision is a gift from God," he said with a smile, "I'll be the first to shake your hand and give you my blessing. But meanwhile"—he gave a theatrical sigh—"meanwhile I have a duty to be sceptical." Effortlessly he began to exude an aura of benign concern. "Now, Jonathan, I'm not going to give you orders about how you should spend your time in between our daily interviews, but I do urge you to relax as much as possible. Ambrose thought a little holiday would do you no harm at all"—this was the first proof I had that Ambrose felt ambivalent about my mental health—"so please don't exhaust yourself in excessive spiritual exercises. Oh, and I forbid you to fast. I don't want you having visions brought on by lack of food."

The interview having thus been terminated on a relentlessly friendly note, I retired with relief to my cell.

MY cell was in fact not a cell at all but one of the distressingly well-appointed bedrooms set aside for visiting abbots. It lay on the same landing as the Abbot-General's sumptuous bedchamber, and faced west across the immaculately tended grounds which were bordered by a high brick wall. Our founder Mr. Ford, an adventurer who had made his fortune from slave-trading before his miraculous conversion to Anglo-Catholicism in the 1840s, had lived in style on his ill-gotten gains, and his Order, supported from the start by the greater part of his massive wealth, had husbanded their resources with skill.

I have no wish to imply that there is anything wrong with a monastic community which skilfully husbands its resources; on the contrary, every abbot has a duty to make ends meet. But I found it unedifying that a religious Order should spend such a large part of those skilfully husbanded resources on maintaining such a luxurious headquarters. I was offended not merely by the antiques in the Abbot-General's office. The atmosphere of debilitating affluence permeated the entire house and even the novices were pampered by having linoleum on the floor of their scriptorium. As I returned to my grossly over-furnished chamber that afternoon I wondered, not for the first time, how I was expected to pray in it, and to counter my disgust I embarked on some alterations.

My first act was to take down the three pictures and put them in the wardrobe. I like paintings but when I am at work I find them distracting. Then I rolled up the carpet, which was woven into a pattern so exquisite that I had already wasted far too much time gazing at it, and tackled the bed, which I knew from past experience during the annual Abbots' Conferences was soft enough to give me back-ache. Having stacked the mattress against the wall I replaced the coverings on the base, which was reassuringly hard, and sat down at the table.

I closed my eyes but not to pray; I was sharpening my concentration in order to plan how I might best master Francis, but the next moment, realising that I was behaving like some buccaneering politician engaged in a seamy struggle for power with his party's leader, I checked myself in shame. How unedifying! I resolved to order my thoughts along more salubrious lines, but the more I tried to think like a priest, the more I despaired of ever being able to concentrate in that distracting house, and at last, abandoning my room, I sought refuge in the garden.

I felt better outside. At first I merely strolled around the lawn and savoured the sunshine, but later my feet carried me through the gates of the cemetery until I found myself standing by the cross which marked Father Darcy's grave.

Desolation overwhelmed me. I felt lost and adrift, unnervingly vulnerable—and the next moment I was experiencing not only a painful grief but a painful rage that I should have been so abruptly abandoned.

The emotion lasted no longer than a second but I was shocked by the glimpse I had received into such a dark, desperate corner of my psyche. I even glanced over my shoulder as if I feared Francis might be spying on me in my weakness, but of course there was no one there and finally, pulling myself together, I withdrew to the chapel to pray.

7

AT four o'clock on the following afternoon I presented myself once more at the Abbot-General's office, and the gross china clock which squatted on the marble mantelshelf chimed the hour as I halted before my superior's desk.

"Today we're going to examine your vision in more detail," said Francis, motioning me to be seated. "So let me start by asking you this: are you sure the chapel was in England?"

I was sufficiently startled to say: "It certainly never occurred to me that it wasn't. The light was so English—that dull greenish light which is so typical of a cloudy English day."

"Presumably the greenish light means the trees were in leaf. But was it spring or summer?"

"Summer. It was too warm to be spring."

"If you were aware of the warmth," said Francis, writing busily, "were you also aware of your clothing? Were you wearing your habit, which we know is hell in hot weather, or were you enjoying the bliss of trousers and a shirt?"

I was intrigued but had to confess: "I don't know."

"Then let's approach the memory from another angle. You said yesterday"—he consulted his notes—"that there were steps leading to the doors of the chapel. Did you raise the skirt of your habit as you mounted these steps?"

"No," I said at once, and added without thinking: "How clever of you, Francis!"

He looked at me over the top of his spectacles. "Father."

"Father. I'm sorry."

There was a pause before he continued: "So it seems you weren't wearing your habit. But that's not evidence that you weren't still a monk. You may have been on an authorised visit to this place, in which case you'd be wearing a clerical suit, just as we all must whenever we journey outside the cloister. So my next question is inevitably: what was your purpose in going to the chapel?"

"I've no idea."

"Was it your impression that the chapel was in regular use?"

"Yes. The lilies—"

"Obviously the lilies prove that it had been visited recently, but was there any evidence that the building was being used for worship? The lack of orthodox altar furnishings seems odd."

"I agree but I'm sure it wasn't deconsecrated. Perhaps I was going there for private prayer."

"The place seemed familiar to you?"

"Yes, I felt no surprise either when I saw the chapel below me in the dell or when I opened the door and saw the interior."

"Why do you consistently refer to it as a chapel as if it were owned by a family or an institution? Couldn't it have been some isolated country church?"

"In my experience isolated country churches are always medieval. This building was Victorian even though it was built in the style of Inigo Jones."

"What makes you so sure it was a Victorian imitation and not the work of the master himself? I thought Victorian architects were in love with medievalism, not classicism."

"Then this must have been the exception that proves the rule. The pews were typically Victorian. Of course they could have been added later, but—"

"If you know so much about the chapel why don't you know what this ruined building was behind it?"

"I'm sure I did know exactly what it was, but my mind's now a blank. Could it have been an ancient castle?"

"In a dell?" Francis was sceptical. "Castles are usually built on mounds."

"Perhaps it was a much older church, then—a church which for some reason had been allowed to fall into ruins."

There was a pause while we both pondered on this mystery but eventually Francis said: "As we know neither the name nor the vicinity of this place it would be well-nigh impossible to track down, but even if we found the chapel really did exist that still wouldn't prove your vision came from God. All the discovery would prove is that you're capable of a certain type of clairvoyance." Drawing a line below his last note he dipped his pen in the ink again. "Let's leave the chapel now and turn to this bag which you believe to be a symbol. Am I right in assuming this wasn't a bag you've ever owned?"

"I'd never have owned such a piece of luggage. It was expensive—and somewhat feminine, pale beige with dark brown corners. In fact it was the sort of suitcase one would associate with a wealthy woman."

Francis raised an eyebrow. "Are you sure you've never seen it before?"

"I was sure at the time. But on reflection . . . Yes, it's not impossible that I've seen it before. I suspect that when my vision required the symbol I didn't invent the suitcase but plucked the forgotten memory from my subconscious mind."

"But why that particular bag?"

"Because it was striking enough to lodge in my memory. After all, one never usually looks at a bag twice."

Francis laid down his pen, took off his spectacles and idly contemplated the chandelier. "Supposing," he said, "just supposing you've got this entirely wrong and it's the bag, not the chapel, which exists in reality."

"I'm absolutely sure—"

"Yes," said Francis, at once leaning forward on his desk and looking me straight in the eyes, "you're a great deal too sure of yourself here, Jonathan, and I think you should proceed with more mental flexibility and very much more humility. Go away now and ask yourself the following questions: first, what was your connection with the chapel? The assumption that you were going there for prayer is plausible, I agree, but it actually explains nothing. What were you doing in that environment? And what were you thinking about during that walk through the woods? Your mind seems to have been unusually vacant. Does your lack of surprise when you saw the chapel indicate that the scene was familiar to you, or is it in truth an example of the curiously dreamlike quality which permeates this experience of yours? If this was a real glimpse of the future, why weren't you thinking of your current problems, the current people in your life, possibly even of your current approach to God? I put it to you that you were drifting along like a somnambulist, and I think you should consider whether Timothy was really so far off the mark when he interpreted the vision as an allegory. Ask yourself if the ruined building might symbolise what you, in your recent disappointment over your lack of preferment, might consider your spent career as a monk. Ask yourself if this chapel, modern but built along classical lines, might represent your subconscious longing for an entirely new career in the Church. Ask yourself if the evidence that you weren't wearing your habit is in fact a manifestation of your subconscious desire to discard it. And finally ask yourself why you should have seen a bag which apparently symbolises not travel and change to you (yesterday's explanation) but (so you now confess) wealth and women. Think on all these questions, Jonathan. Think carefully. And return here at four o'clock tomorrow."

III

I

I HAD by this time planned a course of reading and meditation to occupy the hours when I was neither crossing swords with my superior nor attending services in the chapel. The Fordites have imprinted their own idiosyncratic stamp on the Divine Office of the Benedictines, merging Terce with Sext and None with Vespers, but several hours of each day are still spent in choir; a monk must never forget that his chief work is to worship God. However beyond the hours of worship lie the hours of service to others, and normally I was heavily occupied not only with looking after my community but with giving counsel to those outside the Order who sought my spiritual direction. It was odd, even disconcerting, to find myself suddenly with no work on my hands beyond the hours spent in choir. I might have been advised to rest but anyone who has ever attempted to lead a celibate life knows how important it is to keep oneself constructively occupied, so after a prolonged perusal of the library shelves I selected some books which I judged would engage my mind without unhealthily over-exerting it.

I chose Dame Julian of Norwich's *Revelations of Divine Love,* not merely because it was one of my favourite classics but because I felt I would be cheered by the writings of a sane, practical, good-humoured person whose visions had been recognised by the Church. As a masculine counterpoise to Dame Julian's robust femininity I also chose *The Cloud of Unknowing,* another of my favourite works. Feeling I should then emerge from the woods of mysticism into the more arid plains of modern theology, I avoided the works of Karl Barth, whose preoccupation with God's transcendence is fundamentally hostile to mysticism, and was about to select the latest book by Reinhold Niebuhr, who parted company with Barth in several important ways, when suddenly I spotted Dean Inge's *The Philosophy of Plotinus*.

I was amazed. Plotinus had been a great religious philosopher with a vast influence on Christian Neo-Platonism, but he had been a pagan and Father Darcy had always refused to have Inge's celebrated masterwork in the house. However on opening the cover of the first volume I found the words "Cuthbert Darcy" inscribed on the fly-leaf. The old fraud! It seemed he had acquired the copy secretly and kept it in his room where it had been discovered after his death. Silently paying tribute to Francis's broadminded good sense in placing the work in the library, I added both volumes to the collection already in my hands and prepared to retire to my cell, but on my way out I caught sight of a new section devoted to modern psychology.

Francis and I, enjoying a rare moment of unity, had succeeded in convincing our mentor that not all psycho-analysts should be burnt at the stake, and rising to unprecedented heights of eloquence we had argued that we had a religious duty to understand as much about the human mind as was possible in the light of the latest scientific theories. When Father Darcy had declared that the Devil was corrupting intellectual progress by the writings of his servant Freud, I had even summoned the courage to say to him sternly: "Remember Galileo." The Church has been put in some ridiculous positions in the past by turning up its nose at the scientists.

However although Father Darcy had given us permission to read the books we felt were important, he had been adamant that we should keep any work on psycho-analysis under lock and key, and the sight of Francis's collection now standing bravely on the shelves was certainly a surprise. An even greater surprise was that I felt ambivalent. On the one hand I approved of Francis's resolution to bring the Order openly into the twentieth century, but on the other hand I was aware that monks were very ordinary men in many ways and might not automatically benefit from such intellectual modernism; I could well imagine my drones feasting on certain passages with a curiosity which was more salacious than spiritual. To my horror I saw Francis had even displayed the volumes of Havelock Ellis on human sexuality. This work was not without interest to a serious student of human nature, but there were parts of it which even I, the crusader for modern knowledge, had felt inclined to burn. Certainly I believed such a work could only have an unwholesome effect on the average monk.

I suddenly realised I was perturbed to a degree more complex than might have been anticipated, and retiring to my room I tried to analyse my feelings further. After a while I realised I was worried that Francis might be tempted to compensate himself for his spiritual limitations by relying too heavily on psycho-analytical theory. It was a chilling thought. Psycho-analysis can be a useful tool and it had certainly given me numerous important insights during my work as a counsellor, but it is not a substitute for religion and it should always be a servant, never a master. If Francis intended to rely on Freud and Jung instead of on God as he exercised the charism of discernment, then both he and I could well be heading straight for the most profound disaster.

2

"NO doubt you've composed a host of brilliant answers to the questions I posed yesterday," said Francis when I returned to his room on the following afternoon, "but since my aim at present is not to initiate a debate but to illuminate your situation, I propose we move on to the next topic and discuss your failure to become Abbot-General. I trust you're not going to deny you were disappointed?"

"No, Father."

Francis picked up his pen. "What steps did you take to adjust to this disappointment?"

"I had a long talk with Aidan before the funeral and made a full confession to him. That helped. Aidan's a wily old fox. He never said anything so obvious as: 'You've got to forgive the old boy in order to be at peace with his memory,' but he paved the way to forgiveness by persuading me to admit how much I'd have disliked being Abbot-General and how far more suitable you were for the job."

Francis leant back in his chair. Perhaps he thought his expression was merely quizzical but I found it cynical to the point of being offensive. "Why would you have disliked being Abbot-General?"

"Too much administration. Too much vapid socialising with the upper echelons of the Church. Not enough time to counsel men outside the Order. Not enough time to meditate in solitude."

"A small price to pay, surely," said Francis, "for such enormous gratification to your self-esteem."

"My ego isn't so insatiable as you seem to think! After my talk with Aidan I was happy enough to remain Abbot of Grantchester."

"But were you?" said Francis. "That's the next big question, isn't it? The world beyond our cloister has been turned upside down, the barbarians are at the gates and it's a very unpleasant fact of life, as Machiavelli knew all too well, that war can be immensely stimulating. It kicks people out of their well-worn ruts, offers adventure and provides all manner of enthralling changes—unless, of course, one happens to be in a monastery. Then life becomes increasingly drab."

"I hope you're not implying—"

"Do you deny that the War's been a depressing influence on your work? You lost one of your best young men the other day, didn't you?"

"Barnabas, yes. He's gone into the Army."

"It's always a harrowing experience to lose a good young monk. And meanwhile you still have more than your fair share of boring old drones—Augustine who falls asleep in choir, Denys the glutton—and what was the name of that monk you told me about once, the one who always has to wash his hands when the clock strikes noon?"

"Clement. But a monastery wouldn't be a monastery without its share of harmless eccentrics!"

"Tedious eccentrics. And meanwhile there you are, active as ever but beached like a stranded whale in your Grantchester backwater—"

"I hardly think you can describe a place which is only two miles from one of the great universities of the world as a backwater!"

"Don't try and tell me the War hasn't affected Cambridge! My spies inform me that Air Force officers are now billeted in the colleges and undergraduates are being sucked into the war machine, with the inevitable result that fewer people must be coming to the house to make a retreat or seek counselling. And meanwhile your tedious administrative tasks are increasing—all the irritating war-time regulations have to be mastered, interminable forms have to be filled in—"

"Bernard likes doing all those sort of things."

"—and your frustration must be growing daily. What a contrast to the last War when you were on active service as a chaplain! Then you were making a positive contribution to the war effort, but now all you can do is twiddle your thumbs in your Grantchester backwater amidst all your boring old men—"

"That's a gross misrepresentation!"

"—and it would be only natural, wouldn't it, if you occasionally longed to get out into the world and make some vital contribution to the fight to save England from the Nazis?"

"But even if I went out into the world," I exclaimed, unable to resist the temptation to outshout him and falling straight into the trap he had constructed for me, "I couldn't be a chaplain in the Navy again!"

"No." For the second time Francis leant back in his chair and regarded me cynically. "You couldn't. You're too old, aren't you? You're sixty. *Sixty!* Jonathan"—the trap sprang shut—"why didn't you remind me that the day preceding your vision happened to be your sixtieth birthday?"

I could only say stiffly: "I didn't think it was important."

"No? Could you really regard it as just another birthday? When I was sixty last February I was so sunk in gloom that the old man had to shake me, metaphorically speaking, until my teeth rattled and remind me that to mope about one's age is self-centred, futile and a prime example of that morbid introspection which can so seriously impair one's spiritual health. But the old man wasn't there to shake you till your teeth rattled, was he, Jonathan? He was dead—and that, of course, leads me to my last big question of the afternoon: exactly what effect has his death had on you? It seems to me that you've lost the one spiritual director who was capable of keeping you on the rails."

"That's not true. Aidan's always shown great skill."

"Aidan's skill lay in translating the old man's orders into action. Father Darcy ruled your career from the moment he removed you from Grantchester seventeen years ago, and perhaps now that you're without him you're beginning to feel lost, confused, adrift—even unbalanced—"

This was a line of attack which had to be instantly terminated. "I must insist—"

"No, indeed you must not! You're not here to be dogmatic and opinionated!" Francis, wielding his power with the efficiency of a giant cat bent on disembowelling his prey, was at his most formidable. In self-defence I assumed an expressionless silence, and as the pause lengthened I sensed Francis deciding how he might best complete my demolition. Finally he said in the most mellifluous voice he could muster: "I can see you're a trifle upset, Jonathan. Would you like me to tell you a little fairy story to help calm you down?"

The giant cat was closing in for dinner. With a sinking heart I resigned myself to the inevitable.

3

"ONCE upon a time," said Francis, "there was a hero, but he wasn't a prince as most heroes are in fairy-tales; he was a monk. At his christening long before he became a monk, two fairies were present. The good fairy gave our hero a range of unusual gifts which would one day make him an outstanding monk, but the bad fairy made him proud, arrogant, stubborn, wilful and opinionated. Our hero grew up and had an interesting career in the Church but it was blighted because despite his gifts the bad fairy's curse made him unable to develop them to the full. However when he at last became a monk, the miracle happened and he met his fairy godfather, the godfather who knew how to wave the magic wand so that all those nasty qualities bequeathed by the bad fairy could finally be overcome.

"Our hero endured many vicissitudes but thanks to his fairy godfather, who constantly waved the magic wand, our hero flourished, became happy in his new life and eventually allowed himself to hope that he might climb right to the top of the monastic tree. But then one day a terrible thing happened: the fairy godfather retired to live in fairyland, and our hero suddenly found himself not only abandoned, deprived of the magic wand, but also blocked from reaching the top of the monastic tree.

"Because he was a good monk he did his best to go on as usual, but slowly the bad fairy tiptoed back into his life and all those unfortunate flaws in his personality began to emerge again. Our hero became restless and dissatisfied. He fought to overcome these feelings by diverting himself with hard work, but this only made him exhausted and once the exhaustion began he slipped into a depression. Then slowly, very slowly, as life in the monastery became increasingly dreary, he began to think how nice it would be to abandon the soporific routine of his monastic life and ride off bravely, just as all heroes should, to join the great crusade against the Devil which was currently being waged in the world beyond the walls of his cloister.

"But of course he knew he couldn't leave the Order just to satisfy his own desires so he slogged heroically on—until a really terrible thing happened, so terrible that it sent him into a panic. He had a birthday, a particularly nasty birthday for a man, the sort of birthday which made him realise he wasn't just middle-aged any more, he was OLD. And before he could stop himself he was thinking in terror: I'm old, I've got nothing to look forward to except a few more years of living in this dreary backwater and I can't bear it, I've got to get out, I've got to *live* by joining in the Crusade somehow and proving I'm not as old as the calendar says I am! Because he was such a good monk he did attempt to suppress this thought but at that moment the bad fairy pounced, sneaking into his subconscious and showing him the perfect way to escape from his dilemma. And on the morning after that terrible birthday he had a beautiful vision, just as beautiful as any vision from God should be, so beautiful that he had no doubt at all, in his pride and arrogance, that he was being called to leave the Order."

Francis stopped speaking. With a supreme effort of will I maintained my silence, while far away on the mantelshelf the hideous china clock ticked so abrasively that I longed to smash it to pieces.

"Now, Jonathan," said Francis, smiling at me with great charm, "having, I trust, soothed your nerves by spinning you that quaint little tale which of course you'll deny has any relevance to your current situation, I shall conclude this interview by asking you to meditate on the following questions: how vulnerable are you as a monk now that you've been deprived of your mentor? How vulnerable are you as a man who's just turned sixty? Why did you so fiercely deny to Ambrose that you might be seriously depressed? Why did you resent Ambrose asking about your age? Why, when Ambrose began to talk about carnal matters, were you first withdrawn, then evasive and finally downright annoyed? Why have you been so busy insisting both to Ambrose and to me that everything in the garden's lovely when it's quite obvious that some very nasty weeds have begun to flourish in the flower-beds? Forget that pride of yours for a moment, Jonathan! Try to see yourself for once as the vulnerable man you really are instead of as the superhuman mystic whom your vanity requires you to be—and then perhaps we may have some hope of unravelling this most complex of mysteries . . . Now go away, please, and when you return here tomorrow I trust you'll have made up your mind to display very much more honesty and infinitely more humility than you've deigned to display so far."

4

RETIRING to my room I sat for a long time on the edge of the bed. It was not until after Compline that I was able to read a chapter of Dame Julian's *Revelations* and feel comforted. "And at the end of our woe," Dame Julian had written, "suddenly our eyes shall be opened and in clearness of light our sight shall be full; which light is God, our Maker and Holy Ghost, in Christ Jesus our Saviour. Then I saw and understood that our faith is our light in our night; which light is God, our endless day."

I thought of the light of God in the chapel, and at once my faith was renewed. As a good monk I accepted that I had to consider all Francis's repulsive and degrading insinuations, but my will to survive his attacks was now as iron and it was in a new mood of obstinate defiance that I knocked the next day on his door.

"*I KNOW* this is going to be just as tedious for you as it'll undoubtedly be for me, Jonathan," said Francis in his most businesslike voice as soon as I was seated, "but I'm afraid that today we'll really have to discuss sexual matters."

"I was wondering how long you'd be able to keep off the subject of Havelock Ellis! Are you sure it's wise to allow all your men access to his work?" I was well aware that this critical response represented a gross impertinence, but I was becoming a little tired of standing by meekly while Francis flexed the muscles of his power.

For a moment I thought he would lose his temper, but he controlled himself, and despite all my animosity I was impressed. Dealing with a recalcitrant monk was never easy; dealing with a hostile abbot would without doubt be a nightmare, and the temptation to wield one's power repressively, even violently, would be strong.

"No monk in this house is permitted to take a book from the psychology section of the library without my permission," he said at last, "but I thought it right that everyone should be able to see what's on offer. I wanted to avoid the hypocritical situation sanctioned by Father Darcy in which a select group of men is granted unlimited freedom in their reading while the superior continues to declare virtuously that only devotional and theological books can stand on the library shelves. Now if you've satisfied your urge to be obnoxious in order to prove to me that you're under strain, may we proceed with this interview?"

Finding myself wholly outmanoeuvred by this honest and dignified reply, I could only say: "I'm extremely sorry, Father. I'm afraid I was in error. Forgive me."

"Very well, but let me take advantage of your penitent mood by turning immediately to the subject of your celibacy; perhaps your penitence will encourage a frank response. Have you any comment to make about your past difficulties here?"

I said cautiously: "The difficulties weren't serious. My chief problem as a monk has been in accepting authority, not in doing without women."

"Nevertheless I see from your file that there's been at least one occasion during your career in the Order when you've longed—and I quote your own words, recorded with startling fidelity by Father Darcy—'to chuck it all up and fuck every woman in sight.'"

"I assure you I don't usually use such language, but I was extremely upset when I made that remark and having worked for years among working-class men who used that sort of word with monotonous regularity—"

"My dear Jonathan, just because you've always taken a 'holier-than-thou' attitude to my own occasional lapses into vulgarity, there's no need for you to go into such a paroxysm of embarrassment now that I've caught you out in a rare verbal indiscretion! The truth is, as you well know, that so long as you avoid blasphemy and talk like a gentleman in front of your subordinates I don't care a fig about your language. And now if we may return to the subject of your sexual frustration—"

"I see no point in dwelling on it. All normally-sexed monks feel frustrated occasionally."

"Quite. But would it be fair to say, do you think, that these bouts of difficulty with your celibacy coincided with periods of emotional stress in other areas of your life?"

I said obtusely: "I'm not sure I understand you."

"I think you do but you're playing for time while you try to drum up an innocuous response. Very well, let me be more precise: we all have our different ways of coping with emotional disturbances. When I was in the world I used to cope with them by drinking too much, but I seem to remember you were never greatly interested in food and drink. Your solace always lay elsewhere."

"Only when I was a very young man. But after my call to the priesthood—"

"—you turned over a new leaf, yes, of course you did, but nevertheless isn't it a fact that when you experienced emotional turbulence as a monk you also experienced a period of difficulty with your celibacy?"

"Well—"

"And isn't it a fact that in the emotional stress which followed Father Darcy's death you might have expected to experience yet another bout of discontent with the celibate life?"

I said abruptly: "I thought you assured me at the beginning of these conversations that you didn't intend to behave like a prosecuting counsel."

We stared at each other.

"So!" said Francis. "You sidestep the question! May I remind you that we'll get absolutely nowhere unless—"

"I was aware of sexual tension but it wasn't an urgent problem. It didn't interfere with my work—indeed I worked harder than ever in order to take my mind off the difficulty."

"And no doubt this aggravated the exhaustion which led to your depression."

"I deny—"

"Yes, you would, wouldn't you? But never mind, we've somehow succeeded in establishing that you felt sexually tense. Now let's turn again to that young woman Mrs. Charles Ashworth. How often has she been coming to see you and why does she come?"

I had been prepared for this assault. I said: "I helped her husband through a profound spiritual crisis in 1937 and she was part of that crisis. Without breaking the secrecy of the confessional it's impossible for me to say more than that as the result of the crisis I know facts about them which no one else knows, and in consequence I'm important as a confidant to them both. Indeed Mrs. Ashworth has apparently come to see me as a comforting presence in her life. There's no question of counselling—I've referred her to Dame Veronica at Dunton—but occasionally Mrs. Ashworth finds it helpful to visit me for a short talk and I always try to be available to see her."

"But surely," said Francis, "if you 'rather dislike' the woman—your own words—aren't these visits a bore? Why do you continue to make yourself available?"

I had anticipated this question too. "I feel it's something I can do for Charles," I said. "It's not an easy marriage for either of them and in my unusual position I have the opportunity to exert a stabilising influence."

"Is Mrs. Ashworth so unstable?"

"I was referring to the marriage."

"And I'm referring to Mrs. Ashworth. Any woman in an unstable marriage is liable to be emotionally volatile. Are you in fact telling me that you've been having regular private interviews with a disturbed woman while you yourself were suffering from sexual tension?"

"That gives an entirely false impression—"

"I think not. Could you explain, please, why you've been pursuing a course of conduct which must inevitably have been bad for your spiritual health?"

I knew I had to proceed with great care. After a pause I said: "Perhaps I feel guilty that I dislike her and this guilt makes me feel obliged to bend over backwards to be charitable. To tell the truth, I never wanted her to marry Charles. But on the other hand I fully accepted that he felt called to make the marriage, and since this meant I had to master my dislike in order to accept God's will, my continuing antipathy makes me feel guilty; I feel I'm failing to respond to God's will as I should."

Francis merely said: "Why do you dislike her?"

"I think she's a tough, ambitious little baggage who's fundamentally only interested in herself."

"Tell me what happened at that last meeting."

Obediently I embarked on an account of my interview with Lyle. " . . . and then she left," I concluded in my most colourless voice.

"Did she shake your hand?"

"No."

"There was no physical contact of any kind between you?"

This was the one question which I had prayed he would never ask. The ensuing silence seemed intolerably loud.

"Dear me," said Francis, removing his spectacles, "how very difficult this is. Jonathan, I'm sorry but I'm afraid I shall really have to ask—"

"It was a very trivial incident," I said rapidly. "As I opened the door of the Visitors' Parlour she exclaimed: 'Thank you for always being so kind to me!' and then she stood on tiptoe, kissed me on the cheek and swept out into the hall. Naturally I knew I couldn't possibly see her alone again, so later I wrote to her and—"

"Did you respond to the kiss in any way?"

"No, of course not!"

"I'm not just talking of a voluntary response. Was there any involuntary reaction?"

"Don't be absurd!" I said before I could stop myself, but added at once: "Forgive me, Father, that was the height of disrespect. I'm sorry."

Francis ignored the apology. "Why is my question absurd?"

"Well . . . " To my horror I found myself floundering.

"You were in a state of sexual tension, some saucy little baggage comes along and pecks you on the cheek—"

"My sexual tension had been dowsed by my anxiety. I was worried in case anyone had seen us, I was angry that she should have behaved like a trollop and I was repelled by my fundamental dislike of her."

"Jonathan," said Francis, "you may honestly believe in the truth of every word that you're saying; I'm inclined to think that you do. But I want you to go away and reflect carefully about where the truth actually lies here. Are you sure you've really explained why you dislike this woman so much? Why does an affectionate peck on the cheek turn a clergyman's respectable wife into a trollop? Why did you become so overheated just now when I suggested you might have responded involuntarily to this most fleeting and harmless of kisses? And last of all I'm going to ask you this: can you deny that only a few hours before your vision your sexual tension had been exacerbated and your emotional equilibrium undermined by your encounter with this woman?" He paused but when I remained silent he waved his hand in dismissal and I retired, seething with angry humiliation, from the room.

ONCE again I found myself unable to do anything except sit on the edge of my bed. I had long since drawn up a timetable of work in which simple reading and prayer were interspersed with *lectio divina* and meditation, but now I found that my will to maintain this admirable discipline had begun to flag. Hoping for comfort I turned to Dame Julian again, but this time her joyful optimism had no message for me and halfway through one of my favourite passages I realised I was thinking not of her "showing" but of Francis's appalling "fairy story." Earlier I had protected myself by refusing to dwell upon it, but now, shaken by Francis's remorseless exposure of the Achilles' heel represented by my sexuality, I found my defences had been impaired. In desperation I thrust aside the *Revelations* of Dame Julian and sought to distract myself with the unknown author of *The Cloud of Unknowing*.

But no distraction was forthcoming. Almost immediately I read: "Oftimes the devil feigneth quaint sounds in their ears, quaint lights and shining in their eyes, and wonderful smells in their noses; and all is but falsehood."

Snapping the book shut I gave a convulsive shudder and dragged my way down to the chapel for Vespers.

7

"I LIED to you yesterday," I said to Francis when we met again. "I'm sorry. I know very well I've got to be entirely truthful in order to help you reach the right decision."

Francis never asked what the lie was. That impressed me. Nor did he make any attempt to humiliate me further by embarking on a justifiable reproof. That impressed me even more. Instead he motioned me to sit down and said abruptly: "It's a question of trust, isn't it, and you don't trust me yet."

I forced myself to say: "I do want to trust you."

"Well, at least that's a step in the right direction."

"And I do accept that you're a first-class monk—"

"No, you don't. You accept that I'm a first-class administrator and you accept that the old man gave me a first-class training, but I've still to prove I'm a first-class monk, and that's why it's just as vital for me as it is for you that I should deal with your crisis correctly. I know perfectly well that you believe the only reason why I became Abbot-General was because I knew how to exploit the old man's secret longing for a son. Well, now I have the chance to prove the old man wasn't completely off his head and that I really am the right man for the job, so accept that I have a powerful motive to behave properly here, Jonathan, and do please discard your fear that I'll be unable to wield the charism of discernment unless you regularly throw in a lie or two to help me along."

Yet again I was impressed. I heard myself say: "It takes courage to be as honest as that. Thank you. I can't promise you I'll succeed in matching your honesty, but I can promise I'll do my best to try."

"Then put on your boxing-gloves," said Francis, not ill-pleased by this exchange, "and let's step back into the ring for the next round."

8

"TODAY," said Francis, "we're going to talk about your son." Flicking through the pages of my file he added: "There's not much on record about either of your children. Abbot James noted a few details when you entered the Grantchester house and later when you were at Ruydale Father Darcy made a note—ah yes, here it is—remarking that it was fortunate you were in a remote part of England where your children could only rarely visit you. 'Frequent family visits,' writes Father Darcy, 'would not have been good for Jonathan's emotional equilibrium and would have provided a severe spiritual distraction.' Have you any comment to make on that judgement?"

"Father Darcy knew that like any conscientious father I tend to spend an unnecessary amount of time worrying about my children's welfare."

"But was there so much to worry about once you'd entered the Order? Your daughter's marriage has been a success, you've always said, and your son's certainly not been a failure as an actor."

I said: "I'm very proud of both my children."

"Nevertheless it must have given you a jolt when Martin decided to go on the stage."

"It was hardly a bolt from the blue. He'd always excelled at acting, and when he decided to make a career of it I felt it would be churlish to stand in his way."

"What a model father! If he'd been my son I'm quite sure I shouldn't have behaved with such saintly resignation . . . How old was he?"

"Eighteen. It was the year I entered the Order. Martin was determined to support himself by taking part-time jobs while he was earning a pittance in repertory. My daughter was married. I was free to go my own way."

"Eighteen's very young. Are you absolutely certain there was no row when he declared his thespian intentions?"

"Martin and I don't have rows! Our relationship has always been excellent!"

"Yet last month, on the day before your vision, you and he had what you described as a 'disagreement.' Will you now tell me, please, exactly what happened?"

I had rehearsed this moment many times. "He disclosed to me that he wasn't leading a Christian life. Naturally I was upset."

Francis looked at me over the top of his spectacles. "He's thirty-five now, isn't he? Isn't that rather old to be sowing wild oats?"

I said nothing.

"What's the problem? Trapped in an eternal triangle?"

I heard myself say in an obstinate voice: "Martin must choose how to live his life. He's a grown man and I've no right to interfere."

"But if the life he's chosen to live is un-Christian—"

"Well, of course I pray for him to be brought back to Christ. Of course." Despite my rehearsals I was finding the conversation difficult to sustain.

"Has he been leading this un-Christian life for some time?"

"Apparently."

"Yet you had no idea?"

I shook my head.

"Despite your so-called excellent relationship with him?"

I wanted to shout: "You bastard!" and hit him. The violence of my reaction shocked me. Bending my head I stared down at the obscene luxury of the Indian carpet.

After a pause Francis said gently: "I'm sorry. Obviously the revelation was a great shock to you," and I knew my defences had been destroyed. I could cope with Francis being worldly, cynical, aggressive, snide and downright bloody-minded. But I could not cope with him understanding my misery and being kind.

I stood up. That was wrong. When a monk is seated in the presence of his superior he should never stand until he has been given permission to do so, but now, compelled to turn my back on Francis in order to conceal my emotion, I crossed the room and stood facing the clock on the mantelshelf. My voice said: "I made a mess of that scene with Martin. I should have communicated by showing compassion, by forgiving. How can anyone be brought to Christ if Christ's representative fails to display a Christian face?"

As I stopped speaking I found I was focusing my entire concentration on the clock in an effort to expel my pain by projecting it in a stream of power from the psyche. The clock's hands quivered; I saw the pendulum falter, and as the present began to grind to a halt the past overwhelmed me, not the recent past but the distant past when I had prostituted my powers in order to "get on" up at Cambridge. "I can make your watch stop just by looking at it . . . " The girls had worn watches as brooches in those days, and half the fun of stopping a watch had lain in the erotic adventure of putting a hand on the feminine breast to jolt the mechanism back into action.

In panic I realised I had allowed my psychic discipline to slip. My voice said shattered: "I've stopped the clock," but Francis at once retorted: "Nonsense, it just gave a hiccough. It does that sometimes," and to my relief I realised that the pendulum was still moving. I said confused: "I thought—" but Francis interrupted me.

"Now Jonathan, it's no good trying to play that old parlour-trick because I'm well aware that you never stopped any of those watches in the old days—you merely hypnotised all those gullible girls into thinking that you did. Come back here, sit down and behave yourself—you're acting like a half-baked novice."

This robust approach, so reminiscent of our mentor, at once steadied me. I returned to my chair.

"Have you heard from Martin since the quarrel?" said Francis after allowing me a moment to regain my composure.

"No, but I've written and I know that eventually he'll write back. Martin's always been so good at keeping in touch and sharing his world with me." But of course he had not shared it. Grief threatened to overwhelm me again.

"How old was he when his mother died?"

"Seven. Poor Betty . . . After the scene with Martin I thought how upset she would have been about him, and I kept thinking of her, thinking and remembering—" I broke off. Then I added abruptly: "Forgive me, I'm digressing. My marriage has nothing to do with my present crisis."

But Francis only said: "Hasn't it? Yet you've just confessed that it was most vividly resurrected in your mind shortly before you had your vision," and as we stared at each other in silence we were interrupted by the rapid clanging of the chapel bell proclaiming an emergency.

9

"*AIR-RAID* drill," said Francis casually. "We'd better set a good example by retiring speedily to the crypt. I must say, Jonathan, you've picked the most tiresome time in the history of the world to embark on a spiritual crisis."

After the drill had unfolded in a tolerably well-ordered manner there was no time to resume our interview before Vespers and I found I was greatly relieved by the postponement. I was beginning to be alarmed for the future. If Francis's preliminary talks could so effortlessly destroy my equilibrium, how would I fare when his inquiry became an inquisition? Fear and dread ravaged my psyche, and touring my room I put away all small objects in the chest of drawers. I was afraid that I might be on the brink of generating that activity popularly attributed to poltergeists, an activity caused by bursts of energy from a powerful but poorly disciplined psyche under stress; at such times this energy can move objects, often with considerable force, and if the psyche cannot control itself sufficiently much damage can occur. During my troubled early months in the Order, it had been the poltergeist activity, breaking out in the Grantchester community with alarming violence, which had driven Abbot James to seek help in bringing my disturbed psyche under control.

Memories sprang to life in my mind; I saw myself as a forty-three-year-old postulant summoned to the Abbot's office for an interrogation. I had planned exactly what to say to James to win his soft-hearted sympathy, but when I entered his room I found my plans had gone astray because James was absent and behind his desk sat a stranger, a man in his early sixties, hard-eyed, thin-lipped, ice-cold. The coldness was so extreme that it seemed to burn with heat, and as I at once recognised the powerful psychic aura I experienced a curious mixture of fright and relief. The fear was because I knew this was the one man I could never manipulate and I felt powerless; the relief was because I knew he would heal my disorder. In fact so great was my relief that I forgot to wait for permission to speak but said rapidly: "I'm causing the trouble but I can't help it because my meditation techniques don't work."

He sat in his chair and looked me up and down. Then he said: "Do you know who I am?" and without hesitation I replied: "You're the Abbot-General."

"I'm not just the Abbot-General," he said. "I'm the one man who can get you out of this spiritual cesspit of yours. Now answer me this: do you want to be a monk or don't you?"

When I immediately answered: "I don't just want to be a monk—I want to be the best monk in the Order," he smiled.

"What ambition!" he exclaimed. "But of course your pride would hardly let you settle for less." Then the smile vanished, the aura of ice intensified and he said: "Stand up straight, fold your hands properly, keep your mouth shut until you've been given permission to speak and wipe that arrogant smirk off your face. You've been three months in the Order—are you so unteachable that you haven't yet learnt how to behave? No doubt you think you're such a wise mature priest with your Cambridge degree and your twenty years in Holy Orders, but I'm here to tell you now that psychically you're no better than an ignorant spoilt child and that as a monk you're at present only capable of play-acting."

He waited in case I dared to argue with him but I was speechless. This interview was far removed indeed from my cosy chats with Abbot James.

"Shall I explain to you," said the brutal stranger, "what's really going on here? Like many people whose psychic powers are freakishly well developed, you're used to manipulating people whenever you want your own way. What you want here is to be petted and pampered so you've entranced your Abbot, you've tied your poor Novice-Master into a humiliating knot, and now, just like a spoilt child, you're calling attention to yourself by being disruptive in the hope that by causing chaos you'll make everyone realise how special you are!"

"But I swear I'm not doing this deliberately—"

"Of course that's what you swear! You've hypnotised yourself into believing in your own innocence, hypnotised yourself into believing you can't control these ridiculous outbursts of energy! But this is where the hypnosis ends if you want to survive as a monk. We've no room in the Order for confidence tricksters who perform psychic parlour-tricks. What you've got to understand is that there'll be no spiritual progress unless you learn humility and obedience, no hope of acquiring true charismatic power unless you starve that crude psychic force of yours of the pride which makes it so destructive. How can you expect God to use you as a channel for the Holy Spirit when you not only invite but welcome the Devil into the driving seat of your soul?"

I attempted a defence. I said I was not wicked, merely disappointed and unhappy. I told him the community was lax, that Abbot James was weak and that the Novice-Master was a fool.

Then the stranger rose to his feet. He was not a tall man but at that moment he seemed twice as tall as I was. I flinched. I believe I even took a step backwards. But he never raised his voice. He simply said: "And who are you to pass judgement on this community? Obviously you're in an even worse state than I'd feared and radical measures will have to be taken. You must be taught a lesson in humility, a lesson you'll never forget, and afterwards you must begin your life as a monk all over again elsewhere."

Then he had taken me to London and after a night spent in the punishment cell where I had been taught the lesson I would never forget, I had been dispatched to Ruydale to make my fresh start.

The memory terminated. I returned to the June of 1940, but I continued to think of Father Darcy and after a while I closed my eyes so that I might imprint his image more accurately on the retina of my psyche. To attempt to call up his spirit was out of the question; such practices are dangerous as well as arrogant and in my opinion the Church is entirely right to discourage them. It is not for us to interfere in our hamfisted way with the great reality of eternal freedom which lies beyond our brief existence in the prison of time and space, and such discarnate shreds of former personalities as linger within the prison walls are usually either trivial or demonic.

So I made no attempt to summon Father Darcy, but when I had constructed his memory as accurately as possible I tried to imagine his response to my current dread that stress would seriously impair my psychic control, and at once the word "discipline" was firmly imprinted on my mind. Finding my timetable I stood looking at it. Then sitting down at the table I opened my Bible, made an intense new effort to concentrate and began to read St. Paul's mighty Epistle to the Romans.

I O

"FURTHER to our conversation which was so rudely interrupted," said Francis the next day, "I'd just like to clarify a couple of points about this unfortunate interview with your son. Presumably you were very distressed after he left. What did you do?"

"I dashed off a letter of apology to him. Then I forced myself to make my usual appearances in the chapel and in the refectory, but after Compline I retired to my cell again and read 'Romans.' That always calms me. I think of St. Augustine and Luther reading it and going on to change the course of history; it makes me feel I'm close enough to draw strength from people of great spiritual power. I didn't sleep before the night office but by the time I went downstairs to the chapel I knew I was in control of myself again."

"And after the office?"

"Then I admit I had difficulties." I paused to drum up the courage to be honest. "Once I was faced with the task of sleeping all the symptoms of stress returned. I felt isolated, unhappy . . . If I'd been a married man, I'd have turned to my wife for consolation."

"But as you weren't a married man—"

"I behaved like an ill-disciplined novice and consoled myself, as I implied earlier, with my wife's memory."

"You mean—"

"I gave way to temptation, obtained the relief I needed and fell asleep around three. How Father Darcy would have despised such a failure of the will! I shall always remember him saying that the body should be an obedient servant, not a tyrant balking at the most rudimentary discipline."

"Personally I always found Father Darcy's lectures on the power of the will deeply depressing. After his hypnotic persuasiveness had worn off, I was left contemplating my weaknesses in despair."

"I was certainly depressed when I awoke the next morning at five-thirty—and not just because of the failure of my will. I was depressed because I'd allowed myself to get into such a state that a failure of the will was inevitable, and I was still sitting on the edge of my bed, still well-nigh immobilised by my depression, when the vision began."

Francis said with great delicacy as if he feared one careless word might shatter this miraculous frankness: "When you said just now that you obtained the relief you needed, am I to understand . . ." His delicacy was so extreme that he left the sentence unfinished.

I thought I could understand his difficulty. "You doubt that a sixty-year-old man who was emotionally worn out and sexually spent at three o'clock in the morning could manifest the symptoms of sexual excitement during a vision less than three hours later."

"Not at all," said Francis with an urbanity I could not help but admire. "It's a fact that psychics may command unusual reserves of energy, and anyway where sex is concerned anything's possible, even for sixty-year-old men who ought to be decently exhausted. If I hesitated it wasn't because I was boggling at your energy reserves but because I was thinking that if you did achieve a complete release earlier, it does support your belief that the vision wasn't triggered by a purely physical frustration . . . You're sure you're not slipping in a little inexactitude to help me along?"

"I hope I'm now beyond the stage of deliberately misleading you."

"Then I shall merely conclude the interview by asking you to reflect further on the fact that Martin plunged you into a severe emotional disturbance. The question you should ask yourself, I think, is not: Was this emotional disturbance the direct cause of my vision? Of course you're determined to believe that question can only be answered in the negative. So perhaps it would be more profitable if you asked yourself instead: Exactly why was I so disturbed by Martin's disclosure? What did it mean to me on the profoundest psychological level? You might also ask yourself if there was any hidden significance in the fact that you later began to dwell with a great intensity on the memories of your marriage. For example, when you were manipulating those memories in a certain way, were you merely seeking a release from tension, or were you perhaps expressing a desire to recapture a time when you were leading such an active sexual life that your wife was annually pregnant?"

I stared at him. "Are you implying that subconsciously I felt so disappointed in Martin that I was smitten with the urge to go out into the world and beget a son to replace him?"

"You find that an unlikely explanation of your vision?"

"I find it ludicrous!"

Francis twirled his glasses. I was reminded of an angry cat swishing his tail.

"I'm sorry," I said at once. "That was disrespectful. But I must insist that Martin's still my much-loved son and I've never—*never*—felt so dissatisfied with him that I've longed for a replacement."

Francis twirled his glasses again and swept open my file. It took him some seconds to reach the passage he had in mind, but eventually he found it and paused to look at me. "I'd like to read you an extract from Father Darcy's report on the Whitby Affair," he said. "I think you'll find that it's remarkably pertinent to our present conversation." And clearing his throat he read in a studiedly neutral tone:

"Jonathan then became very distressed. He said: 'I suddenly saw myself as a layman would see me—a pathetic middle-aged monk, starved of women, deprived of a normal masculine life, who was crying, actually *crying* over a cat.' Then Jonathan said: 'Suddenly I hated my life as a monk, hated it—I wanted to chuck it all up and fuck every woman in sight. I thought: here I am, still only fifty years old and feeling no more than forty; I could be out in the world with a young second wife; I could have another daughter, a daughter who wasn't forever reminding me of Betty—and best of all I could have another son, a son who wasn't an actor, a son I could talk to, a son who wouldn't constantly torment me with anxiety. What am I doing here?' said Jonathan. 'Why am I living this impossibly difficult life?' And I said: 'You're here because you're called to be here. You're here because God requires you to serve Him in this hard, difficult way. You're here because if you weren't here your personality would disintegrate beneath the burden of your weaknesses. You're here because it's the only way you can survive.' Then he broke down and cried: 'But how do I bear it?' and I answered: 'Think of the novices who have so recently been entrusted to your care. Think of others, not yourself, and you'll find not only liberation from the dark side of your soul but fulfilment of your ability to do great good and live in harmony with your true self.' After that I made him kneel down and I laid my hands on his head and at last the demonic spirit of doubt departed and he was healed."

Francis closed the file. Then, still using his most neutral voice, he said: "And there you have it all: the emotional disturbance, the profound difficulty with your celibacy, the desire to leave the Order and beget a second family—and finally the healing by the one man who was able to keep you on the spiritual rails, the man who's no longer here to give you the help you so obviously need." He allowed a long silence to develop before adding casually: "Tomorrow's Sunday and I always try to spend the hour between four and five in meditation. But come here directly after supper, Jonathan, make a new resolution to tell me no more lies and then we'll have our last talk before you depart on Monday morning."

II

"I'M worried about your weekly confession," he said when we met the following evening. "Of course you could make one of your bowdlerised confessions to Timothy, but I really feel that would be most unsatisfactory and as I'm reluctant that anyone else in the Order should know about your crisis, I find I've no alternative but to volunteer my own services as a confessor. I needn't remind you of your right under the Order's constitution to decline to make confession to your superior; if you find my suggestion unacceptable I'll ask Ambrose to hear you, but if you could somehow see your way towards waiving your constitutional right, I admit I'd be greatly relieved."

I could not help but sympathise with him in his predicament. "You forget that Father Darcy ordered Aidan to be my confessor after the Whitby Affair," I said. "I'm well used to making my confession to my superior."

"Quite. But one of the vows I made to myself when I became Abbot-General was that I wouldn't ride rough-shod over the monks' constitutional rights as often as Father Darcy did. However if you're willing to waive this particular right without being coerced . . ."

He allowed me time to prepare, and retiring to the chapel I recalled the episodes of pride, anger and falsehood which had punctuated my life that week. Then I returned to his office and the difficult exercise began. I was surprised when it proved easier than I had feared. He kept unexpectedly quiet, refraining from all the obvious comments, and gradually I began to respect his refusal to gloat over me while I was vulnerable. With a certain amusement I wondered if this compassionate behaviour arose not from his desire to be a good priest but from his instinct to act like a gentleman; I could well imagine him deciding that the waiving of my constitutional right was a sporting gesture which demanded that he should be equally sporting in return.

I was granted absolution and assigned a very moderate penance. I thought Father Darcy would have judged this much too soft, and perhaps

Francis too was afterwards convinced he had erred on the side of leniency, for as soon as we embarked on our final conversation he became waspish.

"I want to end these talks where we began—with your vision," he said abruptly. "There's one glaring omission in your account, and I'm sure I don't have to tell you what that omission is."

"It wasn't revealed to me what I'm to do when I leave the Order."

"If you leave the Order."

"If I leave the Order. I'm sorry."

"If this vision is from God," said Francis, examining a well-manicured fingernail in an elaborate charade of nonchalance, "wouldn't you have expected to receive at least a hint about what you're supposed to do next?"

Cautiously I said: "I believe further enlightenment will be forthcoming."

"How wonderfully convenient." Francis held his left hand at arm's length and gave the chosen fingernail another meticulous inspection. Then suddenly he discarded the mask of nonchalance, leant forward purposefully across the desk and said: "Now listen to me, Jonathan. You cannot—and I mean *cannot*—ignore your intellectual faculties in favour of a woolly-minded mysticism when your future has to be considered; you should remember that the best mystics have all been distinguished by their sane practical attitudes to life. As soon as you return to Grant-chester pull yourself together, confront the reality of this alleged call of yours and try to visualise what kind of life would be waiting for you outside the Order. You're a sixty-year-old priest. You've been out of circulation for seventeen years. At first you're inevitably going to find the world confusing, exhausting, depressing and—for the most part— uncaring. Of course we know you can always find work. We know I can always ring up the Archbishop and say: 'Oh, by the way, Your Grace, my best abbot's about to leave the nest—find him a nice little nook in some cosy Cathedral Close, would you?' We know you're not going to be reduced to eating bread-and-dripping in a sordid lodging-house in between bouts of waiting in the dole queue, but Jonathan, if you're going to survive in the world with your equilibrium intact, you absolutely must feel that you're doing what God's called you to do. Otherwise you'll get depressed and fall victim to Monks' Madness, and we both know what that means, don't we?"

We did. It was a notorious fact that monks who left the Order often found themselves psychologically compelled to recuperate in the most unfortunate of ways from their years of celibate seclusion.

"Oh, and while you're grappling with your possible future in the world," said Francis as an afterthought, "do ask yourself what you'd do about women. It's a very important subject and one which must be faced realistically."

"I'd remain celibate."

"Perhaps you didn't hear me correctly. I said: 'It's a very important subject—' "

"Marriage distracts me from serving God."

"In that case you'd better stay in the Order. Oh, go away, Jonathan, before I become really irritable with you, and for goodness' sake take your brain out of those second-rate mystic mothballs so that you can do some constructive thinking! Nothing annoys me more than to hear a clever man talk like a fool."

I rose to my feet. "Do you wish to see me before I leave tomorrow?"

"Yes, come here after breakfast so that I can give you my blessing."

He was so fractious that he made the blessing seem a sinister prospect. Leaving the room I began to count the hours which remained until my departure.

12

FRANCE had fallen, and in England the air-raids had started. At Liverpool Street Station I bought a copy of *The Illustrated London News* in order to see a summary of the week's events, and read about the night attacks on the eastern counties. So the long-awaited, inexplicably delayed battle for Britain had begun. Yet I thought the delay might prove significant. God had appeared to withdraw but as always had been eternally present and now the infusion would begin, the outpouring of grace into those facing the blast of the demonic force, the bestowal of courage and endurance which would ultimately triumph over the nightmare of militant idolatry. Our ordeal had begun. The suffering lay before us, but beyond the suffering lay the power of the Spirit, overflowing eternally— in the metaphor of Plotinus—into the muddied waters of mankind, and against that power the ship of idolatry would ultimately shatter. I could see the shattering. It was not a matter of speculation but of *gnosis,* of knowledge; I knew. Yet still I shuddered at the thought of the ordeal ahead of Britain, standing alone at the edge of a demoralised, demon-infested Europe, and the next moment Britain's ordeal was again fusing with my own until it seemed not merely a struggle for survival but a great spiritual quest which could only be described in the ancient language of religious symbolism.

I saw the powers of light withstanding the recurrent invasions of the forces of darkness, the perpetual conflict of finite existence played out amidst the Eternal Now of ultimate reality. Britain wanted peace yet was obliged to go to war to preserve its cherished values; I wanted to serve God in tranquillity yet was obliged to wage a continuous battle against the qualities which marked the opaque side of my nature, and when I saw myself as a microcosm of the conflict which permeated the very air I breathed, I was conscious of the Devil, not the charming little creature rendered so endearingly by medieval artists, but the unseen climate which periodically bruised my psyche as it sensed the vibrations and emanations of the weather patterns which so many people were apparently unable to perceive. God too can be experienced as a climate, and part of the psychic's *gnosis* lies in being able to read the barometer which reflects not merely the ebb and flow of demonic forces but the unchanging presence of the kingdom of values, the world of ultimate reality that lies beyond the world of appearances.

It was not until I dismounted from the train at Cambridge that I temporarily abandoned all thought of demonic infiltration. I also abandoned *The Illustrated London News;* I did not want my men to know I had been reading a magazine. It was a rule of the Order that the abbots should read *The Times* each day so that they might inform their men during the weekly recreation hour of events in the world, but this was regarded as a necessary duty whereas browsing through even the worthiest magazine could only rank as a distraction.

Resisting the slothful urge to take a taxi I travelled by motorbus from Cambridge to Grantchester and finally, to my profound relief, walked up the drive of my home. I realised then how much I hated that luxurious house which flourished like an anachronistic weed in the heart of drab, dirty, debilitating London. My Grantchester house was neither old nor beautiful; it had been erected late in the nineteenth century by an East Anglian merchant who had shortly afterwards been obliged by his bankruptcy to sell the place to the Fordites, but in its secluded setting at one end of the village it stood in unobtrusive harmony with its surroundings. Returning to it after my enforced absence, I found it refreshingly quiet, modest and serene.

"I've kept all the copies of *The Times* for you, Father," said my admirable prior, welcoming me warmly in the hall. "I thought you might have been too busy in London to read the newspaper."

I refrained from telling him that Francis had not offered his copy for my perusal. Reading a newspaper would have constituted intolerably frivolous behaviour for a monk who was supposed to be concentrating on his spiritual problems.

My relief that I was home expanded into pleasure. My best men were all so glad to see me and even the sulkiest drone achieved a smile of welcome. After dinner I briefly interviewed my officers, attended to the most urgent correspondence, dealt with a couple of domestic matters and toured my five-acre domain of flowers, vegetables, fruit trees, herbs and bee-hives. In the herb-garden the cat came to meet me and I picked him up. A black cat with a white spot on his chest, he had been called Hippo after St. Augustine's city, and was a dull, affectionate animal like the drone who was responsible for his welfare. After stroking the fur behind the ears I set the creature down again but he was captivated; he padded after me as I completed my tour of the garden and even mewed in protest when I eventually shut the back door in his face.

The bell began to toll in the chapel. I displayed myself in choir, but suddenly as I savoured my happiness that I should once more be worshipping God in my familiar place, I remembered my new call and shuddered. How could I bear to leave? My happiness was at once displaced by misery.

However in my own home I found it easier to regain my equilibrium. Reminding myself that my departure was by no means certain, I spent some time reading (the accumulated copies of *The Times* were a great solace) and later made a satisfactory attempt at meditation. When I returned to my cell after Matins that night I was tired enough to feel confident that I would fall asleep without difficulty, and indeed as soon as I had closed my eyes I felt my mind drift free of the fetters I had subconsciously imposed upon it during the difficult week I had spent in London. I began to dream.

13

I DREAMT of Whitby, proud arrogant Whitby, who had stalked through the backyard at Ruydale with his tail pointed triumphantly at the sky. Prowling prancing Whitby, living in his monastery but padding off to the nearby hamlet whenever the celibate life became too uncomfortable, clever cunning Whitby, a little battered and scarred like all successful tomcats but still as striking as a racy buccaneer, tough tenacious Whitby who worked hard and deserved his pleasures, lean lithe Whitby, wonderful Whitby—what a cat! Whitby was walking through my dream towards me but suddenly he faded into a black cat, not Hippo of Grantchester but Chelsea, my mother's favourite cat, serene elegant Chelsea who washed her paws so fastidiously on the hearth. My mother was there too, serene and elegant just like Chelsea, and she was talking to me without words, saying everything she was too reserved to say aloud and making me feel so sorry for my father who was excluded from these conversations because he was unable to hear us in our silence. "How lonely you must be with him!" I said to my mother in my dream, but she answered: "No, I have you and Chelsea."

"My own children can't hear me when I talk to them," I said to her, and in my dream time was abruptly displaced because my mother had never lived to see her grandchildren. "The cat can't hear either." And as I spoke I saw the stupid ginger cat, my children's cat whom my daughter Ruth had named Goldilocks—which was a ridiculous name for a cat although I had never said so—but whom Martin, enrapt by different fairy-tales, had always called Pussy-Boots. In my dream Betty was slopping some milk into a saucer for the cat and as she stooped I could see past the open neck of her nightgown. "You look like a cat facing a bowl of cream!" she said laughing, and as I took her in my arms the ginger cat watched us, a stupid cat, not trained to be clever, but unfortunately I was away too much at sea to ensure his education.

"You're going to talk to me about that cat," said Father Darcy, walking into the scriptorium at Ruydale, and suddenly there was Whitby, proud arrogant Whitby, leaping through the window with an exuberance which made the novices laugh, and Aidan was saying: "I'm not sure I understand; I'm not even sure I want to understand; but whatever's going on must stop."

Then in my dream Ruydale dissolved into London and I was searching the Fordite headquarters for Father Darcy. I searched every room, floor after floor, but he had disappeared and finally I had to confess to Aidan: "I can't go on without him. It's too difficult." But before Aidan could reply in walked Lyle Ashworth, small and slender in an open-necked nightgown, and as she lay down on the bed I turned to Aidan to say: "I lied to Francis—I did have an erection after all," but Aidan had vanished and when I turned back to the bed I found that Lyle had been replaced by Betty. Betty had taken off her nightgown and the next moment I was consummating my marriage, sunk deep in the folds of the most exquisite pleasure, and yet all the time I was so lonely, so isolated, so ravaged by unhappiness and despair—

I woke up sweating.

The room was filled with the dawn light. For some time I prayed for the further revelation which would validate and clarify my vision of the chapel, but no message imprinted itself on my mind and at last, rising reluctantly from my knees, I trudged to the basin to shave.

14

I SHALL not record the mental torment of the next four weeks as I examined each of my interviews with Francis and lurched from confidence to doubt and from despair to hope. Suffice it to say that I meditated on my crisis as conscientiously as I could and somehow, amidst bouts of the most crippling anxiety, contrived to present a semblance of normality to my community as I went about my daily work. Day after day I prayed for a further divine communication, but God, the utterly transcendent God of Karl Barth's repellent anti-mystical theology, appeared to have withdrawn from that scrap of finite time in which my soul was imprisoned, and no matter how hard I prayed for a manifestation of His immanence I was disappointed.

In Europe God also appeared to be absent. The Germans slaughtered thirty thousand people in Rotterdam, bombed the Channel Islands and abolished the famous motto of France, "Liberty, Equality, Fraternity." In their shock and fear the British seemed to find such events almost impossible to digest; they twittered about tea-rationing (my drones were very cross) and talked righteously about the evils of the "chatterbugs" who threatened the national security by their gossiping. But we all listened to Churchill with a new intensity. I fell into the habit of reading aloud his speeches, printed in *The Times,* to my men after breakfast; the national peril was so great that I did not think it right that they should be obliged to wait a full week before hearing the news in the Saturday recreation hour. Monks may live apart from the world but they do not reject it, and day after day we prayed for all those whose lives were being ravaged by the War.

However I was eventually diverted from this urgent work by the inevitable summons from Francis. Three weeks after my return to Grantchester I received a communication which read: "Please confirm that you will return to London on Monday to re-examine the matter which we discussed last month," and at once I sent an obedient message in reply.

The most arduous part of my ordeal was now confronting me.

I began to steel myself for the inquisition.

15

"SO here we are again," drawled Francis, "in spite of Hitler's attempts to interrupt us. I suppose that if the Germans invade they'd shoot all monks on sight? Atheistic Nazism combined with the German folk-memory of Luther's repudiation of religious orders certainly doesn't encourage optimism on the subject."

"At least you'd be spared the ordeal of interrogating me."

"So I would. But perhaps I'm to be spared it anyway. Have you finally succeeded in taking your mind out of those mystic mothballs and deciding your vision was a delusion?"

"I'm sorry but—"

"No, don't bother to apologise. I never seriously allowed myself to hope that you'd walk in here, prostrate yourself at my feet and announce: 'I was deluded.' " Francis swept back his mane of silver hair and allowed himself a theatrical sigh of resignation. Then he said curtly: "Very well. Come back at four this afternoon and I'll start the task of taking you apart."

IV

"St. John of the Cross even said of a nun who claimed to have had conversations with God: 'All this that she says: God spoke to me; I spoke to God, seems nonsense. She has only been speaking to herself.'"

W. R. INGE

MYSTICISM IN RELIGION

I

"BEFORE I wheel on the rack," said Francis when we met five hours later, "I must give you the chance to rebut all the insinuations I made during your last visit, but please, Jonathan, *please* don't offer me any fey mystical claptrap. I want rational propositions from you, not romantic waffle. Now first of all, what makes you think this vision was real and not a fantasy triggered by an emotional disturbance?"

Without hesitation I said: "Apart from the north light at the end there was no obvious distortion of reality—no six naked women, as you put it, dancing in the glade. If the vision had been triggered by a sexual difficulty, I feel some form of sexual symbolism would have shown up."

"What about the rich woman's bag?"

"I don't believe that was a sexual symbol. If it was, then I suspect the lid would have been open to reveal a feminine garment such as a night-gown."

"Very well, but let's stay with the subject of your sexual difficulties. I concede there was no sexual symbolism in the vision but that might have been because you'd obtained physical relief earlier that night. How can you be sure that the vision wasn't triggered by a far more complex sexual malaise arising from a disintegrating adjustment to the celibate life?"

"Primarily because I've been through much worse times without any vision being triggered. The truth is this difficulty with my celibacy wasn't as bad as you're trying to make out."

"And Mrs. Ashworth?"

"With all due respect I think you should guard against turning that particular molehill into a mountain. Obviously I find the woman more attractive than I want to admit and obviously I've been protecting myself from that weakness by stressing my dislike of her, but I'm not in love with the woman, I'm never likely to be in love with her, and such attraction which exists is only of the most trivial kind."

"So might the aging Antony have said when he saw the still youthful Cleopatra—but I take your point. And now we've reached the subject of aging, let me ask you this: why are you so sure that your current crisis isn't the result of your panic when you awoke on the morning of your sixtieth birthday and realised old age was staring you in the face?"

"There was no panic. I'm a mature man, not an elderly adolescent clinging to a lost youth! I admit I disliked the idea of being sixty, but what's so abnormal about that? You yourself admitted that you spent three days sunk in gloom after your own birthday this year—how are *you* enjoying being sixty years old?"

"Well, as a matter of fact," said Francis, "I'm now enjoying myself immensely. But I dare say that's because I've been fortunate enough to acquire this fascinating new career as the Abbot-General."

Conversation ceased. As Francis caressed his spectacles languidly I was appalled to realise that my fists were clenched. Surreptitiously I relaxed my fingers one by one.

"Congratulations!" I said at last. "That was a neat twist of the thumb-screw. Are we reaching the point where you wheel on the rack?"

"Let's first see how well you defend yourself against the charge that you're attempting to storm out of the Order in a fit of pique because you failed to become the Abbot-General."

"I'm neither a fool nor a bad monk. I've got enough brains to see I'd be very miserable here in London, and I'd never request to be absolved from my vows out of mere injured pride." I hesitated, but when Francis remained silent I added: "For seventeen years I've had the strongest possible call to the cloister, and on the one occasion ten years ago when I really did long to leave, my longing had nothing to do with my lack of preferment. On the contrary, at the time of the Whitby Affair I'd just been made Master of Novices and my future in the Order was rosy."

"But on that occasion you had Father Darcy to steer you through the crisis to safety—and that brings us to the next point: how do you deny the charge that this vision is simply a spiritual aberration brought on by the loss of your mentor?"

I had long since decided that I had no choice but to grasp this particular bull by the horns. "I could only rebut that charge by proving there's nothing wrong with my spiritual health," I said, "and since we both know that my spiritual health has recently been impaired by emotional stress, I can't offer a water-tight defence. All I can say is that it never once occurred to me that I couldn't survive in the Order without my spiritual director. Think of my pride! What would Father Darcy have said if I'd chucked in the sponge in such a pusillanimous fashion? No, of course I had to go on. There was no choice."

There was a silence while Francis began to polish his spectacles on the skirt of his habit. I could not decide whether he had no idea what to say next or whether he was trying to rattle me by keeping quiet.

"I suppose," I said to show him I was unrattled, "you now want me to say something about Martin."

"You're inviting me to wheel on the rack?"

"No rack's necessary. I'm willing enough to talk—and willing enough to concede that he thoroughly upset me. In fact I'm even willing to concede that he could have triggered the vision. But I don't think he did, and I'll tell you why: if he'd been the trigger, I believe the vision would have been different—for instance, I'm sure he would have appeared in it, just as Charles Ashworth appeared in my vision of 1937. And there's another point which is important here: why should Martin's problems make me want to leave the Order? Even if I were in the world I could do no more than pray for him, and I can do that equally well in the cloister."

"True. But this is where we wonder if you're subconsciously longing to rebel against old age and wipe out your disillusionment with Martin by taking a young second wife and begetting the ideal son."

"You can't seriously think I'd be quite such a fool!"

"Fortunately for the human race matrimony and procreation aren't confined to fools."

"Yes, but to embark on both at the age of sixty when I know I can serve God best as a celibate—"

"Why shouldn't God now wish you to serve Him as a married man?"

"But I've had no indication of that!"

"You've had no indication of anything! All you've experienced is this mindless urge to leave the Order, and it's quite obvious that this could have been triggered by one or more of a number of circumstances—"

"There was no trigger." I tried not to raise my voice but failed. "This vision came from God!"

"You still have no doubts about that?"

"Absolutely none!" I said with a dogmatism guaranteed to inflame any superior past endurance.

"How arrogant!" exclaimed Francis. "How wholly lacking in humility! How utterly devoid of any willingness to admit you could be wrong!" As he stood up I too rose to my feet and we faced each other across his desk. "Go to your cell," said my superior, "and don't come out of it—unless there's an air-raid—until you're due to return here at four tomorrow. I find your attitude profoundly unedifying."

"Yes, Father." Walking out I somehow resisted the temptation to slam the door.

2

I WONDERED if he intended me to fast, but my supper arrived on a tray and later Ambrose appeared, inquiring about my health. Evidently Francis was taking no chances with my mental equilibrium by allowing me to slide into physical debility.

The knowledge that I had deftly repelled Francis's efforts to undermine my confidence was very cheering; settling down to enjoy my solitary confinement I read, meditated, prayed and retired to bed in a mood which could almost be described as complacent.

However my complacency began to fade when I returned to his office on the following afternoon and was obliged to wait outside the door for ten minutes before he gave me permission to enter. Such a petty exhibition of power I found very irritating, and my irritation increased when he ordered me into the room only to keep me standing in front of his desk while he finished writing a memorandum. I was beginning to seethe with anger when I realised that any loss of temper would constitute a victory for him, and at once I willed myself to be calm.

Eventually he motioned me to sit down. Then he said abruptly: "Now listen to me. There are two things I want to make clear. Number one: I'm convinced this vision of yours had a trigger. And number two: the existence of a trigger doesn't necessarily imply the vision didn't come from God."

I assumed what I hoped was my politest expression and said nothing.

"You believe," pursued Francis, "that in order to prove this vision's from God, you must maintain that it has no connection with anything which was going on in your life at the time. However I'm now certain that this approach is erroneous."

Still I said nothing, but I was aware that my polite expression was becoming strained.

"I'm not denying that God's capable of sending people visions out of the blue," resumed Francis, ploughing on purposefully. "All I'm saying is that I don't think this is likely in your case, and I say that because, as you reminded me yesterday, your call to the cloister was so strong. I think

God would have had to prepare the ground before He gave the blast on the trumpet; otherwise you would have been either deaf to the blast or convinced you were mistaken. So from the point of view of discernment the crucial question becomes: what was the vision's final trigger? I think that once we can answer that question we'll be a lot closer to solving this mystery."

By this time I had given up trying to look polite and was concentrating on achieving a meek expression.

"Jonathan, I find it unnerving when you give a bravura performance of the model monk. Could you please stop acting and venture a comment which isn't entirely lacking in honesty?"

"I find your opinions very interesting, Father, but I can't help wondering if you might be mistaken. If a final trigger had existed I'm sure I'd be able to identify it."

"How typical!" said Francis in disgust. "You think you can do anything, don't you—even read your subconscious mind! It never occurs to you in your arrogance that your subconscious mind may be beyond the reach not only of your intellectual powers but of your tiresome psychic powers as well!"

"Well, of course I'm as capable as anyone else of suppressing a truth I've no wish to face, but all I'm saying is—"

"All you're saying is that you intend to be as arrogant and obstinate as ever! Very well, let me now ask you the question I would have asked yesterday if you hadn't driven me into losing my temper: during your month of reflection at Grantchester did you receive any further enlightenment on the subject of what this call's all about?"

"No. But I'm convinced that if I leave the Order I'll be led to the chapel, and once I get there—"

"Stop!" Francis held up his hand. Then he said incredulously: "Can I possibly have misheard you? Is it conceivable that you seriously believe you'll be led to this place? You imagine a latter-day Star of Bethlehem will be hanging over the chapel, perhaps, to guide you on your way?"

"No, Father. All I'm saying is—"

"That's enough! Be quiet!"

Silence. I folded my hands together and waited.

"I can see it's a complete waste of time talking to you at the moment," said Francis. "I'm beginning to think old age has softened your brain. Go to the workshop and ask them if they can let you have some wood to play with. When people are mentally disturbed they're often encouraged to work with their hands."

"Yes, Father." I did succeed in making a dignified retreat, but I could not help thinking as I left the room that this time Francis had fared far better in the interview than I had.

IN the workshop where four monks made church furniture I introduced myself to Edward the master-carpenter, and informed him that I had been ordered to work with wood. He looked incredulous. Manual labour is encouraged at all levels of the Order and I did my share of gardening alongside my brethren at Grantchester, but nonetheless an abbot is hardly expected to seek work as an artisan.

"I was trained by Alfred at Ruydale," I said.

Edward became deferential. "What would you like to do, Father?"

I did not answer the question directly but said: "Is it too much to hope that you've got some seasoned oak to spare?"

He had the oak. It seemed like a sign. With the wood in my arms I moved in exhilaration to the work-bench and embarked on my first carpentry assignment for ten years.

"I HEAR you're making a cross," said Francis the next day. "Amusing for you. How long will it take?"

"Longer than it should. I'm out of practice."

"What's so difficult about making a cross?" said Francis, deliberately provocative. "Can't you just bang a couple of bits of wood together?"

"No, Father. I have some very beautiful oak and I want to make the cross out of that one piece, taking every chance to display the grain of the wood to its best advantage."

"Well, I suppose that's all very soothing for your equilibrium—maybe I should take up carpentry myself. I've got a novice hearing voices, a visiting bishop who's in a muddle about pacifism, four young shirkers who swear they're called to be monks, Harrods trying to sell me something called a radiogram instead of a modest wireless, twenty unanswered letters requesting advice on topics ranging from the sublime to the ridiculous— oh, and I nearly forgot! An abbot whose psychic powers are running riot! When you return to your cell, Jonathan, go down on your knees and thank God you were spared the ordeal of being Abbot-General."

"Yes, Father."

"Very well, go away, I'm too busy to bother with you at the moment. I'll send for you in a day or two."

Exerting an iron will to control my temper I retired once more to the workshop.

"*I HEAR* you've finished the cross, Jonathan. Of course it's a replica of the cross you saw in your vision, so I suppose all you now have to do is build the chapel, isn't it? Then I can shine a torch through the north window and you can claim a miracle."

"That's right, Father. But before I build the chapel I was hoping we could resume our talks."

"Getting impatient? Patience is in many ways the most difficult of all virtues, Jonathan, and one which I feel it would pay you to cultivate."

"Yes, Father."

"Perhaps you might have another vision while you wait. It would pass the time."

"Yes, Father."

"Jonathan, doesn't it occur to you that this humourless docility is the height of veiled insolence? I detest it—the least you could do to placate me would be to smile at my witty remarks!"

"What witty remarks, Father?"

"Very funny. All right, get out. The Lord Abbot-General is quite definitely not amused."

6

"*CURIOSITY* stirred in my mind this morning, Jonathan, and it occurred to me to wonder what you've been doing since we last met four days ago. Any more enthralling psychic dramas?"

"No, Father. I've been helping Edward to make an altar-table."

"Maybe I can solve your entire problem by ordering you to remain here as a carpenter. Obviously the strain of being an abbot sent you off your head."

"Naturally I shall obey any order you care to give me, Father."

Francis made a noise which sounded like "Arrrgh!" and slumped back in his chair. "Very well, Jonathan, let's have a truce. Sit down."

Once more we sat facing each other across his desk. I was beginning to feel tense again although the relaxation provided by the carpentry had strengthened me mentally, just as Francis had no doubt intended; a nervous collapse would only have made the task of discernment more protracted. Perhaps he had also intended to strengthen me mentally by severing me from the outside world; I had received no invitation to "listen in" to the wireless which had finally been acquired to give him immediate news of the continuing crisis, and I had been granted no access to *The Times*. However fortunately for my sanity the monastic grapevine was active. The postman and the milkman were clay in the hands of the doorkeeper, who with impressive journalistic skill jotted down a few pertinent sentences and delivered the scrap to the kitchens. It usually reached the workshop shortly before the office at noon.

"I've reached the conclusion that we must make a completely different approach to this problem of yours," Francis was saying. "As things stand we're now firmly entrenched behind fixed positions and no further progress is possible, so we must abandon our survey of the recent past, I think, and turn to the more distant past in our quest for enlightenment."

Dutifully I said: "Yes, Father," and assumed an interested expression.

"What I now want to do," pursued Francis, changing the nib of his pen, "is to compare your new alleged call to leave the Order with your old call to enter it and uncover the common denominators."

I was sufficiently startled to exclaim: "But there aren't any!" However I added at once: "I'm sorry. That's not a helpful attitude and I must do my best to be more constructive."

Francis said after an eloquent pause: "Thank you, Jonathan." Throwing the old nib in the wastepaper basket he dipped his pen in the ink and wrote at the top of a new page of foolscap: "THE CALL TO BE A MONK." Then he undid the ribbon which bound my file and opened the folder to reveal the earliest entry.

"The first point of interest about your original call," he said, "is that it's poorly recorded, but I suspect I know why. You were accepted as a postulant by your predecessor in the Abbot's chair at Grantchester, and we all know now that dear old James Reid, God rest him, was so soft-hearted that he welcomed into the Order almost anyone who knocked on his door. I'd wager your call was never comprehensively investigated. In the end that didn't matter, since your call was genuine, but no doubt when you quickly became so disruptive poor James thought he'd made a disastrous mistake."

I felt obliged to say: "He did stand by me; even when I came to blows with the Master of Novices, James resisted the demands that I should be thrown out. When he called in Father Darcy it wasn't because he wanted to get rid of me but because he thought the poltergeist activity demanded a first-class exorcist."

"How Father Darcy must have enjoyed himself! But as soon as he met you, he knew James was right about your potential, didn't he? So he didn't investigate your call in detail either. He was much too busy shaping your future to waste time burrowing into your past." Francis picked up a page from the file and added: "Let me read you part of James's opinion recorded after his preliminary interview with you in 1923 when you were still outside the Order. He writes:

"Jon tells me that he's wanted to be a monk ever since his wife died in 1912. He loved his wife very dearly and they had nine happy years of marriage which were blessed by the gift of two children: Ruth (born 1904) and Martin (born 1905). Jon is clearly devoted to his children and during the eleven years since his wife died he has worked hard to support them even though his call to the cloister was becoming increasingly strong. He tells me that despite his happy marriage he realised that a life of domesticity, charming and rewarding though it might be in many ways, proved difficult to combine with his unusual and distinctive spirituality, and when his wife died he knew he must remain celibate in order to serve God best. He is also convinced that in the world he will always be tormented by the temptation to marry to satisfy his carnal inclinations, and he believes that only in a monastery will he be able to serve God without distraction and develop his spiritual gifts to the full. In my opinion he is patently sincere, mentally well-balanced despite his psychic powers and is obviously a man of high intelligence and considerable pastoral ability. In the past he has been led astray by a desire to exploit the glamour inherent in those psychic powers, but I believe that with sufficient training and dedication a truly charismatic power can be developed for the service of God. I told him I would accept him as a postulant, and I believe that in time he will prove a considerable asset to the Order."

Francis closed the file. For a long moment we looked at each other in silence. Then he said mildly: "Jonathan, I don't want to appear cynical but it sounds to me as if you manipulated that unworldly man with all the skill your 'glamorous powers' could command. During those nine years of happy marriage, what exactly happened which made you feel the trip to the altar was the one journey you never wanted to repeat?"

7

"*JAMES* spells out the truth clearly enough," I said. "I came to realise that despite my successful marriage I could serve God best without the distraction of family life."

"But was your marriage really so happy as James apparently believed it was?"

"No, of course not. My marriage was like the vast majority of marriages; sometimes it was heaven and sometimes it was hell. Betty and I enjoyed the heaven, survived the hell and on the whole rubbed along very tolerably together. I certainly felt I was entitled to present the marriage to James as a success."

"Tell me about the times when the marriage was hell."

"You're most unlikely to understand how unimportant our difficulties really were. If you'd ever been married yourself—"

"Oh, good heavens!" Francis was suddenly at his most theatrical. He groaned, shaded his eyes with his hand and twisted his mouth into a mournful grimace. "I did hope I'd never hear a monk of your calibre try to trot out that hoary jibe of the snide layman. If you're not careful you'll drive me to trot out the equally hoary gibe of the Roman Catholic priests that the onlooker sees most of the game."

Despite my tension I laughed and apologised.

"I can see I must tiptoe up to this delicate subject by another route," said Francis. "How did you meet your wife?"

"After I was ordained in 1903 I went to work at the Mission for Seamen in Starmouth, and a week later I met Betty in the park. She saw me, failed to look where she was going and stumbled over a patch of uneven ground. Naturally I rushed to assist her."

"Just like a romance from Mudie's Library. What was her background?"

"Her father owned a tobacconist's shop."

"Dear me, how awkward! What did your schoolmaster father think of your desire to marry below your station?"

"How could he complain? He'd married a parlour-maid—as Father Darcy never ceased to announce to all and sundry whenever he wanted to rub my nose in the mud and induce a spirit of humility."

"Am I to deduce that you married a working-class woman because you wanted a wife who was just like your mother?"

"No, you can forget your obsession with Freud and deduce that I married a working-class woman because I couldn't afford to marry a lady on my modest salary as a chaplain."

"If you had no private means I'd have thought that any marriage would have been out of the question for a young man of twenty-three. Surely your father advised you to wait!"

"My father was a quiet scholarly man who didn't find it easy to talk to me—indeed I both mystified and frightened him. His predominant reaction to my desire to marry seemed to be relief that I wanted to settle down."

"And your confessor—who, of course was none other than dear old James himself at our recently founded Grantchester house—what did he think of your decision?"

"He was the one who urged me to marry as soon after my ordination as possible."

Francis said dryly: "It's amazing how dangerous these unworldly holy men can be. However I mustn't be too harsh on poor old James—after your shady career at the Varsity I suppose it was inevitable that he should doubt your ability to stay chaste for long . . . Did you continue to see him regularly between your ordination in 1903 and your entry into the Order twenty years later?"

"No, there came a point when I realised he was incapable of counselling me, so I decided to dispense with a confessor."

"You mean you had no direction at all?"

"Oh, I was never completely adrift! I always had some older priest with whom I could discuss spiritual matters, but I never made a formal confession and I never talked in detail about my private life."

"In other words you abandoned Anglo-Catholicism."

"Not entirely. It was easy enough to drift back into the fold later when I realised I wanted to be a monk. I never lost my admiration for Bishop Gore and the High Church party."

"What was the matter on which James failed to give you acceptable counsel?"

"Contraception." I hesitated but when Francis merely waited I said: "Betty could barely manage two children under two. The strain was affecting her health as well as our marriage, and when she threatened to seek an abortion if she became pregnant again I saw contraception as the lesser of two evils."

"Meanwhile James, I suppose, had told you to behave like a eunuch. How far were you able to share the spiritual aspects of this dilemma with your wife? Was she devout?"

"No. She believed in God as children believe in Father Christmas— with a mindless innocence. Religion for her was little more than a charming superstition."

"How very difficult for you!"

"Not at all," I said at once. "She supported me by coming to church on Sundays and she was very good in bed. What did I have to complain about?"

"Well, Jonathan, I'm just an ignorant old bachelor, as you tried to tell me a moment ago, but I seem to remember hearing somewhere that there should be more to marriage than sexual intercourse and I'm quite sure there should be more to being a clergyman's wife than turning up in church on Sundays. Tell me, was your wife intelligent?"

"No, she was really rather stupid. But that didn't matter. I prefer to discuss intellectual matters with men, and anyway when a man gets home after a hard day's work the last thing he wants is to hear his wife expounding on intellectual or spiritual matters. He wants a kiss and a hot meal and the latest report on the domestic front, the more banal the better."

"The wife you're describing seems to be little more than a housekeeper," said Francis. "Or is it a glorified parlour-maid?"

"If you're still clinging to the theory that I wanted to marry a woman just like my mother, I assure you that you couldn't be more mistaken! Betty and my mother were utterly different."

"Tell me about this mother of yours. Were you the only child?"

"Yes, but she didn't spoil me. She trained me much as she used to train her cats—firmly and without sentimentality."

"How old were you when she died?"

"Fourteen. Can we stop this digression now, please, and return to more relevant matters?"

"Why are you becoming so flustered about your mother?"

"I'm not flustered! It's just that one doesn't always welcome the opportunity to share cherished memories, particularly if one's in the middle of an inquisition. Why are you so obsessed with the Oedipus complex?"

"You don't ask the questions, Jonathan; you answer them. Why do you suppose you married a woman who was so utterly different from your mother?"

Losing patience I said with sarcasm: "No doubt you'd advance the theory that when I failed to find my mother's replica among the women I met through my Cambridge acquaintances, I married my mother's opposite in despair."

"Never mind the theory I'd advance. Let's hear you advance a theory of your own."

"I don't have a theory; I have knowledge. I married Betty because I loved her, and although the marriage had its difficult aspects I must absolutely insist that it was happy and successful."

"But my dear Jonathan," said Francis, "can't you see that you're trying to harmonise two statements which are fundamentally incompatible? On the one hand you're insisting that you were happily married—yet on the other you're insisting that the marriage made you so maimed spiritually that you were unable to serve God to the best of your ability. I put it to you that either you were happily married and not spiritually maimed; or that you were spiritually maimed and unhappily married. But a priest like you can't possibly be both spiritually maimed *and* happily married. That would be a psychological impossibility." He terminated the interview by laying down his pen. "Now go away and consider what I've said, please, and when you return tomorrow I trust you'll be a good deal more explicit about your curious marriage than you've deigned to be today."

8

AFTER supper I retired to my cell to examine the new development in my ordeal. I could now perceive the dimensions of the rack, just as I could sense that Francis was steering me towards it, and I knew I had to take defensive action. I felt no guilt in admitting this because I knew Francis was on the wrong track; my duty at this point was clearly not to wave him on his way but to do my best to steer him back onto the right road.

I sat plotting how I might best deflect him and escape the rack. Of course I could not tell lies. I had to be as truthful as possible but that meant I had to calculate with precision where the boundary between the possible and the impossible lay. It would be unfortunate if I were to discover in mid-sentence that I had allowed myself to be strapped to the rack despite all my efforts to avoid it.

I saw then that the next interview would be fraught with danger, and on the following morning in the workshop I barely glanced at the doorkeeper's daily news. The war beyond the cloister was receding in my consciousness. I was too busy fighting a desperate private war of my own.

9

"I'M sorry you thought I was being so paradoxical yesterday," I said to Francis when we next met. "With your permission I'd now like to explain my marriage in a more comprehensible way."

Francis kept his expression bland and motioned me to continue.

"What I was really trying to imply," I said, "is that I was probably as happy with Betty as I would have been with any other woman. The problem wasn't Betty; it was marriage itself—the whole business of living in close proximity to another person. The truth was I shouldn't have married at all, but as I was neither a eunuch nor a homosexual it never occurred to me at the tender age of twenty-three that I'd be better off as a celibate. So I married and was often very happy. It's true that I did find my spiritual vitality was being sapped, but since I loved my wife and children I was prepared to tolerate that. All marriages involve some degree of compromise and mine was certainly no exception."

But Francis merely said: "I do see the distinction you're trying to make when you blame your discomfort on the institution of marriage rather than on your wife, but nevertheless if living in close proximity to another person was so difficult for you, one can't help but wonder if that other person might be part of the problem. Forgive me for asking, but did you in fact marry her for any reason other than the sexual and the economic?"

"No, but that doesn't mean the marriage was doomed. Most marriages founder over either money or intimacy. It was our modest bank balance and our intimate relationship which held the marriage together."

"Well, there wasn't much else to hold it together, was there?" said Francis bluntly. "She shared none of your intellectual interests; she was spiritually illiterate; she came from a different class, a fact which must have complicated your professional and social life in all kinds of difficult ways—"

"But I've told you—I didn't care about any of those disadvantages! All I wanted was a morally acceptable outlet for my sexual inclinations—"

The trap sprang shut.

"How very humiliating for your wife," said Francis brutally, and at once I was slammed on the rack.

I O

FRANCIS saw his shot had hit the mark and allowed me no time to regain my equilibrium. "Tell me more," he said, "about how unsuited you were for matrimony. I can quite believe that an immature young man who treats his wife merely as a cheap sexual receptacle would make a far from ideal husband."

I tried to devise a strong response but I was unable to think clearly. I began to twist my Abbot's ring round and round on my finger.

Francis said briskly: "The truth is, isn't it, that you made each other very miserable. When did you first realise you'd made a mistake?"

"You're completely misrepresenting the situation—"

"How can I be when you admit marriage left you cold?"

"It didn't leave me cold. It left me deprived of psychic space. That's different. It wasn't Betty's fault. As I keep telling you, it was marriage, not Betty, that made me unhappy." I had stopped twisting my ring but my fingers were tightly interlocked. "Even before I entered the Order," I said, "I needed a great deal of time alone in order to meditate and pray, and frankly I had no idea that the daily routine of marriage would be so hostile to any attempt to sustain a rich inner life. Nothing had prepared me for such chaos. My parents were quiet people; our home was very orderly, very peaceful, very conducive to developing a talent for using solitude constructively. But as soon as I married I found myself in a different atmosphere. Betty was seldom still. She was always rushing hither and thither, continually invading my psychic space, laughing, crying, endlessly chattering . . . And then the children came. Of course I was pleased and proud, but the noise, the mess, the constant destruction of any interlude which encompassed peace and order—"

"You were born into the wrong class, Jonathan. My parents cheerfully abandoned their children to nannies and governesses and enjoyed numerous delightful interludes with their lovers."

"My dear Francis!"

"Will you kindly stop trying to undermine my authority by addressing me by my Christian name?"

"I'm sorry, but I was so appalled by your lighthearted attitude to such adulterous irresponsibility—"

"Good heavens, can't you see I was trying to signal my sympathy to you by making a joke about my own melancholy experience of family life? No, obviously you can't and I must apologise. I shouldn't have forgotten how sensitive you are on the subject of class . . . But let's return to your marriage. You've admitted you were in a situation which would have driven me, if not you, to drink. How did you make life bearable for yourself?"

The rack creaked. Once more I found myself groping unsuccessfully for a strong response.

"Come along, Jonathan! Obviously you had to take drastic measures to preserve your sanity—"

"I volunteered for service at sea."

"What a brilliant solution! But didn't the authorities try to tell you that a married chaplain should remain ashore with his family at the Naval base?"

"I talked them out of that. I said I'd been called to serve on board ship. I was very convincing."

"And how did your wife feel about being abandoned?"

"She was no more abandoned than any other Naval wife! Anyway I made it up to her—whenever I came home our reunion was as good as a honeymoon."

"But how did you get on at sea? There was little privacy and peace, surely, on board ship."

"I had my own cabin. Once the door was closed I had the psychic space I needed and I was happy. That was when I finally faced the fact that I couldn't serve God properly as a married man, yet on the other hand—"

"—on the other hand you had a wife and two children and no doubt you still couldn't imagine giving up intimacy entirely. What an exceedingly difficult spiritual position! You led this divided life, you had no adequate spiritual direction, you must have become increasingly isolated—"

"But I'm a psychic! I was used to isolation, used to no one understanding, used to struggling unaided with my problems."

"Nevertheless what a relief it must have been when she died!"

Silence fell after this ultimate turn of the screw. My psyche, jarred and jolted by the rack, flashed a warning to my brain that the strain was proving too much, but before I could stop myself I was saying: "It was terrible when she died. *Terrible.* If you think I was glad you couldn't be more wrong."

"The dark side of bereavement lies in the guilt beneath the grief."

"Why should I have felt guilty? She loved me, I did everything in my power to make her happy—"

"You're wonderfully convincing, Jonathan, and I can almost smell the red roses and hear the Strauss waltz, but unfortunately my sceptical streak means that I have a deep-rooted resistance to romantic fantasies. However, I'm always willing to listen. Come back tomorrow and spin me another romantic fantasy about your chaste life as a widower."

I stared at him. He stared back. I was acutely aware of my file bulging on the desk between us.

"Francis, I really can't see what relevance such a conversation can possibly have to my present predicament."

"It's my business to see the relevance, not yours—and for heaven's sake stop calling me Francis! That's a privilege I'll allow you if you ever leave the Order, but meanwhile I'm your superior and I don't want either of us to forget for one moment that I'm responsible for the care of your soul . . ."

I I

I DREAMT about Hilda that night. In my dream she was committing suicide by hanging herself, but I was bound hand and foot, unable to save her. She was hanging herself on the gallows of the prison where I had worked as a chaplain, and as I watched the body twitching on the end of the rope I realised that I was lying in a pool of blood.

"You look a trifle pale," said Francis when I returned to his room the following afternoon. "I was sorry to see when I passed your door at three o'clock this morning that your light was on."

"Why were you spying on me at three this morning?"

"Why should you automatically assume I was spying on you? What vanity! As it happens, I was summoned to the infirmary to attend to my poor little novice who hears voices. I'm afraid his place is in a hospital, not a monastery."

"I'm sorry."

"It was a salutary reminder that ninety-nine-point-nine percent of the people who hear voices and see visions are mentally ill. Now," said Francis, having tested the rack and found it in good working order, "let's return to the subject of your past. We'd established that your marriage was a nightmare—"

"It was not a nightmare! It simply had difficult aspects!"

"Were you faithful to her?"

"Of course I was faithful to her! How could I have gone on as a priest if I'd committed adultery?"

"Was she faithful to you?"

"Yes, she loved me."

"Even after you ran away to sea? It sounds to me as if she was either mad or mesmerised. Were you abusing your psychic powers to keep her under control?"

"Certainly not, and if you hadn't known me during the most shameful period of my life it would never have occurred to you to ask such an obscene question! After my call to the priesthood no woman ever played Trilby to my Svengali—and anyway there was no need for me to play Svengali to ensure Betty's devotion. She loved me almost too much as it was."

Francis at once made a note. I tried to read it but could only decipher the words "unreciprocated love" and "additional strain."

I said: "I think you've still got quite the wrong impression of my marriage."

"Have I? Then before you start getting upset all over again let's now leave the subject of your marriage and examine your life as a widower." Opening my file he turned to the page he had already marked. "I'm going to read you another passage from James's notes," he said. "The dear old boy writes:

"Today Jon made a full confession prior to his entry into our house tomorrow. I must admit I was privately shocked and saddened that he should have drifted so deeply into error, but I remain certain that life in the Order will solve this problem of his by preserving him from temptation, and my original opinion that he will make a good monk remains unchanged."

Francis closed the file and waited, but when I remained silent he said not unkindly: "Jonathan, I promise I shan't be censorious. You confessed these sins to James, he gave you absolution and from a spiritual point of view the matter's closed. I only raise the subject now because I want to see how far your difficulties as a widower contributed to your desire to be a monk."

"Yes, Father." I tried to pull myself together. "I'm sorry," I said. "If I hesitate it's because I'm still ashamed, even now, that I failed to live as a priest should."

"I can quite see how difficult it must have been for you. You were accustomed to an intense intimate relationship and you were in a state of spiritual weakness after years of a divided life . . . Did you never consider remarriage?"

"Never. I did try hard to avoid women and for most of the time I succeeded. But at the end . . ." I fell silent again.

"Yes?" said Francis. "What happened at the end?"

"I met this woman. It was 1923 but I didn't know when I met her that I was going to be able to enter the Order later in the year. I thought I was going to have to support Martin up at Cambridge. If I'd known he had no intention of going I might have resisted the temptation, but as it was . . . I felt I couldn't bear my unhappiness any longer."

"But you'd had mistresses before 1923, surely?"

"I wouldn't call them mistresses. There were incidents during the War when I was on my own somewhere a long way from home. But Hilda . . . that was quite different. She did voluntary work for a charity which aided discharged prisoners. I met her when I was calling at the home of a prisoner who'd just been freed and she was there too, visiting the wife and children . . . We were both immediately attracted. Chastity soon became quite impossible."

"Did you ask her to marry you?"

"No, I told her from the beginning that I was only marking time until I could be a monk. But of course she never believed I'd go through with it."

"How did you eventually extricate yourself?"

"I . . . No, I really can't describe the ghastliness of it all except to say that she threatened suicide and I nearly died of guilt. I hadn't hated myself so much since that poor girl died up at Cambridge."

Francis printed: "GUILT. HATES HIMSELF" on his sheet of foolscap and said without expression: "Did she in fact commit suicide?"

"No." I wiped the sweat from my forehead. "She married someone else eventually."

"And during this agonising time did it not once occur to you, *not once,* that you might give up all thought of being a monk and marry this woman?"

"Oh no," I said. "The affair with Hilda confirmed what I already knew: that I couldn't stay in the world and remain a good priest. My only hope of fulfilling my vocation lay in entering a monastery."

"Obviously your call was very strong but a satisfactory intimate relationship is no mean driving force either. I'd have thought—"

"Marriage was an impossible dream," I said impatiently. "I could never have borne the burden."

Francis's pen paused in mid-sentence. "Burden?"

"The burden of guilt that I'd married despite my knowledge that I was unsuited to married life." Unable to look at him I glanced around the room until my gaze rested once more on the clock. The temptation to reduce my tension by projecting it in a stream of power from the psyche was very strong.

"But you've just admitted that you nearly died of guilt when you jilted her," Francis was saying. "Are you now implying—"

"Yes. The guilt would have been even worse if I'd married her. I chose the lesser of two evils."

"How far were you able to set down the burden of all this guilt when you entered the Order?"

"The relief was instantaneous. I was finally at peace after years of torment."

"How very odd! I wouldn't have thought that merely walking through the door of the Grantchester house would have made so much difference—in fact surely your problems were only exacerbated when you wound up in such a mess as a postulant?"

"I agree I got in a mess and was miserable, but it was a different kind of mess and a different kind of misery. Grantchester was quite the wrong house for me, of course—but not, as I thought at the time in my arrogance, because it was spiritually slack. It wasn't, not then; James ran the place well enough in his own mild, idiosyncratic way until old age made him lose his grip, but I was beyond being helped by a mild, idiosyncratic rule. I needed the austerity of Ruydale, and Father Darcy realised that as soon as he met me."

"So, once you met Father Darcy—"

"I was happy."

"Even when he followed that first meeting by flogging you in the London punishment cell?"

I stopped staring at the clock and swivelled to face him. "Nobody enjoys being flogged!"

"No?" said Francis. "I rather thought that according to modern psychology some people do."

I finally lost patience with him. "Can we forget the modern psychology for a moment and concentrate on the spiritual dimensions of what was going on? The flogging was necessary because I was so deeply sunk in pride that I was unable to learn humility and obedience in any other way—I was being forcibly turned around and redirected along the correct spiritual path. But once that had been done I was set free to realise my full ability to serve God at last—and *that's* why I can say with truth that an enduring happiness only began for me when I met Father Darcy."

"And your happiness continued when he kicked you north to Ruydale, the toughest house in the Order—are you sure you don't enjoy suffering, Jonathan?"

"Is that another of the witty remarks which I'm supposed to find amusing? I can't tell you how irritated I'm becoming by your psycho-analytical poses—shouldn't you now pause to remind yourself that you're a priest and not a Harley Street quack? If you did you'd have no trouble understanding that the suffering I had to endure—*endure,* not enjoy—was a necessary part of my development into a good monk, and I endured it—*endured* it—because my call to be a good monk was so strong."

"Yet now you have what is apparently an equally strong call to stop being a good monk—and why, Jonathan, *why?* Has your life at Grant-chester become too soft and easy for you? Do you think you'd suffer more if you went out into the world?"

"You're being deeply offensive. I absolutely deny—"

"Save your breath. Come back at four o'clock tomorrow and—hullo, the clock's stopped! Ah yes, of course—I forgot to wind it this morning." Francis rose to his feet, moved to the fireplace and produced a key from a china vase on the mantelshelf. Then he looked back at me over his shoulder. "What are you waiting for?" he demanded. "You're dismissed."

Retiring to the chapel I futilely tried to pray.

I 2

I WAS now convinced that Francis was determined to reduce my call to a delusion by burying its spiritual dimensions beneath the rubble of a garbled psycho-analysis. I could see all too clearly the theory which he was developing. Deciding that I was a masochist who had finally exhausted the potential for suffering offered by the monastic life, he was toying with the idea that Father Darcy's death had been the mythical "final trigger" which had sent me over the edge of sanity. Having suffered the delightful humiliation of being rejected by my mentor and the exquisite pain of failing to become the Abbot-General, I had realised that the Order now offered me nothing but an intolerably pain-free life at Grantchester, and unable to face a monastic future without my favourite sadist I was chafing to return to the world where with any luck I might acquire a wife who would beat me every night. How delicious! All I would have to do was buy a whip and a chain or two and then I could live happily ever after.

This atheistic vision of a maimed psyche so appalled me that I even wondered—and this was the final horror—if there could be a grain of truth in it. Surely if the theory were quite inapplicable I should be laughing at its absurdity? But my whole future was at stake. How could I laugh when the future I knew I had to have was now threatened with abortion? Indeed all thought of both present and future had suddenly become so agonising that instinctively I took refuge in the remote past. Closing my eyes I reached up to clasp my mother's hand as we walked down the garden to find Chelsea, serene, elegant Chelsea, who washed her paws so fastidiously before the sitting-room fire on the long winter evenings when my father read his books and my mother sewed in silence and I sat listening to her thoughts.

"You and your cats!" said my father to my mother. "In the old days you'd have been burnt as a witch!" And the high clear voice which had belonged to me long ago said in panic: "They won't burn her now, will they? I don't want her dying and going away."

My memory shifted. I felt Martin's small sticky hand in mine and heard him say: "I don't want you going away any more."

I said aloud in 1940: "Martin—"

But then the light was switched off in my memory, and stripping off my habit I went to bed and willed myself into unconsciousness.

13

"WE'VE discussed your relationship with your wife," said Francis, "we've inspected your relationship with your mistress and now today we're going to examine your relationship with your children. What happened to them after your wife's death?"

"My mother-in-law took charge."

"I detect a lack of enthusiasm. How did you tolerate her living in your home?"

"She didn't live there. She took the children into her own home and I moved to bachelor quarters on the Naval base. But I wasn't there much. I still spent most of my time at sea."

"Did the children mind not living with you?"

"I told them that the quality of time fathers spent with their children was more important than the quantity."

"Are you good with children?" said Francis idly, but I could feel his large, sleek, powerful psyche prowling around mine as he sought to induce a fatal relaxation. "Are you one of those gifted adults who always know what to say to anyone under sixteen?"

"It depends on whether there's any psychic affinity."

"And does such an affinity exist between you and your children?"

"No. I can't communicate with them without words as I used to communicate with my mother."

"Disappointing for you. How you must have longed for a couple of little replicas of yourself instead of these two people whom you obviously found so alien!"

"You couldn't be more mistaken. I despise parents who long for replicas—I consider such a desire indicative of gross selfishness and an inflated self-esteem."

"Aren't you reacting rather strongly? It's a very human trap for a parent to fall into, I've always thought, and it's certainly not an uncommon one . . . However I won't press that point; we already know from Father Darcy's record that even if you didn't long for replicas you were nonetheless capable of finding your children a disappointment. But what about your grandchildren?" said Francis, sweeping on before I could argue further with him. "Any affinity there? I notice you never mention them, but perhaps that's because you're so sensitive about your age that you dislike being reminded you're a grandfather."

"Nonsense! My silence is because my grandchildren are strangers to me. They were born after I entered the Order so I've seldom seen them."

"What kind of a man is your son-in-law?"

"He's an outstandingly boring atheist who earns his living as an accountant in one of Starmouth's shipbuilding firms."

"Tedious for you! If he's got to be an atheist he might at least have the grace to be an amusing one," said Francis, and made a note which included the words "strangers," "antipathy" and "disappointment."

"Something tells me," I said, "that once again you're forming quite the wrong impression of my family life. Let me stress that I'm devoted to both my children and I've always tried to do my best for them."

"Of course. You palmed them off on a woman you disliked and occasionally dropped in to see them whenever you weren't far away at sea."

Once more I was slammed on the rack.

I 4

"SO I wasn't mistaken," I said as I clenched my fists to endure the pain. "You have indeed formed quite the wrong impression of my family life.

I wrote to my children frequently. When I was ashore I saw them as much as possible and when I left the Navy after the War I even undertook a very hard, difficult chaplaincy at Starmouth Prison so that I could be near them during their adolescence. I cared deeply about their welfare, I—"

"Dear me, I seem to have drawn blood! What a sadist I am! But perhaps you only enjoyed sadism when it came from Father Darcy."

"I most strongly deny—"

"Why did you really take on that hard, difficult chaplaincy at the prison? I suppose that once the War was over and there was no chance of you being killed or maimed the Navy had nothing left to offer, so you deliberately sought an environment where you could suffer vicariously with all the men condemned to be flogged or hanged!"

I said with great precision in my clearest voice: "I'm deeply opposed to both corporal and capital punishment. I have never received a perverted sexual pleasure through either watching or receiving physical punishment. I have never either sought or welcomed flagellation."

"You certainly gave me the impression you welcomed that flogging from Father Darcy. And if you're so deeply opposed to corporal punishment, how did you reconcile yourself to compulsory self-discipline as a novice?"

"Self-discipline! Nobody could hurt themselves with the kind of scourge the Order provides, and anyway even at Ruydale we often used to thump our beds to make the required sounds while the Master turned a blind eye—"

"I agree that for normal people self-discipline is little more than a symbolic act, but for a masochist entranced with punishment even a Fordite scourge could provide some interesting possibilities."

"*I am not a masochist entranced with punishment!*"

"You certainly seem to be entranced with Martin who's giving you some heavy punishment at the moment! How did you really feel all those years ago when he kicked over the traces, cocked a snook at the Varsity and went off to daub himself with greasepaint?"

"I've already told you—"

"You've told me nothing! You mouthed a few platitudes, the sort of platitudes saintly fathers are expected to utter, but now I think it's time we heard the truth. How did you take this rejection by your son of you and your way of life?"

"He didn't reject me."

"He has now! You've been a failure there, haven't you? You were a failure as a husband and a failure as a father—and while you were sleeping with your mistress you were a failure as a priest. No wonder you entered a monastery! After all those disasters the only way you could repair the damage to your self-esteem was to go through hell in order to be a success as a monk!"

Leaping to my feet I shouted: "Damn you, that's a bloody lie!" Then I covered my face with my hands and somehow managed to say: "I'm sorry, Father, that was unforgivable."

"Vulgar behaviour—even blasphemous language—I can forgive," said Francis, "particularly when I was providing great provocation, but what I find hard to forgive is your persistent evasiveness. If you do have a genuine call instead of a mere emotional problem that could be solved with competent counselling, you'll want to be absolutely honest with me, and being honest in this context means giving frank answers to my questions about Martin."

"Yes, of course. I'm sorry."

"Very well, I accept your apology, but if your repentance is genuine you'll now go away, pray that you may be granted a genuine humility which will prevent you lying to preserve your pride, and return tomorrow prepared to tell me all about that son of yours—and when I say all, Jonathan, I mean *all*, from Alpha to Omega."

V

"The silence of God has at all times been a great trial to mankind."

W. R. INGE
MYSTICISM IN RELIGION

I

I WAS in such distress that for a long time I could do nothing but pace up and down my cell. Francis was now behaving as if he suspected the quarrel with Martin had been the final trigger, and the most terrible aspect of this new development was that I myself, becoming increasingly aware of how deeply Martin had disturbed me, was beginning to wonder if he might not be connected with my vision despite all my previous doubts. However once I admitted the call was rooted in a psychological disturbance, I remained convinced I would be doomed. Francis, ruthlessly setting aside any possibility of divine involvement, would speed ahead to a neat psychological conclusion and dispatch me to Ambrose for weeks of medical supervision; possibly I might even be ordered to resign as Abbot. And all the time the chapel would be waiting for me in some corner of England which I would never find . . .

Or would it be waiting? My psyche froze as the demon of doubt finally encircled it. I remembered that I had received no further word from God either confirming my vision or clarifying it. I still had no idea what work I was being called to do.

Perhaps there was no chapel.

Perhaps I was deluded.

Closing my eyes with a shudder I knew I was in hell.

HOURS later I fell asleep, and as I lost my grip on consciousness my life unfurled beyond finite time until past and present streamed side by side, interweaving and interchanging, while the future was the blank mirror waiting to reflect their final image. I dreamt I was studying the visions of Ezekiel and feeling frightened because my vision was so dull in comparison. Then Francis said as he removed my Bible: "If your vision was genuine, God would have ordered you to perform a symbolic act—remember Ezekiel!" But I answered: "I performed my symbolic act. I entered the Order." And I added to Father Darcy: "I have to live in imitation of Christ. There's no other way I can live with myself and stay sane."

Then Father Darcy took me to the punishment cell and on the wall hung the crucifix, the image of Christ crucified, Christ atoning, and I knew then, knew beyond any shadow of doubt, that for my children's sake all the suffering would have to be borne.

I said to my children: "I'm doing it all for you!" but as I spoke I realised they had vanished and I was making a cross in the workshop at Ruydale. I worked and worked at my crucifix, that image of Christ crucified, Christ atoning, until at last Alfred the carpenter who had trained me said: "You can put that aside now, lad. Martin no longer needs it. Just make a cross instead for the chapel in the woods."

So I put aside my crucifix, image of Christ crucified, Christ atoning, and I began to make a different cross, a plain, pure cross, an image of faith and hope—THE CROSS OF THE RESURRECTION—and then as I became one with the risen Christ, Christ redeemed, Christ liberated, I knew my long Good Friday was over at last and the sun was finally dawning on my long-awaited Easter Day.

3

I AWOKE in a daze of happiness which dissolved with lightning speed into confusion. I tried to remember Alfred's exact words. Had he really mentioned Martin? To my horror I realised the question could only be answered in the affirmative, and although I told myself the dream was a mere illogical aberration of the mind, I knew the mention of Martin's name was significant. I tried to make further deductions but failed; I was too frightened of coming face to face with the fact that my call was a delusion. I did wonder how I was going to survive my next meeting with Francis, but soon I could no more think of Francis than I could think of Martin because I had suddenly realised I was feeling ill. I forced myself to attend Prime and Mass, but as soon as the services were over I avoided breakfast and retired to my cell where I tried—futilely—to will myself to feel better. Five minutes later a note arrived which read: "I have not given you permission to fast. Come to the refectory immediately." With a great effort I reached the refectory, drank a cup of tea and swallowed a mouthful of bread, but afterwards I knew I had no choice but to drag myself to the infirmary.

"This is just a physical manifestation of severe mental strain," I said to Ambrose. "Give me a couple of aspirin and I'll be well again by dinner-time."

"I always enjoy your bold diagnoses, Father. Sit down, please, and I'll take your temperature."

"It won't be more than ninety-nine."

The thermometer registered a hundred and two.

"Obviously it's broken," I said.

Ambrose smiled at me as if I were a wayward child who needed humouring and examined me for further symptoms but there were none. "I doubt if you've got anything infectious," he said at last, "but take the corner bed away from the other patients."

As I hauled myself from his office into the ward, a long, light room with six beds flanking each side of a central aisle, I was aware of feeling very, very old indeed. This unnerved me, and as I removed my habit I started to worry about the damaged defences which had allowed my body to slide from the ease of good health into the dis-ease of physical impairment. I slid into bed. Ambrose gave me three aspirins, and after swallowing them I tried to stroke my psyche by recalling peaceful memories of the scenery at Ruydale. However I was too ill to concentrate on this exercise for long, and within minutes I had drifted into sleep.

When I awoke I knew it would be wiser to keep my eyes closed, and the next moment I heard Francis muttering: "It's entirely self-induced! He's trumped up this illness to avoid a distressing interview with me—in fact this is a typical example of a psychic controlling his body with his mind! What a shady, shoddy little parlour-trick!"

"With all due respect, Father, I'm convinced it's not a conscious willing of the mind. He was genuinely surprised to find he had a high fever."

"You mustn't be too credulous, Ambrose. Don't let him manipulate you. These sort of people can be appallingly plausible. How are you going to treat him?"

"If the illness is psychosomatic, perhaps the laying-on of hands would help."

"Absolutely not!" said Francis, keeping his voice low but allowing it to shudder with rage. "I'm not pandering to his psychic tantrums by authorising any charismatic healing which would enable him to claim a miraculous cure! You mark my words, Ambrose, that man can heal himself perfectly well if he wants to—give him orthodox medical treatment and stand absolutely no nonsense whatsoever!"

Francis stumped off. I could hear the slap of his boots on the linoleum, and the atmosphere, which had been swirling with turbulence, immediately became smooth. I opened my eyes, and when he saw I was awake, Ambrose sat down at my side. Ambrose exuded a calm, benevolent aura, just as a physician should; I felt my mind being enfolded by his sympathy.

"All set to stand no nonsense from me?" I murmured, and he smiled before saying: "Father Abbot-General's very concerned about you."

"Father Abbot-General!" I wanted to smile too but it seemed less effort to sigh instead. "When I first met him up at Cambridge he was called Lord Francis Ingram. He had a greyhound which used to drink champagne. Nasty animal. I don't like dogs. Too much like dependent humans. But cats . . . ah, cats are quite different! One day, Ambrose, one day I'd so much like to tell someone about Whitby."

"Ah, that was the cat up at Ruydale, wasn't it, the cat Wilfred mentioned in his letters . . . Father—"

"Call me Jon, Ambrose. I'm too ill to be Jonathan the Abbot at the moment."

"—Jon—did you really raise that cat from the dead?"

"Careful, Ambrose. Superstition. Blasphemy. Shhh."

"I suppose he was actually still alive—"

"That's what some people said about Our Lord in order to explain the Resurrection, but he did die. I've died too and now I've come here to wait for my own resurrection, but oh, how ill I feel! It's hard work being dead, and Whitby probably knew that. He didn't want to die—he had a great fighting spirit. Ah Whitby, Whitby, Whitby, what a cat you were, what a cat!"

Ambrose clasped my hand and released it. "Try and sleep again, Jon. Try and rest your body and mind as much as possible."

"I feel better already. A healing presence, a little conversation, someone calling me Jon . . . You must have good results with the laying-on of hands, Ambrose."

"I can't channel power through my hands as Wilfred can."

"That doesn't matter. The charism of healing doesn't always come in the form of power channelled through the hands. In your case the laying-on of hands would be a sacramental gesture symbolising the healing action of your psyche as it enfolds another psyche in love and prayer." I suddenly felt exhausted. As my eyes closed I murmured: "Dear old Whitby, he was so pleased to be better," and the next moment I saw Whitby, proud arrogant Whitby, stalking through the backyard at Ruydale with his tail pointed defiantly at the sky.

"May God bless you, Jon," I heard Ambrose say from a long way away, "and may he restore the strength you so badly need."

I murmured an automatic "Amen" and stooped to take Whitby in my arms.

4

WHEN I awoke again I heard someone calling: "Ambrose! Emergency—a scalding in the kitchens," and turning my head I saw Ambrose hurry away clutching the Gladstone bag in which he kept his first-aid equipment. I sat up, drank some water and glanced around the room. There were three other occupants, including a restless youth whom I had seen break his ankle while descending too rapidly to the crypt at the start of an air-raid. He looked bored enough to flout the rule of silence, and his restlessness created a succession of eddies in the atmosphere until I felt as irritated as if I had been trapped with a fly who persistently evaded the swatter.

I closed my eyes to ward off any illicit attempt he might make at conversation, but my psyche, raw and vulnerable, continued to be lacerated by the unpleasant emanations. I was only saved from losing my patience by the return of Ambrose, hurrying back into the ward with his Gladstone bag and making a rapid inspection of his patients as if he feared we might all have taken a turn for the worse in his absence.

"Awake again, Jon?"

"I think I've recovered."

Ambrose set down his bag on the empty bed next to mine and produced a thermometer. "It's most unlikely that you're wholly recovered," he said, taking the instrument to the window and examining the mercury to make sure it was low in the glass, "but let's see if you're right in thinking there's been an improvement." And he turned aside from the window to place the thermometer in my mouth.

It was then that my perceptions tripped. I had just glanced at the Gladstone bag which was no more than six feet away from me, but the next moment I was seeing not the bag but the suitcase of my vision. All sound immediately ceased. My entire being was directed towards perceiving the pale beige leather suitcase with the dark brown corners. I could see the triangular label clearly now, far more clearly than I had seen it in my vision, the label which showed a black and white ship floating above three wavy blue lines and six scarlet letters, the letters which spelt CUNARD. Then I saw another label, a label attached to the handle, a brown label fastened by string, but when I reached out to discover the name of the owner the entire suitcase vanished and the Gladstone bag was solid beneath my shaking hands.

I sank to my knees, squeezed my eyes shut and began to shudder from head to toe.

"Jon, it's all right—you're in the infirmary, you're quite safe, absolutely safe—" His words made me realise I had conveyed an impression of fear but in fact all my fears had vanished. The shuddering ceased. As Ambrose helped me back into bed I tried to speak but he said at once: "No, don't try to talk. You've had a shock. Take this extra blanket to keep you warm and I'll make you some tea."

Across the room the young monk was boggling, but as I lay limply on the pillows I found his restless aura failed to irritate me. My psyche was infused with light. I closed my eyes but the light still shone in the darkness. I was at peace.

In the distance Ambrose said to someone: "Tell Father Abbot-General I need to see him urgently," but the words stirred no anxiety in me and later I never even flinched as the swirling tornado of a disturbed presence swept down the corridor into the infirmary. The tornado was deftly deflected by Ambrose into his office, and as my fellow-patients watched enrapt I slid out of bed, padded into the passage and noiselessly opened Ambrose's door an inch.

" . . . so whatever he saw he couldn't have seen for more than five seconds."

"And your diagnosis?"

"Some sort of psychic experience. It couldn't be a hallucination unless his fever's got worse and he'd just said he felt better."

I pushed open the door to reveal my presence.

Both men jumped. Then Francis exclaimed in fury: "What the deuce do you think you're playing at, making an entrance like the demon-king in a pantomime?" and Ambrose said severely: "Go back to bed at once and stop straining your heart by unnecessary exertion!"

I said to Francis: "I saw the suitcase," and walked out. Then I returned to bed and waited. After some minutes Ambrose appeared, bringing me the promised cup of tea, and took my temperature before I attempted to drink. The thermometer registered ninety-nine degrees.

"No hallucination," I said, satisfied. I began to drink the tea but it had been liberally sweetened to fortify me against the effects of shock, and

I was still grimacing in disgust when Ambrose said: "Father Abbot-General wishes to talk to you in private and as your temperature's almost normal I'll allow you to get dressed and sit in my office. But you must finish that tea and you must wrap yourself in the extra blanket to ensure you keep warm."

Downing the tea I pulled on my habit, swathed myself in the blanket and strode to the office where Francis, sitting in Ambrose's chair, was staring blankly at the blotter. It occurred to me that the sweet tea had been administered to the wrong man.

"If you think for one moment," he said, rousing himself sufficiently to motion me to sit down, "that you can convince me this call is genuine merely by producing a new parlour-trick—"

"The gifts of the Spirit can be recognised by their fruits. Gauge the effect this experience has had on me before you start accusing me of parlour-tricks."

"You're being intolerably impertinent—how dare you lecture me about this new aberration!" said Francis, now overwhelmed by the most painful insecurity, and I saw my first task was to calm him down.

I tried to enfold his mind with my own, but such an enfolding is impossible without love and, as everyone knows, it is difficult to generate even the most modest fraternal concern for someone whom one has never liked. However I exerted the power of my will, and remembering what little I knew of his early days, I tried to approach him through a different psychological avenue.

I imagined him being brought up by some hired woman in his parents' vast mansion; I speculated that it had been his craving for affection as well as attention which had drawn him to a life of decadence; I thought of him enjoying every material comfort while his soul starved, and suddenly I was seeing him stumble across the Order, across different values and different people who would care for him in an entirely different way. Then I found I could easily picture him thriving at last in response to Father Darcy's powerful interest, and in a moment of enlightenment I realised that his bereavement when his mentor died must have run precisely parallel to my own.

At once I was conscious not only of sympathy but of empathy; I was seeing us for the first time not as rivals, but as the twin aspects of Father Darcy's complex personality, the mystical and the worldly, not in opposition but complementing each other, and then I understood at last why Father Darcy had taken such care to yoke us together, despite all our antipathy, in the years preceding his death.

I became aware that Francis was speaking. He had overcome his inner chaos sufficiently to say: "Tell me exactly what happened," and I found

I could obey him calmly in a manner which could neither exasperate nor threaten him. "It wasn't a vision," I added when the moment came to comment on the experience. "There were no physical symptoms preceding it, no dislocation of time and space. I believe it was what Julian of Norwich would have called a 'showing.'"

Francis finally managed to recapture his favourite defence, the debonair theatrical manner. "You alarm me exceedingly! Can we keep Dame Julian out of this?"

"You'll understand my state of mind better if we bring her in. After her own 'showings' she felt so happy, so confident, so convinced that all would be well—"

"Am I to deduce from these somewhat emotional utterances that you feel you've received a divine reassurance?"

"You can deduce that I now see my recent behaviour—all the lies and evasions, all the fears and anxieties—as demonstrating the most shameful lack of trust in God. I know now that all I have to do is have faith and trust that all will be well. If the vision's genuine, I'll be led to a new life in God's service. If the vision's false you'll arrange for me to be cared for until I can continue to serve God in the Order. So my task here's not to worry about whether you can exercise the charism of discernment; my task is to trust God by trusting you because only by putting myself without reserve in your hands can God's will for me ever be conclusively revealed."

In the silence which followed I sensed Francis's wordless thanksgiving but all he eventually said was: "That sounds like a promising approach. Am I then to assume—"

"Yes," I said, "I'm going to tell you everything at last. Everything from Alpha to Omega."

5

"THE truth's so painful," I said, "that over the years I've buried it by reconstructing my memories into a pattern which I could endure. You suspected this, of course, but I couldn't dispense with the defence this reconstruction offered; I had neither the courage nor the faith to do so."

Francis's sleek, powerful psyche, which always reminded me of a giant member of the cat family, was now entirely still and the stillness was mirrored in his motionless body. He had surmounted the acute strain generated by the burden of his responsibility, and having turned inward to dwell upon his own ordeal he was now turning outward to dwell with a new strength on mine.

I said: "Everything I told you about my marriage was true, yet it was all false because I couldn't paint the past in the right colours." As I groped for the right words I again ignored the rule which forbade a monk to stand while his superior was seated. I moved to the window. The dark events of 1940 were being enacted against the background of a brilliant summer, and instinctively I tried to fight my way through my own darkness by staring at the light sky beyond the rooftops.

"My marriage was hell," I said. "I hated my life as a husband. I was miserable, isolated, trapped with this woman who hadn't the faintest idea what my life was about. Sexual intimacy was the only compensation and even that in the end became a mockery underlining my loneliness. But the real nightmare was that this tragedy was all my fault. Betty was a nice girl in her own way and she tried hard to be a good wife. She really did love me—but I couldn't love her, not after the romantic passion was gone, and of course she came to realise that. People always know when they're not loved. She became angry, possessive, demanding—and the more demanding she became, the more I withdrew from her. I couldn't help myself—not when my psychic space was being continually invaded and my whole inner life was cut to ribbons . . . If I hadn't gone away to sea the marriage couldn't have survived, but at sea I could recuperate until I had the strength to face another harrowing spell ashore—oh, what hell it was! And all the time I felt cut off from God by my failure to love as I should. I was in despair."

I paused to calm myself. I examined the pattern of the rooftops with care. I even counted the chimney-pots.

"When she finally died," I said, "the full horror of the tragedy dawned on me. She'd died after I'd psychologically abandoned her, and I'd abandoned her for no valid cause. She'd loved me; she'd committed no sin, but I'd made her suffer and suddenly as I saw the exact dimensions of my cruelty I felt unfit to live. That was when the crushing burden descended upon my psyche—I talked of the burden, didn't I? And I admitted the burden was guilt, but I only revealed a fraction of it, the guilt I felt when I jilted Hilda. My guilt was far deeper than I disclosed to you. It was a huge, crippling, back-breaking guilt, and I carried it with me during all those years I spent as a widower.

"At first," I said after a rapid recount of the chimney-pots, "I thought I saw how I could alleviate the guilt. I decided I'd do my best to love my children by being an exemplary father to them.

"But I couldn't.

"I should have applied to work ashore so that I could be at home with them—it was two years before the War so I didn't have to be at sea—but I couldn't face the thought of either my mother-in-law or a hired woman keeping house for me, destroying my psychic space—and worse still I knew I wouldn't be able to cope with the children, all the noise, all the mess, all the emotional demands—I couldn't do it, I just couldn't do it, I wanted to but it was beyond me, I'd have gone mad, broken down utterly—no, I felt it was quite impossible for me to be permanently ashore, but oh, how I despised myself, and oh, how guilty I felt! So I never alleviated the burden after all. What happened, in fact, was that I doubled it.

"My meetings with my children became so awkward; I tried hard to show them I cared and I did care, but . . . I couldn't express my love adequately. The guilt crippled not only my power of expression but the love itself. Perhaps if the children had been more like me communication would have been easier, but Ruth, reminding me of Betty, only exacerbated my guilt, while Martin remained beyond my reach no matter how hard I tried to build an understanding between us. I did make an effort to share my life with him when he was an adolescent; I talked of the Church and my work and how happy I was in God's service, and there was a time when I thought he might become a priest—it was around the time of his confirmation—he was genuinely devout—I hoped . . . even prayed . . . which was stupid of me because I was just praying that my own selfish wish should be granted and not pausing to ask that God's will might be done. However I was still hoping that he might become a priest when he told me he wanted to be an actor—an *actor*—" I could no longer continue.

"Yes," said Francis. "Yes. There's no need to explain how you felt." And as he spoke I felt his psyche brush mine faintly in the dark.

I had to pause to focus my gaze on the view again. The sky beyond the chimney-pots was a radiant blue.

"I should have discouraged him," I said. "I should have insisted that he went up to Cambridge before making any decision about the future. But I didn't. And I wasn't being a noble, understanding father. I was being a bad, selfish one. I wanted to enter the Order so desperately that I put my needs before his welfare—I let him go into a notoriously amoral world so that I could have the life I wanted. How bad a father can a man be? I abandoned Martin—and I abandoned Ruth too; I let her marry a man I disliked because I wanted to get her off my hands and be free . . . And so I failed my children, failed them as I'd failed my wife, and the burden of my guilt lay unredeemed.

"But by that time I'd worked out how I could finally exorcise the guilt. I knew I had to atone for what I'd done, atone for all my sins and my terrible failures. I had to live in imitation of Christ and suffer as he suffered on the Cross—it was the only way, Francis, the only way, and

I know that sounds as if I enjoy suffering but I didn't, I don't, I hated it, I hardly knew how to bear it, but I endured it because I knew it was the only hope I had of setting down that appalling burden which had been crushing me for so long.

"However there were two aspects of my call to the cloister, and unless I describe them both you won't understand the exact nature of the force which has kept me in the Order for all these years. The first and most obvious aspect involved this exorcism of the guilt by a spiritual purification. But the second aspect . . . well, I hardly know how to put this, I feel so embarrassed, but as the years passed and my children flourished, I came to believe that my atonement, my suffering, was somehow enabling them to live free of the shadow of my past sins. I came to think . . . Francis, I know this sounds superstitious to the point of blasphemy, but I thought I'd succeeded in driving a bargain with God. I was desperately afraid my children's lives would go wrong because I'd been a bad father, so I told myself that so long as I remained a good monk God would repay me for my sacrifice by keeping my children safe. What pride, what intolerable arrogance to think that one can ever drive bargains with God! What a theological perversion ever to see the concept of atonement in those self-centred primitive terms—"

"Nevertheless it was still an attempt to raise up and reconcile all things in Christ. The form of the attempt might have been misconceived but the desire to atone was obviously genuine enough." Francis's psyche, heavy and blunt, yet trained to move with an elegant delicacy, encircled mine and supported it. Again his body mirrored the psychic action. Rising to his feet he crossed the room, guided me back to my chair and moved his own chair around the desk so that he could sit at my side.

"Last May," I said when I could speak again, "I was so pleased to see Martin on my birthday. He looked so happy too. I thought: how wonderful it is that he's doing so well! And I felt all my sacrifices had been worthwhile.

"Then he told me.

"Of course I can see now how brave it was of him, but I was so shattered I couldn't respond to that gesture of trust. Then in his pain he started making accusations, saying it was all my fault, saying I'd never been there when he needed me, saying everything which underlined my guilt until in the end I could bear it no longer. I told him to get out—my son—*Martin*—I rejected him absolutely, but as soon as I was alone I thought: how *could* I have treated him like that? And I hated myself. But then a very strange thing happened. Once the shock had faded I felt everything changing, as if the world was turning itself inside out. Instead of thinking: how deeply I've failed! and hating myself, I thought: how desperately hard I've tried to succeed! And I resented that Martin should be oblivious of all the suffering I'd endured for his sake. My anger was no longer turned inward upon myself; it had turned outward at last, and then as my self-hatred finally began to disintegrate, I saw my superstitious bargain with God for what it was: superstition.

"The first aspect of the atonement represented by the monastic life had indeed been essential for me; I'd genuinely needed to assuage my guilt, purge myself of my sins and achieve the spiritual development which I could never have achieved in the world, but for me then to say to God: 'I'll keep on atoning if you keep my children safe,' was not only pathetic but futile. Ruth and Martin had gone their own way in the world and Martin at least hadn't been preserved from harm. The truth was I'd tried hard to be a good parent, I'd done my best, pitiful and inadequate though that was, and now there was nothing more I could do." I hesitated, then heard myself whisper in imitation of Christ on the Cross: "It was finished."

Silence fell, and this time Francis's psyche encircled mine not merely with efficiency but with compassion. Reaching out with his right hand he briefly covered my interlocked fingers.

At last I was able to say: "Of course I can see now that I'm just emotionally disturbed. The meeting with Martin destroyed my need to atone and this triggered such an upheaval in my mind that I imagined I was being called to leave the Order. But in fact what was happening was that God, in His great mercy, had finally seen fit to relieve me of my self-hatred because He had realised that my call to serve Him as a monk was so deeply entrenched that I no longer needed to be kept in the Order by a psychological compulsion. At the same time He had also seen fit to purge my call of the superstition which had become attached to it; indeed one could regard the whole experience as a further spiritual purification." I paused. I was feeling calmer. Beyond the window the chimney-pots were bathed in a brilliant light.

"I'm sure now," I said, "that the vision was an allegory. I believe the ruined building behind the chapel represents my failure during my life in the world, and the chapel represents my life in the Order. The mysterious suitcase still represents change, but it's a change from a call underpinned by guilt to a call flowing from a psyche at peace. And the light at the end of my vision represents the confirmation of my call, just as Timothy said—the assurance that I'll be able to serve God as a monk even better than before now that I'm fully reconciled to the past."

Francis slumped back in his chair but when I steeled myself to look at him I saw that although he was limp with exhaustion, the expression in his eyes was friendly. Presently he even smiled.

"So that's how you finally see your situation, is it?" he said.

"Yes, Father." As an afterthought I added: "Please forgive me for calling you Francis just now when I was upset."

But Francis, no longer intimidated but exuding an unmistakable air of confidence, merely waved this apology aside as if my offence were too trivial to be worth mentioning. "You've no doubt you're right?" he persisted. "No doubt at all?"

"No, Father. Not now."

"Ah, Jonathan, Jonathan"—Francis heaved a massive sigh—"are you never to be cured of your intolerable arrogance?" And as I stared at him he added casually: "Your new call is quite obviously genuine. You must leave the Order without delay."

PART TWO

THE REALITY BEYOND THE VISION

"Rightly or wrongly [genuine mystics] are convinced that they have been in contact with objective reality, with the supreme spiritual Power behind the world of our surface consciousness. If they are right, this intuition must be a factor in what we believe about reality; it means that reality is spiritual."

W. R. INGE
MYSTICISM IN RELIGION

VI

I

AT first Francis refused to discuss his judgement and when I begged stupefied for an explanation, he merely ordered me back to bed in the infirmary. Then he relented. Motioning me to remain seated he said: "The turning point was when I realised that I had to examine your original call to be a monk."

"Yes, but—"

"Be quiet!" snapped Francis, revealing his exhaustion. "If you want an explanation don't irritate me with ill-judged interruptions!"

I said at once: "I'm very sorry. Please go on."

Francis waited until he was calm before continuing: "The point about your original call was that it was indisputably genuine. As you yourself said at the start of this conversation: the gifts of the Spirit can be recognised by their fruits—or, as a layman would say, the proof of the pudding's in the eating. You've become an outstanding monk, your skill as a spiritual director being acknowledged both inside and outside the Order. Clearly God called you to serve Him in this way, and it seemed to me that if only I could discover how He had called you to start being a monk I'd be able to discern whether He was now calling you to stop being a monk; I suspected that this new call, if it were valid, would be a negative reflection of the old."

Francis paused, grappling again with his exhaustion, but I took care not to distract him and at last he said: "You had no vision calling you to be a monk, but contrary to what many laymen believe, calls from God aren't normally manifested by psychic or supernatural phenomena. Much more common are the cases where a man is put in a psychological vise and God proceeds to tighten the screws. This is what happened to you. You had this tragic private life which went so disastrously wrong that you felt your only hope of survival was to serve God in the Order.

"It seemed logical to assume that if God called you to enter the Order by imprisoning you in a psychological vise, His first step, on calling you to leave, would be to loosen the screws and set you free. Your call to the Order, as you yourself pointed out, had two aspects. First, you wanted to set down the burden of your guilt, purge yourself of sin and achieve the spiritual development which you were unable to achieve in the world. And second, you thought you could drive a bargain with God to keep your children safe. The first aspect drove you into the Order; the second aspect kept you there. No matter how hard the life was, you couldn't leave. You had to be a monk. No other option was open to you.

"However when you achieved that spiritual development which you could never have achieved outside the cloister, the role of the Order in your life became redundant. You were now fit to serve God in the world, and all that remained for God to do was to remove the various psychological fetters which were chaining you to the cloister.

"Father Darcy died, a death which liberated you from supervision by a mentor. You failed to become Abbot-General, a failure which represented the termination of any all-too-human ambition to reach the top of the Fordite tree. And finally, most vital of all, your so-called bargain with God was shown during your quarrel with Martin to have been an illusion.

"All these devastating blows rained down upon you within the space of a month, and while they were happening you were being goaded by the minor troubles, the recurring difficulty with your celibacy, the unfortunate birthday, the adverse effects of the War on your community and your work. It seems to me that you were being remorselessly manoeuvred into position to receive the knock-out blow with which Martin finally demolished your compulsion to remain in the Order.

"However you were a good monk. Out of sheer conscientiousness you were going to fight this systematic destruction of your old call, and so even after the knock-out blow had been delivered the new call had to be spelt out in a way you couldn't misunderstand: you were granted the vision.

"Now"—Francis sighed as if he still found my vision a heavy cross to bear—"it's impossible to say for certain exactly what was going on during this strange experience of yours, and the difficulty is exacerbated because you and I represent two quite different religious types. I'm not a mystic; I can only discern God through reason and logic. As far as philosophy goes I have the greatest respect for Platonic Idealism, but it's the respect of a man blind from birth for colours: when many good honest people tell me colours are beautiful, I deem it reasonable to believe that this fact is true. Therefore as far as Neo-Platonic mysticism goes, I'm prepared to believe it's a symbolic expression of experiences which the mystic can recognise, but to me it's just a foreign language which I'll never master.

"I'm essentially a Pragmatist of the school of William James. I recognise the will to believe, acknowledge that it can have beneficial results and conclude that there's a form of religious truth here based on my subjective experience. To put it crudely, I'm a Christian because Christianity works for me; it enables me to live my life in a happy, productive, spiritually satisfying way. Intellectually I can recognise the absolute objective truths which lie beyond the Platonic veil of your own philosophical approach to God, but experientially that approach isn't mine. All I can say is that it works for you and therefore it's true for you. That's a truth I can deduce by using rational powers of observation, but when I'm obliged to deduce the meaning of a vision, an experience not grounded in logic, I find my intellectual powers quickly become no more use than a broken sword. 'Spiritual is most rational,' says that Cambridge Platonist Whichcote. Yes—but there comes a point in spiritual matters beyond which reason is unable to go.

"So having stressed my limitations in this field, let me now venture a very tentative opinion on this vision of yours. I don't think you saw the future. It strikes me as being much more like a dream than a concrete experience. I know the detail was very striking but detail can be striking in dreams, too. Of course I'm not saying it *was* a dream, just that it was like a dream—not a glimpse of an actual happening and certainly not an allegory, which has always struck me as a contrived literary device requiring intellectual planning.

"I believe that many years ago you read about this chapel in a book, perhaps even saw photographs of it, and that the memory was retained by your subconscious mind. During the psychic earthquake you experienced in May, this memory was regurgitated and used as a medium for conveying the word of God. Now, I'm perfectly prepared to concede that one day you may actually come across this chapel—one must always allow in life for the one truly extraordinary coincidence—but I don't think it will have anything to do with your new call. To me, the Pragmatist, the only thing of importance in your vision is the light at the end which imprinted the word of God on your mind; nothing else is relevant.

"When this call to leave the Order was imprinted on your mind, God completed, in my opinion, the necessary sequence of events: you were called to enter the Order, you achieved the required spiritual development, the psychological compulsion to remain was then destroyed and you were called to leave. In short, the whole sequence is all of a piece; the two calls are mirror-images of each other, and if your first call was genuine then this second call must be genuine too."

As Francis sank into an exhausted silence I had the chance to speak, but now the words refused to come. Emotion mingled with my own exhaustion. I had to shield my eyes with my hand.

"You need food, drink and a great deal more rest," said Francis abruptly, rousing himself. "Go back to bed and we'll talk again tomorrow."

But I was immobilised. I felt so old, so tired, so utterly overwhelmed not only by my recent battle but by the enormity of my unknown future that I even whispered: "I don't want to leave the Order any more," as if I were a spoilt child begging to be excused from the ordeal of being sent away from home to boarding school.

"Who cares what you want?" said Francis brutally. "It's what God wants that's important. Stop snivelling and pull yourself together!"

I forgot the shame of my uncontrolled emotion. I exclaimed startled: "You sound just like the old man!" and I added in disbelief: "You're even beginning to look like him!"

"I suppose you'll be claiming next that you've seen his ghost—oh, for heaven's sake, Jonathan, go back to bed before you get up to any more convoluted psychic antics!" said Francis, and striding out of the room in a paroxysm of exasperation he banged the door violently behind him.

2

"*I MUST* apologise for that graceless exit," said Francis when we met in his office the next morning. "As you no doubt realised I temporarily succumbed to jealousy. I've never had a vision from God, nor, I dare say, am I ever likely to have one."

I hardly needed to point out to him that God can communicate with man in numerous other ways. Nor did I need to tell him that the mystics are united in distrusting psychic experiences and usually treat them as either irrelevant or seriously misleading. The truth is that although psychic powers are a gift from God, like the power to express oneself through art, they are not by themselves any guarantee of either holiness or religious genius. In fact psychics, like artists, are usually conspicuously less than holy, subject as they are to any passing demonic force which can exploit their characteristically inflated pride and self-centredness.

However if the psychic powers can be harnessed by rigorous discipline and put to work in the service of God, they can be used to supplement the charismatic power, that gift of the Spirit which God may bestow on anyone, psychic or otherwise. Francis knew very well that he was not excluded from hearing calls from God or from wielding charismatic power merely because he had no psychic gifts, but I sensed that his statement represented more than a simple confession of jealousy. In an oblique way he was admitting an old anxiety about his spiritual limitations, an old dread that he might not live up to Father Darcy's high hopes for him, perhaps even a lifelong insecurity that he would be overlooked or judged second-rate unless he exerted his flair for calling attention to himself, and suddenly I recognised the isolation of the man of power who yearns for an equal in whom he can freely confide.

Making every effort to express sympathy without condescension I said: "I'm sure your own call to enter the Order was in its own way just as powerful an experience as any vision granted to a psychic."

"Possibly. But nevertheless I can't help feeling that to receive a vision of a beautiful chapel must be a more profound spiritual experience than to wake up hung-over in a strange bed one morning with the thought: if I don't become a monk I'll be dead within six months. The trouble with Pragmatism," said Francis dryly before I could comment, "is that it has absolutely no glamour. How I've always envied you those 'glamorous powers,' Jonathan! When we were up at Cambridge, how *I* always longed to tell fortunes, conduct séances and hypnotise pretty girls into fulfilling my wildest dreams! And now, forty years later, I see to my shame and dismay that very little has changed. The envy's still there and it's there because I'm still hopelessly addicted to glamour. The old man did try to cure me, of course, but that was a case of the blind leading the blind—he was too addicted to glamour himself, the old rascal, to conduct the necessary purging effectively."

"I'm surprised he even tried."

"His efforts were certainly half-hearted. But at the end he said: 'I should have sent you too to Ruydale instead of keeping you here like a pet poodle cocooned in vintage claret, visiting archbishops and vulgar chandeliers!' He knew he'd been too soft with me, but poor old boy, he was lonely at the end when all his favourite brothers started dying off, and he did suffer considerable pain from his arthritis. I could quite understand why he needed an amusing pet poodle to keep him company."

"What an unjust description!"

"You think so? I wonder. I've got a weakness for luxury and a mind like a cash-box—how on earth have I ended up as a spiritual leader? And how on earth am I going to manage in future without my arch-rival stimulating me to do my spiritual best with the very limited talent at my disposal?"

I said briskly: "I'll tell you exactly how you'll manage: you'll use the energy you've always wasted on our rivalry to rise to new heights in exercising the charism of leadership. The old man foresaw the exact dimensions of that charism, of course. He didn't choose a pet poodle to be the kind of leader the Order has to have. He chose the managing director with the financial brain, the organising skills and the spiritual education which he himself had personally supervised. How obvious it all seems to me now! In fact I feel amazed that I could ever have resented his decision."

"For a man who's just survived the rack you're being extraordinarily charitable—"

"No, not charitable. Honest."

"—but now I must call an end to all this delectable fraternal flattery in order to discuss practical matters," said Francis firmly. However he was much cheered, and conquering the melancholy which had prompted his unique confession he embarked on the task of bringing clarity to my clouded future.

3

"THE Church authorities at Westminster tell me that they can't trace this chapel without knowing the name of the owner," he said, "so we have no proof that it exists, and in my opinion it would be the greatest possible mistake if on leaving the Order you sat around waiting for the chapel to materialise. On the contrary, your first task, it seems to me, is to set aside all thought of the chapel and try to work out exactly what you're being called to do."

I could hardly deny that this was sensible advice so I had no difficulty in replying tactfully: "Yes, Father."

"One must never demote the faculty of reason in favour of a dubious mystical *Schwärmerei*," said Francis severely, suspicious as always of my meekness and perhaps still wondering if I were envisaging a latter-day Star of Bethlehem to guide me on my way. "You must approach your unknown future rationally—starting from now."

Despite the fact that I had had experience of the sad task of assisting a monk to leave the cloister, I was surprised by the depth of my confusion when I found myself on the receiving end of an abbot's ministrations. I hated the talk of money, although I knew it was essential that I should have some means of support. I hated the thought of leaving my brethren, although I knew the departure from Grantchester would have to be faced, and I hated the prospect of making a plan for the immediate future, although I did realise I could hardly emerge into the world with the mindless naïveté of a chicken hatching from an egg; I had to acquire—at the very least—a roof over my head, the prospect of hot meals and the services of someone who would do my laundry.

" . . . and you must buy some modern underclothes," added Francis.

"Why?" I was becoming impatient with these worldly trivialities. "Surely I can make do with what I have!"

"Do you want to be a laughing-stock to your laundress?"

Despite my impatience I could not help but be impressed by this all-embracing attention to detail. I had never told any of my departing monks to buy new underclothes.

"Now we must decide exactly where you're going to go," said Francis, continuing to exercise his indefatigable talent for the practical. "I always think that a departing monk should if possible spend his first few days in a normal home so that he can be reminded what life's like without people praying all over the place. Would your daughter have you to stay?"

But I had already decided to go to Ruth for a week. In a recent letter she had mentioned that my grandson would be visiting a school friend in mid-August, but my granddaughter would be at home and I liked the idea of discovering more about her. I wondered if I were being sentimental in assuming it would be easier to be a grandfather than a father.

"And where will you go for the next three weeks before you return to London to review your situation with me?" pursued Francis.

"I'd thought of Allington Court. I stayed there once before I entered the Order."

Allington Court in Devon was the former home of a wealthy bishop who had bequeathed his estate to the Church of England under a trust which stipulated that his house should become a hotel offering inexpensive holidays to clerical families. The house boasted a remarkable library, several comfortable reception rooms and a chapel—though not a chapel built in the style of Inigo Jones. Nowadays the hotel was seldom patronised by clerical families with children, but clerical widows, retired priests and interested laymen arrived regularly, theological students came to recuperate from examinations and a variety of church-workers appeared in the hope of renewing their spiritual energy. The establishment was run by a warden, always a priest of distinction, and he employed two assistants who helped him to organise retreats, to respond to any requests for counsel and, on a more mundane level, to generate a sociable atmosphere.

I wrote to the warden to ask if he could offer me accommodation at such short notice in August, but there was no difficulty; the War had depleted the ranks of his regular visitors. I also wrote to my daughter and received an ecstatic reply by return of post. Of course I could come to stay. I could stay for as long as I liked. She could hardly wait to see me. My news was so wonderful, so marvellous, so exciting. What did I like to eat? What did I drink? Did I want to meet anyone? Would I hate a party? Had I got anything to wear? (I thought of my underclothes.) Had I got any possessions at all? Would I like a book from Boots' Library? I was to tell her everything I wanted so that my every whim could be gratified.

After telling myself how fortunate I was to have such a devoted daughter, I decided I found this flurry of questions curiously exhausting. With caution I wrote back to inform her that I would eat anything that was put in front of me and drink anything except spirits. Then I wrote even more cautiously that I would prefer not to meet strangers at this time since readjustment to the world would inevitably be difficult and I would need to channel all my gregarious inclinations into renewing my acquaintance with my family. I concluded by writing that if Boots had the latest detective story by Miss Agatha Christie, I would be most interested to read it.

That night I went to bed depressed, although when I tried to analyse my feelings I could not decide whether I felt depressed because Ruth had reminded me of Betty, showering me with trivial questions, or because the reality of leaving the Order was at last impinging on my consciousness. However I allowed myself no respite from that particular reality; the next morning I embarked on the difficult task of writing the letters which would inform my friends in the world of the new turn my life had taken.

To Charles Ashworth alone I allowed myself to hint at the ordeal I had undergone. "As you can imagine," I wrote, "I have been experiencing a most difficult time, but I trust that eventually, when I'm settled in my new life, we may meet and resume our friendship." But even to Charles I wrote no word of my vision or of my utter ignorance about the nature of my new work.

With my letters completed I then reached the most arduous part of my severance from my old life: the parting from my brethren at Grantchester.

FRANCIS and I travelled to Grantchester in the height of luxury in the Abbot-General's Daimler, inexcusably purchased by Father Darcy to convey him on his annual visitations well before arthritis had confined him to a wheelchair. Our chauffeur was my friend Edward the master-carpenter, who drove us at such a stately pace up the Great North Road that I thought we would take all day to reach our destination. I even told Francis frankly that we should have travelled by train, but Francis, his weakness for glamour well to the fore, merely told me not to be such a spoilsport.

I will not record the scene in the chapterhouse at Grantchester as my resignation was announced; the memory affects me too deeply even now. Later, after Francis had organised the election and installed my prior as the new Abbot, there were various emotional moments as I took my leave. David the beekeeper gave me a pot of our famous Grantchester honey. The novices proffered a hastily-written scroll of appreciation. My officers presented me with one of my favourite books from the library, *The Cloud of Unknowing,* and as I accepted it with gratitude I thought how appropriate it was that the title should so accurately reflect my current spiritual condition. I was much moved.

Eventually when all the farewells had been concluded in the chapterhouse, the new Abbot escorted me to the front door. I was hoping he would restrict himself to a few formal phrases in order to lessen the awkwardness of the parting, but to my dismay he blurted out: "If only we knew what you were going to do, Father! It would make your loss so much easier to accept!"

I could not speak. Not only was I paralysed by emotion but he had echoed my own sentiments with such precision that I could not have attempted to argue with him. However Francis exclaimed with a severity worthy of our mentor: "If Jonathan can accept this new call from God with courage and dignity, Bernard, I really fail to see why you can't do likewise! This mawkish outburst can't be excused just because I've judged it unfitting at present to disclose further details of the call to you!"

Poor Bernard was crushed. He managed to say with the obedience of a good monk: "Yes, Father," but his grief remained as deep as my own.

In the Daimler Francis muttered: "I know I was harsh, but it's no good allowing a new abbot to sink into sloppiness when his brethren are in an emotional state. He simply has to set a good example, keep a stiff upper lip—" He broke off as he saw my expression. Then: "Sorry," he said. He sounded uncharacteristically abashed. "It was harrowing, wasn't it? Poor Bernard. Poor brethren. Poor you."

But I was sunk too deep in misery to reply.

5

IN our final conversation which took place before I left the Order, Francis said with the robust common sense which I had come to respect so profoundly: "Jonathan, I know this is a difficult subject but I'm reluctant to close our talks without speaking my mind to you on the subject of women—and don't, I beg of you, now mutter some idiocy such as: 'Oh, I'll be all right.' I do accept that you've got the strongest desire to live as a priest should, but what I think may well happen is that once you're back in the world you'll soon be so busy wrestling with all manner of temptation that you'll be unable to concentrate on the vital task of listening for any further word from God about your call. Then once you're in such a debilitated spiritual state, it's possible—not inevitable but possible—that you'll eventually start drifting into error."

Here indeed was a harsh and painful reality. I said: "You're tactfully reminding me that my last attempt to live a celibate life in the world ended in disaster."

"Yes, but don't misunderstand. I'm not actively counselling you to marry; it may be that your new life in God's service will be so absorbing that celibacy becomes not only essential but easy. On the other hand, neither am I actively counselling you to remain celibate; it may be that your new life will require the presence of a wife. But what I *am* strongly advising you to do is to keep an open mind on the subject of marriage." He paused to choose his words with care before adding: "Remember that you're a very different man now from that young priest who got into such a harrowing emotional mess. Remember that your marital problems arose not merely because at that time you were unsuited to marriage but because you'd made the mistake of marrying the wrong woman—and don't, whatever you do, automatically dismiss the possibility that somewhere in the world there may well be a woman who could enhance your life instead of diminishing it."

Without hesitation I said: "That's good advice. I'll do my best to be sensible."

"That's not good enough."

"I promise I'll pray that by the grace of God—"

"That's better."

"—I may be wise enough to make the right decisions and strong enough to live according to His will."

"That's much better. Very well, you're ready to leave and tomorrow I'll release you from your vows."

6

THE release from my vows took place before two witnesses, Ambrose and the prior, in the privacy of the Abbot-General's office. The mercifully brief ceremony was set out in the constitution of the Order and Francis made no attempt to deviate from the text, but when I handed over my habit, that symbol of the way of life I was abandoning, I was overcome by such a profound sense of loss that I might not have known how to continue if we had not all been diverted at that moment by the chimes of noon ringing out in error to announce the half-hour.

"I must get that clock overhauled," said Francis blandly when the ceremony had been completed. "It's become much too temperamental lately." And as the other two men left the room after wishing me well, he handed me a large brown envelope. "Here's the first instalment of your loan together with your identity card, ration book and the standard sheet of advice about the old-age pension, how to sign on at the Labour Exchange and where you can go for help if you're destitute. There's also an additional sheet giving information about war-time conditions—I expect you've read about 'Cooper's Snoopers' from the Ministry of Information and how the Local Defence Volunteers can ask you for your identity card, but you should also know that road signs and the names of railway stations are all being removed in order to confuse any invading Germans. I'd advise you to get hold of a map before the booksellers destroy their stocks."

Again I was impressed by his attention to detail. Thanking him I stuffed the envelope in my pocket and groped for my suitcase.

"Not so fast!" drawled Francis, and he then gave me not only copies of the Bible, the Book of Common Prayer and the Fordite Missal, but also Father Darcy's copy of *The Philosophy of Plotinus*.

The last offering touched me deeply. I had neither expected any memento of my mentor nor anticipated a gift which embraced the subject of mysticism. "What a very liberal and courageous choice!" I said, ever mindful of Plotinus' dubious status as a pagan.

"The old man would have given you St. Augustine's *Confessions*, of course," said Francis, pleased by my response, "but I can see I must fight the urge to turn myself into a replica of the old man."

We left the house together, and as we crossed the courtyard to the main gate I was aware of the hot sunlight on the cobbles, the dull roar of the traffic beyond the wall and the glint of an aeroplane far above us in the cloudless sky.

"More trouble brewing," said Francis, glancing up as he drew back the bolt on the gate. "I don't know how much you've heard on the grapevine but the Luftwaffe have been making a big attack on the South-East during the last few days. However we seem to be holding our own."

"Still our Finest Hour?" I said, remembering one of Mr. Churchill's felicitous phrases.

"Apparently." He turned to face me and suddenly I realised that with the formal blessings all exchanged and the cenobitic rituals completed we were at last free to be ourselves. "Make sure this is *your* finest hour," he said bluntly, not as a superior preaching to his subordinate but as one man giving encouragement to another. "Make sure *you* hold your own during all the inevitable assaults on your spiritual strength." Then with a swift change of mood he exclaimed laughing: "Something tells me we should now cut short this conversation before we both wind up as shattered as poor Bernard!" and I too somehow contrived to laugh as I clasped his outstretched hands in mine.

So all I said in the end was: "Thank you, Francis," and all he said was: "Good luck, Jon." Then the monastery gate swung wide, our hands slipped apart and tightening my grip on my suitcase I walked out at last into the world.

VII

"The young have their own ideas, which are not ours. 'The conversation of the young and old,' says Dr. Johnson again, 'generally ends with contempt or pity on either side.'"

W. R. INGE
A PACIFIST IN TROUBLE

I

UNLIKE the majority of monks who return to the world after many years of an enclosed existence, I had journeyed from time to time beyond the walls of my cloister and in consequence the shock of a permanent return was alleviated; there was no danger, for example, that I might be un-nerved by the sight of a woman smoking a cigarette in public. Yet despite my persistent contact with the world, the fact remained that I had lived apart from it and I knew I should expect to find my surroundings not only alien but possibly repellent. It was with wariness that I approached my visit to my daughter, and although I felt elated that I was free to respond to my new call, I was at the same time conscious that disillusion-ment might lie no more than an undisciplined thought away.

Reaching Waterloo I boarded the train for the South-West and won-dered how many changes I would see when I arrived at my destination. Ruth had lived all her life in Starmouth, where I had begun my ministry thirty-seven years ago, but although I knew the city well I had never liked it. Unlike the county town of Starbridge, which possesses great beauty and much historical interest, Starmouth is an ugly product of the Industrial Revolution, and as the train approached the city centre that morning I wondered how soon the shipyards would be pock-marked by bombing. Closing my missal I said a brief prayer for all those who lived and worked near the docks.

The train entered the station. Thrusting my missal back in my suitcase I abandoned my newspaper for the next occupant of the carriage,

smoothed the creases from my unfamiliar trousers and adjusted my clerical collar. By the time the train halted I was ready to spring down on
to the platform with a vigour which I hoped demonstrated courage as
well as youth, but I knew this air of bravado was mere play-acting; as
always I was aware of the dread that I would fail to live up to Ruth's
expectations of how an ideal father should behave.

I soon saw her. She came rushing forward, stumbling in her ridicu-
lously high-heeled shoes, and then hesitated as if she were shy. Immediately I felt anguish that I should arouse such diffidence, and in an effort
to sweep aside all constraint I dropped my suitcase and held out my arms.

"Daddy!" As she hurled herself against my chest I reflected, not for
the first time, how odd it was to be called "Daddy" when normally
everyone under the sun addressed me as "Father." I could remember Betty
and I arguing about how our children should address us. I had favoured
"Mama" and "Papa" for infancy, "Mother" and "Father" when the
children were able to pronounce "th" without lisping, but Betty, to my
horror, had shortened "Mama" and "Papa" to "Ma" and "Pa"; moreover,
when I had criticized these abbreviations as intolerably common she had
called me a snob and burst into tears. After this stormy scene "Mummy"
and "Daddy"—then names which were becoming fashionable—seemed
the only possible compromise, but I had never liked being "Daddy," and
after Betty's death I had been tempted to ask my children to call me
"Father." However my nerve had failed me. I had been too afraid they
would interpret the request as a retreat into an unloving formality, so the
name "Daddy" had not only persisted but had even degenerated into
"Dad" (a vulgarity almost as bad as "Pa") when Martin entered adolescence.

All these memories flashed through my mind in seconds and by the
time I gave Ruth the required paternal kiss I found I was thinking not
of Betty but of my mentor. Ruth was the only woman I had been
allowed to embrace during my years as a monk; Father Darcy had of
course thought I should have no embraces with any member of the
opposite sex, but since he had been unable to invent a justifiable excuse
for depriving an innocent woman of the chance to show her natural
affection for her father, the embraces which marked Ruth's visits had
continued. Yet Father Darcy had been right in judging them undesirable.
They had not only recalled memories of intimate moments with Betty
but—far worse—stirred up complex feelings of guilt.

Ruth was one of those women who are almost beautiful but somehow
only succeed in being pretty. She was taller than Betty and slimmer
around the hips (Betty had been proud of her hour-glass figure), but she
had the same small elegant waist and the same disconcertingly lavish

bosom. Her dark hair was immaculately curled; I deduced she had recently emerged from a hairdresser's salon. She was wearing a blue coat and skirt, a spotted blue and white blouse and a matching blue hat, but this smart assortment of clothes was ruined by the fact that she was also wearing lipstick, rouge and a very pervasive scent. I resent having an odour deliberately imposed on my sense of smell. I am also, I confess, quite unable to overcome the conviction shared by many men of my generation that the use of cosmetics other than powder is most improper for a respectable woman.

"My dearest Ruth, how very fashionable and alluring you look!" The long compromise with the truth, in the name of what the world deems to be good manners, had begun.

"Darling Daddy, how lovely to see you in real clothes instead of that ghastly habit—and how excited you must be to return to the world at last after being cut off for so many years!"

"I wasn't in the least cut off!" I was trying not to take offence, since I knew she meant only to be affectionate, but I was unable to suppress an indignant protest.

"But you couldn't do any of the *real* things, could you, like going to the shops or listening to the wireless or chatting with the neighbours about the weather."

"That's reality?"

"Oh Daddy, stop teasing me! I can't tell you how lovely it is to see you here—I was only saying this morning at breakfast . . . " Ruth chattered away, just like Betty, just like the vast majority of people in the world, talking about everything but actually saying nothing. The constant talk was going to prove arduous, I could see that, but I knew I had to stop thinking like a monk; I had to make the effort to respond even to the most banal remarks without writing off the conversation as a tedious frivolity that trapped me in the world of appearances when I longed for the world of reality, the reality that lay beyond time and space and the puny perceptions of the five senses.

"What a smart motor car, Ruth! Is it new?"

"No, we got it last year. Don't you remember me telling you about it?"

"Ah yes, so you did . . . " I had been listening with only half an ear at the time because I had been worrying about someone else's spiritual problem.

"Fortunately there's no difficulty at present in getting petrol—the allowance is quite generous—but Roger says rationing's bound to be severe eventually . . . "

Roger was my son-in-law. At forty-five he was too old for active service so Ruth was at least spared the constant anxiety which so many wives had to endure at that time. Dutifully I inquired after his health and was told that he was flourishing; the War had resulted in a promotion to a post of greater importance in his expanding firm of shipbuilders, and as I murmured the necessary words of approbation Ruth began to talk with enthusiasm of the consequent increase in salary which had permitted her to purchase a new refrigerator.

Meanwhile we were driving through the streets of Starmouth and I was feeling exactly as if I had returned from the dead to inspect the haunts of my previous existence. A painful nostalgia, liberally laced with poignant memories of Betty, seared my psyche and temporarily diverted me from my alarm that I should be travelling in a motor driven by a woman. My alarm was exacerbated since Ruth was too excited to drive well, but eventually when we passed from the centre of the city into quieter districts, I was able to surmount both my nervousness and my nostalgia. I saw we had reached the former village of Hartley, now transformed into a select suburb where houses reposed in spacious gardens on either side of roads entitled "The Bower," "The Spinney" and "The Mount" by authorities determined to breathe a 1930s life into the concept of *rus in urbe*. My daughter's home, I discovered, was distinguished by a wealth of half-timbering which was no doubt supposed to recall memories of Tudor architecture. I wondered what an Elizabethan would have thought of such a parody.

Inside everywhere was spotlessly clean and immaculately tidy. I wondered if Ruth had made a special effort to impress me or whether she really was a far more orderly housewife than her mother.

"I love housework," she was saying, answering my unspoken question. "Of course I have a daily—the neighbours would think it odd if I didn't—but I spend my whole time trying to think of things for her to do." With pride she ushered me into the spare room where a double bed lay marooned on a spongy pink carpet. The counterpane was not only frilled but flounced. On the walls hung a series of pictures reminiscent of the sentimental daubs which so frequently adorn the lids of chocolate boxes. There were net curtains.

"What a beautiful vase of flowers!" I said, relieved to see at least one item I could admire, and immediately Ruth blurted out: "Oh Daddy, you're not secretly hating everything, are you?"

"My dearest Ruth—" I saw with foreboding that her eyes shone with tears.

"You're so silent—I never know what you're thinking—"

"I'm thinking how exceedingly lucky I am to have such a good daughter," I said truthfully enough but somehow I only succeeded in sounding stilted and embarrassed. "The house is most striking," I said fervently in despair, "and I'm sure I shall be very comfortable." Giving her a kiss of gratitude, I realised with relief that I had finally succeeded in behaving as she wanted me to behave, and seconds later my relief was expanding as I was left on my own to unpack.

Immediately I took down all the pictures and put them in the wardrobe. Then I hung up my other black suit, put away its clerical accompaniments and my change of underclothes in the chest of drawers and arranged my books on a shelf by the bed. The pot of honey I set aside to give to my granddaughter. Having completed my unpacking I then read a psalm and prayed that I might be given the grace to overcome the guilt which so inhibited my relationship with my daughter, the guilt which stemmed from my past inadequacy as a parent and which so distorted my genuine affection for her that I found it impossible to express my feelings in a satisfactory way. Certainly I knew Ruth was never satisfied, just as I knew that her obsessive attention to me sprang not primarily from her innate warm-heartedness but from a deep-rooted subconscious fear that I had no love for her at all.

However my prayer for the grace to be the ideal parent was disjointed and, as I soon realized, ill-conceived, based on a self-centred desire to avoid the debilitating emotional scenes which would arise if Ruth found me inadequate. Rising from my knees in shame I tidied myself, visited an effete lavatory which even had a frothy piece of material covering the lid like a tea-cosy, and went reluctantly downstairs for luncheon.

2

LUNCHEON consisted of an excellent shepherd's pie followed by cheese, and I began to feel more cheerful. Ruth and I were alone. Roger was at his office, my grandson was still on holiday with his school friend and my granddaughter had been dispatched to Roger's sister nearby.

"I wanted to have you to myself for the first couple of hours!" confessed Ruth, touching me impulsively as if to make sure I was not a mere figment of her imagination.

After luncheon I was given a tour of the house, but although I had wanted most particularly to see the children's rooms, I found them disappointing. Colin, covering his walls with pictures of aeroplanes and motors, had revealed a passion for machinery not uncommon among boys of sixteen who never open books except when forced to do so at school, but the pictures reinforced my suspicion that I shared no interests with him. My granddaughter's room indicated a fractionally wider outlook on life, but its very femininity only emphasised the gulf which must always exist between the sexes; I noted an assortment of dolls, no doubt retained only for sentimental reasons now that Janet was twelve, a large picture of Princess Elizabeth and Princess Margaret Rose, and two shelves of storybooks bearing titles such as *Mimsie in the Upper Fourth*. In neither room did I see a Bible, a prayer book or even a volume of biblical stories for children.

"Now I'll take you to the kitchen," Ruth was saying. "I've been saving it up till the last because I'm so proud of it. I'm longing to show you my new fridge!"

It was clear that the refrigerator interested her greatly, and as she talked about it with animation I noticed that she finally became relaxed. I stood listening in courteous silence and thought how baffling the scene was. If she had said to me: "I have this serious difficulty which is disrupting my spiritual life," I would have known exactly what questions to ask. But to be told the virtues of a refrigerator and to be expected to make an intelligent comment was a trial indeed. I found the dialogue quite impossible to sustain.

I eventually contrived to escape from the kitchen by asking to see the garden, but when Ruth continued to chatter interminably about trivialities I began to feel very tired. However my spirits revived when my granddaughter appeared at the back door and skipped down the path into my arms. We had not met for some months and I was disappointed to see that she was going through a plain stage. Her pale hair was scraped back from her face into pigtails and she wore a brace on her teeth, but her grey eyes sparkled and I thought for a moment that I had caught a glimpse of my mother, although it was impossible to be sure.

We had just retired indoors when the telephone bell started to ring. At once I wondered if the call came from Martin but in the hall Ruth exclaimed: "Pam, how lovely to hear you!" and began to talk about a forthcoming whist-drive in aid of the Red Cross. Hiding my disappointment I sat down at the kitchen table.

"Mummy's in an awful flap about your visit," confided Janet impulsively as she sat down at my side. "So's Daddy. They can't understand why you've left the Order when you were such a success in it."

"But I could hardly have made it plainer in my letter that I've been called by God to work in the world again!"

"Have you really? Gosh, how interesting! Neither of them told me that. Did God speak to you from a cloud like in the Bible?"

"No, he entered my mind and arranged it in certain patterns." It occurred to me that this was the first conversation I had ever had with my granddaughter on her own and I hastened to make the most of Ruth's absence. "Do you really enjoy your Scripture lessons at school?" I said. "When you told me at our last meeting about that ex-missionary teacher of yours, I thought she sounded a bit of a bore. And what about your local vicar? I didn't ask you about him. Does he take a special interest in helping children of your age to take part in the life of the Church?"

The child became wary. "I don't think so."

"Think? Don't you know?"

She was immediately intimidated, and cursing myself for becoming too inquisitorial in my eagerness to discover more about her spiritual life, I added swiftly: "Of course I know your mother doesn't take you to church every Sunday but surely when you do go—" I stopped. A bitter enlightenment had dawned. "Don't you go to church at all nowadays?" I demanded. "Not even at Christmas and Easter?"

The child was now tongue-tied with a guilty shame which, I knew, would later make her feel resentful and cross. I had made a mess of my first real conversation with a grandchild. In distress I groped for the words which would put matters right but before I could speak Ruth exclaimed angrily behind me: "Really, Daddy, can't you talk about *anything* except religion? Can't you ask Janet about her friends and her hobbies instead of cross-questioning her about whether I'm being a good mother and taking her to church every Sunday?"

"My dear Ruth, I'm well aware that there are plenty of good mothers who have some difficulty which makes church-going impossible, and of course I quite understand how hard it is when a husband can't share his wife's spiritual life—"

"And now I suppose you're going to criticise me for marrying a man who isn't religious!"

"Ruth, is this really the wisest of conversations to conduct in your daughter's presence?"

The child saw an opportunity to channel all her confused resentment into an aggressive question. "Mummy, why didn't you tell me that Grandad had had a call from God to leave the Order?"

"Oh, that's what he always says when he wants his own way!" cried Ruth, her insecurity rendering her quite unable to endure even the mildest disapproval from me, and in a storm of emotion which reminded me sickeningly of Betty she rushed out of the kitchen into the scullery and slammed the door violently behind her.

I STOOD up and at once the child said desperately: "Please don't be cross with us because we don't go to church."

I sat down again. Ruth could wallow in her tiresome tantrum; Ruth could wait. I saw clearly that to reassure the child was my first task, and taking her hand in mine, I said: "I certainly shan't love you less just because at present you're not a church-goer. However . . . " I hesitated but was unable to resist adding: "Church-going can be useful in helping one to approach the task of worshipping God. It provides a structure which makes the task easier—just as your teacher made the task of learning to write easier years ago when she gave you specially lined paper to help you form your letters."

The child stared at me wide-eyed. Possibly no one had ever talked to her about worship before. In a home where a refrigerator was treated with reverence no doubt all the occupants would be seriously out of touch with reality, but although I enfolded her with my sympathy she remained unaware of it. To my acute disappointment she withdrew her hand and said in a voice which told me her earlier guilt had turned to anger, just as I had foreseen: "Mummy's very upset and you don't care."

"Of course I care," I said, but my voice sounded much too austere and suddenly I saw myself as I must appear to her, a tall, intimidating stranger, cool, aloof and baffling, the very reverse of the cosy old grandfathers who inhabited the best storybooks for children. I knew I had to project warmth in order to win her confidence, but I felt chilled by a sense of inadequacy. I could only add in a stiff voice: "I'll talk to your mother. Don't be upset. I'll soon calm her down."

"Mummy's very difficult to calm down when she's in a state. Daddy just gives up and goes off to play golf."

"I don't play golf and I'm used to dealing with people who are upset." I managed to smile at her. "Sometimes I used to feel that being an abbot was like being the captain of a ship. I was forever steering my passengers and crew through troubled waters."

I could see this description interested her and although she remained grave I sensed her resentment ebb. However she retorted severely: "You wouldn't have been an ordinary captain—you'd have been a pirate, swinging a cutlass and shaking up everyone in sight." And having described with a startling accuracy my mysterious talent for disruption, she slipped away out of the room before I could attempt a reply.

I COULD postpone the moment no longer. Nerving myself to enter the scullery, I found Ruth crying and took her in my arms.

"Oh Daddy, I didn't mean to be so rude but you made me feel so guilty that we don't go to church—"

I was acutely aware of her alien femininity, the lush, loosely-corseted flesh, the pervasive odor of cosmetics, the unnaturally curled hair, the high voice and—most unnerving of all—the undisciplined emotion. How did one deal with such a creature? If she had been a disturbed relation of one of my monks, I would have been kind but implacably austere, allowing no physical contact whatsoever; I knew exactly how an abbot should behave in such circumstances, but how a father should behave towards such a mysterious version of his own flesh and blood was a problem which quite defeated me. I suddenly found myself wishing the old useless wish that Ruth could have resembled my mother, and the next moment in my memory I could see my mother, serene, silent and self-possessed, never making exhausting emotional demands which could only fill me with a resentment born of guilty despair.

Carefully putting the precious memory aside I said to my daughter with all the kindness I could muster: "Poor Ruth, I'm so sorry." I was just wondering what I could possibly say next when I was saved by the ringing of the telephone bell, but although I again hoped the caller was Martin I again hoped in vain. Ruth began another conversation about the forthcoming whist-drive, and slipping past her I padded upstairs to my room.

I could not remember when I had last felt so overpowered by the need to be alone.

THE next hurdle to be surmounted was the reunion with my son-in-law, who had always abstained from visiting me in my cloister not, as he would have had me believe, because he could never manage to take sufficient time off from his work, but because he had a horror of an enclosed religious life; I suspected that even if he had found me the most delightful of fathers-in-law he would still have fought shy of visiting a monastery in order to pay his respects.

When he arrived home that night at half-past six, his first act after the ritual of handshaking was to ask me what I wanted to drink. Possibly he had no idea what else to say to me. Equally possibly he could not face the reunion without a stiff dose of alcohol. Feeling sorry for him and realising that I had to offer more than a meticulous politeness, I requested a dry sherry in order to appear convivial. I have, I confess, never been attracted to alcoholic beverages as I dislike having the sharp edge of my psyche blunted, but as a Naval chaplain I had learnt the value of nursing a glass in order to repel any accusation of priggishness, and certainly I have never thought that a priest should feel under any obligation to be a teetotaller. Our Lord, after all, is indisputably on record as enjoying his wine at social gatherings.

My son-in-law was a bald man with an unremarkable countenance and when I saw how stout he had become I thought how lucky he was to have such a pretty wife. I hoped he appreciated his good fortune. However he paid scant attention to Ruth and aided by a very dark whisky-and-soda he began to talk in a boastful manner about his blossoming career. Since he had been at a public school, albeit a minor one, I thought he should have been trained to exhibit more modesty, but I realised that this childish desire to impress me sprang from his extreme nervousness. Clearly I needed to soothe him by making a friendly gesture, but it was not until he said to me after dinner: "Can I offer you a glass of port, sir?" that I saw what form the friendly gesture should take.

"Roger," I said, "it was all very well for you to call me 'sir' when you were a young man engaged to my daughter, but I feel it's high time we dispensed with such formality. Please call me Jon in future. And yes, I will have some port, although I'd prefer the measure to be a small one."

We were alone by this time. Ruth and Janet were washing the dishes, and although I had volunteered to help my offer had been received with a horror which I had forgotten would be inevitable. As a monk I had become so used to men performing all manner of domestic work that the traditional family practice of excluding males from the kitchen now seemed like an archaic custom, droll and not without charm but creating an artificial division between the sexes which could only foster the widespread delusion that the function of women was to wait on men hand and foot. I remembered one of my novices complaining at Ruydale: "I want to be outdoors with the men—I don't want to be in the kitchen doing women's work!" and I remembered too my severe response: "Men and women are of equal worth in the sight of God and all work, even the most menial task, becomes worthwhile when dedicated to His glory." I wondered what my son-in-law would have thought of such a philosophy, but I could no more imagine Roger agreeing that men and women were of equal worth than I could imagine him washing dishes contentedly in the kitchen.

" . . . and may I ask," Roger was saying, still not bold enough to address me as Jon despite the large amount of alcohol he had consumed, "if you're about to land some important post in the Church of England?"

It would have been useless to explain that a priest should be uninterested in obtaining a position which the world deems important. Instead I said neutrally: "My only plan at present is to adjust to the world as quickly as possible."

"But you surely must have some idea of what you're going to do!"

"Apart from serving God, no. None at all."

Roger was at once disturbed by my failure to behave like a normal person, and sensing the source of his anxiety I moved swiftly to soothe him. "The Order has kindly granted me a loan to tide me over the next three months," I said, "so there's no danger that I'll starve—and certainly no danger that I'll be a financial drain upon you."

"Well, of course if there's anything I can do to help . . . " His relief was almost palpable.

"It's extremely helpful that I'm able to spend my first week here, and I'm most grateful to you for your hospitality."

No father-in-law could have behaved better. The last swirl of tension faded from the atmosphere as Roger was finally able to relax.

"Tell me," I said before he could voice any insincere pleasure that I should be staying beneath his roof, "have you heard anything from Martin?" This was a question which I had avoided asking Ruth because I had been too nervous of arousing her jealousy.

Roger's air of relaxation was abruptly dissipated. "I'm afraid that's a difficult subject"—he nerved himself to take the plunge—"Jon. He turned up here two weeks ago, drank all my whisky, and became pretty damned unpleasant when I refused to lend him money. I had to ask him to leave."

At first I was surprised that Ruth had concealed this incident from me; her jealousy ensured that I usually heard promptly whenever Martin had been disagreeable, but then I realised that she had not wanted me thinking of Martin when for the first time for many years she had me all to herself.

"He's asked for money before, of course," Roger was saying, "but he never pays it back and this time I decided to put my foot down. I dare say you'll think me uncharitable, but—"

"Not at all. Charity isn't always synonymous with giving money. It may be better for Martin if he's taught that he can't continue to extract money from you on demand."

Making the mistake of thinking I was entirely unsympathetic to my son, Roger said aggressively: "Perhaps he'll now make more effort to get a job. Why can't he seek appropriate work like any other decent pacifist instead of loafing around as an out-of-work actor? In my opinion it's a pity he can't be press-ganged into the Army tomorrow—it would straighten out his drinking and make a man of him. I can't stand all this weak-kneed pacifist talk, and if you ask me I think Martin's decision to swim with the pacifist tide is just his immature way of showing off and calling attention to himself."

I waited for five seconds until I had myself absolutely in control. Then I said in a voice which was devoid of emotion: "Personally I'd rather Martin stood up for his beliefs by talking weak-kneed rubbish than compromised his integrity by talking strong-armed claptrap."

Ruth, re-entering the room seconds later, found us sunk deep in a hostile silence. "Coffee's ready!" she said brightly, trying to conceal her dismay, but I could only profess my need for an early night and escape once more to my room.

6

THE next day I did not present myself in the dining-room until Roger had departed for his office. It was curious to be confronted by a cooked breakfast again. I was torn between finding the bacon and eggs repulsively rich and savouring such a nostalgic reminder of my youth.

Ruth was closeted with her "daily" and Janet was playing with her friend next door, so in my solitude I was free to read the newspapers which had already been delivered to the house. Setting aside *The Daily Telegraph,* I began my first inspection for seventeen years of that popular rag *The Daily Express.* Amazed, aghast and wholly absorbed by the bold headlines and even bolder photographs, I marvelled at the violent, sex-obsessed, trivia-infested world I had been called to rejoin. This was indeed a world far removed from the decorous columns to which I had become accustomed. Guiltily I wondered what Father Darcy would have thought as I skimmed through the latest society divorce case and allowed my glance to linger on a picture of an exceedingly fetching actress, but I did not think of Father Darcy for long. I was too busy imagining the actress in one of the astoundingly brief modern bathing costumes which were displayed in an adjacent advertisement, and I was just wondering in alarm if I could be experiencing the onset of Monks' Madness when Ruth returned to the room.

"Now, Daddy, it's quite obvious you need a woman to take you in hand," she said, sublimely unaware of the image which this normally innocuous phrase at once conjured up in my disordered imagination. "I'm going to drive you to the shops. You simply must have some more clothes, and Roger and I have decided to give you a suit as a coming-out present."

"How very kind," I said, "but the two suits I have at present are quite sufficient."

"What utter nonsense! Daddy, you can't possibly go off to this hotel next week with no decent clothes—do come down to earth and be realistic for a moment! You must have a dressing-gown, pyjamas, slippers, some ties, a couple of ordinary shirts, some grey flannels and a sports jacket—and oh my goodness, I nearly forgot! Daddy, your *underclothes!* When we met outside the bathroom this morning—"

"I concede," I said with dignity, "that I need new underclothes, and of course if you and Roger truly wish to give me a suit it would be most ungracious of me to refuse to accept it, but the other items will have to wait. I can't possibly put you to such expense."

"Yes, you can—we're not poor, and it's very important that you should get everything you need before they bring in clothes rationing. Stop being so huffish and proud!"

Realising that any further argument would only upset her, I refrained from any mutinous comment, but I found Ruth demonstrating her love by well-meaning bossiness almost as exhausting as Ruth demonstrating her love by staging an emotional scene.

Half an hour later we motored to the centre of Starmouth, and there I was firmly led, like a small child dragooned by a nanny, to the gentlemen's tailors and outfitters' shop which I had patronised earlier in my life. There a surprise awaited me. I had expected merely to be measured for the suit, but it had already been bespoken. My measurements had been on file, Ruth had placed the order as soon as she had received word of my return to the world, and the little tailor, who remembered me well, was now beaming as he offered me his latest sartorial masterpiece.

I said: "It's navy-blue," and somehow succeeded in keeping the horror out of my voice.

"Isn't it lovely?" said Ruth pleased. "So much nicer than dreary old black!"

The tailor said soothingly to me: "The navy-blue is very dark, sir, and perfectly seemly for a gentleman of your calling."

Realising I was on the brink of behaving badly, I pulled myself together. "I'm extremely pleased," I said. "This is a wonderful surprise. May I try it on?"

I was shown into a curtained alcove and abandoned with my new suit. The colour still looked unbearably frivolous and common but I told myself I had to stop thinking in such ascetic terms and that my snobbery was not only unattractive but in all probability out of date. Perhaps nowadays even aristocratic clergymen ran around in blue suits during their leisure hours. I held the material up to the light. The colour was indeed very dark. Perhaps at night or on a wet day it might be mistaken for black. That prospect seemed the best I could hope for.

Keeping my back to the looking-glass I slowly exchanged the old for the new, the sacred for the profane, but despite my antipathy I had to admit the suit felt a perfect fit. I allowed myself a moment of unedifying pride as I reflected how little my figure had altered in seventeen years, and then, fortified by my vanity, I nerved myself to face the glass.

I was appalled. A layman, smart and barely recognisable, confronted me. He looked like a successful actor playing the role of a celebrated politician—or possibly of a celebrated surgeon. Pride, arrogance and an aura of reckless, ruthless individuality emanated from the reflection with a force which recalled all my most horrific memories. I felt I was glimpsing again the young undergraduate who had so unscrupulously used his gifts for his own aggrandisement, and this sinister exposure of the dark side of my personality made me yearn in panic for my black and white habit which, like some metaphysical corset, had encased my faults and concealed them behind the facade of a corporate identity.

"Does it fit?" Ruth was demanding, reminding me of Betty as she slashed my consciousness with the razor of her conversation. "Can I come in?"

"I suppose so." I disliked all this womanish bustling.

"I was sure you hadn't put on any weight, but even so I—*Daddy!* Darling, you look stunning, just like a film star! What a wonderful transformation!"

This was exactly the judgement I had no wish to hear. The last thing I wanted was to be transformed; that way lay danger, error and nightmare. "It's a most generous gift, Ruth. Thank you very much," I said with difficulty, but all the time I was longing for my pectoral cross and my Abbot's ring.

"Daddy, is anything wrong?"

"No, I just feel odd dressed as a layman. I'll be fine once I'm back in my clerical suit."

"But aren't you going to wear—"

"I'll save it for later." I got rid of her, changed back into my familiar clothes and felt better, but when I emerged from the cubicle I found she had been rapidly buying a host of other items, shirts and ties to go with the new suit, the promised grey flannels and sports jacket, the pyjamas, dressing-gown, slippers—and even the underclothes.

"You need new shoes too," she said. "We'll leave everything here and just slip across the road to the shoe shop."

"Ruth, I'm quite sure you can't afford all this gross and unnecessary expenditure—"

"Now don't start being proud and huffish again!"

I gave up and allowed myself to be marched to the shoe shop, but as soon as we left I asked to be taken to the nearest church.

"Church!" She was much taken aback but after a moment's hesitation she said uneasily: "I'll take you to the one nearest the house so that it'll be easy for you to walk home . . . Daddy, what is it? What's wrong?"

"Nothing. I just want to be in church for a bit, that's all. It feels so odd not to have been in church yet today."

"I suppose you want to be alone. I can remember Mummy saying to Grandma: 'In the end no matter what I do he always has to be alone.'" And as I flinched she added in a rush: "I'm sorry, I know talking about Mummy always upsets you. I'll shut up now and give you some peace."

She left me at the church, a Victorian replica of the conventional Norman design, and drove away looking injured. I dragged myself inside. The interior was dusty and dark. Kneeling in a corner by a pillar I wrestled with my misery for a long time but eventually I sat back in the pew, took my missal from my pocket and read the noon office. That soothed me, and afterwards I was at last able to concentrate on framing my personal prayers.

"What on earth have you been doing?" cried Ruth, opening the front door as I toiled up the drive in the middle of the afternoon. "You've been gone for hours! I've been so worried—I thought you'd got lost, had an accident, suffered a heart attack—I even went down to the church to look for you but you weren't there—"

"I went for a walk. Then I found another church and—"

"Well, you might at least have telephoned to say you were missing lunch!" Once more she was deeply hurt. It was tempting to express my guilt and despair by shouting at her in exasperation, but of course there could be no shouting, so scenes, no reaction other than a saintly contrition.

"I'm so sorry, how very thoughtless of me."

"And now I suppose you'll say you want to be alone again!"

With a supreme effort I managed to say levelly: "My dear, you mustn't take it as a personal insult. The truth is I'm just not used to the world yet and I need time to recuperate. Please try to understand and make allowances."

Silently she stood aside to let me pass, and awkwardly, feeling guiltier than ever, I slunk away up the stairs to my room.

THE depression began, stabbing deep deadening fingers into my psyche and casting a dark dragging shadow over my powers of reason. I knew that I was suffering from a reaction to the elation I had experienced when I had found myself free to respond to my new call; I knew I was emotionally dislocated, deprived of my cherished way of life; I knew I had to calm myself not only with prayer but with the knowledge that my distress would almost certainly pass, but I found prayer so difficult in that alien environment and the belief in my ultimate recovery was of small comfort. Meanwhile my psychic vitality was continually sapped by the unfamiliar noise of the world, from the meaningless conversation at mealtimes to the irritating stream of sound on the wireless. I began to feel increasingly debilitated and desperate.

However after three torturous days Sunday arrived and I had a chance to conquer my apathy by embracing the disciplined structure of corporate worship. I attended the early service of Holy Communion, which was tolerably well conducted, and later went to Matins and Evensong. Both sermons struck me as slipshod and unedifying. So did the music; the choir made much noise but sang flat. I felt saddened by the lack of men in the congregation and the predominance of elderly women, but at least I was participating in some form of familiar routine. It had a stabilising influence on me, and as I walked home after Evensong I made up my mind to stop pining for my Grantchester chapel, for the voices of my brethren singing the office, for the ascetic atmosphere which I had found so conducive to a rich inner life. To recoil from the world was to fall into the trap of Dualism. No one could deny, in 1940, that evil was present in the world, but the world itself was good, a place to be loved and cherished, and it ill became a priest to regard the work of God with despair.

The next morning I found I had the will to battle against my melancholy, and although I was still tempted to incarcerate myself in my bedroom, I left the house, took a motor bus into the countryside and went for a long walk. Fields, hills, valleys, streams—all seemed radiantly beautiful in the summer light, and as I walked I felt the depression loosen its stranglehold on my mind. I was wearing one of my new shirts with my new grey flannels, and so for the first time in seventeen years I was able to enjoy hot weather without being burdened by heavy robes. I decided that there might after all be compensations for relinquishing the monastic life, and later when I stopped at a village inn for a pint of ale,

I sat peacefully in the small, spare, masculine saloon without once wishing myself back in the cloister.

When I returned to Ruth's house in the early evening I felt physically tired but mentally strong enough to surmount any emotional hurdle which my family might heave across my path—or so I thought. I did not ring the front doorbell. I sensed little Janet was waiting for me in the back garden, so I strolled around the side of the house and pushed open the tradesmen's gate. However as I entered the garden I found that my intuition had been only partially correct. Someone was indeed waiting for me but that someone was not Janet.

It was Martin.

8

HE was drunk, of course, but to my surprise I found this was a challenge I could meet without flinching. Women like Ruth might baffle me, but I was thoroughly experienced in dealing with men afflicted by Martin's problems, and no doubt the fact that I at last felt on familiar ground gave me additional strength. Having allowed myself three seconds to pray for the required pastoral skill, I said with a smile: "What a splendid surprise—I couldn't be more pleased to see you!" and firmly shook his hand.

This was evidently the right approach; as we sat down together on the garden-seat he offered me his hip-flask and said benignly: "Have a swig."

I recognised the olive branch, and as I went through the motions of accepting the whisky I was careful to swallow to create the illusion that I had consumed a large mouthful. It was a technique I had perfected in the Navy.

"Sorry I didn't write," he said in between gulping several large swigs of his own, "but I couldn't face it."

"The only thing that matters now is that you're here. When did you arrive?"

"An hour ago. Then Ruth and I had a screaming match and I was put out like a bloody cat that's made a mess, but at least Janet smuggled the whisky decanter to me so that I was able to refill my flask . . . No, don't ask me how I am! I know damn well you'll have guessed why I'm so conspicuously drowning my sorrows! So much for my dramatic declaration that I'd settled down and was as good as married—he walked out a week after I saw you and the last thing I heard of him was that he was living with a French chef. *A French chef!* Christ, how low can you get! I hate all those bloody pretentious messes which the Frogs push around their plates. Give me bangers-and-mash any day . . . Have another swig."

"No, obviously you need the swig more than I do. I'm sorry you've been through such a rough time—"

"Balls! You're secretly cheering with relief, but if you think I'm going to react to this disaster by taking up with some frightful female—"

"Martin, I've spent many years of my life praying that you wouldn't take up with a female who was frightful."

"Well, if you really want to know how I'm going to react to this disaster I'll tell you: I'm going to kick pacifism in the arse, bugger my way into the Army and bloody well get killed. That would solve all my problems nicely."

I realised that this extravagant statement was an appeal for love and attention, but nevertheless it is exceedingly upsetting when one's child expresses the wish to be killed. I felt my professional poise begin to slip. "Martin—"

"I didn't really believe in all that pacifist rubbish anyway, not after Munich. I just put on an act because Bob was so keen on pacifism and I didn't want to be separated from him if we were called up."

"But will you be accepted for the Army?"

"Don't be naive, Dad! If they excluded from the Army all the men who'd ever committed buggery, England would be entirely defenceless!"

"I was actually thinking of your age—"

"No, you bloody weren't! But perhaps you're hoping I'll change my mind yet again and become a monk—which reminds me, why on earth have you chucked it all up?"

"I told you in my last letter. I've had a call from God to serve Him in the world again."

"Yes, but for Christ's sake, what does that *mean?* What are you going to do? Oh God, I can't stand it when you do your Holy Mystic act!"

"I don't know yet what I'm going to do."

"Then you must be crazy. You had that nice little nook at Grantchester, you were well-fed and well-housed with nothing to do all day except play the Holy Mystic, your favourite role, and yet you decide to chuck it all up in order to bugger around in this bloody awful old world again! It must be sex. There's no other explanation, but all I can say is that you'd better watch out. Don't turn into one of those nasty old men who get sentimental about girls of Janet's age—"

I stood up, crossed the lawn and began to contemplate the nearest flower-bed. No matter how healthy it was for him to vent his rage and misery, it was important that I controlled the conversation by demonstrating exactly how much offensive talk I would tolerate.

He came after me and tugged at my sleeve like a child begging for

attention, the little boy who had never grown up. "Dad—wait a minute—*Dad*—oh damn you, don't go all cold and silent—"

I swung around. "When I want to look in a sewer, Martin, I'll pull
up the cover of the nearest manhole. I've no intention of listening to such
filthy conversation, and moreover I'm under absolutely no obligation to
do so."

"You bloody old prig!" yelled Martin and retreated to the garden-seat
to seek solace in his hip-flask.

I waited till we were both calmer. Then I too returned to the garden-
seat and said quietly: "How can I help you?"

"You can't help me. You despise me."

"How could I despise someone who's brave? You were brave to be
an actor, brave to live your life as you felt you ought to live it, and above
all you were brave to tell me about Bob—"

"I only did it to hurt you. I thought if I hurt you I'd make some sort
of contact, get some sort of genuine reaction instead of this ghastly
saintliness you project whenever you're playing the role of Father with
a capital F—"

"Martin, this behaviour is unconstructive and it's induced by a surfeit
of alcohol. Come into the house and I'll make you a sandwich."

"I don't want a bloody sandwich!"

"Then what do you want, Martin?"

Without warning his bravado crumbled and his eyes filled with tears.
"I want you to tell me you don't mind me being the way I am. I want
you to tell me it doesn't matter."

"I can't tell you that," I said, "because it would be a lie. I do mind
and it does matter, but that doesn't mean I no longer care about you—
indeed it's because I care for you as much as ever that I want to do all
I can to help. Look, I can see how much you've suffered, but suffering
needn't be destructive. If you could only use it as a spur to begin a new
life—"

"Oh my God, we're knee-deep in crucifixion and resurrection!" He
struggled to his feet. *"I don't want your bloody religion!* All your bloody
religion ever did for me was to give me a man who was more interested
in being a bloody clergyman than a bloody father!" And as Ruth finally
gave way to the temptation to erupt from the house in fury, he blundered
away through the tradesmen's gate without looking back.

VIII

"Religion, so far from being a disease, is essential to mental health, and if we may trust those who in other fields would be called experts in their subject, there is one thing of which they feel increasingly certain, and that is that in prayer and meditation they are actually in contact with a spiritual reality which is not a projection of their own thought and will."

W. R. INGE
LAY THOUGHTS OF A DEAN

I

DURING the last part of my conversation with Martin I had been aware that Ruth was listening at the open scullery window so I was far from surprised when she decided to intervene. Nevertheless I was angry. I found her bright-eyed excitement unedifying and I was reminded of nursery scenes long ago when she had rejoiced at Martin's transgressions in the hope that she might consequently win extra favour.

"Poor darling Daddy—oh, how could he have said such horrible things to you, how could he!"

"He's intolerably unhappy."

My response disappointed her; at once she became angry. "I should have known you'd always stand up for him—even now he's a drunken pervert you're still busy pretending he's wonderful!"

So overwhelmed was I by my misery that I was unable to order her to be quiet. Retreating to my room I tried to pray, but I felt cut off from God and memories of my marriage, all hellish, screamed through my consciousness until my entire psyche was a dense ball of pain.

Half an hour later I was still groping for the will which would enable me to perform the simple task of changing for dinner when there was a mouselike tap on the door.

It was the child, her small face pale and grave. "I'm sorry, Grandad. It was all my fault. I gave Uncle Martin the whisky and the whisky made him beastly."

With unutterable relief I recognised a familiar situation: someone in distress had come to me for help and I had the opportunity to rise above my own pain by thinking of someone other than myself. Scooping her across the threshold, I sat down with her on the edge of the bed. "Uncle Martin had already decided to share his unhappiness with me," I said, "and the extra whisky merely made it easier for him to do so. You mustn't blame yourself. I know you wanted only to be kind."

I was aware of her gratitude. She said confidentially: "Mummy's livid with me because she says I made Uncle Martin drunk and Daddy's livid with me because he's just arrived home and found there's no whisky."

"Both your parents are upset and not thinking clearly. It's only natural that you should feel hurt and cross, but in fact you're not the real source of their anger. They're angry with Martin for behaving badly, and although they may not realise it they're angry with me for being the pirate who boards their orderly ship and causes chaos."

She was intrigued. "But Grandad, how do you manage to cause such chaos? You're always so quiet and polite! Why is everyone reeling in all directions?"

I laughed. "Perhaps I should offer myself to the Army as a secret weapon!"

"Gosh, what a ripping idea! You could knock out Hitler!"

"Exorcism would be more effective, I think."

"Exorcism! I've read about that. But does it work?"

"Certainly. No demon can withstand the power of Christ."

Far away in the hall Ruth called tensely: "Dinner's ready!"

"Grandad."

"Yes, Janet?"

"It's all real, isn't it? Religion, I mean."

"Of course."

"But why doesn't everyone understand that?"

"One of our limitations as human beings is that we find it exceedingly difficult to grasp reality—the ultimate reality which is spiritual."

"Daddy thinks it's religion that's unreal. He thinks it's a sort of illness."

"It's hard for people who operate on only five senses to perceive a reality which they can't hear, see, touch, taste or smell. However there's a vast mass of evidence which suggests that not only does this ultimate reality exist but that it can be perceived by man. For instance, Plato (who was a mystic) said that the fully real is fully knowable, and by that he meant—"

"Dinner!" shouted Ruth.

"What's a mystic?" said Janet.

"A mystic is someone who can perceive ultimate reality, the ground of our being, known variously as God or the Absolute or the One.

Mysticism isn't confined to Christianity; it's the raw material of religion and exists independently of creeds and sects and religion in an organised form. But in my opinion a mystic should work within an organised Church because he needs the discipline of a stable framework in order to remain spiritually healthy. It's a very regrettable fact of the spiritual life that a mystical approach to God is peculiarly subject to demonic influences."

"I wish you taught us Scripture at school," said Janet. "I know you're old but you still look nice and you talk about such interesting things."

It was the kindest remark I had received for some time. I gave her a kiss and somehow found the strength to face dinner.

2

THE sixth and penultimate day of my visit dawned at Starmouth. I had still not succeeded in sleeping through the night; old habits die hard, and when I awoke I read the office of Matins. Later at half-past five I rose, shaved, dressed and read the office of Prime before spending two hours in prayer and devotional reading. Every day I longed to receive the sacrament, but during the week there was no Mass in Starmouth beyond the walls of the Roman Catholic Church. In my desperation I was tempted to attend Mass there, but I knew the inevitably voluptuous interior of the church and the stream of garbled Latin would distract me so much that the exercise could only be unedifying.

Ironically it was my time as a High Church monk, not my career as a Broad Church Naval chaplain, which had nurtured my antipathy towards the Church of Rome. The Anglo-Catholics' flirtation with ecumenism in the form of a reunion with Rome is a relatively recent development, and the Fordite Order, founded in the 1840s before Mr. Ford's hero John Henry Newman had seceded to Rome, had remained true to the original spirit of the Oxford Movement as it re-established Catholicism as a powerful force within the Church of England. This famous ethos had consisted in part of an outlook which saw Anglo-Catholicism as truer to the Early Church than the Catholicism of Rome, which was judged to have been corrupted over the centuries. The Oxford Movement's later, more charitable view—that the true Catholic Church was tripartite, consisting of Anglo-Catholics, Roman Catholics and the Orthodoxy of Eastern Europe—was eventually accepted by the Fordites, but the anti-Roman bias lingered on and in fact the Fordites were still distinguished by the strong stress they laid on their separation from the Roman Orders. As a leading High Churchman, Father Darcy had felt bound to encourage the reunion talks at Malines in the 1920s between the Anglo-Catholics and the Roman Catholics, but later in private he had told me he considered the entire exercise not only a waste of time but thoroughly undesirable. However this deep antipathy had probably been rooted in the fact that he considered his Order to be vastly superior to any of the Roman Orders and had hated to think that in the event of reunion he would have had to be servile to some foreigner called a Pope who would almost certainly have regarded him with disdain.

My own feelings on the subject were as mixed as my mentor's. As a Christian I did my best to regard the authoritarian monolith of Rome with charity; as an Englishman I could not help but regard it with distaste, and as a mystic I could only regard it with horror. Profound religious truths are eternal; the man-made divisions of Christendom, trapped in time, are subject to corruption, and because of this no man-made institution should be allowed to interpose itself in a dictatorial fashion between the mystic and his God—indeed no man-made institution can effectively do so, and this, of course, explains why mysticism has so often been a running sore on the body politic of the Roman Church. No authoritarian regime likes the rebels who by circumventing its power cut it down to size.

Mystics, as I had told Janet, need the framework of organised religion, but when the organisation can only offer a framework that insists on conformity at all costs, then mysticism, if not crushed or driven underground, will flourish not because of the organisation but in spite of it. The monastic life of the Fordites certainly had its authoritarian aspects, but the watchwords of the Church of England are liberty and tolerance, and certainly no one in the Order had tried to suppress or distort my spiritual gifts in the name of dogmatics. I had known then that although I was a Catholic I would remain an English Catholic and that the Church of Rome would always be alien to me.

So I abstained from attending Mass at the local Roman Catholic church, but on the penultimate day of my visit to Starmouth I padded downstairs after reading Prime, stole a crust from the bread-bin in the larder, filched a drop of sherry from the drawing-room decanter and retired to my room to celebrate the Holy Communion. Afterwards I felt comforted, and it was in a strong tranquil frame of mind that I once more nerved myself to face the breakfast table.

"Daddy," said Ruth purposefully as she delivered my eggs and bacon, "I want to talk to you."

My strength and tranquillity instantly evaporated. I had, of course, realised by this time that Ruth's devotion to housework and her new refrigerator could indicate the existence of a vacuum elsewhere in her life, and I had, of course, noticed that she and Roger talked only on the most facile of levels, but I had instinctively pulled down the shutters over my perceptive powers—and not because of any praiseworthy parental desire to avoid meddling in an adult daughter's private life. I had been driven by sheer cowardice buttressed by a strong sense of self-preservation; so debilitated did I feel by Martin's problems that I shied away from debilitating myself still further by embracing Ruth's.

"There's no need to look so alarmed!" she was saying with an exasperated affection. "I just wanted to tell you about a lovely idea that I've had. Do you remember me mentioning last year that we thought of converting the space over the garage into a games-room? Well, we never actually got around to it, but why don't we now convert the space into a little flat for you? I know living *en famille* doesn't really suit you, but if you had a room of your own, quite separate from us, with your own bath and a little pantry-kitchen—well, you might come to visit us regularly, mightn't you, and later when you've retired . . . Well, Daddy, let's be realistic! You've got no private income and no prospect of any money when you retire except for the old-age pension and some pittance from the Church, and I simply can't bear to think of you all alone and miserable in some sordid old peoples' home—"

"Isn't this fantasy a little premature?"

"Premature! How could it be? Daddy, you're sixty—*sixty years old*—"

"Quite." I somehow managed to muzzle my rage.

"—and there might well come a time in the not-too-distant future when you'll need to be looked after, and as I like looking after people and as we do have the space over the garage—"

By a superhuman effort I mastered my temper and said in my gentlest voice: "It's certainly not impossible that one day I might welcome such a generous and unselfish offer, but meanwhile I feel I've plenty of work to do before I can consider retirement and so it seems only sensible that I should continue to stay here *en famille* during my visits. I wouldn't want to put you to the expense of providing separate accommodation for me only to find that I was seldom able to use it."

Her face crumpled.

"Ruth . . . " I was in despair. The memory of Betty encircled my psyche with a strangler's grip, and suddenly the guilt that I could not love her in the way she wished was more than I could bear. Pushing aside my untouched plate of eggs and bacon I stood up. "Ruth, please—no more emotional scenes—"

"You hate it here—the visit's been a failure—"

"Nonsense!"

"Then why can't you accept my offer?"

"The real question is not why can't I accept your offer but why can't you accept my refusal." Suppressing the urge to walk out, I sank down again in my chair. That cost me so much energy that I barely had the strength left to say: "The truth is that your distress here isn't rooted in my response to your offer. It lies in the fact that your children are growing up, Roger's absorbed in his own activities and you've begun to feel your family don't need you any more."

But this glimpse of reality was much too painful for her to face, and at once she rushed sobbing from the room.

3

THE fault was entirely mine; I had committed the error, unforgivable in an experienced counsellor, of confronting Ruth with a truth she was unable to digest, and I knew I had to give her time to resurrect her damaged defences. Accordingly I retired to the garden with my copy of *The Cloud of Unknowing,* but I made no attempt to read. I merely waited and after a while she came outside to join me.

"I'm sorry," I said, standing up to meet her. "Your offer was so good and kind and I feel almost criminally at fault for being unable to find the right words to refuse it. But you mustn't think I'm either ungrateful or uncaring."

She struggled with her tears again but at last she said: "I just wish I didn't find you so baffling. I don't understand a single thing you do— why you went into the monastery, why you've come out of it, why you've got to go off tomorrow into the blue when you could stay here with your family and be comfortable and loved and well looked after—"

"I think my monks at Grantchester felt much as you do and I can only tell you what I told them: I must do what I believe God requires of me. But how guilty I feel that you've never been able to express your bewilderment until now! I must try and make it easier for you to talk to me."

"But I talk to you all the time!"

"I wasn't referring to the kind of conversation in which you tell me all about your new refrigerator. I was thinking of the kind of conversation in which you'd tell me your problems and I'd do my best to be helpful."

"But I don't have any problems! I'm so lucky—I've got so much to be thankful for!"

"Yes, but—" Automatically I fell back on a technique of which I was a master. Combining my practical experience with my psychic eye I picked a hidden subject, a subject which had hitherto remained unmentioned between us, and trailed it in front of her to lure her into self-revelation. "But this is a frightening time, isn't it?" I said sympathetically and paused before adding the key words: "Particularly for mothers of sons."

At once she shuddered. "If there's no invasion perhaps the War may last for years, and there's Colin, eighteen in two years' time—"

We were, as I believe they say in racing parlance, "off and running," galloping away down the opening strait. I murmured: "That's certainly a terrible prospect for you," and waited, not unpleased by my skill, for the confession inevitably to unfold.

"I try to shut out the anxiety," said Ruth, "I try not to think about it, but I worry and worry and worry and Roger says I must stop, worrying does no good, I'm simply making myself ill, but it's easy for him to say that, he's got plenty of distractions, out all day at the office or at the golf club, and I've got nothing to divert myself with except cleaning, and I clean and I clean and I clean, but sometimes I feel I can't bear the strain, I love Colin so much—well, I love Janet too, of course, but she's been a bit peculiar lately, I suppose it's the onset of the awkward age and I've got to accept that she's not a little girl any more, but—oh, how I wish I had another baby! I always did want another but when we had our boy and our girl Roger said all right, that's it, that's all we can afford if we want to live comfortably in a nice home—although as things have turned out we could perfectly well have afforded one more, and now sometimes when I'm cleaning I find I'm thinking about it, the baby, I mean, the baby that never was, and I feel so sad and I start crying but that makes Roger so irritable and off he goes to the golf club and then I feel worse than ever, so sad and so alone, although of course I keep telling myself how lucky I am to have such a nice home and lots of smart clothes and the very latest refrigerator—"

"Why don't you go ahead and have it?"

"Have it? Have what?"

"The baby. You're only thirty-six. There's no problem now about money. What's stopping you? Would Roger object?"

"No, no, of course not!" she said at once, but when I saw her hands clench in her lap I knew the intimate side of their marriage had ceased. "It's a lovely idea, certainly . . . I'll have to think about it." Giving me her brightest smile she rose to her feet. "Well, I mustn't sit here gossiping about trivialities when I've got all the washing to do! If you'll excuse me, Daddy . . . "

"Of course," I said, and feeling profoundly distressed I watched her hurry away across the lawn.

MY first reaction to Ruth's pathos was the primitive one: I felt angry with the man who had made my daughter unhappy. But then I remembered those stern words: "Judge not, that ye be not judged," and found myself asking whether Roger's failure to be an attentive husband was any worse than my own failure thirty-five years ago; when I had failed to make Betty happy I had regularly abandoned her for a far longer time than it took to play a round of golf.

Scraping together a professional detachment—a well-nigh impossible exercise in the circumstances—I tried to imagine why marital intimacy should have ceased. Late nights at the office and repeated absences at weekends did not necessarily indicate an adulterous husband; perhaps after years of over-indulgence in food and drink Roger had been plagued by recurring impotence until in humiliation he had abandoned sexual intercourse altogether. His absorption in his work and his golf could thus be seen not merely as a device to avoid his wife but as a method of blotting out his sense of failure.

I toyed with this plausible theory for some time. I liked it because it enabled me to regard Roger with compassion and to see Ruth as an innocent victim, but after a while it occurred to me to speculate how far the marriage had been dislocated by Roger's inclination to acquire inanimate possessions instead of additional children. Such behaviour by a husband could have a crippling psychological effect on the wife; I could well remember the sailor who had confided to me many years ago: "As soon as my wife was told she couldn't have more children, padre, she lost interest in you-know-what." However before I could dwell on this new theory another memory seeped into my mind. I saw a young priest whom I had counselled at Ruydale and heard him saying to me in despair: "I've tried so hard, Father, but she absolutely hates it." I could remember his wife too. He had brought her to see me once; I had told him I could not counsel a woman but I had thought it might help me to counsel him if I had some idea what kind of woman she was, and I could see her now, young and pretty, charming and delightful, a girl who had responded to my friendly enquiry about her parents by talking reverently, eyes glowing with hero-worship, about her father.

Standing up abruptly I began to walk around the garden. The top layer of my mind was still thinking of the poor young priest, one of my failures, someone I had been unable to help, but the next layer of my mind was contemplating my own guilt. By not loving my daughter adequately

I had aroused in her an obsessive need for an attention which was paternal, not marital, and the need had destroyed the core of the marriage. Ruth's troubles were all my fault, I could see that now, just as I could see that Martin too was still suffering from my shameful failures as a father long ago.

Depression overwhelmed me again and sapped the last shreds of my spiritual strength. I wondered how Francis could ever have counselled me to keep an open mind on the subject of marriage, and as I sank down once more on the garden-seat I decided my mind had to be not open but resolutely closed. Remarriage was impossible. I was utterly unfit. A celibate life was the only answer, but how was celibacy going to be possible for me outside the walls of a monastery?

I knew myself too well not to experience another wave of despair at this point, and suddenly I was reviewing with a bleak clinical eye all my sexual responses to the world to which I had returned. They had ranged from the innocent pleasure of watching a pretty girl cross a road to the salacious stimulation of seeing scantily-clad women in newspaper photographs, from the harmless day-dreams of courting an ideal woman to the obsessive knowledge that it was now within my power to dress as a layman, take a 'bus into central Starmouth and commit fornication. In the cloister I could have confessed all the "impure thoughts," poured out all my difficulties and somehow, with sympathetic counselling, won the battle for serenity and self-control. I would have been helped also by having my work to distract me, and in caring for others I would have been too busy to waste time agonising over myself. But now I was alone, without work, without regular spiritual counselling, without, so far as I could see, any hope of a conventional happiness in the future. For one long moment, as my spirits hit rock-bottom, I doubted my ability to survive as a priest.

Then in my imagination Father Darcy exclaimed: "Disgusting! What a weak, self-centred, cowardly, maudlin exhibition of ill-ordered, unedifying feelings! Pull yourself together this instant!" And my vision cleared. I saw that I could not be alone when God was with me; nor was I without work for I still had the task not only of worshipping Him but of discerning what He required me to do. I was hardly deprived of spiritual counselling either, since Francis had promised to write to me regularly, and certainly I was not without hope of happiness in the future; I would be serving God, and without serving God no lasting happiness, conventional or otherwise, was possible.

Meanwhile I could wage war against despair by committing my anguish to paper and seeking advice.

I retired to my room to write to Francis.

MY train to Devon departed from Starmouth at half-past nine the next morning, and Janet came with Ruth to the station to see me off. Disliking protracted goodbyes and fearful that Ruth might use the opportunity to stage yet another emotional scene, I managed to part from them outside the ticket office, but as I hurried onto the platform it was hard to avoid the conclusion that yet again I had wound up running away from my family.

My shame enveloped me all the way to the Devon border and manifested itself in the demon sloth; I was unable even to open my Bible. Then just as I was once more struggling to recall the saving image of my exorcist, I glanced up at the luggage rack—and saw not my battered old suitcase but the elegant bag of my vision.

I leapt to my feet but it was already gone. I sank back, numb with shock, and some seconds passed before I realised that the Bible was now open in my hands. "I have fought a good fight, I have finished my course, I have kept the faith . . . " The famous words of St. Paul instantly vanquished the demon, and with my courage renewed by the second "showing" I travelled on into the unknown.

I ARRIVED at Allington Court shortly before luncheon and was warmly greeted by the warden, Dr. Sheen, who two years before had made a retreat under my direction at Grantchester. After a successful career as a schoolmaster he had suddenly decided in his mid-fifties that he was tired of teaching Scripture to adolescent boys, and his retreat had taken place shortly before he had become Warden of Allington. I had had no doubt that the change had been right for him, and occasionally after his departure from Grantchester I had pictured him ministering briskly, though perhaps a trifle too heartily, to his varied collection of guests.

I was shown to a large room overlooking the garden and possessing only one picture, a print of Masaccio's *The Tribute Money*. As no women were depicted in it I decided it was insufficiently distracting to merit an incarceration in the wardrobe. I pressed the bed surreptitiously. The mattress was hard. Glancing around I noted a plain brown carpet and unobtrusive curtains. My spirits rose. I decided that this was a room in which I could feel at home.

"Now, sir," said Dr. Sheen, exuding the most worthy desire to put me at ease, "don't be afraid that I'll pester you with questions about your new life. I've no intention of prying, and the only question I'd like to ask is how you'd care to be addressed now that you've left the Order. Obviously I shan't go around calling you 'My Lord Abbot'—well, I never did, did I?—but do you wish to be Father Darrow or just plain Mr. Darrow nowadays?"

"I don't want to raise any hackles among your Broad Church and Low Church guests. Let it be 'Mr.' "

Dr. Sheen, mindful of the constant need to maintain harmony in his community, congratulated me on my charity in the face of possible bigotry. It never occurred to him that my request might have arisen not from a saintly wish to avoid irritating others but from a selfish desire to obtain peace and quiet. Church of England priests who welcome being addressed as "Father" too often wind up in debilitating debates about the value of the Oxford Movement, the evils of Popery and whether the use of incense is a valid aid to worship or merely a thoroughly nasty piece of un-English mumbo-jumbo. Anglo-Catholicism was capable of arousing strong passions among those who opposed it as a betrayal of Protestant values.

"I'd also be most grateful," I added, "if I could be allowed to blend in with your other guests as unobtrusively as possible. Of course there may well be people here who either know me or know of me, but I'm most anxious to avoid being treated with any fuss or fanfare."

"My dear Darrow, I'm afraid my wife and I have already trumpeted your arrival to all our favourite guests! We were so excited at the thought of having you here, but don't worry, we've got a good bunch of people here at the moment and I'm sure they won't submit you to any tactless interrogation. I've already made sure you've been put at a civilised table—or do you want to sit by yourself at mealtimes?"

I did, but I had already made up my mind that I must make an effort to be sociable in order to hasten my adjustment to the world. The dining-room at Allington, in common with the dining-rooms of ocean liners, had few single tables, and guests on their own were encouraged to share a table with others.

I had been considerably taken aback by Dr. Sheen's carefree confession that he had already revealed my identity on such a sweeping scale, but I suppressed my exasperation by reflecting that my dream of anonymity had always been unlikely to come true. Warily I went down to luncheon. In the dining-room the warden's wife, hair firmly coiffed, front teeth well exposed, swept me to one of the central tables for six and introduced me to my fellow-guests as Mr. Darrow. When the introduction had been completed I found myself in the company of a retired priest called Staples and his wife, a clerical widow called Mrs. Digby, a professor of theology called Haydock and a most fetching American called Miss Tarantino who told me she had arrived at Oxford before the outbreak of war to do research and had decided to stay on; she gave no reason for this decision but I thought it not unlikely that she had been influenced by some romantic attachment, now defunct, which had resulted in her being stranded in a foreign country at such a crucial time. Enquiring about her research I learnt that she was writing a book about the influence of the Black Death on fourteenth-century religious thought. I would have asked more questions but at this point little Mrs. Staples, wife of the retired priest, could no longer contain her curiosity.

"Dr. Sheen's told us all about you, Mr. Darrow!" she said, beaming at me with a disarming innocence. "How very strange you must find it here after being locked up for so many years!"

"The Fordite monks aren't locked up, my dear," said her husband hastily, "and indeed Fordite abbots go all over the place. I believe the Abbot-General actually has a chauffeur-driven motor at his disposal."

"Something tells me," said the clerical widow Mrs. Digby shrewdly as she noted my expression, "that this particular abbot doesn't approve of chauffeur-driven motors for monks."

I said in my firmest voice: "I'm no longer an abbot. I'm just an ordinary clergyman of the Church of England now."

"The last thing you could ever be, surely," said the alluring Miss Tarantino with a flutter of her very long eyelashes, "is just an ordinary clergyman, Mr. Darrow."

I nearly knocked over my glass of water.

Professor Haydock, exhibiting a remarkable imperviousness to both Miss Tarantino's allure and my confusion, demanded abruptly: "Do you have a degree in theology?"

"Yes."

"Perhaps you feel called to teach!" said ingenuous little Mrs. Staples. "I'm sure an abbot would know just how to keep order in the classroom. Or do you feel called to serve in some quite different field? Do tell us, Mr. Darrow—I'm sure we're all fascinated to know what happens to monks when they go back into the world!"

A heavy silence enveloped us as the others wrestled with their embarrassment that Mrs. Staples should be so sublimely tactless and I wrestled with my embarrassment that they should be embarrassed. However eventually Miss Tarantino saved the situation by drawling: "What he's going to do is have a wonderful vacation sizing up exactly how much this wicked old world has to offer!" But just as I was relaxing with relief she gave me such a brilliant smile that I was again plunged into confusion.

Somehow I managed to restrain myself from bolting unfed from the room, but I was already wondering how I could survive for three weeks in such an atmosphere of gossip, curiosity and rampant carnal temptation.

7

THIS state of horror, born of nervous anxiety and nurtured by the sheer novelty of lunching in unknown mixed company, was soon alleviated. I found that the warden had not underestimated the essential good manners of my fellow-guests and eventually even Mrs. Staples retreated into a conscientious discretion. Deciding that my panic had been both ridiculous and unnecessary I retired after luncheon to the library, which was as handsome as I remembered, and settled myself at one of the writing tables.

On my arrival at Allington I had found a collection of letters waiting for me, and I now took the opportunity to read them at leisure. My correspondents included people to whom I gave spiritual direction; all regretted my departure from the Order and the majority asked if they could continue to consult me by post, but a small minority displayed their disturbed psyches by berating me for "leaving them in the lurch" when they needed me most. I decided these gentlemen needed a prompt response.

I also received a number of letters from the monks, ranging from the most eminent to the most humble. Most of them wished me well and promised to pray for me, but there were a few monks who wrote not out of charity but in a self-righteous fury, claiming that I was "letting the side down," "throwing in the sponge" and "dyed deep in apostasy." One Yorkshire officer even raked up the Whitby Affair and said he had always known I would come to an unedifying end. I mention these examples of antagonism because I may have given the impression, in describing my departure from Grantchester, that I was universally loved by my brethren, but the truth is that as a controversial figure I have always had my enemies, and unfortunately monks are as liable as the rest of mankind to be invaded by the demons of envy and dislike.

The most important letter came on the morning after my arrival. In response to my unhappy communication from Starmouth, Francis wrote:

I'm inclined to think that in your despair you came to some highly questionable conclusions. I would regard the harrowing dramas of the past week not as confirmation that you should never remarry but as a salutary reminder that you should never again attempt marriage to the wrong woman for the wrong reasons. With regard to Martin and Ruth, I'd like to remind you of a remark you made to me once during a discussion of psycho-analytical theory. "I entirely disapprove," you said, "of the Freudian habit of blaming all a child's woes on its hapless parents." How wise you were! And how unfortunate that this wisdom should have been swept away by the hurricane of guilt which has temporarily reduced your rational faculties to rubble! In my opinion Ruth and Martin must be allowed to assume at least some of the responsibility for their errors and shortcomings—to deny them that responsibility in order to assume it all yourself is actually a perverse form of vanity. Besides, are you really such a complete failure as a father? Both your children seem to care deeply what you think of them, and if you were a complete failure they surely wouldn't give a fig for your opinion.

This letter was a great comfort to me, and after reading it many times I embarked on a reply late that night in my room.

Again Francis answered by return of post. Knowing how busy he was I was impressed by this scrupulous attention to my welfare. After the opening paragraph, in which he professed himself relieved that his earlier letter had provided a steadying influence, he wrote:

I'm delighted to hear that you're making the effort to be sociable at mealtimes. I know how difficult this must be for you, but I do wholly endorse your opinion that the effort should be made in order to accelerate your adjustment to the world.

Don't be too frightened of the fetching American damsel. If she were what I believe is now called a "vamp" and what in our young day would have been called a "hussy," she would hardly have buried herself in a clerical playpen in Devon. The time to worry about the lady, I think, is when she invites you to her room to inspect her manuscript—or when you lure her to a secluded corner of the grounds in order to stop her watch. Meanwhile it's inevitable that you should find all women intensely interesting at present, particularly foreign women who appear to stand outside English conventions, and instead of fighting your interest in panic you might do better to accept it with a moderate amount of amusement. Remember that a reed which bends before the wind survives intact whereas an unyielding tree can be ignominiously uprooted.

I spent much time pondering this excellent advice but I continued to find Miss Tarantino, who in fact was as well-behaved as she was charming, almost unbearably distracting. She had only to walk into the library and any serious attempt to read was destroyed. However within forty-eight hours of my arrival Miss Tarantino's effect on my equilibrium was less disturbing to me than the knowledge that I had become a centre of attention.

Unfortunately I have always tended to stand out in a crowd and this is not merely because I am six foot three and somewhat hard to overlook. At Allington people were primarily intrigued because I was an ex-monk, but even if my past had remained unknown to them I suspect I would still have attracted as much attention as a lighthouse in a desert. This mysterious aura, generated by my psychic powers under the pressure of mental stress, was part of what Father Darcy had called my "infinite capacity for disruption," and the harder I tried to be unobtrusive the more readily every head would turn whenever I entered a room.

Finally the worst happened. Guests arrived who were incapable of either tact or discretion, and I was obliged to engage directly with their curiosity.

I had arrived at Allington Court on a Wednesday. On Saturday several guests departed and various newcomers took their place. At my table the retired priest Mr. Staples and his ingenuous wife left after breakfast and at luncheon I found that their vacant chairs had been claimed by a middle-aged churchwarden called Braithwaite, a tiresome officious fellow who I had no doubt was a sore trial to his vicar, and by his wife, a woman who made Trollope's Mrs. Proudie seem humility personified. As soon as they found out who I was they besieged me with questions. Why had I become a monk? What was the point of it? Didn't I think it wrong for an able-bodied man to be idle when he could be doing something socially useful? Didn't I think the monastic hatred of women was unhealthy? Didn't separation from women and the world lead to a grossly abnormal existence? How had I survived for seventeen years in such an environment? Significantly it occurred to neither of them to ask why I had left the Order; they merely leapt to the conclusion that I had at last come to my senses after a prolonged aberration.

When I was given a chance to reply to their bigoted, ignorant and ill-natured tirade, I said with an iron courtesy: "First, I became a monk because God called me to do so; argument would have been not only impertinent but irreverent. Second, the point of being a monk is primarily to obey the great commandment: 'Thou shalt worship the Lord thy God with all thy heart and with all thy soul and with all thy might,' so I most certainly wasn't idle. Also, in addition to worshipping God for several hours each day, I worked at various times as a domestic servant, a farmhand, a carpenter, a teacher, a counsellor and a managing director. I could even claim to have been 'socially useful,' since I helped various people in the world to overcome their problems, but even if I hadn't been 'socially useful,' why should that have invalidated my work for God?

You can't define what God requires of us in terms of social utility, and indeed it's perfectly possible for work to be socially useful yet spiritually irrelevant. As for monastic misogyny I can assure you that if monks do hate women they shouldn't, and indeed from my experience I believe that monks are more inclined than their brothers in the world to believe the great Christian proclamation that men and women are of equal value in God's sight. Does separation from women and the world lead to a grossly abnormal existence? It leads to a fundamentally different existence, certainly, but I suspect the people who would call it grossly abnormal are merely frightened of a non-conformity which calls their own so-called normality into question. You ask how I survived for seventeen years as a monk, and I'll tell you: I survived because I was happy and fulfilled, doing the work which I had been called by God to do, and because I was healthier in mind, body and spirit than I had ever been in my life before."

"Well said, Darrow!" exclaimed Professor Haydock, who had clearly taken a dislike to the newcomers. Only the previous day he had been mooting the idea that monasticism had no place in the modern world.

"Well, I'm sure none of us would question your sincerity, Mr. Darrow," said Braithwaite, grudgingly retreating an inch from his entrenched position, but his wife had resolved to stand firm. "I still say," she declared, "that it's not a natural life for a man."

Professor Haydock said dryly: "I rather doubt that it's theologically possible for God to call a man to an unnatural life. How would you define 'natural,' may I ask, madam?"

"Being natural," said Mrs. Braithwaite, bristling with hostility, "means living with a wife and two children in a nice little house and going to church on Sundays—and if you'd ever done *that*, Mr. Darrow," she added, turning on me, "we might find your defence of the monastic life more convincing."

"My dear Mrs. Braithwaite," I said, "before I became a monk I spent nine years of my life living with my wife and two children in a nice little house and going to church on Sundays." Tossing aside my napkin I rose to my feet, murmured: "I wish you all a pleasant afternoon," and walked away.

"Game, set and match . . . " breathed Miss Tarantino enrapt, and I heard the Professor give his short caustic laugh.

Ten minutes later, feeling thoroughly disturbed, I sat down on the trunk of a fallen tree which lay by the lake on the far side of the grounds, and contemplated my latest failure to adjust satisfactorily to the world. I was well aware that I had behaved badly. I should have resisted the urge to make Mrs. Braithwaite look ridiculous; I should have met her bigotry with a charitable silence—or at the very most with a quiet observation that I had once been a married man—and feeling not only ashamed of the anger which had impelled me to humiliate an ignorant and possibly unhappy woman, but also profoundly worried by my persistent sense of alienation from those around me, I decided to retire to my room to pray.

Retracing my footsteps I entered the house by the garden door and walked down the corridor to the hall. No one was about. In the middle of the afternoon at Allington the guests were either reading, resting or outside enjoying the hot August weather. I was deep in thought as I endeavoured to recall a suitable text for meditation, and as I crossed the hall I might well have remained unaware of my surroundings if some mysterious antenna had not twitched in my psyche.

I stopped. I knew I could not go on without glancing around the hall. Slowly, very slowly, I turned my head towards the front door and there, far away by the door of the warden's reception-room, stood the beige suitcase with the dark brown corners.

I waited for it to vanish but it remained visible and—apparently— tangible. At once I thought I was hallucinating. I knew I was in a troubled, psychically unreliable state. If this vision was another "show-ing," sent by God to strengthen my faith, why was the suitcase still visible? It should have been wiped from the retina of my mind within seconds, but there it remained, as solid and three-dimensional as any other object which existed in a temporal spatial world. My mouth was dry. Sliding my tongue around my lips, I squeezed my eyes shut, took a deep breath and nerved myself to have another look.

The suitcase was still there. Moreover every other item in the hall looked wholly real. I saw no distortion of colour, no six naked women prancing on the carpet. My heart was now beating with unprecedented violence. Moving awkwardly, in the manner of a man wading upstream against a swift current, I reached out to touch the bannisters. They were solid. I edged forward just as the grandfather clock chimed three. With-out doubt I was in finite time, and the suitcase, already substantial, became even more substantial as I edged closer. I could see the CUNARD label clearly enough to realise that it was exactly as I had perceived it during my spasm of clairvoyance in the infirmary, and tied to the handle was the brown label which I knew would reveal the name of the owner.

Running the last six paces I sank down on one knee and grabbed the suitcase with both hands.

It was real. The expensive leather, a little scuffed in places but still in good condition, was sumptuously smooth beneath my fingers, and as I caressed it I was suddenly overwhelmed by the knowledge that God should have finally brought His communication out of my psyche into the world of the five senses. For a second I was well-nigh paralysed with relief, wonder and above all an intense gratitude. Then just as I had pulled myself together sufficiently to grab the brown label to unlock the mystery of the owner's identity, a cool voice demanded behind me: "Can I help you?" and I knew the intuition I had voiced to Francis had been correct.

The owner was a woman.

IX

I

I LEAPT to my feet. The woman had obviously just emerged from the warden's reception room for the door was now ajar, but my absorption in the suitcase had been so deep that I had failed to hear either her approach or the distant voice of the warden as he conducted a telephone conversation which, as I now realised, was still in progress.

I stared at her. If I had expected to see someone as alluring as Miss Tarantino—and of course I had—I was doomed to disappointment. This woman was tall and somewhat stout. She wore a felt hat crammed down over short dark hair, horn-rimmed spectacles, a coat and skirt of a severe shade of grey, a white blouse devoid of frills, thick brown stockings and a pair of heavy walking shoes. I classed her as a forty-five-year-old spinster, probably a schoolmistress, possibly a missionary newly returned from organising the natives in some obscure corner of the Empire. Then I noticed that her neck was unlined, her skin was fresh and her eyes were uncrinkled at the corners. Knocking fifteen years off her age I decided she was a business woman, the private secretary of some gentleman who required a plain employee in order to allay the fears of a jealous wife. On the other hand the woman's voice, which was not merely well-bred but "county," suggested I was confronting a lady of leisure. I was aware then of a mystery, a conundrum.

All these thoughts raced through my mind in seconds while simultaneously I tried to decide how I could explain my bizarre embrace of her suitcase. At last I said: "I do beg your pardon but I thought I'd seen this bag somewhere before." It takes a great deal to make me behave like an embarrassed schoolboy, but I felt more gauche than I had felt for over forty years. I even wondered in horror if I were blushing. My face felt abnormally hot.

The warden chose that moment to emerge from his room. "So sorry to keep you waiting!" he said to the woman. "It's amazing how often the telephone goes at the wrong moment—ah, I see you've just met Mr. Darrow! Or are you perhaps already acquainted? No? Then let me introduce you: Mr. Darrow, Miss Fielding; Miss Fielding, Mr. Darrow." He beamed at us, stooped to pick up the suitcase, winced at its weight and set it down again. "One moment, Miss Fielding—I'll just summon Arthur," he said, naming the burly yokel who was employed to flex his muscles when required, and bustled off toward the green baize door.

I said to Miss Fielding: "How do you do," and held out my hand.

"How do you do," said Miss Fielding, clasping and dropping it without enthusiasm. Behind her glasses her eyes were a cold, suspicious blue.

"Arthur! Arthur!" the warden was calling in the mellow bass voice which resonated so impressively in the chapel during the daily prayers.

I said to the woman: "If you'll excuse me—"

"Of course." She turned aside as if she had completely lost interest.

I have no memory of the journey to my room. All I remember is slamming the door, slumping on the bed and shuddering with amazement as I asked myself if the key to my future could possibly lie in the hands of such an exceedingly unprepossessing young woman.

2

SINCE my arrival at Allington I had consistently avoided afternoon tea, a meal which I found both tedious and unnecessary, but that afternoon I was already loafing in the drawing-room as the waitress wheeled in the urn. The decision had been made to serve the meal on the terrace in order to take advantage of the fine weather, and I was just helping the warden's wife to steer the trolley of crockery and cucumber sandwiches through the French windows when Dr. Sheen himself crossed the lawn towards us.

Having cornered him I asked what connection his latest guest had with the Church, but to my disappointment he was vague.

"She comes from Starbridge where everyone seems to live in the shadow of the Cathedral," he said, "but otherwise I know of no reason why she should stay at a clerical establishment like Allington."

"This is her first visit?"

"No, she's stayed here every August for the past five years, although of course I only met her when I took up my appointment in '38. However I regret to say I know her no better now than when I first met her. She keeps herself very much to herself and I'm afraid she's dreadfully shy, poor girl."

"She didn't strike me as shy. In fact I thought she was unusually self-confident," I said, but the warden had been diverted by a summons from his wife and at that point our conversation ended.

Accepting a cup of tea at the urn I waited for Miss Fielding to arrive, but all that happened was that I was buttonholed by various guests with whom I had no wish to converse. Finally Miss Fielding made her appearance, but before I could detach myself from my group she had collected her tea, grabbed a sandwich and retreated to a seat on the far side of the lawn.

"That's Miss Fielding," said the shrewd clerical widow Mrs. Digby unexpectedly. "She was here last year—a very strange woman, anti-social to the point of rudeness. Puzzling, I thought, because she's definitely a lady and one would expect her to behave with more grace."

"Maybe she's shy," said Miss Tarantino. "I'm shy myself sometimes— it's so disabling." She smiled up at me. "Why are you so interested in the new arrival, Mr. Darrow? You've been watching her ever since she came out of the house."

"Anti-social people interest me," I said vaguely, and beat a swift retreat to my room.

From my window I continued to observe Miss Fielding. When she returned her cup and saucer and headed back across the lawn towards the woods, I padded downstairs again, slipped out of the garden-door and made an elaborate detour to avoid being seen by the people on the terrace. Then I plunged into the woods in pursuit of my quarry.

3

I FAILED to find her. The grounds were extensive and the woods prevented me from seeing more than a few yards in any direction. Reaching the fallen tree by the lake for the second time that afternoon, I wiped the sweat from my forehead, took off my jacket and told myself to calm down. Numerous opportunities to talk to Miss Fielding would undoubtedly arise in due course and meanwhile I was being given more time to consider my situation. I decided to write to Francis.

Yet again he replied by return of post. After the necessary paragraph in which he marvelled at my clairvoyance, he had written:

But be careful. The temptation to jump to conclusions will be very strong, but it's possible that this bag has no connection with the chapel at all; you always said, remember, that it seemed superimposed on the chapel's reality.

I'm relieved to hear that this mysterious woman is unattractive. That eliminates the risk of you being lured into some dangerous romantic fantasy, and personally I'm inclined to think that if she's of any real significance here, that significance will be revealed to you without any effort on your part. I'm not suggesting that you do nothing until Miss Fielding sidles up to you like an espionage agent and enquires *sotto voce* if you're interested in a chapel built in the style of Inigo Jones. Obviously you'll wish to converse with her in order to give the mystery a chance to unravel, but walk delicately, like Agag, and be prepared for the solution to be more obscure than you're at present inclined to suppose.

I received this letter in the afternoon post on Monday. I had tried a couple of approaches to Miss Fielding on Sunday but had been rebuffed on each occasion; after Matins I had said: "What did you think of the sermon?" and she had replied: "I ceased to listen after the first five minutes," while during tea I had ventured to enquire: "What are you reading?" and she had retorted: "Shakespeare," before reburying her nose in a battered volume of the Bard's complete works.

"I know why Mr. Darrow's so intrigued by Miss Fielding," said the shrewd Mrs. Digby after Miss Tarantino had again commented on my interest in the newcomer. "She's the only person here who doesn't pay the slightest attention to him."

That, as Shakespeare himself might have phrased it, was "a palpable hit." I began to wonder how far an affronted masculine vanity was exacerbating my curiosity, and the speculation was not a pleasant one.

However when Miss Fielding appeared in chapel on Monday morning before breakfast, my curiosity reached new heights and I forgot to worry about any unedifying masculine vanity. Holy Communion was cele-brated only on Wednesdays and Sundays at Allington, but Matins and Evensong were recited daily, and apart from one or two devout laymen it was the clergy who attended. I was most surprised when I entered the chapel and saw Miss Fielding already seated in a pew; I thought the warden would have mentioned if she had been unusually devout in her religious observances, for it would have explained her regular patronage of a hotel such as Allington. Choosing a pew across the aisle from her I was aware of her turning her head as I sat down. But her glance was brief and throughout the service she gave no further hint that she was aware of me.

After the blessing I remained kneeling for some minutes, not to pray but to avoid any vapid conversation, and it was only when I judged my solitude to be guaranteed that I rose to my feet to leave.

She was waiting in the porch.

"Is it my imagination," she said, "or are we bumping into each other abnormally often? I don't usually attend weekday Matins but I found I couldn't resist the urge to discover if it would lead to yet another encounter—and here we are."

"But since you decided to lie in wait for me, wasn't an encounter inevitable?"

"Not at all. If you'd come out with the others you could have stalked by without a word. It's all very odd—or maybe it's simply that *you're* odd, Mr. Darrow. I suppose you do realise that you're like a giant magnet? You enter a room and all the little pins start twinkling and twirling in your direction." I laughed but before I could comment she was musing: "First of all I thought people were fascinated merely because you're an ex-monk, but then I became more aware of that very peculiar atmosphere you exude—"

"Who told you I was an ex-monk?"

"Everyone from the warden to the waitress."

"How interesting," I said at once. "I was under the impression you talked neither to the warden nor to the waitress nor to anyone else."

"Then at least you now know I'm capable of speech." Abruptly she turned away.

"Yes, but what I still don't know is why you're so keen to remain silent," I said, following hard on her heels as she walked out. "Do you have to talk a great deal in your profession with the result that on holiday you promptly sink into an exhausted silence?"

As she swung to face me I saw the astonishment in her eyes. "What makes you think I have a profession?"

"Your self-confidence. You're not shy; you simply have no wish to be sociable. And you have an air of authority too which makes me think you're used to dealing with people on a business level. Ladies of leisure, who so often can define themselves only in relation to the men in their lives, tend to display more malleability and self-effacement when projecting their identity."

"In other words you think I'm just a bossy old spinster unredeemed by any conventional feminine grace!"

"That's what you want me to think, isn't it? That's what you want everyone to think. But why are you going to such lengths to create an identity which I suspect is a grossly exaggerated distortion of your true self?"

She stared at me incredulously. Then turning her back on me a second time she fled back to the house as if pursued by the Furies.

4

SHE succeeded in eluding me for some time after that, but on Wednesday morning we met, taking each other by surprise, in the remotest bay of the library, a corner at the far end of the gallery which flanked one side of the room. I was sitting on the window-seat with a copy of *Lux Mundi* in my hands and remembering how much Bishop Gore had influenced me in my youth. Miss Fielding, apparently also in search of seclusion before embarking on a nostalgic intellectual journey, entered the bay with her battered volume of Shakespeare's complete works and before she could recoil in dismay I said swiftly: "Congratulations on finding the quietest spot in the house. May I offer you half my window-seat?"

"Thank you, but I'd be too afraid of twinkling and twirling like one of your magnetised pins."

"What nonsense! Sit down and read your Shakespeare!"

"A bit bossy, aren't you?" said Miss Fielding, but she sat down. "I can't remember any bossy abbots in Shakespeare's plays, but there are a couple of very wicked cardinals."

"Beaufort in *Henry VI* and Wolsey in *Henry VIII*."

As her eyes widened I knew the fish was hooked. Stealthily I began to reel in the line. "My father was a schoolmaster," I said smiling at her. "His volume of Shakespeare's complete works was more precious to him than the Bible, and naturally some of his enthusiasm rubbed off on me."

"But surely nowadays you only read religious books?"

"Not entirely. Last week I read a detective story by Miss Agatha Christie. I admired her grasp of the reality of evil but I'm afraid I found the plot improbable."

"Life *is* improbable," said Miss Fielding. "It's improbable that you should have been so mesmerised by my bag when I arrived and it's even more improbable that you should have been prowling along in my wake ever since. Will I spoil your fun if I now ask you frankly what on earth's going on?"

Our voices had risen above the level of a murmur, and below us at one of the writing tables someone hissed: "Shhh!" Closing *Lux Mundi*, I stood up. "Come into the garden," I whispered, "and all will be revealed."

"That sounds like a literary marriage between Agatha Christie and Lord Tennyson."

Numerous heads swivelled to look at us as we left the library and to my surprise I noticed that Miss Fielding's cheeks had become pink. Perhaps the shyness did exist after all beneath the outer layer of self-confidence. Reminding myself of the danger of rushing to conclusions, I said to her as we left the house: "Let's sit on that seat on the far side of the lawn."

"I'm not sure I want to bask in your peculiar limelight in full view of all the old dears on the terrace! I come to this place for a quiet life—"

"An unusual aspiration for a young woman."

"What makes you think I'm so young?"

"Your neck's unlined. I doubt if you're thirty."

"I'm thirty-two."

"Then why on earth are you trying to look forty-five?"

"Why are you embarking on an interrogation? You're supposed to be answering questions, not asking them!"

"Getting impatient? As my superior said to me the other day: 'Patience is one of the most difficult of all virtues and one which I think it would pay you to cultivate.'"

"I shall hit you over the head with Shakespeare's complete works in a minute," said Miss Fielding, and when I laughed she smiled at me.

Providing deep interest to all the guests languishing on the terrace, we crossed the lawn and sat down a respectable two feet apart on the wooden seat.

"Now," said Miss Fielding in the tone of one who is determined to stand no nonsense, "about my bag—"

"I'd seen it before in a psychic experience."

The inevitable silence fell. I waited for the equally inevitable amazement, scepticism, even fear—all those reactions which make the psychic shun the well-nigh impossible task of translating into words an experience which is ultimately beyond translation—but nothing happened. Miss Fielding meditated without expression on the statement which most people would have judged outrageous, and eventually said: "I should have guessed you were psychic. For five years I've been coming here and everyone has accepted me at face value. Yet you take one look and see a mile farther than anyone else." She hesitated before asking: "In this psychic experience did you see me as well as the bag?"

"No." I waited, but still no conventional reaction occurred. I was inflicted by no ill-judged questions, no banal comments, no torrent of feminine chatter. Miss Fielding's face was grave as she stared at the book in her hands, but at last she raised her head and said abruptly: "You don't want to tell me any more, do you? It's too private. But that's all right, I understand. I've got a great respect for other people's privacy because

I value my own privacy so much." And without giving me the chance
to reply, she rose to her feet and walked away across the lawn.

5

AT luncheon I declined pudding, excused myself from my fellow-guests
and lurked in the hall until Miss Fielding had abandoned her solitary
table.

"At the risk of making a thorough nuisance of myself," I said, waylay-
ing her, "may I ask when you can accompany me for another stroll in
the grounds?"

"When? Not if? Here comes the bossy Abbot again!"

"Before I was a bossy abbot I learnt how to be an obedient monk.
Name the time and place and I'll be there."

"Somehow I have trouble picturing you as meek and submissive—did
you find life very difficult when you entered the Order?"

There was a long silence.

"Sorry," said Miss Fielding rapidly at last. "I didn't mean to give
offence."

"You haven't. I was merely surprised. Every layman I've ever met has
always blithely assumed I took the monastic life in my stride."

Silence fell again. Then Miss Fielding said abruptly: "Let's meet by the
lake. I hate all the old dears spying on us from the terrace."

"Five o'clock by the fallen tree?"

She nodded and we went our separate ways.

6

SHE arrived on time. That impressed me; women so often feel obliged
to be late. She was wearing a floral-patterned dress which appeared to
have been designed for a woman of fifty who had lost her figure, and
I was wearing my clerical suit. I pictured us both looking irreproachably
seemly as we seated ourselves well apart on the fallen tree, and I thought
how odd it was that we should be linked by the far from seemly fact of
my clairvoyance.

"I wanted to thank you for your extreme tact earlier," I said. "It would
have been so easy for you to have made my confession an awkward one."

"By showing scepticism? Or resorting to ridicule? No, I leave that to
the scientists—the ones who can't bear to admit they don't know all the
answers."

I smiled. Then I said: "It's not only the scientists who find clairvoyance disconcerting. It raises questions about the nature of time which baffle even the philosophers and theologians."

"Does it?" said Miss Fielding intrigued, and I knew that once again the fish was hooked. As her defences relaxed I tightened my grip on her psyche.

"The crucial question," I said, "becomes this: how can one see the future unless there's a reality beyond what is colloquially described as reality—an ultimate reality in which all time is eternally present?"

"That's the sort of question which makes my head spin. But go on."

I continued to smooth away her defences as I gently stroked her psyche. "You remember, of course, that Plato said time was the moving image of eternity?"

"No, but never mind."

This time we both smiled before I said: "The key word is 'moving.' We live in a world of movement, of change, which is reflected in the words 'past,' 'present' and 'future,' but beyond this world is another world to which we're inextricably linked but which we can only dimly perceive. This world is a kingdom of values, the absolute values of Goodness, Truth and Beauty, and it's these unchanging values, present in our changing world of time and space, which reflect the other world, ultimate reality, which is beyond space and time."

"It's hard to imagine something which can't be described in spatial and temporal terms."

"That's exactly why any meaningful description of the other world really lies outside the scope of our vocabulary. For example, I call the time of this world 'finite time' to distinguish it from the everlasting Now which is the only way we can conceive of eternity, but this terminology isn't wholly satisfactory because there are philosophers who argue that even our time is infinite. But that argument only stems from the fact that they can't imagine being at the edge of time with a blank wall instead of a future ahead. The truth is that if the universe is running down like a clock—"

"Stop!" said Miss Fielding. "I can't cope with universes running down like clocks. Are you trying to say that when you're clairvoyant you step out of finite time into some form of eternity?"

"Perhaps one should phrase that more cautiously. All I know for certain is that I step out of time as we understand it where the past is always behind us and the future is still to come."

Miss Fielding said suddenly: "It must be like escaping from a prison. Isn't it strange how unaware people are of being locked up in time?"

"You find an unconscious awareness of this in the widespread longing to be immortal. Yet isn't it equally strange, when one remembers that we're also locked up in space, that no one seems to long to be ubiquitous?"

She laughed, and knowing she was now thoroughly relaxed I glided forward into my inquisition.

"Talking of eternity," I said, "I'm reminded of your home town of Starbridge, the only city I know which possesses an Eternity Street. Do you worship at the Cathedral?"

Immediately her defences were resurrected; she displayed no hostility but I was aware of her extreme stillness. "My aunt prefers to worship at St. Martin's-in-Cripplegate," she said, naming the church in the centre of the city which had originally been erected for the benefit of the workmen building the Cathedral.

"You live with your aunt?"

"My parents are dead," said Miss Fielding, looking at the lake, the trees, the sky but not at me. "My aunt has a house in the section of the city called St. Stephen's Fields. It's between Eternity Street and the river."

"You work in the city?"

Her studied nonchalance disintegrated. "What business is that of yours?"

"Absolutely none. Forgive me."

We fell silent but gradually I became aware of her psyche, encased in an iron band but yearning to be free. As soon as I saw the iron band with my inner eye, I visualised a file and pictured myself whittling the fetter apart.

"I work on a farm," said Miss Fielding abruptly as the band snapped in two.

"Do you?" I said. "I worked on a farm once. I was assigned to the cowman when I was a novice in Yorkshire, but I unconsciously projected so much antipathy towards the cows that the milk yield dropped and I had to be removed from the farmyard."

She was amused and not unsympathetic. "I'm not much good with farm animals either," she said, and added after a hesitation: "I work in the estate office."

"I must confess I didn't quite see you as a land-girl—"

"—so you peeped into my mind and saw I was an administrator!"

"No, I can't read your mind like a book! If I could, I wouldn't be asking all these impertinent questions!"

"I think you're just asking the questions to confirm your psychic suspicions."

"I have my psychic suspicions certainly—I can't help myself—but they could be dead wrong. If I were to make any deductions about you I'd base them on reason and experience before allowing my intuition free rein."

She said sternly: "And what are your deductions based on reason and experience?"

"I deduce that your aversion to normal social intercourse stems from the fact that at one time you trusted people far more than you do now—and paid a heavy price. I deduce that this deep wound in your psyche has remained unhealed, with the result that you're periodically driven to play the kind of role you're playing here at Allington, a role which you can use as a shield to protect your true self." I shrugged my shoulders to signal that I had no inclination either to criticise or to condemn. "Neither of those deductions involves any psychic intuition whatsoever, of course. They're merely conclusions which any experienced counsellor might reach."

"And what happens when you give your psychic intuition free rein?"

There was a pause while I debated what I had to lose by responding to the question and decided that I had everything to gain. "I could be quite wrong," I said, careful to maintain a casual tone of voice, "but I think the traumatic incident in your past involved a massive loss and it was all connected with water. Perhaps someone close to you was drowned? Or perhaps someone you loved sailed away and never came back?"

As she stared I had a most uncomfortable memory of Francis warning me against exercising my psychic powers with a woman in a secluded corner of the grounds. "I'm sorry," I said rapidly, "I'm behaving like a charlatan in a fortune-teller's booth on a seaside pier and I must stop at once. Let me now give you the rational explanation for those wild and no doubt inaccurate guesses: I saw the CUNARD label on your suitcase. I've associated you with travel by water. I've now fused that association with the deduction that you've suffered in the past, and one of the most traumatic forms of suffering is bereavement. You see? There's really no psychic intuition going on at all. It's just the kind of mental sleight-of-hand which can be made to look so effective in a parlour-trick."

For a long moment Miss Fielding was silent as she stared across the lake, but at last she said: "When I was twenty-six my fiancé broke off our engagement and sailed away on one of the transatlantic liners. My brother then took me on holiday to Cornwall to help me recover, and three days later he drowned while swimming in the sea." She stood up, smoothing the creases from her dress. "After that I knew my life had to change completely," she said. "The old life was burnt out and the new life had to begin." She turned to face me and as I too rose to my feet I saw that her eyes were a clear, tearless blue. "That's what happens when someone becomes a monk, isn't it?" she said. "They die to the old life and are born again in the new. There's some Greek word for it—"

"*Metanoia*. Miss Fielding—"

"It's all right," she said. "I don't mind you knowing because I'm sure you'll respect my confidence. But in future, Mr. Darrow, could you somehow keep your psychic powers in check? My mind doesn't like being X-rayed with such horrible accuracy. It quite definitely doesn't like it at all."

7

AFTER that conversation I exerted my will-power, curbed my burgeoning curiosity and for two days made no attempt to seek another interview with her.

" . . . so you needn't worry," I wrote as I concluded a long letter to Francis.

> I have the situation well in control and can say with perfect truth that I'm not in the least in love with Miss Fielding, who has no waist to speak of (I am exceedingly partial to waists) and is elsewhere too large when she should be small and too small when she should be large—not that I wish to be uncharitable, for she's obviously highly intelligent and sensitive, but my point is that since she's so lacking in conventional feminine allure I run no risk of making a fool of myself.

I posted this most sensible letter on Friday morning, but as soon as the envelope had dropped into the village pillar-box I realised I could no longer endure to keep Miss Fielding at arm's length and that afternoon I succeeded in luring her back to the lake.

"It seems almost indecent that we should be somewhere so peaceful at a time like this," said Miss Fielding unexpectedly as we again settled ourselves on the fallen tree.

"That's a phenomenon of war—the non-combatant's guilt. But you shouldn't let it oppress you. Better to look upon our peaceful oasis here as a gift from God and give thanks for it."

"I suppose that as you're a prayer expert you can now automatically send off a perfectly-phrased prayer of thanksgiving. All I can do is mutter a fervent 'thank you' and feel inarticulate."

"A fervent 'thank you' would be entirely admirable," I said pleased, "and you must never think for one moment that a trained religious necessarily prays more effectively than a devout layman. Prayer's the great leveller. Anyone can do it, and the only pity is that more people don't try." By this time I was so consumed with curiosity about her spiritual life that I risked saying: "Are you High Church, Broad Church or Low Church?"

"I'm not at all sure what all those awful labels mean. If High Church means the Anglo-Catholics and Low Church means the Evangelical Protestants and Broad Church means the vast majority of church-goers between the two extremes, then I suppose I'm Broad—I'm certainly a Protestant. I don't like anything which suggests the Reformation martyrs died in vain. I'm not saying all Anglo-Catholics should be burnt at the stake—well, that would be a bit tactless in present company, wouldn't it?—but I don't like parsons calling themselves priests and Communion being called Mass, and personally I think the use of incense is a nasty piece of un-English mumbo-jumbo."

"The glory of the Church of England," I said at once, "is that you and I, despite our very divergent views, can both belong to it." But as I spoke I was thinking with delight: what a challenge! and wondering if I could convert her to my point of view.

Having reassured her that I was capable of conducting a normal conversation without oppressing her with my psychic peculiarities, I remained silent as we journeyed back from the lake, but when we reached the house I said: "Mrs. Digby leaves tomorrow afternoon and there'll be a spare place at my table. Will you join me for dinner?"

Without hesitation she answered: "I'd rather not."

"Very well."

We entered the house.

"I'm sorry," said Miss Fielding quickly after struggling with her conflicting emotions. "That was abominably rude of me. Thank you for the invitation—in many ways I'd like to accept but nevertheless I'm going to ask you to excuse me."

"Of course."

"I seem to be making a complete fool of myself," said Miss Fielding at last. "Anyone would think you'd made an indecent proposal. Thank you, Mr. Darrow, I accept the invitation and apologise for being so ungracious."

I retired in triumph to my room.

8

"I UNDERSTAND the mysterious Miss Fielding will be joining us tonight," said Miss Tarantino, who was already seated at the table when I arrived in the dining-room the following evening. Allington Court was by no means "smart," but Miss Tarantino, sleek in dark red satin, exuded a glamour which was almost operatic. I was vaguely reminded of *Carmen*.

"Miss Fielding will indeed be joining us," I said, "and I intend to pamper myself by sitting between the two of you and luxuriating in your combined feminine attention." I had, it will be noticed, travelled a considerable way from the tense, wary ex-monk who had wanted to bolt from the dining-room ten days previously.

Miss Tarantino was prevented (perhaps fortunately) from replying by the arrival of the Braithwaites and the Professor. The warden was already chafing to say grace, and I was just wondering if Miss Fielding's nerve had failed her when to my relief she entered the room. She was wearing another shapeless item from her dowager's wardrobe, a funereal black gown. I saw Miss Tarantino give it a look of pitying amazement although I sensed that the Braithwaites were more interested in the diamond necklace which Miss Fielding had slung around her neck. The diamonds had the effect of reducing Miss Tarantino's allure to a tinsel glitter and underlining the ugliness of Mrs. Braithwaite's cultured pearls.

The meal proceeded uneventfully until the middle of the main course. Miss Fielding and I said little; Miss Tarantino and the Professor argued fitfully about Luther's view of the sacraments, and the Braithwaites talked in consequence about a handsome Lutheran church which they had inspected during a holiday in Germany in 1936. It was the mention of Germany that sealed the fate of the evening. The conversation drifted inexorably towards the War until we were discussing the prospect of increased rationing.

"Another thing we can expect to increase," said Braithwaite, vigorously sawing his portion of chicken, "is immorality." He seemed to find the prospect stimulating.

"Oh don't, dear!" said his wife with a shudder. "Every time I see those girls in uniform living like men I feel cold inside. A woman's place is in the home."

Miss Fielding said: "Are you implying that women are so lacking in moral backbone that they risk corruption the moment they step outside their front door?"

"It's a well-known fact," said Braithwaite, using the phrase which in my experience so often heralds an old wives' tale, "that once women stop being wives and mothers and start working alongside men, there's an immediate decline in moral standards."

"You mean," said Miss Fielding, "that if women are obliged to work alongside men there's a possibility that they may become as promiscuous as the men they meet—always assuming the men they meet are promiscuous. But the hole in your argument, Mr. Braithwaite, is that promiscuity doesn't automatically follow the opportunity to be promiscuous. If immorality does increase as the result of the War it won't simply be because women are working alongside men. It'll be because both sexes are frightened to the point of instability in a time of great danger."

Miss Tarantino said: "Sure!" emphatically and the Professor grunted his acceptance of this rational contribution to the conversation, but Mrs. Braithwaite was rigid with disapproval and Braithwaite himself clearly could not bear to be worsted in an argument with a woman. "You talk with a great deal of authority, Miss Fielding," he said harshly, "but what do you really know about the ways of the world? Your argument might sound•more convincing if it didn't come from an unmarried lady whose attitude to the opposite sex appears to be characterised by ignorance and dislike!"

I said: "Braithwaite—" at the same moment as the Professor exclaimed in disgust: "Great Scott!" but Miss Fielding needed no one to defend her. She said strongly: "The ignorance and dislike are all on your side, it seems! You know nothing about me except for the fact that I'm not married, and your dislike is obviously because unlike most women I have the nerve to argue with you when you start slandering my sex!"

"There was no slander!" said Braithwaite, scarlet with rage. "And I consider I'm justified in objecting to rude opinionated females who give spinsters a bad name!"

I leapt to my feet but so did Miss Fielding. Flinging down her napkin she said fiercely to Braithwaite: "My God, you're a stupid man!" and stormed from the table.

All conversation in the dining-room ceased. I had a fleeting impression of the warden's appalled face, but I ignored it and the next moment I was saying to Braithwaite in a voice calculated to travel the length of a sizable church: "As a gentleman your conduct was beyond the pale and as a churchwarden your conduct was beyond belief. Reflect on your behaviour. Examine your conscience. And I shall expect an apology to my guest within the hour."

I made a superb exit, and it was only when I reached the hall that I allowed myself to pause. I could not remember when I had last felt so angry. Heading for the stairs I decided to pursue Miss Fielding all the way to her lair, but then I remembered that I did not know her room number, and as I paused again I was aware of the antenna twitching in my psyche.

I strode to the library and found her sitting on the secluded window-seat where she had interrupted my perusal of *Lux Mundi*. She had removed her glasses, but as I sat down beside her she rammed them back on her nose as if they could hide all evidence of her tears.

I said: "You were right. He's a very stupid man, and like so many stupid men he's pathetic, trying to bolster his self-esteem by telling himself that his gender makes him superior to fifty percent of the human race. But you're not stupid—and you're not pathetic either. You've got the brains and the courage to look back on that scene and see that it wasn't you but he who was so irretrievably diminished by it."

While I spoke she took off her glasses again, but by the time I had finished she had brushed the tears aside. Passing her my handkerchief I said: "He's due to leave tomorrow so you won't have to endure his presence here much longer. In fact when tomorrow comes, breakfast in your room and then I'll take you out for the day."

"If that's an offer made out of pity—"

"It's made out of admiration for your courage in standing up to that man, and how better could I demonstrate my admiration than by asking you to share my solitude?"

She could not speak, but when I took her hand in a gesture of comfort, her fingers closed trustfully on mine.

9

WE completed our dinner in the privacy of the warden's sitting-room after a subdued Braithwaite had proffered the required apology. Then the next morning the warden drove us into the nearby town of Ashburton where, armed with a picnic-basket, we boarded the motorbus which climbed up the winding country roads onto the high plateau of Dartmoor. We reached the church at Widecombe in time for Matins, and by one o'clock we were sitting on a hillside overlooking the village as we embarked on our luncheon. The sun shone fitfully over the hills that ringed the valley, and below the outcrop of rocks which marked the summit of the nearest ridge a breeze ruffled the manes of the wild ponies.

After a prolonged silence in which we ate our sandwiches, sipped our tea and watched the shifting patterns of light playing on the vast expanse of heather around us, I said suddenly: "This reminds me of Ruydale. I lived there for fourteen years. It became home. Being transferred to Grantchester in '37 was a great wrench."

"Is it usual for monks to be transferred?"

"No, it's rare—and my transfer was like a bolt from the blue. The wire arrived from the Abbot-General at ten o'clock one morning and by two I was on the train to London."

She was appalled. "But how horrible to be uprooted from your home so suddenly!"

I said nothing as I remembered how nearly my anger and misery had destroyed my will to obey orders without question. There had been no mention of Grantchester in Father Darcy's wire. I had thought I was being transferred to London so that I could be more accessible to the increasing number of clergymen who sought my spiritual direction.

"Why was there such a rush?" Miss Fielding was asking in bewilderment.

"The Abbot of Grantchester had just died and his death revealed urgent problems which required swift attention." I had intended to say no more about the Order's private affairs, but when she said: "Was there a scandal?" I felt obliged to quash any melodramatic suspicions.

"From a monastic point of view it was scandalous," I said, "but I don't think a layman would have found the disorder particularly titillating. The main problem was that Abbot James had become very withdrawn during the last year of his life—it would be unfair, I think, to use the word senile—and all power had passed to the prior, whose previous heavy drinking then flowered into full-blown alcoholism. As a result discipline became disastrously lax and soon everyone, even the good men, spent too much time wallowing in sloth."

Miss Fielding said with a most disarming sympathy: "How on earth did you set everyone back on the rails?"

I was lured into further confidences. "First of all I ordered everyone to clean themselves up; men get slovenly without either women to look after them or a discipline to keep them up to the mark. Then we all took part in cleaning the house from top to bottom; nobody can work well in a filthy environment." I paused, remembering the odors of stale sweat, stale urine, stale food and the sight of thick grease, thick dust, thick grime. The details came back to me abruptly: the underclothes in holes at the garment inspection; the stained chamberpots used as shaving bowls to enable their owners to avoid "the trough," the long narrow basin in the central wash-room where all monks but the Abbot (who had his own basin in his cell) were obliged to shave; the sheet of noughts-and-crosses tucked under the hassock in the chapel to betray how at least two of the brethren had spent the time supposed to be devoted to worship; the dog-eared copy of *The News of the World* which lined the basket of the flea-bitten cat; the three-tiered cream cake brazenly sitting in the larder; the chocolate box hidden behind the blackboard in the scriptorium, and—worst horror of all—the empty brandy bottles stacked high in the crypt.

"Then I changed the diet from a gourmet cuisine to predominantly vegetarian meals," I heard myself say to Miss Fielding, "restricted wine to feast-days and ordered that everyone, even the oldest monk, was to take some exercise every day. I'm afraid that at the start of my rule I was highly unpopular with the lazier members of the community."

"I'm sure the good men were relieved to have a firm hand at the helm again."

"The relief was mixed with resentment. They didn't like the Abbot-General's decision to bring in someone from outside to rule the community," I said, and the next moment I was remembering my debilitating sense of isolation, my homesickness for Ruydale, my struggles to avoid any self-centred expression of misery as I wrote the weekly report Father Darcy had demanded for the first six months of my tenure.

However I was diverted from these difficult memories when Miss Fielding asked with curiosity: "What happened to the alcoholic prior?"

"He was transferred permanently to London so that the demon drink could be exorcised by the Abbot-General."

"A fate worse than death?" said Miss Fielding with a smile, and I laughed before replying: "Father Darcy was certainly formidable."

"Darcy!"

"No relation to the famous Jesuit. Different spelling."

"I was thinking of Jane Austen's hero."

"Father Darcy was a hero to many of his monks but heaven only knows what Jane Austen would have thought of him."

"Was he a hero to you?"

"No, he was my mentor. That meant our relationship had to be grounded in reality, not fantasy."

"Well, I hope he gave you a pat on the back after you'd transformed the Grantchester house! How long did it take you to put everything right?"

So she had sensed I had no inclination to say more about my complex relationship with Father Darcy. With gratitude I answered readily: "The worst difficulties were ironed out quickly enough but it took at least six months to reduce the minor irritations—the endless pettiness, the foolish squabbles, the incessant twittering in corners whenever the slackers thought their superior was out of earshot . . . The Fordites aren't Trappists and the rule of silence is never rigidly enforced, but gossiping is forbidden and personally I can't endure people twittering about nothing."

Miss Fielding at once said: "How difficult you must have found it to adjust to all the twittering at Allington!" and before I could stop myself I was confessing: "To be honest I'm beginning to wonder if I've adjusted to Allington at all. I'm supposed to be giving serious consideration to my future, but so far I've found my attempts at meditation singularly unproductive." But as soon as these words had been uttered I felt driven to exonerate Allington. "The fault's mine, of course," I said. "I'm failing to make a satisfactory adjustment to normal society and that's why I persistently feel that I'm in the wrong place."

"But maybe you *are* in the wrong place," said Miss Fielding unexpectedly. "I can see why you came here, but surely in your case a community like Allington can only seem a travesty of the type of community where you've learnt to feel at home? I almost wonder if you'd be better off in some remote rural guest-house where you'd be the only visitor."

This struck me as a most perceptive observation. "You may well be right," I began, and then broke off as I suddenly realised which way the conversation was drifting. My heart seemed to beat a shade faster as I said with immense care: "Miss Fielding, please don't take this amiss; I wouldn't like you to feel that I was engaged in some form of unwanted pursuit of you, but do you by any chance know of a remote spot in the Starbridge area where I might find the peace and quiet I need?"

There was a long silence. Miss Fielding was staring at the wild ponies grazing in the distance and she was still staring at them when she eventually said: "I think I do know of a place which would suit you."

I waited, not hurrying her, and at last she turned to face me. "It's a manor house," she said. "It's at Starrington Magna, twelve miles from Starbridge." Looking away from me again she began to trace a pattern on the grass with her finger. "The owner lives there alone apart from the servants," she said. "It's a big house. You could be as secluded there as you wished, and there are twenty acres of walled grounds which are ideal for solitary strolls."

Five seconds elapsed before I was able to say with a theatrical calmness: "Can you tell me . . . is there a chapel in the grounds?"

Her eyes widened. "Yes," she said surprised, "as a matter of fact there is."

"And is there a ruined ivy-clad building behind it?"

I saw the colour fade from her face. "The chantry," she whispered. "Yes."

"And is the chapel Victorian but built in the style of Inigo Jones?"

By this time she was beyond speech. She was barely able to nod.

My voice said: "Miss Fielding, forgive me for playing what must appear to be yet another psychic parlour-trick, but this place is of the greatest importance to me. Who's the owner of this manor house? I'd like to get in touch with him straight away."

In the silence that followed, the world seemed entirely still; it was as if even the breeze had ceased to blow. But as Miss Fielding took off her glasses at last, like a soldier removing his camouflage after some complex battle, the truth hurled itself against my shuttered mind and smashed awake my sleeping psyche.

"It's you, isn't it?" I could hardly speak. "The chapel belongs to you." And when, mesmerised by my emotion, she offered no denial, I covered my face with my hands and silently thanked God for this great deliverance from the torment of my doubts.

X

"Our real self is not the captive of Space and Time."

W. R. INGE
MYSTICISM IN RELIGION

I

MY emotion was so profound that I felt a need to be alone, and rising to my feet I crossed the heather to the stack of rocks which crowned the Tor. The wild ponies regarded me with mild interest but soon resumed their grazing. I looked back. Miss Fielding had been watching me but I saw her avert her gaze as if she wished to give me every privacy. Slowly I circled the rocks before retracing my steps through the heather.

When I reached her I began: "Miss Fielding—" but she interrupted me.

"My name's Anne Barton-Woods," she said. "Fielding is the name of my aunt who lives in Starbridge. I'm sorry I lied to you but I have such a horror of fortune-hunters that when I'm on holiday I find I can't relax unless I take on a false identity." And as an afterthought she added: "Of course you'll now think I'm a hopeless neurotic."

Again I was aware that there was a taut, fearful underside to the psyche which existed beneath the veneer of her self-confidence, and at once I said: "I suggest we forget the word 'neurotic,' which is one of those fashionable modern words that are so frequently misused, and consider your situation from a calmer, more rational perspective. If you have a horror of fortune-hunters, how clever you are to retreat to an ecclesiastical backwater like Allington where any normal fortune-hunter would die of boredom within twenty-four hours! And how sensible to adopt a false identity so that no abnormal fortune-hunter, lurking among the clerical collars, can pursue you once you leave! This all sounds most closely reasoned to me."

Miss Barton-Woods was sufficiently encouraged to say: "I wish I could dispense with holidays altogether, but I find I need them. I work very hard running my estate."

"No doubt you're wise to take an annual rest, but I do see that it must be an ordeal to spend two weeks among strangers."

"Shakespeare helps," said Miss Barton-Woods. "After I arrive I always read *Henry V*—"

" 'Once more into the breach—' "

"Exactly. Then later I read the light-hearted plays, *Twelfth Night, The Comedy of Errors*—"

"The plays in which a lost brother is found."

She gasped but before she could speak I asked: "How long have you been running your estate?"

"Since my brother died six years ago." She hesitated, then added: "The estate's been in the hands of my family since the Civil War—we were Roundheads taking over from Cavaliers—but now the family's died out and there's no one left except me. My aunt in Starbridge is on my mother's side of the family." She began to clear up the debris of our picnic, and as she tilted her cup to spill the dregs of her tea on the ground the gesture seemed to emphasise the bleakness of her situation, drained as it was of family life. "For a while I thought I would marry," she said, "but when I was engaged I found I wasn't much good at all that sort of thing—so you see, I don't just put on this mask to avoid the fortune-hunters. I put it on to keep all men at arm's length because I never want to get engaged again."

"Of course. That makes perfect sense."

She gave me a suspicious look. "You're probably now thinking I'm just suffering from sour grapes because my fiancé broke off the engagement."

"That would be Braithwaite's explanation, no doubt, but I'm not Braithwaite. My explanation would run like this: your broken engagement, combined with the loss of your brother, brought you profound suffering; you transcended that suffering by using it as a base on which to build a new life set in opposition to the old—a move which made celibacy not only desirable, after the tragedy of your broken engagement, but essential to complete the process of *metanoia,* the turning aside into the new life which would enable you to survive."

She said simply: "You're the only person who's ever understood," and opening the picnic-basket she replaced the thermos as if she feared it might shatter in her hands. "But I knew you'd understand," she said, "and that's why I'm willing for you to stay at the Manor. You won't be a nuisance and you won't mind me being"—she bit back the word "neurotic"—"eccentric."

"My dear Miss Barton-Woods," I said, "if you're still willing to offer me hospitality after my psychic parlour-trick just now, I shall think you're the most courageous of women and you can be just as eccentric as you please! But now let me follow your confession about your identity with a far more bizarre confession of my own . . ."

2

I MADE no attempt to translate the spiritual quality of the vision into words, but this was not only because mere words could never have reflected satisfactorily that glimpse of ultimate reality as I journeyed beyond the borders of finite time. It was also because I was aware that my story was already so unusual that I shied away from any inadequate descriptions which might well have aroused her incredulity. Indeed so outrageous did my clairvoyance sound as I recited the bare facts that I feared she would inevitably judge me either mad or wicked or both, using my psychic powers to slither my way first into her confidence and then into her bank account.

" . . . and a light began to shine through the north window. As the light increased in power I knew it was the light of God. I then realised I was called to leave the Order," I said colourlessly in the tone employed by the gentlemen reading the weather forecasts which I had heard on Ruth's wireless. I had been amazed when the announcers had droned on with such impressive lack of emotion about the numerous gales poised to ravage the North Sea.

Miss Barton-Woods was silent and inscrutable. I watched the breeze disturb her short dark hair which was shaped into a point at the nape of her neck. Her skin was lightly freckled; I noticed the small mole above the square line of her jaw, the shine on the tip of her wide nose, the dull unpainted red of her mouth. She looked no prettier without her glasses but there was a stronger impression of a striking individuality. I thought it not unlikely that she was one of those women who appear at their best not in youth, when their unusual looks preclude them from conforming to fashionable notions of beauty, but in middle age, when the unusual looks can be seen as distinguished or even handsome. Picking up the glasses I saw that the lenses were clear. The glasses had been part of the camouflage she had worn to protect herself, part of the degrading of the personality perhaps not so different from the degrading I myself had employed when to protect the privacy of my inner self I had referred to my vision as a parlour-trick.

At last I said abruptly: "Do you believe me?" and she answered surprised: "Of course."

Greatly relieved I confessed: "I was afraid you might think I was a confidence trickster."

"That thought had, of course, occurred to me," said Miss Barton-Woods, "but the warden knew you when you were at Grantchester, so obviously you are who you say you are. I suppose it's just possible that you might now be sinking into iniquity, but I think if that were the case you'd have taken care to get the details of the chapel right."

I forgot my fear of her distrust. "What did I get wrong?"

"There's no wide space between the doors and the last pew; the pews do go all the way back. There's no plain altar-table with a wooden cross; the chapel's not deconsecrated but it hasn't been used since my grandmother died, and my father, who wasn't a believer, gave the altar-table to a local church before selling the altar-furnishings at Sotheby's. As for the memorial tablet . . ." She hesitated before saying: "That's really most odd. It does exist; it commemorates my uncle who was killed in the Boer War, but no one's placed lilies there since my grand-mother died in 1919."

"So the past was mixed up with the present and future. That happens sometimes." I was so absorbed by these new facts that I barely noticed the astonished lift of her eyebrows.

At last she ventured awkwardly: "This is all very—" but she could not find the word which would have expressed the quality of her amazement and fascination. "I suppose I should feel frightened," she said, "but I don't feel in any way endangered." She groped for words again before conclud-ing: "It's because you're benign. There's no wickedness here for me to fear."

"Father Darcy would have said that's because the vision came from God and not from the Devil."

"In that case is it vulgar to say I feel exhilarated?"

"Certainly not! No one thought a spiritual exhilaration in the least vulgar until the religious philosophers of the Enlightenment made 'en-thusiasm' a dirty word."

We smiled at each other before Miss Barton-Woods closed the picnic-basket and stood up. "I'll leave tomorrow," she said. "Give me twenty-four hours so that I can talk to my housekeeper and have one of the spare rooms made habitable."

I stared at her. "But you can't possibly cut short your holiday!"

"Why not? I'm fed up with Allington and after last night I've got the perfect excuse to leave."

"Yes, but—"

"If you take the noon train on Tuesday from Ashburton to Star-bridge, you can get the three-thirty train from Starbridge to Starrington Magna. I'll send my chauffeur to the station to meet you. You don't want to walk a mile with your baggage, and the village taxi's always breaking down."

I almost balked at the prospect of a chauffeur but managed to pull myself together. "How very kind," I said. "Thank you so much. But are you sure that my arrival won't cause awkwardness for you?"

"What kind of awkwardness?"

"Well . . ." I found myself floundering in the face of what I suspected was an aristocratic indifference to certain conventions. "I was thinking of your neighbours," I said. "Might they not judge it a little unseemly if you were to grant hospitality to a man whom you've only just met?"

"Oh, good heavens!" exclaimed Miss Barton-Woods, confirming my suspicions. "Surely it's only the lower classes who spend their lives worrying about what the neighbours might think!"

Old wounds broke open in my psyche. "Possibly," I said, "but my background is very different from yours, Miss Barton-Woods, and I'm afraid you must make allowances for my tediously bourgeois anxiety."

She looked stricken. Furious with myself both for upsetting her and for revealing my ineradicable sensitivity on the subject of class, I said rapidly: "I'm sorry. You were being refreshingly honest and I was being tiresomely inhibited."

"No, I was being snobbish and you were quite right to reprove me for it. But don't worry about the neighbours," said Miss Barton-Woods, resuming the casual confidence which can only be acquired from an upbringing in privileged surroundings. "They wouldn't cut me unless I did something quite beyond the pale."

"I think offering hospitality to a clairvoyant cleric might be construed as pressing the pale to its utmost limits."

"We'll keep quiet about the clairvoyance and play up the clerical collar," said Miss Barton-Woods smiling at me, but added in panic: "Or are you trying to create an excuse for refusing my invitation?"

"Absolutely not!" I said with a robustness worthy of Francis. "The very last thing I want to do is refuse! Thank you for displaying your hospitable inclinations so generously, Miss Barton-Woods. I can only confess I find your offer irresistible."

3

LATER on the motorbus which took us back across the moor to Ashburton, some confused impulse prompted me to say: "I'm sorry I embarrassed you earlier by displaying the chip on my shoulder," but she answered tranquilly: "You weren't embarrassed by my chip—why should I be embarrassed by yours?"

"But to be over-sensitive about class is so tedious and common-place—"

"A chip is never tedious or commonplace to its owner. It's always quite unique and utterly beastly. Fortunately I've never suffered from class prejudice, but I'm sure that if I had, I wouldn't think a chip about class was tedious or commonplace at all."

The motorbus began to growl up a steep hill. When we reached the summit there was a brief pause as if the engine were gasping for breath, and at that moment my voice said: "My mother was an orphanage girl who became a parlour-maid. When I was growing up I found that what the neighbours thought so often made the difference between happiness and misery."

"Beastly old neighbours! I suppose they couldn't bear to think that your parents had not only married in defiance of the conventions but had actually had the nerve to live happily ever after."

I smiled before saying: "My parents were certainly devoted to each other."

"I remember you saying your father was a schoolmaster. Did he teach at a public school?"

"Yes—but that was before he was married, of course. When he became engaged the headmaster suggested to him that my mother might find it difficult to fit in with the wives of the other masters in such a closed community, and so naturally my father resigned. After that he taught at the local grammar school for some years, but although that was a step down the educational ladder he never complained."

"Beastly headmaster! Beastly public school! If you ask me, both your parents were well out of it. Did your mother manage to make many friends in her new life?"

"Good heavens, no! None of the neighbours would call. But she didn't mind. She'd got what she wanted."

"And your father?"

"Oh, he never complained."

"All the same—"

"They were happy enough. She had her household and her cats, he had his study and his books, and both of them were content in their isolation. *I* was the one who minded when the neighbours' children weren't allowed to play with me and the big boys tried to bully me at the local dames' school where I began my education."

"Beastly, *beastly* children!"

"Fortunately I was big for my age and soon became more than a match for the bullies. Then eventually I went away to boarding school where no one knew my mother's background so I had no trouble living happily ever after."

"Just like your parents . . . I'm glad your mother was happy in spite of the neighbours."

"I suspect she wrote off their lack of charity as the price she had to pay for her security." As soon as the word slipped out I knew I had made a mistake. I should have said "romance" or "happiness," but before I could attempt to gloss over the error Miss Barton-Woods commented sympathetically: "I'm sure all orphans must long to feel secure in a nice home with someone they love," and the next moment I heard myself saying: "I remember her talking once about her favourite cat. 'There sits Chelsea,' she said, 'washing her paws in front of the fire. She wouldn't be here if she didn't love us, of course, but what she really loves is sitting in front of that fire on winter evenings and knowing she'll never be one of those alley-cats left outside to starve in the cold.' She often used to express truths—truths which she could never have expressed directly—by talking about her cats. I remember—" But I broke off. I had begun to wonder if old age had finally caught up with me by producing an urge to be garrulous in the company of sympathetic young women.

"Go on," said Miss Barton-Woods, but I was silent, remembering the time over fifty years ago when Chelsea had given birth to four kittens, three of which had died. "It's for the best," my mother had said casually, mopping up my tears. "If there are too many kittens the mother doesn't have enough love for them all and they're not brought up properly. Better to have one kitten who becomes a splendid cat than a bunch of nuisances who yowl around asking to be drowned." And I had known then that she had never wanted another child after I was born. "Of course her greatest sorrow," my father had said after her death, "was that she was unable to give me more children." I could still recall the exact quality of my amazement as I realised how imperfectly he had known her.

"I mustn't bore you with my past," I heard my voice saying to Miss Barton-Woods, and at once she responded: "There's no question of boredom but you mustn't think I want to pry. Why don't we sink into one of our restful silences?"

I smiled and said no more, but the atmosphere was neither awkward nor uncompanionable.

The motorbus roared on towards Ashburton.

"... BUT may I hasten to reassure you," I wrote that night to Francis,

that although I shall be staying beneath the same roof as an unchaperoned young woman, I shall be in no danger of succumbing to Monks' Madness. Miss Barton-Woods is so much younger than I am that I can unhesitatingly think of her as a daughter, and even if she were older I would still be quite safe as I have no inclination whatsoever to respond to her in any carnal way. In short, I am in complete command of this situation.

I reread this letter and decided that I had never sounded more sane. However the copious underlinings troubled me. I added: "Forgive the emphatic style but I'm sure you're worried about me and I'm most anxious to allay your fears." I almost continued: "I know I myself would be worried if I were in your shoes," but I thought better of it. I had quite enough to occupy my mind without trying to put myself into Francis's shoes.

Nevertheless I was unable to stop asking myself what he could possibly be thinking.

THE next morning I said to the warden: "I've received an unexpected invitation from a friend who lives near Starbridge, so I regret to say I shall be leaving Allington earlier than I'd planned."

To Miss Tarantino, who playfully accused me of plotting a secret elopement with the departing "Miss Fielding," I said: "So you've guessed my guilty secret!" and to Miss Barton-Woods herself I said as she left: "I look forward immensely to tomorrow." Then I retired to the chapel to meditate, but I was so excited that I made a sad hash of my spiritual exercises.

The train reached Starbridge a quarter of an hour late on the following afternoon, but I still had five minutes in which to change platforms and pace up and down like a tiger at the zoo. Repeatedly during my pacings I stared at the spire of the Cathedral, soaring in the distance above the cluttered railway yard as if to symbolise my faith triumphing at last over my disordered doubts, but at last my view was interrupted by the arrival of the train to Starrington Magna.

The chauffeur was waiting when I arrived. His extreme age gave a venerable air to his peaked cap and gaiters, and infused his welcome with dignity. The motor was equally dignified; despite my ignorance on the subject of mechanised transport I did realise that I was about to complete my journey in a Rolls-Royce, and my automatic judgement was that it was a most unsuitable vehicle for a monk. But then I remembered that I was no longer a monk, and suddenly for the first time the full awareness of my liberation exploded in my consciousness. It was as if my psyche, long burdened with the strain of leaving the Order, had finally somersaulted free, and my depression now seemed not only remote but fantastic, a mental aberration which could not possibly be repeated.

We drove through a long village built in that pale golden stone which is quarried in the Starbridge area. Many of the houses had thatched roofs and were set beside a stream which for half a mile ran parallel with the road. There was no green but I glimpsed a Norman church tucked away down a lane, its steeple rising above the trees like the prow of a ship breasting the waves. I also noted two public houses and the usual assortment of shops, including a post office where I could cash my weekly money order.

At the end of the village the road began to encircle the high brick wall of the estate and a minute later we were driving up the curling drive of the Manor. To my disappointment I saw it was not a beautiful house but its varied features, accumulated over the centuries, gave it a certain eccentric grace. It appeared well-kept but not smart; I realised I was moving into a quiet, casual, effortlessly well-bred world where smart country houses were considered the hallmark of the nouveaux riches, and for a moment I remembered my home long ago, the respectable little villa with the respectable little front garden where my mother had grown well-behaved flowers in order to impress the neighbours. I had never been allowed to play in the front garden; only working-class children played so near the street, but I had been happy in the back garden where my mother moved dreamily in a bewitching silence among the undisciplined shrubs and the aromatic herbs and the wild lawn studded with daisies. I could see her long skirts trailing across the grass as she listened to her thoughts, and Chelsea was there too, sharpening her claws on the peach tree in preparation for a new adventure, serene, elegant Chelsea who savoured her security by the fire on dark winter evenings and was quite content with the one kitten who sat bright-eyed at her side.

The door of the motor was opening. Returning from the 1880s with a jolt, I alighted just as the butler opened the front door.

He was very old, like the chauffeur, and had a mild, innocent expression which reminded me of Timothy at Grantchester. I was given a civil welcome and ushered deferentially across the threshold before I was informed of the absence of my hostess. "But she hopes to be back within the hour, sir," he added after waiting for my murmur of regret, and began to lead the way upstairs.

I was taken to a large corner chamber with extensive views to the south and west. The furnishings were Victorian; my glance encountered a handsome brass bedstead, an elegant washstand and a vast but noble wardrobe. The carpet was probably beyond price but had faded into a distinction that rendered it mercifully unobtrusive. Noting the plain curtains and the war-time black-out blind with approval, I saw that the only picture in the room was an austere engraving of Starbridge Cathedral and at once I decided that this was one of those rare pictures which could not be automatically consigned to the wardrobe. Sighing with pleasure I became aware that the butler was asking me whether I required tea immediately.

"No, thank you." All thought of food and drink seemed unbearably irrelevant. "Can you please direct me to the chapel?"

The old man looked startled but led me to the south window and indicated the woods on the far side of the lawn. After pointing out the indentation among the line of the tree-tops and describing the dell he added: "You'll find the path behind the summer-house, sir. You can't miss it."

Immediately I was on my way.

6

AS soon as I joined that part of the path where my vision had begun, I realised I was in the wrong time; at that moment my vision was not to be exactly reproduced. In the time in which I was now moving the sun was shining and the wood-pigeons were silent in the trees.

But the chapel was the same. I looked down upon it, just as I had in my vision, but this time I was so stunned to see it that I stopped dead. However the chapel remained, neither vanishing nor fading, no mere imprint on the retina of my psychic eye but a three-dimensional building accessible to the five senses, and hurrying on down the path I crossed the floor of the dell, bounded up the steps to the porch and flung wide the main door.

The pews stretched before me on either side of the central aisle and I saw the empty space below the east window where the altar should have stood. Then I found I could see no more. Slumping down on the nearest pew, I covered my face with my hands and shuddered beneath the impact of the knowledge that three months ago I had journeyed through time and space in a manner which defied the known laws of physics.

After a while I became calm enough to notice the evidence of the chapel's disuse. The pews needed polishing. So did the brass memorial tablet. Cobwebs festooned the windows and dirt lay ingrained on the floor. There was also a pervasive musty smell, conjuring up images of long, damp winters. The thought formed in my mind that I had to effect a restoration, but whether this was a mere emotional reaction from within or a faint call from without I had no idea.

I knelt to pray. At first I prayed in words, thanking God again for His guidance and asking that His will be fully revealed. Then I prayed in images: the classical architecture of the chapel, symbol of Beauty, one of Plato's three absolute values; the spire of the Cathedral at Starbridge, symbol of another absolute value, Truth; the cross on the summit of the spire, symbolic of Christ and of that third absolute value which Plato had called Goodness and which the Christians had exalted as Love. The images quickened. I saw Christ crucified, Christ resurrected, the old life giving way to the new, but then even the familiar images faded beneath the power of my desire to communicate with God, and I found myself praying in stillness, waiting upon the silence, my mind open, my senses in repose but alert for the slightest tremor of psychic movement.

Yet nothing stirred. No wordless message formed in the blankness and in the end my concentration broke as my mind, overstrained, eased its way painfully back to a normal level of consciousness in the manner of an athlete slowing down from a fast sprint to a walking pace. My first reaction, not unnaturally, was to be disappointed; I had been so confident that once I reached the chapel I would receive a further revelation. My next reaction was to be baffled; here I was at the chapel and yet nothing was happening. My third reaction was to be cross; I had struggled through three exceedingly difficult months only to be kept in the dark when I could expect to be enlightened. However I then realised I was being preposterously arrogant, nagging God for another revelation like a spoilt child whining for a sweet, so my final reaction was to be ashamed. Father Darcy, I knew, would have said that in my arrogance I was in no fit spiritual state to receive a revelation, and Father Darcy, as usual, would have been right.

With regret I resigned myself to the fact that the way forward was to remain hidden. But then, just as I was about to slide despondently back into the pew, I heard the click of the latch and knew that my hostess was entering the chapel.

WHEN she saw I was kneeling she immediately withdrew, and although I wanted to stop her the door closed before I could utter a word. At once I rose from my knees and strode outside.

She was waiting on the steps of the porch, and immediately I was startled because for the first time in our acquaintance she was wearing clothes which fitted her. I saw she had a waist—not a small waist and certainly not a wasp-waist, but nevertheless a waist. I also saw that the other attributes of her feminine figure were by no means as ill-proportioned as "Miss Fielding's" wardrobe had led me to suppose. Of course she was still too stout and of course there was no possibility that I might find her sexually attractive, but I realised that it was not after all so surprising that she should have had a fiancé and I even felt it was not beyond the realms of possibility that one day she might have another.

My surprise gave way to a detached observation. Miss Barton-Woods was wearing a pale grey coat and skirt with a dark blue blouse and she looked, in a discreet way, the wealthy landowner that she was. Ruth would have dressed up such plain clothes with fussy costume jewellery; Miss Barton-Woods wore a single cameo at the neck of her blouse. Ruth would have worn flimsy shoes with high heels; Miss Barton-Woods had exchanged "Miss Fielding's" ugly walking shoes for a pair of brogues so elegant that I felt certain they had been hand-made. Ruth would have painted her face and dowsed herself with perfume; Miss Barton-Woods presented merely a powdered nose, a trace of pale lipstick and a faint fresh aroma which indicated that her uncurled hair had recently been washed. I admired her good taste, applauded her lack of pretentiousness, and wished with a vague, guilty unhappiness that Ruth would refrain from concealing her natural advantages beneath such a vulgar layer of artificiality.

Meanwhile Miss Barton-Woods had succumbed to an unexpected bout of shyness. Immediately I gave her my warmest smile and held out my hand, but when she could do no more than clasp it and mutter: "Welcome to the Manor," I realised I had quite failed to alleviate her discomfort. I wondered what I was doing wrong. As far as I was aware I was merely standing innocently in the sunshine, six foot three inches of faultless masculine propriety. However before I could inquire what the matter was, she managed to reclaim her confident manner and ask in her most businesslike voice: "Is the chapel as you saw it?"

"Apart from the differences you mentioned, yes."

I could see that she too was moved by the thought of my vision being translated into the world of finite time, and sitting down abruptly on the top step of the porch she stared across the sward to the trees.

I sat down beside her. For a time we were silent but at last she decided that further comment was too difficult, particularly as I was offering her no encouragement, and that a retreat into more mundane matters was required.

"I'm sorry I wasn't here when you arrived," she said, "but I suddenly decided I should slip down the road and take the cat to the vet. The trouble's only an ear infection but it seemed better not to delay treatment when the poor creature was obviously in discomfort."

A lark began to sing in the woods as I said: "You didn't tell me you had a cat. What's his name?"

"William."

"After Shakespeare, naturally," I said smiling at her again, and to my relief I found she was now sufficiently relaxed to smile readily in return. "What kind of a cat is he?"

"Just a tabby. But he's very clever."

The lark was singing and singing. I heard myself say: "I knew a tabby-cat once. He was very clever too." And suddenly I realised that at long last I was going to talk about Whitby, proud arrogant Whitby, who had belonged to the community at Ruydale but who had obeyed no man's orders but mine.

8

"*HE* was the house-cat up in Yorkshire," I said. "Soon after I arrived at Ruydale the old cat died and one of the local people gave us Whitby out of an unwanted litter. A new keeper was appointed to look after him, but I soon realised the man had no idea how to bring up a kitten. Whitby quickly became wild and useless, but cats are kept for a utilitarian purpose in a monastery, just as they are on board ship; they're not kept to chase their tails while the mice eat all the food in the larder.

"Eventually I decided to report the keeper's mismanagement to the Abbot—an unorthodox move because a novice is supposed to take all problems to his Master, but I was afraid my Master would simply tell me to mind my own business. Mature, well-educated novices are always a cross for a monastic nanny to bear—they're too ready to think they know everything—and I was well aware that my monastic nanny thought I was 'a handful.'

"So I went to the Abbot and told him the kitten was fast becoming a useless monster. Aidan immediately sent me back to the scriptorium, but because he was a good Abbot, interested in even the most minor detail of his community, he investigated my complaint and the first thing he saw as he entered the kitchens was Whitby urinating in the flour-bin. Immediately the keeper was relieved of his responsibilities and I was assigned the task of training the monster.

"I was tough with him. I wasn't unkind—but I certainly wasn't sentimental either. It doesn't do to be sentimental about cats; the best ones don't respect you for it, but Whitby respected me and I understood him and before long he was a first-class cat, intelligent, efficient and resourceful. He soon decimated the rodent population. He used to leave the corpses piled up by the back door with the entrails of the ones he'd eaten arranged neatly on the mat. Once before he was fully trained he caught a bird, but I rubbed his nose in the feathers and smacked him and he never did it again. Whitby learnt fast. Ah, what a cat he was, what a cat!

"Our partnership lasted nearly six years. Then I was promoted from the carpenter's work-bench to the Master's desk in the scriptorium and Aidan said to me: 'Since the novices will take all your time I'll appoint someone else to look after Whitby.' Of course I couldn't argue. One can never argue when one's superior is laying down the law, but I did say: 'I don't think Whitby will care for the change at all.' Then Aidan gave me a hard look and said: 'Whitby's here to serve the community, Jonathan, not to dictate to it, and Whitby will have to learn to accept the change, just as you will.'

"So that was that.

"But I hated to think of Whitby pining for my company and being fobbed off on a stupid new keeper who didn't understand him. I couldn't disobey orders, of course. That was out of the question, but as the days passed I thought I saw how I could demonstrate conclusively that Whitby was resisting Aidan's decision.

"When I'd entered the Order I'd been forbidden to make any conscious use of my psychic powers, not just because such powers can fuel one's pride to the point of spiritual unhealthiness but because any psychic manifestation can have a disastrous effect on an enclosed community by triggering a hysterical reaction. But now I thought: no one will ever know. And I began to manipulate Whitby with my mind.

"Animals are more open to unseen forces than humans, and often they seem far less deaf than humans to psychic communication. Certainly Whitby was far from being deaf; he was perfectly in tune with me, and when I projected orders with my mind he picked them up with an amazing consistency. Well, you can guess what happened. Gradually everyone began to notice that wherever I was, Whitby would seek me out and leap purring into my lap. 'Whitby's pining for Jonathan,' people were soon saying, exactly as I'd planned, but the new keeper was so jealous that in his rage he accused me of sorcery.

"That made Aidan sit up. Sorcery's not a word which an abbot wants to hear in his monastery, and finally Aidan said to me: "I'm not sure what's going on. I'm not even sure I want to know what's going on. But whatever's going on must stop—and that's an order, Jonathan.' He knew he couldn't prove I'd been using the powers, but he knew too that I wouldn't disobey a direct order. So I found I had to face the fact that I'd failed in my efforts to be reappointed Whitby's keeper.

"But then it seemed Whitby genuinely began to pine.

"He became ill. I heard he was lacklustre, not eating, lying all day in his basket, and eventually a delegation arrived from the kitchens to beg me to intervene to save his life.

"Aidan was much exasperated but he told me to attempt a diagnosis, and as soon as I saw Whitby's bedraggled fur I knew what was wrong: he had a stoppage caused by a fur-ball. Whitby had unusually long hair for a tabby and he needed to be combed once a week to prevent him licking too many hairs into his stomach when he cleaned himself. The stupid new keeper hadn't combed him—probably out of a jealous spite towards me just because I'd stressed how important the combing was.

"I picked Whitby up and took him outside. The delegation tried to troop after me, but I didn't want an audience so I told them to stay in the scullery. Carrying Whitby to the nearest patch of earth, I dug a hole and sat him on it. Poor Whitby! He was too weak to dig a hole for himself. In fact he was barely conscious, but I knew he recognised me because when I'd picked him up he'd started to purr.

"I stroked him for a while. It's important, before any attempt to heal, that the patient should be calm and relaxed. Then I prayed hard and pressed down my hands on him. I can't explain how the power is channelled, but when I laid my hands on Whitby, he yelped and his fur stood on end and the next moment he was getting rid of everything, fur-ball and all, and we both knew he was cured.

"When he stopped mewing I picked him up, but Whitby didn't want to be carried now that he was well. Whitby had great pride. When he struggled I set him down again, and seconds later we were entering the kitchens in triumph, I swaggering along like a master-magician who's just pulled off a magnificent trick and Whitby staggering along beside me with his eyes shining and his tail held high. The monks were absolutely agog. No magician could have wished for a better audience, and suddenly in my pride I was unable to resist 'playing to the gallery,' as they say in the theatre. I ordered: 'Give him something to eat and drink!'—and from that moment we were all doomed. Do you recognise the order? After Our Lord had raised Jairus's daughter from the dead, he advised that she be given food and drink, and of course every monk in the kitchens at Ruydale that night was instantly reminded of that miracle. A second later some fool was shouting: 'Whitby's been raised from the dead!' and I was being treated as a wonder-worker. But I knew I'd gone beyond the pale and would have to try to redeem my mistake.

"I assured Aidan there had been no resurrection from the dead but I kept quiet about the charismatic healing. I said only that Whitby had cured himself while I'd been holding him, and Aidan, who's a wily old fox, decided to leave the necessary cross-examination to my confessor and thus seal up all the sordid details in the confessional. However his plan misfired. I was so gripped by the guilty urge to cover up what had happened that I remained silent on the subject when the time came for me to make my confession, and my confessor, although an excellent monk in many ways, was unfortunately no match for me once I felt compelled to manipulate him away from the subject of Whitby's miraculous cure.

"After I'd survived the confessional I thought I was safe. But in fact the real scandal of the Whitby Affair was just about to begin.

"The word 'miracle' was still reverberating around the house, and soon the community was divided into my allies, who called me a blessed healer, and my enemies, who called me a wicked sorcerer. Fanatical feelings were aroused on both sides, and before long the community was fully poised to go sliding down the slippery slope into hysteria.

"The more ignorant laymen often think that hysteria is endemic in a religious community—they even think hysteria's welcomed as a necessary adjunct to the mystical experience, but in fact the best mystics are all characterised by their rationality and their down-to-earth common sense. The sensational manifestations of an over-stimulated psyche are shunned or at best treated as a tiresome inconvenience by those who are experienced travellers along the spiritual way.

"The hysteria at Ruydale following the healing of Whitby began when a group of monks fell to their knees in the chapel and tried to kiss the hem of my habit as I passed by. At first I was so startled that I could only let them slobber over me, but just as I was making the effort to detach myself there was an outburst of speaking in tongues—a well-known charism but one which is peculiarly subject to demonic infiltration. At once I knew this was no gift from God. This was hysteria triggered by the Devil, and that was when I realised the situation was quite beyond my control. I turned to Aidan, but before he could act the unlatched door of the chapel creaked open and in walked Whitby. In my disturbed state I must have unwittingly sent out a distress signal which he'd picked up, clever cat, and now there he was, prancing down the aisle to meet me.

"One of my enemies screamed: 'It's his familiar!' and pandemonium broke loose, but at once Aidan acted. He snapped at me: 'Remove the novices!' and as I left, I heard him shouting orders to the other senior officers. In the end the hysterics were all either locked up or confined to the infirmary, but the whole place remained in chaos—and all because I'd disobeyed orders, used my powers and healed that innocent cat.

"The Abbot-General arrived three days later to mop up the mess.

"We needed him by that time. Aidan's a strong abbot but even Aidan felt he had to have help. A modern psycho-analyst would say we needed an exceptionally forceful personality to impose control upon all those dissociated minds, but Father Darcy didn't talk like a psycho-analyst. He talked about the Devil's presence, and he talked as one who *knew* the Devil existed, just as you and I can talk of Hitler and know we're discussing someone who's real. Father Darcy said: 'We must trace the source of the demonic influence in order to exorcise it,' and the spiritual purging of Ruydale began.

"He interviewed all the monks, beginning at the bottom and working his way to the top. Eventually I received my summons, and as soon as I walked into the room I knew that he knew. He'd ordered Aidan to be there as an observer, and I realised he wanted to teach him exactly how to deal with a high-ranking officer who had caused an entire community to go off the rails.

"For a while I tried to fob Father Darcy off with partial truths but I was wasting my time. He simply took my mind, psychic powers and all, washed it, scrubbed it and hung it up to dry. At the end of the interrogation I was in such a state that I could barely think straight, but I remember being certain that he'd strip me of my office and possibly even transfer me to London so that he could keep an eye on me. I was in despair.

"However the situation was far more complex than I in my panic supposed. The truth was that Father Darcy didn't want my career to be ruined. He was convinced I could be a great asset to the Order and he remained determined that nothing, least of all a lot of nonsense over a cat, was going to demolish his plans for me. Yet obviously I deserved a severe punishment; it wouldn't be enough merely to dole out the mandatory punishment for disobedience and then send me back into action. What was needed at that point, as Father Darcy came to realise, was a master-stroke, an action that would teach me a lesson I'd never forget, complete the mass exorcism of the community and ensure that the incident never happened again.

"That night when I was asleep Whitby was waylaid outside his favourite mousehole, taken to the water-butt and held under the water till he drowned. The next morning I was summoned to the Abbot's office but Aidan wasn't there. Father Darcy was alone and on the table in front of him was Whitby's corpse. Father Darcy just said: 'I performed the execution but *you* were the one who killed that animal with your disobedience, your vanity and your utterly intolerable pride.' Then he rang the bell and Aidan came in. Father Darcy pointed to the corpse and said: 'Burn it in the furnace,' and without a word Aidan picked up Whitby and took him away.

"I was sent to my cell to reflect on what had happened and at the end of the second hour Father Darcy came to me. He said: 'You need to be healed, don't you?' and I broke down, spewing out all my grief and rage. I even said I couldn't go on as a monk. Father Darcy let me talk, but gradually I became aware of his silence stroking my psyche, soothing it, until at last the verbal haemorrhage stopped. Then he said a few sentences. There wasn't a single wasted word and although the words were firm, even severe, his voice was kind. While he was speaking I saw clearly that in order to keep my powers under control I had to live within the disciplined framework he offered me, but although I tried to tell him that, I couldn't find the words. I could only kneel down in front of him, and when he laid his hands upon me in a formal sacramental gesture to complete the healing, I knew I'd be able to go on in the Order. He knew it too, but afterwards all he said was: 'Keep away from the next cat and never, never discuss this incident again.'

"And I never have discussed it. Even now I never talk of Whitby. Indeed why should I? Who could possibly understand? He was just a cat who came to an untimely end. It happens all the time everywhere, so what's so remarkable about the incident and why should it matter now after all these years? I often ask myself those questions and tell myself the answers are no longer important, but then sometimes when I lie awake at night I think of him—proud arrogant Whitby, such a wild, undisciplined kitten and yet such a first-class gifted cat—and it's as if he's reflecting my own career as a monk until suddenly *I'm* the one who's drowning in the water-butt and *I'm* the one who's burning in the furnace, and I grieve over his death as if it were my own."

I stopped speaking.

I had not been looking at her during my long monologue. I had been watching the sunlight as it slanted through the trees, and when I stopped speaking I was too ashamed to face her. I saw I had been behaving in a most unbalanced manner, talking for minutes on end about a dead cat, and in horror I asked myself how I could possibly have been so stupid. No doubt she had long since regretted her offer of hospitality.

The silence which followed my monologue lasted ten seconds. Ten seconds can seem a very long time when one is inwardly writhing with humiliation, but at last my torment ended. She said unsteadily: "How very dreadfully you must have suffered when he was killed and how very dreadfully you must have missed him since he died."

Struck by the passion in her voice I turned to look at her, and it was then, as I recognised the profound understanding etched in every line of her face, that the scales fell from my eyes at last and I saw that she was beautiful.

XI

"Love is the great reality."

W. R. INGE
MYSTICISM IN RELIGION

I

"I'VE fallen in love," I said eight days later to Francis.

"At the risk of infuriating you I must say that I'm not in the least surprised. Every time you wrote insisting that you found the lady unattractive I wondered how long you could possibly go on deceiving yourself."

I had presented myself as planned at the Fordite headquarters at the conclusion of my first month in the world, and Francis had welcomed me not in his office, which was in the enclosed section of the house, but in the Abbot's Parlour, the room in which he received guests from outside the Order. It was so opulently furnished that I was reminded of the gaudy chambers of Brighton Pavilion. Francis, resplendent in his perfectly cut habit and bejewelled pectoral cross, looked quite at home there.

A young monk chose that moment to bring us some refreshment but as soon as he had departed I said: "Of course I've fallen victim to Monks' Madness."

"Do you take sugar in your tea?"

"You know perfectly well that I don't take sugar in my tea!"

"I thought you might have acquired a taste for it along with falling in love."

"Francis—"

"Now Jon, you must calm down. You seem to be expecting me to show violent disapproval but at the moment I have insufficient information to show anything except a profound curiosity. Why don't you bring me up to date with what's been going on? Begin: 'I arrived at Starrington Magna,' and proceed from there."

I talked in a disordered fashion for some minutes. Francis sipped his tea and looked inscrutable.

"Of course I can't possibly marry her," I concluded in despair after I had reached the point where the scales had fallen from my eyes. "Yet how can I endure it if I don't?"

"Let's set all speculation aside for the moment and stick to the questions which can be answered with hard facts. Have you been to bed with anyone yet?"

"No. And maybe—this is a terrible thing to say, but maybe this is exactly why I've lapsed into such insanity."

"That doesn't necessarily follow at all; grand passions can strike the lechers and the chaste with equal ferocity. But don't let's make *a priori* assumptions. We haven't yet established either that you're insane or that you're in the grip of a grand passion. To what do you attribute your chastity?"

"Prayer."

"Yes, yes, yes," said Francis impatiently, very much the worldly priest. "Of course you prayed and of course your prayers were important— obviously, since they've been answered—but we both know that the sexual drive of a man who's been celibate for a number of years is capable of grinding even the most cherished moral principles into the dust no matter how hard he prays for self-control. How do you explain your chastity in psychological terms?"

"I don't. It's all been a matter of luck. As soon as I met Miss Barton-Woods and realised she was the key to the mystery, sex—for once—took second place. Of course I was still plagued by impure thoughts—"

"Of course, but nevertheless I think you're being a little hard on yourself when you say your chastity's been a matter of luck. In the circumstances a month's self-control represents a considerable achievement, and I can't help thinking that if you were genuinely suffering from Monks' Madness you'd have bedded at least half a dozen women by this time. Now tell me this: why do you believe Miss Barton-Woods is so unsuitable for you?"

"Francis, she's thirty-two. *Thirty-two!* I don't mind people whispering that I've sunk into an undignified dotage, but it would be so terrible for Miss Barton-Woods if her neighbours decided to cut her—"

"Why should they? They'd probably be delighted she'd at last got off the shelf, even if her rescuer did turn out to be a man twenty-eight years her senior. Contrary to what you seem to suppose, the real question here is not: what on earth will the neighbours think? But: what does Miss Barton-Woods think of you being sixty?"

"She doesn't know that I'm sixty."

"My dear Jon—"

"I know, I know, but I just haven't yet found the opportunity to tell her—"

"Then create one fast! She'll feel deceived if you frolic around like a forty-year-old and then reveal, as you eventually must, that your children are in their mid-thirties. But let's leave the problem of age now and consider any other difficulties. What else makes this marriage undesirable?"

"The difference in class. I don't want to marry into the landed gentry and live in a big house littered with servants."

"Jon, I'm well aware of your sensitivity on the subject of class, but are you really saying you'd have trouble facing the landed gentry in order to marry the woman you love?"

"I trust I'm gentleman enough to face anyone, prince or pauper, with equanimity whenever the need arises," I said grandly, pride well to the fore, "but I'm just pointing out how ill-suited I am by background, experience and inclination for that kind of life. And I couldn't talk about agriculture with Miss Barton-Woods, couldn't help her run the estate—"

"That would probably suit her very well. If she's been successfully running her estate for some years, the last thing she'd want would be a husband who interfered. She's hardly a helpless little miss, is she?"

"No, she's a rich woman with a horror of fortune-hunters, and here I am, poor as a church-mouse—"

"Yes, but from her point of view all that matters is that you're obviously a man of integrity who wouldn't dream of marrying her for her money. However"—Francis, who had been enjoying the challenge of demolishing my difficulties, now became more cautious—"don't misunderstand; I'm not saying the disparity in your financial and social positions is unimportant. Nor am I saying that the difference in age doesn't matter. All I'm saying is that these very real problems needn't be prohibitive. Is there, in fact, any difficulty which you regard as truly insuperable?"

"She's resolved to be celibate."

"But surely she'll be willing to change her mind!"

"She may be psychologically incapable of changing it."

"Ah, I see. What an alluring challenge for you!"

"I hope," I said, trying not to sound annoyed, "I don't see her merely as a challenge."

"I don't believe you do, but nevertheless it might be salutary for you to be reminded that men who are successful with women are always fascinated by the ones who don't fall grovelling at their feet. However let's suppose that all inhibitions are overcome on both sides and that you marry Miss Barton-Woods. What makes you think you won't wake up one morning and find that she's 'invading your psychic space,' as you put it to me once?"

"She couldn't. She's too sensitive. She always knows when to be quiet and she never pesters me with unwelcome questions—and that's why I know beyond any doubt that I could be happy with her."

"And would you remain happy when she was bearing your children?"

After a pause I said: "If God should choose to bless the marriage with children I'd accept the situation and pray for the grace to be a good father."

"That's the sort of pious remark," said Francis, "which I suspect has very little to do with the painful and complex reality to which it's supposed to correspond. Is this where we reach the one insuperable difficulty?"

"Certainly not! It's simply a bridge which I'm sure I'll be able to cross when I get to it."

"Well, make sure you have your bridge-crossing ability developed well before the wedding. Presumably at some stage you intend to confide in her fully about your past?"

"Of course!"

"You greatly relieve my mind. So the crucial question at the moment, I think, becomes this: will Miss Barton-Woods help you or hinder you in the pursuit of your new call? Obviously it's no good if you marry a woman who's deeply entrenched in her family home and then find you've been called to be a missionary in China."

I said in despair: "I've received no enlightenment."

"None? Are you sure?"

I stared at him. "That sounds as if you disagree."

"I can have no worthwhile opinion until you complete your account of your recent activities. So far we've only reached the point eight days ago when you made your long speech about the unfortunate Whitby and Miss Barton-Woods revealed herself as irresistible. What have you been doing since?"

Taking a deep breath I resumed my narrative.

2

"AS soon as I realised I was in love," I said, "I knew I had to expend as much energy as possible elsewhere, so that evening I asked Miss Barton-Woods if I could clean the chapel. She was horrified at the idea of a guest on his hands and knees with a scrubbing brush, but when I reminded her that as a monk I'd often done heavy cleaning and when I assured her that I'd enjoy making the chapel sparkle, she reluctantly gave her consent."

"You must be enthralling the servants. But don't let me interrupt you. There you were, scrubbing away in your clerical suit—"

"I bought a pair of dungarees. For a while I wondered if I might uncover serious structural decay beneath the grime, but the place seems to be in reasonable condition despite the years of disuse." And I told him how Miss Barton-Woods's grandfather had quarrelled with the local vicar, who had been influenced by the Oxford Movement, and had built the chapel in order to avoid being subjected to "Papist ritual" at the village church. "He picked the site next to the ruined chantry," I added, "because he thought he'd be building on consecrated ground. The chantry, of course, was destroyed at the time of the Reformation." I hesitated but eventually concluded: "I can't help wondering if I'm to have a ministry centred on the chapel, a ministry which will require the removal of the back pews so that the chapel corresponds in every detail to my vision."

Francis said briskly: "That sounds most improbable. Although you may—*may*—have seen the future state of the chapel in your vision, that doesn't mean your own future necessarily has any connection with it. The chapel could be just another signpost along the way, like the bag."

"Yes, but—"

"What are you going to do when you've exhausted the possibilities of your scrubbing brush?"

"I thought I might build an altar-table."

"And how long do you intend to go on inventing amusing little tasks for yourself at the Manor?"

"My dear Francis, please don't think I haven't been considering how I could occupy my time in a more appropriate manner for a priest! I was thinking that I might offer to help at the local church. The vicar's gone into the Army, there's no curate and the services are at present being conducted by a decrepit, semi-blind, retired canon who's anxious to be relieved of his responsibilities."

"In that case I see no reason why you shouldn't help out on a voluntary basis for a couple of months while you wait for your call to unfold."

"But what on earth am I going to do about Miss Barton-Woods?"

"I don't really have to spell out the most obvious advice, do I?"

I said reluctantly: "You want me to leave the Manor."

"Yes. Take a room in the village. I think it's important—even vital— that you should continue to see Miss Barton-Woods, but your bedrooms must be at least half a mile apart."

"You think it's *vital* that I continue to see her?" I was astonished.

"Of course. In my opinion the key to your future lies not in the chapel but with Miss Barton-Woods, and the only reason why you've been unable to see that is because you've jumped to the guilty conclusion that your attraction to the lady is just a piece of elderly self-indulgence which can have nothing to do with God's purpose for you. But now think again. What's actually happened here? Almost as soon as you leave the Order this woman is thrust across your path with the result that you eventually reach the chapel. You then pray for a revelation—at which point Miss Barton-Woods reappears and some impulse drives you to break a ten-year silence on the subject of that murdered cat. And then you do have your revelation: you realise that you love this woman and want to marry her. Of course a cynic would explain all this by saying you're in an unstable state after years of celibacy, but in fact this explanation won't do because Miss Barton-Woods's remarkable arrival in your life and her connection with your vision are both facts which exist independently of your emotional state, stable or otherwise."

"So what you're saying is—"

"I'm saying it's possible that this is a genuine call to matrimony. Of course I'm not suggesting God's called you back into the world solely in order that you should marry, but it does begin to look as if matrimony could well be an important element in a much larger call which at present we still can't perceive. However," said Francis, smiling at me as he approached the most difficult part of his advice, "the fact that you may be called to marry doesn't mean that you can sit back and leave it to God to preserve you miraculously from temptation while you await your journey to the altar. How far have you actually travelled with the lady? Have you allowed yourself, for example, a modest squeeze of the hand?"

I was so overwhelmed that he should be advancing the theory I had not dared believe that I could not immediately frame a coherent reply. But at last I was able to say: "I've concealed my feelings. I was afraid that once I'd started to display them I wouldn't be able to stop."

"Quite. How wise. Is she a virgin, do you think? I'm trying to gauge how likely she'd be to say no if your wisdom suddenly decided to expire."

"I suspect there was a disastrous attempt at intimacy with the fiancé. If I'm right then the odds against her allowing herself to be seduced again would be high."

"Good, but remove yourself from her house as soon as possible, I beg of you, Jon, and don't, whatever you do, propose to her in a rush of romantic enthusiasm before you know a great deal more about your future as a priest than you do at the moment. In fact I feel bound to say," said Francis, looking me straight in the eyes, "that in my opinion it's out of the question that you should marry either Miss Barton-Woods or indeed anyone else until you've been in the world for at least six months."

It was the soundest possible advice. At once I answered: "I wouldn't dream of marrying in haste!" but as Francis relaxed in relief I thought of Father Darcy turning my mind inside out, washing it, scrubbing it and hanging it up to dry. Father Darcy would have said: "You're saying what you want me to hear but I hear the words you can't bring yourself to say." And he would have talked of lust and pride and wilfulness, of the Devil striking at me through the Achilles' heel of my sexuality, until at last I would have confessed to him that I wanted to go to bed with Miss Barton-Woods that very night and that the possibility of a further five months of chastity was the beautiful dream of a monastic mind, a dream which had no hope of coming true.

3

I SPENT the night in one of the guest-rooms of the Fordite headquarters, but the sober masculine atmosphere, which I had looked forward to sampling for a few hours, seemed so bleak in contrast to the glowing aura infusing Starrington Magna that on the following morning I was relieved to depart. Francis, who perfectly understood that I could hardly wait to return to Miss Barton-Woods, remarked that at least he was spared the worry that I might be pining for the cloister.

"And how was London?" enquired Miss Barton-Woods when we met that evening; as usual she had been out all day at the estate office. "Did you see much evidence of the bombing?"

I described my fleeting visit to Westminster Abbey, where the great west window had been destroyed, and told her how the nocturnal air-raids murdered sleep. "It's not just the bombs," I said. "It's the guns. My friend Father Ingram—who incidentally was looking just like one of Shakespeare's wicked cardinals—said that one got used to the noise after a while, but I suspect he was merely putting a brave face on what must be a tedious as well as a nerve-racking ordeal." Exasperated by the tenacity of the RAF, Hitler had recently turned aside from his efforts to destroy the fighter-bases in Kent and had unleashed his fury on the capital. But although hundreds of barges had been accumulated along the coasts across the Channel, although the tide had favoured the enemy, although the Home Guard had even been called to stand to arms, the long-awaited invasion had never come.

"Thank goodness you're safely back in Starrington!" Miss Barton-Woods was saying. "But what happens next? Did Father Ingram approve of your plan to help out at the village church?"

"Yes, he did—and that means, I'm afraid"—I allowed myself the luxury of a deep sigh—"that I must leave the Manor. If I'm to work in Starrington in a pastoral capacity, I must live in the village among my flock."

"Ah yes, of course," said Miss Barton-Woods without hesitation, but just as I was wondering in alarm if her alacrity indicated relief, she stooped to pick up her tabby-cat and said: "But what a pity you have to leave! William will miss you so much when you're gone."

At once I said: "I hope I'll still have the opportunity to see him regularly," and I reached out to stroke William behind the ears.

As our chaperon purred loudly between us Miss Barton-Woods murmured: "Call whenever you like." But then she added, steering the conversation back on course as if she feared the atmosphere were becoming too impregnated with confusing possibilities: "Are you sure you'll be allowed to work here? Supposing the Bishop thinks you could be more useful somewhere else in the diocese?"

I realised startled that this was a valid point. In my arrogance I had been so confident of getting my own way when I sought the episcopal permission to work in the village that it had never occurred to me that I should approach not only the Bishop but the Archdeacon with care. The Archdeacon in particular might be offended if an itinerant ex-monk invaded his territory and ignored him by dealing directly with his superior.

"I'm sure Dr. Ottershaw will understand that as I'm still adjusting to the world I can at present only manage part-time work in a rural parish," I said cautiously, "but the Archdeacon, who would inevitably know this part of the diocese better than the Bishop, might well feel I could be of more use elsewhere."

"Would it help if you met him?" said Miss Barton-Woods unexpectedly. "I can easily arrange it. His name's Neville Aysgarth and his wife happens to be a friend of mine—I'm godmother to her latest baby."

I said surprised: "Aysgarth married late to a young wife?" My fascination must have been very obvious but Miss Barton-Woods answered tranquilly: "No, he married in his twenties and he's still under forty."

I was even more surprised. "That's young to be an archdeacon! Is he a protégé of Dr. Ottershaw?"

"Not Dr. Ottershaw," said Miss Barton-Woods. "Dr. Jardine—our famous fire-breathing Bishop who had to retire in 1937 because of ill-health."

"Ah." At once I adjusted my mental image of Aysgarth. Since I had heard that Jardine and Ottershaw could hardly have been more dissimilar, I deduced that their taste in protégés was unlikely to coincide.

"I met the Aysgarths through my aunt," Miss Barton-Woods was saying. "The Archdeaconry's attached to the benefice of St. Martin's-in-Cripplegate so she's one of Aysgarth's flock."

"Is he a local man? It's a Yorkshire name."

"I think he was born in some town near Huddersfield, but he keeps very quiet about it. He's a self-made man—which may have been one of the reasons why Dr. Jardine favoured him. Dr. Jardine's a self-made man too, as you probably know."

I did in fact know all about Dr. Jardine, but it is not a priest's business to gossip about churchmen who are either famous or—as in Jardine's case—notorious, so although it would have been delightful to remain cosily *à deux* with Miss Barton-Woods, I terminated the conversation by standing up. At once Miss Barton-Woods exclaimed in alarm: "Have I been repulsively snobbish again?" but I said firmly: "It would be quite impossible for you to be repulsively anything," and excused myself from her presence for five minutes.

Retreating to my room I retrieved the box in which the monks of the London workshop had packed my cross, and swiftly rejoined her downstairs. "This is something I made before I left the Order," I said, "so it belonged to the monks, but Father Ingram today insisted that I should offer it to you as a gift for the chapel." And setting down the box I removed the lid to reveal the glowing oak within.

Miss Barton-Woods was overwhelmed. "Is it the same as—"

"Yes."

"It's beautiful." She lifted the cross and was surprised by its weight. "How very satisfying it must be to have the skill to make something so beautiful," she said. "Thank you, Mr. Darrow. Thank you very much." And still clasping the cross she smiled radiantly at me.

The desire was almost annihilating. How I succeeded in excusing myself from her presence in order to change for dinner I shall never know.

4

I SHALL refrain from describing my mental and physical reactions as my carnal urges, exacerbated by years of celibacy, ploughed remorselessly through every particle of my being. As Francis had pointed out, never do moral convictions seem so insubstantial as when a man is invaded by a powerful sexual desire. Suffice it to say that after a sleepless night I took a cold bath, rejected the possibility of eating breakfast and walked to the post office to enquire about accommodation in the village. By this time

I suspected that Miss Barton-Woods's visitor who talked like a gentleman and scrubbed floors like a skivvy was the talk of the parish, and my suspicions were confirmed when the postmistress, a stout, plain, eminently respectable married woman, did not refer me to the nearest guest-house but offered me her own spare room with all the satisfaction of someone bringing off a coup guaranteed to stun the neighbours.

The room was not large but it was clean, and as it faced the garden at the rear instead of the high street at the front I judged it would be tolerably quiet. I made arrangements which encompassed the provision of breakfast and an evening meal. Then I retired to the chapel to pray.

5

AS soon as I moved to my new lodgings that evening I missed my large, light, airy room at the Manor. I also missed not only the house itself but the grounds—the flowers, the lawns, the woods, the dell, the chapel, the chantry—and above all I missed Miss Barton-Woods. This moping was quite uncalled for since I had an open invitation to visit the Manor whenever I pleased, but nonetheless I regret to record that I gave way to the urge to behave like a lovesick swain and I moped. Trailing around the village after dinner I wound up loafing morbidly in the churchyard among the tombstones. A priest has no business speculating on how much longer he has to live; his duty is to get on with the task of serving God, not to sink himself in self-centred introspection. But that evening I contemplated the tombstones and reflected that as I was no longer a young man I might well drop dead before I had been to bed with Miss Barton-Woods. The thought was intolerable. A feverish urgency engulfed me. I did not like to enter the church when I was in the grip of thoughts so unbecoming to a priest, but I sat down on the stone bench in the porch and for the first time began to grapple ruthlessly with the future.

It did not take me long to confront the fact that I had to marry Miss Barton-Woods immediately and that "immediately" could by no remote stretch of the imagination be construed to mean "after six months in the world." That decision promptly brought me face to face with a most unpalatable fact: a man who is both unemployed and living on borrowed money is not in a position to marry. No consolation lay in the knowledge that Miss Barton-Woods had enough money for both of us. Even the idea that I might be "kept" by a rich woman made me shudder in horror, and besides, I was already haunted by the recurring fear that Miss Barton-Woods might decide I was a sponger and refuse to marry me.

Abruptly I tossed aside the notion that I should engage in unpaid part-time pastoral work as I waited for my call to unfold. I needed to be employed. I needed to be employed immediately. And I needed to be employed on my future wife's doorstep in the parish of Starrington Magna.

Rising to my feet I opened the ancient oak door and stepped into the church. For a long moment I stood gazing at the altar but unfortunately my thoughts were very far from spiritual. I was wondering where the parish stood in the financial structure of the diocese and how difficult it would be to dredge up enough money for a curacy.

It occurred to me that these were questions an archdeacon could answer, and sitting down in the nearest pew I began to plot my conquest of young Neville Aysgarth.

6

I MET Aysgarth a week later at a luncheon-party given by Miss Barton-Woods. I had expected to find a man of obvious ability, perhaps someone who would reflect the wit and worldliness of his benefactor Dr. Jardine, but when I first saw Aysgarth I could detect no remarkable qualities in him.

He was short, no more than five foot seven, and somewhat ill-proportioned, his shoulders too broad for the rest of his frame; it occurred to me that he needed to be half a stone heavier to create a more fetching effect. He had waving brown hair, a high, handsome forehead, blue eyes set deep, a Roman nose and a thin, straight, brutal mouth. It was an odd face, a face of conflict, a face which even I, experienced as I was at summing up people, found it difficult to judge with confidence. I had an impression of an iron will juxtaposed with a shy, sensitive, possibly even a deeply emotional nature, and these seemed explosive attributes for a priest. In fact the more clearly I sensed that he had the determination that is essential to achieve worldly success, the more acutely I wondered, as a director of souls, about the quality of his spiritual life. It occurred to me that the sensitive side of his nature—if indeed it existed—would need to be carefully nurtured to save it from being trampled underfoot by the other, less desirable features of his personality.

His wife, on the other hand, was clearly a much less complex character, a dark, pretty woman who preferred to talk of her home and children, as so many wives do, but who was also capable of discussing an eclectic collection of books with Miss Barton-Woods. Aysgarth was evidently adored. Her conversation was littered with sentences which began: "Neville thinks . . ." or "Neville feels . . ." or "Neville says . . . ," and her adoration made me take a more respectful second look at the Archdeacon who by achieving a happy marriage had succeeded where I had failed.

The other guests at the luncheon-party consisted of another young woman in her thirties, Mrs. Wetherall, who was the wife of Starrington Magna's absent vicar, and three people of my own generation, a couple called Maitland who owned the second-largest property in the parish, and Miss Barton-Woods's solicitor from Starbridge, a gentleman called Musgrave. The latter at first regarded me with a wariness which suggested he feared I might be a fortune-hunter, but after an exquisitely veiled cross-examination over the pre-luncheon sherry he decided, to our joint relief, that I was an acceptable acquaintance for his client.

The Maitlands too had regarded me with a certain bemusement when I first entered the drawing-room, but this startled response could no doubt be attributed to the fact that I had decided to wear not my clerical uniform but my new lounge suit. My vanity had of course preserved the memory of Ruth saying that the suit made me look like a film star, and I regret to record that I had now given in to the dubious desire to "make a splash," surprising the other guests who had probably expected a desiccated old man in a dog-collar, and dazzling (so I hoped) Miss Barton-Woods who had never before seen this secret sartorial weapon in my armoury. I did dimly remember how I had earlier hated the suit so much that I had longed for my monk's habit, but that eccentric behaviour now seemed part of a very remote past.

When the ladies withdrew at the close of the meal, Colonel Maitland was put in charge of the decanter but Aysgarth and I, declining both port and cigars, wandered away from the table towards the nearest open window. As Maitland and Musgrave began to debate how much longer the Luftwaffe could continue to bomb London every night, I said to the Archdeacon: "I think I find smoking the most difficult habit to tolerate now that I've left the cloister."

Aysgarth murmured a sympathetic response but I wondered if he himself smoked in private like my friend Charles Ashworth. The younger generation of churchmen seemed to have fewer scruples about "lighting up" once their clerical collars had been discarded than the priests of my age.

Opening the window wider I remarked idly: "What a pleasant parish this is! But since it's so extensive I'm surprised Mr. Wetherall was obliged to manage without a curate."

"It's the usual story," said Aysgarth with a shrug of his shoulders to indicate resignation at the passing of the old order. "Changing economic conditions have resulted in the vicar being barely able to keep himself, let alone a curate."

"But I understand this parish is in the Bishop's gift. Can't the endowment be improved by prising open the diocesan coffers without trying to tap the funds of the Church Commissioners or Queen Anne's Bounty?"

"I'm sure Dr. Ottershaw would feel that in war-time there were more urgent demands on the diocesan coffers."

"Quite. But"—I decided to lay my cards on the table—"it had occurred to me that I might contribute to the war effort on the Home Front by taking care of this parish while the vicar's in the Army. Of course I'd prefer to work on a purely voluntary basis but unfortunately I do need some form of stipend."

Aysgarth's expression immediately became so inscrutable that I felt uneasy. "I'm sure, sir," he said, "that Dr. Ottershaw could find work for you which was a great deal more commensurate with your distinguished career in the Order."

Impatience elbowed my uneasiness aside. "My dear Archdeacon, since Our Lord was content to wash the feet of his disciples without wondering whether or not it was commensurate with his career as a teacher, surely it would ill become even the most distinguished priest to turn up his nose at serving God in a country parish?"

"I take your point, sir," said Aysgarth politely, refusing to be intimidated, "but I put it to you that we nonetheless have a duty to serve God to the best of our ability, not to squander that ability in work which is unsuited to us."

I found myself becoming increasingly annoyed. "You think I'm unsuited to work in a country parish?"

"That's not for me to judge. I'm only fit to judge whether in view of the war-time shortage of clergymen it's essential for this parish to have a parson, and in my opinion—"

"Supposing I were to tell you that I'd been led to this place by God? Would you continue to close your mind to the possibility that I might have been called to serve here?"

I expected Aysgarth to capitulate at this point. It is hardly easy for a young archdeacon to stand his ground when a distinguished ex-abbot starts talking forcefully about God, but Aysgarth's obstinate mouth only hardened and I felt his will confronting my psyche with the strength of a steel wall.

"If you feel called to serve in this parish, sir," he said in a voice devoid of emotion, "then of course you must discuss your position with Dr. Ottershaw. But I can't help thinking that if you really want to do some worthwhile war work, you'll acknowledge that the Home Front extends beyond the boundaries of Miss Barton-Woods's estate."

So he had noticed Miss Barton-Woods's expression when she had seen me in my new lounge suit. Cursing the vanity which had betrayed me I simultaneously marvelled at his nerve in administering the rebuke. I had been a Fordite abbot, the equal in rank (so it was usually held) of a bishop. Within the Church there was even a school of thought which held that an abbot was superior to a bishop. Yet here was this young archdeacon not only lecturing me about war work but even daring to imply that my humble aspiration to be a country curate might be rooted in an aspiration that had nothing to do with humility at all! In my rage I almost felt that his perspicacity was more intolerable than his insolence. I was seething.

"May I suggest," I said in my coldest voice, "that you think a little less about the worldly power you wield as an archdeacon and a little more about the spiritual needs of the untended souls in your Archdeaconry?"

"And may I suggest," said Aysgarth instantly, "that you think a little less of your own needs and a little more about the needs of our war-time Church?"

In the deep silence which followed I suddenly realised I had not only involved myself in a most unedifying skirmish but had made a potentially dangerous enemy. Shame mingled with consternation and bred in-credulity as I tried to work out how I could have allowed my pride to lead me so far astray, but I decided that a full analysis of the disaster could wait. My immediate task was to patch up the damage.

"This conversation does neither of us any credit," I said tersely, "and I must apologise for raising such an obviously difficult subject. It was hardly my intention to sabotage what I'd hoped would be a cordial relationship."

"I've certainly no wish for our relationship to be other than cordial," said Aysgarth with a primness which I found quite repulsive, "but I'm not one of your monks, Mr. Darrow, and you shouldn't expect me to humour you with unquestioning obedience."

I felt not only as if he had spat on my olive branch but as if he had had the impertinence to flagellate me with it. Before I could stop myself I said: "I assure you, Archdeacon, that if you'd been one of my monks this conversation would have taken a very much more Christian course." And turning my back on him I rejoined Musgrave and Maitland at the dining-table.

7

"*WHAT* on earth was going on between you and Aysgarth?" said Miss Barton-Woods when I was at last alone with her in the drawing-room. "Mr. Musgrave told me the clerical fur was flying *sotto voce* by the window and brotherly love appeared to be conspicuous by its absence!"

I achieved a casual laugh. "I'm afraid Aysgarth and I made a very clumsy attempt to explore each other's personalities," I said, "but no doubt we'll become more adroit in time. I must say, I'm surprised he didn't volunteer to be an Army chaplain. He's obviously the sort of priest who enjoys a fight."

"Isn't the age limit between twenty-eight and thirty-eight? I think he must be a fraction too old. Philip Wetherall's forty, but he had a military uncle who pulled strings for him as soon as war was declared."

"The Church has the final word in recommending a man as suitable." I thought of Charles Ashworth who was now also forty; he had had to slip around the official age limit, but Charles, a former protégé of Archbishop Lang, had friends in high places.

"In that case I suppose Dr. Ottershaw decided that Wetherall could be spared and Aysgarth couldn't," Miss Barton-Woods was speculating. "After all, an archdeacon's more important than a country vicar . . . I say, I'm awfully sorry if you found Aysgarth heavy going! I've heard he's occasionally a bit stiff with men—some form of social insecurity, perhaps—but I assure you he can be charming, especially with women."

"Ah!" I said, wondering if I were now detecting a resemblance between Aysgarth and his benefactor Dr. Jardine other than a breathtaking capacity for insolence.

"Of course he's always the soul of propriety," said Miss Barton-Woods hastily. "He's devoted to his wife. But sometimes I suspect that beneath that rather prim exterior there lurks a secret hankering for wine, women and song. He adored the dinner-parties at the palace when Dr. Jardine was Bishop—and Dr. Jardine, of course, was famous for his titled ladyfriends and his vintage port."

"At the risk of sounding insufferably priggish I feel bound to say that an interest in titled ladies and vintage port is best left to laymen."

Miss Barton-Woods laughed. "You weren't one of Dr. Jardine's admirers?"

"I'm afraid not."

"Aysgarth hero-worships him, although I don't think they see much of each other now that Jardine's retired to Oxford. They think alike on clerical matters—Aysgarth always supported Jardine against the Archbishop of Canterbury and the High Church party."

"Yes, I sensed his antipathy to Anglo-Catholicism when he persistently refused to address me as 'Father,' referred to priests as 'parsons,' and displayed an open contempt for monks."

"Heavens, how boorish!" exclaimed Miss Barton-Woods, and in her annoyance she turned a most becoming shade of pink. "I am sorry!"

"It's hardly your fault that internecine strife is common between the different wings of the Church!" I retorted, making her laugh again, and the conversation turned to other matters but the memory of my clash with Aysgarth continued to make me feel uncomfortable. It was not the kind of prelude I wanted to my new career in the diocese of Starbridge.

8

MISS Barton-Woods had evidently been intrigued by the fact that Aysgarth and I represented different wings of the Church, for when we next met she said tentatively: "I must admit I find it hard to connect you with Anglo-Catholicism—I'd have thought you'd favour a more austere approach, just as Aysgarth does."

"I'm austere in my private worship, but public worship is quite a different matter." I hesitated, not wanting to bore her with a religious polemic, but when I saw she was genuinely interested I said: "A rich liturgical tradition can play a vital part in providing symbols for truths which can't easily be expressed. In my opinion ritual can make complex truths more accessible—and particularly to people who lack the education to receive truth in the form of complex word structures. Hence the effectiveness of the Anglo-Catholic slum-priests."

"But have you always been an Anglo-Catholic?"

"No." I thought of my father, an agnostic who could only tolerate Sunday worship when it came in the form of an intelligent sermon and the minimum of ritual. Then I remembered my mother, a deeply religious and spiritually gifted woman who had had little interest in organised religion. "My parents went to church as a concession to middle-class respectability," I said, "but they always attended Matins, never Communion. As a child I found church-going very boring. I did become more interested in worship when I was introduced to Holy Communion at the time of my confirmation, but the ethos of my public school was Protestant Evangelical and I just couldn't connect this expression of religion with my private *gnosis,* the knowledge which I sensed in every fibre of my being but which I couldn't express verbally. It was only when I went up to Cambridge, where there was a variety of churches to choose from, that I discovered Anglo-Catholicism and saw at last how my private *gnosis* could achieve a full, meaningful public expression."

"Were the Fordites in Cambridgeshire then?"

"They'd just opened the Grantchester house. I used to visit them regularly, and soon I was enrapt by the whole Anglo-Catholic ethos. My hero was Charles Gore—"

"Bishop Gore? He was very important and famous, wasn't he?"

"He was one of the greatest religious leaders of the Church in this century. It was Gore who adapted the Anglo-Catholicism of the Oxford Movement to a more modern era when he enabled it to meet and master biblical criticism, Gore who encouraged young Anglo-Catholic priests to work among the poor, Gore who founded a brotherhood of celibate priests, Gore who seemed, when I was a young man, to have his finger on the pulse of an up-to-date, dynamic version of Christianity, Gore who laid the foundations of the twentieth-century Anglo-Catholic tide which is sweeping through the Church of England—" I had run out of breath. I broke off, recovered myself and laughed. "But I must stop at once! What a sermon! Forgive me, I'm afraid preaching is a terrible clerical vice."

"I like good preaching," said Miss Barton-Woods generously, "and I've no objection to hearing more about Anglo-Catholicism."

"But you still doubt that I could convert you!"

"On the contrary, I'm sure you could convert me to anything if you put your mind to it!" she said amused, and I knew I should leave at once before I lost all control and started converting us both to the pleasures of fornication.

It was on the next morning that I received my letter from the Bishop of Starbridge. I had written to him directly after the luncheon-party. I can write very clever letters when I choose and this letter had been exceptionally clever. I had not mentioned Aysgarth.

In his reply Dr. Ottershaw declared how delighted he was to hear from me and how he quite understood why I had not presented my compliments to him earlier; naturally I had needed time to adjust to the world after my years in the cloister, and how very wise I was to stay in such a quiet, beautiful spot while I was engaged in laying the foundations of my new life. However he would deem it a great honour if I would "dine and sleep" at the episcopal palace as soon as I felt prepared to venture forth from my rural retreat. "My wife and I are simple people," concluded the Bishop modestly, "so you need not fear being inundated by a tidal wave of worldliness as soon as you cross our threshold. Moreover war-time austerities have forced us to close both wings of the palace and manage with only a few servants, so lavish hospitality, I fear, is very much a thing of the past. Nevertheless I trust we can offer you a quiet, comfortable and possibly not unstimulating evening should you wish to visit us."

On receipt of this letter I obtained Miss Barton-Woods's permission to use her telephone and rang the Bishop up. Dr. Ottershaw was delighted. He sounded exactly like the benevolent holy man which all prelates should be but so few are. I guessed him to be seventy, silver-haired and stout, and when I met him a couple of days later at his episcopal palace I found my guess had not been inaccurate.

I dined at Starbridge on Saturday night. On Sunday I attended the morning services in the Cathedral, but by tea-time I had returned to Starrington Magna and at five o'clock I was walking up the Manor's drive to call on Miss Barton-Woods.

9

I FOUND her reclining on the drawing-room sofa as she browsed through the unread corners of the Sunday newspapers. Her long legs, clad in the sheerest of silk stockings, were coiled in a manner that displayed her slim ankles to perfection. I belong to a generation which was brought up to regard the occasional flash of a feminine ankle as erotic, and at that moment I found the sight of those two elegant ankles, so generously displayed, almost overpoweringly alluring. She had discarded her shoes in order to put her feet up, and now for the first time I could feast my eyes on her toes which sloped from the inner to the outer edges of her feet with remarkable symmetry. She was wearing a dark blue afternoon frock with a severe cut that emphasised the generous lines of her bosom, flattered her waist and offered tantalisingly veiled vistas of her hips. Her dark hair again exuded its aromatic newly washed aura of purity, and her skin, radiating that quality which the florid poets call "the bloom of youth," was worthy of a Shakespearean sonnet. Indeed so banal did any speech not written in blank verse seem at that moment that I had great difficulty in making my opening remark. It was: "I hope I'm not interrupting."

"Of course not!" She tossed *The News of the World* casually onto the floor. Miss Barton-Woods ordered all the papers on Sunday. I thought it was magnificently extravagant of her and showed a broad charitable interest in human nature, even the human nature reported so pruriently in the paper she had just discarded. My eye caught the headline: RUNAWAY VICAR: NEW SCANDAL: CHAMBERMAID TELLS ALL.

William was purring around my ankles and I stooped to pick him up. He was not a handsome cat but he had that subtle air of distinction which intelligence always confers.

"I'm glad to report," I said in response to her eager inquiry, "that Dr. Ottershaw was really most obliging. He saw no difficulty about opening the diocesan coffers, and suggested that I begin work in mid-October as soon as the inevitable bureaucratic details have been sorted out."

Miss Barton-Woods's pleasure was delectable to behold. "Wonder-

ful!" she exclaimed. "So you'll be running the parish until Philip Wetherall comes home from the war!"

"Precisely. Miss Barton-Woods"—I set down William as carefully as
if he were made of bone-china—"now that I'm no longer a penniless
ex-monk but a priest with a respectable stipend, I hope you won't think
it too great an impertinence if I tell you how very much I want you to
be my wife. Will you marry me?"

She never hesitated. She said simply: "I thought you'd never ask!" and
the next moment we were in each other's arms.

XII

"The psychical man, for St. Paul, is the self of our normal experience. . . . He may rise to the spiritual man, or he may sink to the carnal man, or, as most of us do, he may fluctuate uneasily between the two."

W. R. INGE
MYSTICISM IN RELIGION

I

THERE followed an interlude characterised by fragmented conversation, unfettered exuberance and a succession of embraces so stimulating that I felt no more than thirty-five. My fiancée certainly could have passed for eighteen, but eventually proved sophisticated enough to suggest we might cool our ardour with champagne.

" . . . Oh, and Mr. Darrow and I are getting married, Portman," said Anne as an afterthought after giving the order.

The ancient butler, who had been padding away towards the door, stopped dead, revolved slowly to face us and beamed from ear to ear. "That's very pleasing news, I'm sure, madam," he said with verve. "May I offer you my congratulations, sir, and express the wish that you and Miss Barton-Woods will be very happy?"

"Thank you, Portman." My secret uneasiness with servants meant that I was relieved as well as touched by his sincerity.

When Anne and I eventually drank to the future I was delighted to be reminded that champagne, a beverage which I have rarely encountered during the course of my ministry, tastes very much more intriguing than dry sherry.

"When can we get married?" I said, emboldened by my first sip. "I hope you'll agree that the only possible answer to that question is 'soon.' "

"As soon as possible," said Anne, having taken three gulps in rapid succession. With a shudder she added: "I must tell you everything now.

His name was Hugo. We had a long engagement. A huge wedding had been planned at the village church."

"In that case I'll get a special license and we can be married at the end of the month. I suggest a plain ceremony at the chapel in front of a handful of close friends."

Suddenly she began to weep. "I was putting on my wedding dress when the letter arrived. It was vile—everything was vile—a cruel, horrible nightmare—"

As I took her in my arms I said: "There's no need to say any more."

"Oh, but there is!" As she raised her tear-stained face to mine I saw the painful honesty in her eyes. "There's one thing I simply must tell you before we go any further. He—I—" But the words refused to come. Breaking down she clung to me again and I waited, stroking her hair until she was calmer. Then I said: "Since he was a fortune-hunter I've no doubt he did everything possible beforehand to get you into his power and secure his future. So of course he would have done his best to break down a door which should never have been opened."

"So you guessed." But she was no longer upset; she was only relieved that I could accept that sad truth without expressing either censure or distaste. "Oh, if only I could describe how *polluted* I felt afterwards when I realised how little I meant to him—"

"Someone you loved breached your trust and treated you with contempt. Naturally you felt polluted—the very centre of your psyche had been laid waste. But from his point of view, what went wrong? Why didn't he go through with it?"

"With my consent he had a meeting with my solicitors before the wedding in order to discuss money, and Mr. Musgrave told him that much of my capital's tied up in trust. I hadn't mentioned that; I hadn't thought it mattered. Hugo said he had a large private income of his own . . . But he hadn't. He didn't mention money in the letter he wrote me, of course—it was Mr. Musgrave who told me later how shattered Hugo had been at the meeting. The letter just said—" But again she was unable to go on.

"If he had the kind of maimed, stunted psyche I suspect he had," I said, "he would have made some disparaging remark about the way you demonstrated your love for him, and declared that you could never have made him happy—and of course he would have been right; that kind of deformed psyche is always impossible to please and no woman would ever have satisfied him. Clearly it was he, not you, who failed in the intimate relationship, but by slandering you in such a wicked way he was able to hide from his own inadequacies and run off like a coward to leave you bearing the burden of his failure." And as she stared, astounded by this radical reinterpretation of her past, I added in my most authoritative voice: "It's plain he had a hatred of women and you should on no account think ill of yourself just because an emotional cripple made a cruel remark designed to boost his self-esteem."

Her gratitude was so overwhelming that it was some time before she could speak, but at last she whispered obscurely: "Do you mind?"

"I mind that you suffered. I mind that any man could treat a woman so badly. But I don't mind about you not being a virgin. Love's too important to mar with quibbles about physical technicalities, and as for the moral aspect of the tragedy your repentance is so obviously genuine that no priest would hesitate to grant you absolution."

She said: "I love you so much I can hardly bear it," and struggled again with her tears.

"Bear it," I said, "and have another glass of champagne."

That made her smile, and we sipped in companionable silence until I had summoned the courage to say: "There's a lot I too must tell you about the past."

"I hope I shan't feel as intimidated by your first wife as Mrs. de Winter felt by Rebecca."

An interval followed while the reference to Miss Du Maurier's novel had to be explained to the ignorant ex-monk, but at last I was sufficiently enlightened to exclaim: "What a distressing example of marital misunderstanding! Why couldn't he have told the new wife straight away that he'd been so unhappy?"

"I suppose it was guilt—and the fear that she'd be horrified by what he'd done."

"Ah." I paused before saying sternly: "You're on no account to visualise Betty as a goddess on a pedestal!" and after another pause I added: "Of course I'll tell you all about my marriage one day."

To my great relief Anne said: "I'm more interested in Ruth than in Betty—after all, Ruth's the one I'll eventually have to meet. Has she been married long? I suppose if you've got no grandchildren that must mean—"

"I do have grandchildren. Ruth has a son called Colin and a daughter called Janet."

The inevitable question followed: "How old are they?"

"Growing up fast." For several agonising seconds I wrestled with pride, vanity, shame and sheer fright before I forced myself to add: "Ruth herself is thirty-six now."

"Thirty-six?" exclaimed Anne amazed.

"Thirty-six." I drained my glass of champagne. "I'm afraid—very much afraid—that I'm probably a little older than you suspected. I married at twenty-three. Ruth was born a year later. So as far as my age is concerned . . . well, it seems quite fantastic—indeed sometimes—well, fairly often—I can hardly believe it, but in actual fact—well, the truth is—"

"You're sixty. How distinguished! I wouldn't have you a day younger. More champagne?"

Now it was my turn to be overcome with gratitude. Speechless with relief I turned my back on old age and once more pulled her into my arms.

2

TWENTY-FOUR hours later I was still wreathed in euphoria but I felt sufficiently composed to communicate with those concerned for my welfare. Deciding to tackle Francis first I wrote:

You will be aghast to learn that I have proposed to Miss Barton-Woods and we are to be married on October the first. You will also be startled, if not aghast, to learn that I've decided to work here full-time as a curate, and I'm glad to report that when I volunteered my services to the Bishop of Star-bridge he couldn't have been more willing to produce a stipend. Let me hasten to add that I'm sure I haven't been called back into the world solely to be a country priest; my true call will no doubt unfold in due course, but while I wait it seems better that I should be fully occupied.

Don't be too cross with me, my dear Francis, because knowing myself as I do I'm convinced that an early marriage is the best safeguard against the error to which I'm particularly prone. Moreover since I have no doubt now that you were right and that I'm being called not only to marry but to marry this particular woman, I see no point in prolonging my celibacy for a day longer than necessary.

Allowing myself to relax after the ordeal of informing my spiritual director that I proposed to toss his advice to the winds, I then penned a request to Charles Ashworth. Charles was now stationed with his regiment less than forty miles away on Starbury Plain, and I hoped that he might obtain leave not only to attend my wedding but to conduct it. Anne did not care for the retired canon who had been taking the essential services since the vicar's departure, and having heard me talk of Charles she was anxious to meet him. There were other priests whom I might have asked to conduct the ceremony, but Charles had a special place in my affections; I often felt that the crisis which I had helped him surmount in 1937 had indissolubly linked us together. He had been the first priest who had sought my help after my arrival in Grantchester, and the absorbing complexity of his case had helped relieve the acute stress which had burdened me as I had struggled to bring my lax community to order.

Having written a long, affectionate letter to Charles with ease, I was then confronted with the ordeal of breaking the news to my children. My heart was already sinking at the prospect of either of them attending the wedding; I found it all too easy to imagine a nightmare in which Martin arrived drunk while Ruth staged some emotional scene, and I knew I wanted no reminders of my first marriage as I embarked on my second. Could any paternal attitude have been more unworthy of a Christian priest? I thought not, and in a paroxysm of guilt I began the required letter to my daughter. Eventually I produced a communication which read:

My dearest Ruth:
You will be greatly surprised to hear that I am to be married to someone I met at Allington Court. Her name is Anne Barton-Woods. The wedding will be on October the first in the family chapel of the manor house where she lives here at Starrington Magna, and I do hope that you, Roger and the children will be able to attend. I have just been appointed curate of this parish while the vicar's absent in the Army, so my new life is rapidly taking shape. As for Miss Barton-Woods, she is a woman of your own generation, a fact which encourages me to hope that in due course you will become friends. Meanwhile I send you my love and blessing, and in assuring you that you're always in my prayers I remain your devoted father,

J.D.

I sent a copy of this letter, amended where appropriate, to Martin and tried to suppress the hope that neither he nor Ruth would find the invitation irresistible.

The first response to all this arduous letter-writing came in the form of a wire which read: DELIGHTED BY YOUR NEWS FLATTERED BY YOUR REQUEST HONOURED TO ACCEPT EAGER TO SEE YOU MANY CONGRATULATIONS CHARLES.

In contrast to this happy communication Ruth wrote:

Darling Daddy,
I have just received your rather worrying letter. Of course I wish you every happiness but I can't help wondering if you're being wise in rushing into marriage with a girl half your age whom you've only known for a few weeks. It's none of my business and I wouldn't dream of criticising you, but it does all seem a little undignified, and I do feel it's my duty as your daughter to point out that there are plenty of people less loyal to you than I am who

will make some very snide remarks behind your back. In fact speaking as one who loves you, I feel bound to say that in my opinion a man of your age should approach marriage with the greatest caution—if indeed he should approach it at all.

Yours in deepest love and concern,
RUTH.

P.S. Thank you for the invitation to the wedding, but in the circumstances I think it would be less awkward for Miss Barton-Woods if we didn't accept. I'm sure she wouldn't want to be reminded on her wedding day that she's marrying a grandparent who's old enough to be her father.

I wondered if Martin would write a letter that was equally unspeakable, but to my relief he failed to reply.

However Francis was hardly the man to abandon me to my fate without comment. He took longer to respond than Ruth, but I knew the delay arose because he had been praying and meditating on the problems I had posed him. Finally he wrote:

My dear Jon:
Did I really expect you to wait until you had been in the world for six months? Probably not. But I felt I had to set you a goal, even if it proved to be a goal which you chose to repudiate. You would not have respected me, I think, if I had murmured indulgently: "Yes, yes—marry the lady tomorrow!" and you would not respect me now if I were to respond to your news by writing: "Bless you, my friend—run off and live happily ever after!" But before I start making you uncomfortable, let me congratulate you on abandoning your earlier conviction that you should live the rest of your life as a celibate. I myself have always been convinced that despite your sad past you should live in the world as a married man, and therefore I'm delighted that you've coaxed an apparently sympathetic, compatible woman to promise to accompany you to the altar.

My main anxiety—and this is where I start to make you uncomfortable—is not that you're rushing to the altar in such haste. I think you're being precipitate, certainly, but after all you're a man of considerable experience and you should be granted at least some liberty to act with an incisiveness which in a young man would deserve the description "hot-headed folly." No, my main anxiety is that you may be busy glossing over all the difficulties which inevitably surround your situation. I'm just an ignorant old bachelor, of course, but I seem to remember hearing somewhere that a honeymoon can be a time of profound disillusionment if either partner has failed to be as honest as the rules of the game require.

Let me complete your discomfort by asking you a series of questions: (1) Have you talked frankly to your fiancée about why your marriage went so wrong that you felt you could never marry again? (2) Have you explained why the subject of parenthood is peculiarly painful to you? (3) Have you even discussed the subject of parenthood? (4) Have you made any attempt to describe Ruth and Martin in terms which bear at least a passing resemblance to reality? (5) Have you talked to your fiancée in detail about your spiritual needs so that she has a true idea of the amount of time you devote daily to prayer, meditation and devotional reading? (6) Have you warned her that in order to satisfy your spiritual needs you're obliged to spend much time being what the world deems unsociable? (7) Have you discussed the contribution she might make to your work in the parish? (8) Will she in fact be able to give you the support you need when she's busy running her estate? (9) How are you going to resolve the conflict arising from the fact that you belong to different wings of the Church of England? (10) Have you had a frank conversation with her about money? (11) Have you had a conversation with her, frank or otherwise, about marital intimacy, a matter which could create grave difficulties if the emotional damage proves hard to heal? (12) Have you in truth paused long enough to imagine what this marriage will really be like, or are you at present only capable of imagining how charming Miss Barton-Woods will look in her nightgown? (13)—

But no. Twelve awkward questions are quite enough, and meanwhile I trust I've made my point: when one's in love one's instinct is to present oneself in the best possible light, but I can't counsel you too strongly to present yourself "warts and all" to Miss Barton-Woods at the earliest opportunity. But perhaps you've already done so. In which case I humbly beg your pardon and offer you my sincere congratulations.

There's a great deal I could say to you about your sinister acquisition of the curacy, but I'd prefer to explore the spiritual dimensions of this when we meet—and I trust we can meet soon. You will, of course, be as keenly aware as I am that there's much you need to discuss before the wedding, so I beg you to write by return to suggest a date for your visit. Meanwhile . . .

And he concluded with the formal reference to prayers and blessings before signing himself my devoted friend and brother in Christ.

I could not help thinking that this letter was a masterly example of how to conceal rampant disapproval beneath a diplomatic expression of trenchant common sense. Indeed it took me some hours to rouse myself from my admiration but at last I composed a reply which read:

My dear Francis:
As usual you've given me excellent advice and I must thank you for it. I must also thank you for your support of my decision to marry. In the circumstances I regard this as very generous.

I find your reference to the curacy somewhat strange. I hardly think the spiritual dimensions of its acquisition are so pregnant with menace that I need to be hauled immediately to London! In fact it's extremely difficult for me to get away at present as there's so much to do before the wedding, and indeed I may be obliged to postpone my next visit to you until after the honeymoon. However please don't think I intend to approach my wedding in a murky spiritual state; Starwater Abbey's no more than fifteen miles from here, and I shall see Cyril soon to make my confession.

May I thank you again for your letter and repeat how much I value your advice.

I did not expect a swift reply, but Francis, meticulous as ever in his pastoral care, wrote back promptly:

My dear Jon:
So be it! But may I leave you with two more questions to consider during your very limited spare time? (1) What was your exact motive for seeking this curacy, and (2) precisely how did you obtain it? The second question is the interesting one, of course; I fear the answer to the first is painfully obvious. As a churchman experienced in financial matters I can only regard your success in coaxing the Bishop to produce a stipend out of thin air as miraculous—in fact I'd have been less surprised if you'd told me that he'd produced six white rabbits out of his lawn-sleeves! Of course we all know that dear old Ottershaw, like our own late Abbot James, finds it almost impossible to say no to anyone, but nevertheless I can't help thinking that this latest triumph of yours puts even stopping watches in the shade. My dear Jon, beware of those "glamorous powers"! Once you start twisting bishops around your little finger you stand at the top of a very slippery slope indeed, so step back from the brink, I beg of you, by reminding yourself of the truth no priest can afford to forget: we're here to serve God, not ourselves.

I sat thinking about this letter for a long time. Then I wrote to Abbot Cyril to suggest a date when I could visit Starwater to make my confession.

3

"I'M rather worried about all these Anglo-Catholic habits of yours," confessed Anne when I told her of my decision to visit Starwater, and in a rush she added: "Are you secretly cross because I don't want to go to confession too?"

"Good heavens, no! Anyway, you've made your confession—to me. And even if you hadn't you have a perfect right, as a member of the Church of England, to abstain from confession to a priest."

"Yes, but since you're always doing it—"

"My case is quite different from yours. I've spent many years living in an environment where a weekly confession was built into the structure of my spiritual life, and in returning to the world I'm certain to have problems which could lead to spiritual debility unless they're regularly aired with someone skilled in giving advice."

I paused. We were in the chapel some hours after I had received Francis's second letter. I had been working on the new altar-table, and Anne, arriving home from the estate office, had walked through the grounds to exchange news with me before I returned to the village for my evening meal. We were now sitting hand in hand in the front pew.

"Anne, talking of confessions—" I stopped, took a deep breath and began again. "Talking of confessions I really must tell you all about Betty and my children," I said with commendable determination, but then found to my horror that I was unable to continue. This ordeal was much worse than merely confessing my age, and as Anne waited, the model of patience and tact, I realised that part of my difficulty lay in the fact that I could not discuss Betty frankly without referring to the one subject on which Anne was so painfully sensitive; it would hardly be good for either her morale or my honeymoon prospects if I were now to reveal that her predecessor's forte had been sexual intercourse.

In panic I scraped together a few pale platitudes. "It was a typical romance of youth," I said. "I was attracted by her looks but in fact we were utterly mismatched and made each other very miserable. I did my best to be a good husband"—the terrible half-truths ran on and on—"but life was difficult. One of the reasons why it was difficult was because"—I reached for the whole truth but knew it was going to slither through my hands; I was too afraid she might think me an Anglo-Catholic fanatic—"was because I need a certain amount of time alone for prayer and meditation and devotional reading, and Betty could neither understand nor accept that." I hesitated, knowing I should specify the amount of time I needed, but the next moment my voice was saying: "However the situation was eased when I felt called to serve at sea." I told myself I really could not let the lie about a call pass. But I did. I was too frightened of being judged a deserting husband who had walked out on his loving wife.

"Once I was no longer at home all the time we got on much better," said my voice with despicable glibness. "It was a case of 'absence makes the heart grow fonder.' However nothing could change the fact that the marriage produced tensions which interfered with my spiritual life, and when Betty died I knew I could serve God best as an unmarried man. I wanted to be a monk straight away but of course I had to stay in the world to provide for my children." Too late I corrected myself by saying:

"To care for my children." Sweat prickled the nape of my neck. I dared not look at her. "However when they were grown up and going their own way in the world—" I told myself I really could not gloss over my difficult years as a widower. But I did. I was terrified that she might recoil when she heard how I had not only failed to live as a priest should but had even jilted the woman who loved me. "When my children no longer needed me, I joined the Fordites. For years I remained convinced that I should be celibate, but recently when I was called to leave the Order I realised that my marital unhappiness had arisen not because I was unsuited to marriage but because I'd married the wrong woman when I was too young to know better."

I told myself I could go no further, but in my imagination Father Darcy was looking at me with contempt and at last my pride came to my rescue. I really could not allow myself to be such a coward. Making a mighty effort I said: "That's not much of a confession. The truth's far darker than that. I was haunted by guilt that I couldn't love Betty as she loved me and I conceived of becoming a monk as a form of atonement. Later I did fall in love but I rejected the woman by entering the Order. I've done appalling things, Anne. I hurt my wife. I hurt my"—balking at the word "mistress," I grabbed a term which in my youth had been capable of an innocent meaning—"my lover. And of course I hurt my—" But at that point cowardice reclaimed me. My courage was exhausted and I could not utter the word "children."

In the silence which followed, Anne's fingers intertwined comfortingly with mine and I felt so grateful for her silent sympathy that a few shreds of my courage rose phoenix-like from the ashes. Remembering Francis's letter I resolved to embark on a realistic description of Ruth and Martin.

"Of course my difficulties have affected my children," I said in a resolute voice, the voice of a man determined to tell the truth, the whole truth and nothing but the truth, "and they've been through certain awkward times. But I couldn't wish for a more devoted son and daughter and I really am tremendously proud of them. I know Ruth's being silly about the wedding, but she's only acting out of a misguided concern for my welfare. And I know Martin should have replied to my letter by now, but I can only conclude that for some reason he hasn't received it. Martin always replies to my letters—and replies very amusingly too, I might add. He's got an excellent sense of humour, and women always seem to find him very attractive and charming."

I stopped speaking, and gradually as the silence lengthened I became aware that I was staring at Anne's engagement ring, a Victorian circle of gold set with garnets, which I had bought at a small jeweller's shop in Starbridge. The ring was so pretty that I had not felt ashamed that it was cheap, and at the time of the purchase I had thought the garnets symbolised the fire of love. Now I was aware only that they were the colour of blood. I felt as if I were suffering some profound haemorrhage.

"Darling!" said Anne warmly, and suddenly the garnets flashed past my eyes as she slipped her arms around my neck. "How lucky your children are to have a father who obviously cares so much for them!"

Shame nearly annihilated me. "Anne, I really can't let you believe . . . you really must understand that I . . . I mean, I can't possibly let this conversation end without stressing my terrible faults and weaknesses—"

"Silly man, I don't expect you to be a saint!"

"But I have such crippling peculiarities—"

"My dear Jon, if I'd wanted to marry the dead-norm of English manhood, would I have looked twice at anyone who'd just spent seventeen years being a monk?"

"But maybe you'd be a great deal happier with the dead-norm of English manhood—"

"Absolutely not! It was a man claiming to be the dead-norm of English manhood who jilted me! Now stop agonising about yourself in this morbid fashion and come up to the house for a drink before you sail back to your doting postmistress—I think you need a very stiff sherry to set you back on the rails of optimism . . . "

4

THAT night I reflected for a long time on this harrowing conversation with Anne, but eventually I told myself it was neither possible nor desirable to attain an absolute honesty in a single interview. There was too much emotional constraint on my side and too much emotional vulnerability on hers. To subject her to a single prolonged and inevitably turgid confession of my failures would only upset her, and it seemed to me that I had a moral duty not to strain her love by wallowing self-indulgently in guilt. "Stop agonising about yourself in this morbid fashion," she had said, and I was neither so stupid nor so insensitive that I could not detect her antipathy. Women, I knew, did not like self-indulgent wallowing. It filled them with impatience and contempt.

"Thank God your father's not the complaining sort," said my mother in my memory. "I can't abide men who moan and groan."

"You won't believe this," said my father to me lightly, years after her death, "but because I was so much older than your mother I was always haunted by the dread that she might find me an elderly bore. Silly of me, wasn't it? Of course she was as devoted to me as I was to her, I can see that now, but I always guarded my tongue to ensure we never exchanged a cross word—with the result that despite the differences in our age and rank we were able to live happily ever after, as of course you remember."

I shuddered suddenly, then cast the memory aside, but that night I dreamt that William the tabby-cat had disappeared, abandoning those who loved him to a hell of loneliness and desolation, and my mother was saying severely: "You've no one to blame but yourself. You shouldn't have moaned and groaned about your past like that," while my father said urgently: "Guard your tongue. Never exchange a cross word. Never complain."

I awoke sweating in the dark.

After a long while I repeated to myself that I would, of course, tell Anne everything; it was unthinkable that I should even consider not telling her everything; but I would not tell her everything just yet. The revelations had to be made little by little at carefully judged intervals, and meanwhile a long, healing silence seemed called for.

Drifting back into sleep I found to my relief that William was purring peacefully in my arms.

5

THE next morning I forced myself to reread Francis's letter in order to confirm that I had addressed myself to all of the many problems he had listed.

I had dealt with question (1), my unhappiness with Betty. The subject of parenthood, which had occupied questions (2), (3) and (4), would have to wait. I examined question (5). Had I talked to my fiancée in detail about my spiritual needs? No, but I had made it plain that I required time to satisfy them and Anne had appeared to accept this without complaint; after all, unlike Betty she had her work to occupy her and would not expect my undivided attention twenty-four hours a day. Had I warned her that my spiritual needs often made me unsociable? No, but that was of no consequence since Anne was hardly a social butterfly, cramming her calendar with frivolous engagements. Had we discussed the contribution she might make to my work in the parish? No, but I had already decided that the nature of her contribution should be given time to evolve; I had no wish to burden her immediately with parish matters when her war work was so important. Nevertheless, in answer to question (8), I felt confident that she would eventually support me to the best of her ability, just as a good wife should.

How was I going to resolve the conflict arising from the fact that we belonged to different wings of the Church? There was no conflict. She was willing to learn about Anglo-Catholicism and eventually I would educate her to share my point of view.

Had I had a frank conversation with her about money? No, but what was there to say? She would manage her money and I would manage mine and naturally I would not dream of interfering in her financial affairs. Had I had a conversation with her about intimacy? Yes, and further conversation would at this stage be inappropriate. Any sexual problems could be sorted out on the honeymoon. Had I paused long enough to imagine what this marriage would really be like or was I at present only capable of imagining how charming Anne would look in her nightgown? How impertinent! But Francis had merely been trying to needle me into confronting the difficulties, and now that I had indeed confronted them this final question did not require a serious answer.

Deciding that I had made a tolerable, if not entirely perfect, response to my spiritual director's interrogation, I happily began to count the hours which separated me from my first glimpse of Anne's nightgown.

6

ON the afternoon before the wedding all four Ashworths arrived, accompanied by the children's nanny. Realising how much I wanted to see Charles Anne had insisted that they be invited to dine and sleep at the Manor, and when I reminded her that such an offer would compel us to abandon the tradition that the bride and groom should not meet on the night before the wedding she displayed an admirable contempt for superstition. So the matter was settled, much to my delight, and I began to look forward to the luxury of a long talk with Charles.

When I saw him again I felt I was being granted a new insight into the misguided but all-too-human weakness which had led Father Darcy to keep Francis by his side in London. How delightful it was to have a friend twenty years one's junior who so exactly fulfilled one's specifications of the ideal son! Charles had his faults; as his spiritual director I knew that better than anyone, but he was an able priest, a loyal husband and a devoted father—all the things Martin would never be—and there were times when I was tempted to jettison the detachment which made me so successful as a counsellor and manifest a paternal affection. But that would have been unforgivable. It was my detachment which made me valuable to Charles as he wrestled with his problems; he needed a spiritual director, not a father, and besides I was quite astute enough to see that my paternal impulse was primarily selfish, springing not from an altruistic desire to benefit Charles but from an urge to compensate myself for the agony of Martin's shortcomings.

All these thoughts passed through my mind as we greeted the Ashworths and showed them into the drawing-room, but at last I roused myself sufficiently to hear Charles say to Anne: "I can't tell you how grateful I am for your invitation! It's hard to brave a hotel with two children under three, and although Lyle suggested leaving the boys behind in Cambridge with Nanny I hated the thought of missing them when I had leave." He added that although he had considered the idea that they might all stay with a local acquaintance of his, a doctor who lived in the village of Starvale St. James, the doctor's wife was unfortunately not the most hospitable of women.

"Is that Dr. Romaine?" said Anne interested. "I've never met him but one of my friends is always saying how wonderful he is with mothers and babies." And as the inevitable comments followed about what a small world it was, I saw Charles had put her at ease. One of Charles's gifts—a very useful one for a clergyman—was his ability to be immediately and effortlessly charming to people from all walks of life.

Later I took Charles down to the chapel and after he had expressed the most gratifying admiration we settled down in one of the pews for our talk. I had no wish to compromise my detachment by disclosing too much personal information, but of course I had to tell him how I had met Anne, particularly when he pressed me for details. However I somehow restrained myself from talking about my vision. My role in Charles's life was not to burden him with my spiritual problems—nor to enthral him with my spiritual challenges—but to help him along his own spiritual way.

"I realise now how much I've missed our regular meetings at Grantchester," he said after we had discussed his problems. "And what a relief it is to find you still as rational and serene as ever despite all the turmoil you must have gone through! In fact one of the things I most admire about you, Father, is that you never seem to have any serious difficulties—or if you do you apparently always have the strength and wisdom to overcome them without effort."

"My dear Charles!" I shall never cease to be amazed by how imperfectly we are known even by those closest to us. "You're very flattering, but I hardly think Father Ingram would recognise me from that description!"

"That's the new Abbot-General, isn't it? I hear he's a Cambridge man—did he read theology?"

"No, French novels and Oscar Wilde," I said, making him laugh, and began to talk about Francis's rise to monastic power from such remarkably inauspicious beginnings.

To my delight the dinner-party that evening proved a most happy occasion, apart from one incident which revealed a tension that no doubt the Ashworths would have preferred to conceal. Halfway through the last course the elder boy pitter-pattered into the room in search of entertainment and both his parents gave exclamations of dismay.

"Why aren't you asleep?" demanded Lyle, but the little boy, ignoring her, ran straight to Charles and scrambled up onto his knees.

"He says he feels sick."

"He's always saying that. It's his new ploy to get attention. Come along, Charley—back to bed—"

"No!" cried the child, and hid his face in Charles's jacket.

Lyle, whose normal manner was one of cool confidence, suddenly became ruffled. "Stop being so naughty this instant! There's Michael upstairs, fast asleep, good as gold—"

As the child screamed with rage Charles exclaimed: "Stop throwing Michael's name in his face! Can't you see he hates it?"

"Well, I hate him misbehaving! He plays up to you, Charles—he knows perfectly well you're as soft as butter with him—"

"Who's as soft as butter with Michael?"

I stood up to terminate this disturbingly abrasive exchange, and moving over to the child I began to stroke his hair.

He looked at me in surprise. Unlike Michael, who was the kind of infant guaranteed to excite much admiration, Charley was a plain child who was probably unused to special attention from strangers. His sullen mouth hinted at a temperamental nature but his eyes, bright now with unshed tears, reflected his intelligence and I could sense his little thoughts flashing anxiously hither and thither as he tried to understand what I wanted. Very gently I enfolded his mind with my own, and a second later he was stretching out his arms towards me.

"Well!" said Lyle, sufficiently astonished to forget her tension. "I've never seen him respond to a stranger like that before!"

I picked the child up and he relaxed against my chest with a sigh. Stroking his hair again I was acutely aware of Anne's enrapt admiration and I was also acutely aware that I enjoyed it.

"You're going to sleep now, Charley," I said. "You're tired, very tired, so tired that your eyelids feel heavy."

His eyelids promptly drooped over his pale brown eyes. His thumb rose to his mouth. He was at peace.

"Well!" said Lyle again, matching Anne's admiration. "That's the kind of magic I wish I could bottle and take home!"

She came with me upstairs to put him to bed, and when we had tiptoed from the room she said: "Thanks—that was amazing." For a moment I thought she had no intention of saying anything else but then she blurted out: "I'm sorry I got so irritated but I feel under frightful strain at the moment."

I assured her in my most neutral voice that there was no need for her to apologise, but with a sinking heart I realised she was unable to resist the urge to confide.

"I'm just no good without Charles," she said. "I get so depressed, so afraid—and don't tell me I'm just one woman among thousands with husbands in the Army and that we all have to make sacrifices in war-time; that sort of platitude does no good at all."

"Then what exactly do you want me to tell you, Lyle?"

She stopped at the top of the stairs. "Tell me it's not all some ghastly punishment."

"It's not all some ghastly punishment. War-time life is simply a difficult challenge which you must surmount as best you can. Don't you have any friends in Cambridge?"

"They're all *his* friends, and anyway all the nice men are away and all the women are absolute cats—"

"Then if you have no friends to offer support, you must turn to your family. I know you have no family of your own, but Charles has parents to whom he's devoted—why don't you take a house near them in Epsom?"

"Charles doesn't know this, but his mother and I can't stand each other."

"Why doesn't Charles know? Why haven't you discussed such an unfortunate problem with him?"

"I'm afraid of him being upset. I'm afraid he'll stop loving me. If Charles stopped loving me I think I'd kill myself—I'd feel so worthless, so contemptible, so—"

"There's no need to resort to talk of suicide—I can hear what you're trying to say. You need someone who'll blot out those feelings of worthlessness by making you feel cherished and special."

"But there's no one." The tears started to fall. "No one, I swear it. No one except Charles."

I regarded her in silence as she found a handkerchief and dabbed her eyes daintily. Then I said: "The real solution is to exorcise that guilt which is giving you these unbearable feelings of worthlessness. You should go to seek help from Dame Veronica again."

"I can't. She dislikes me." More tears fell. "*You're* the only one who can help because you're magic and you always know all the answers."

I sighed, partly because she was exasperating me, partly because I felt sorry for Charles being burdened with such a troubled wife and partly because I did feel a genuine compassion for her in her misery. Abruptly I said: "You need a sympathetic older man who'll offer you a Platonic paternal friendship. Try Dr. Romaine. He'd do anything for Charles." And without giving her time to reply I strode away downstairs to the dining-room.

At the end of the meal when the ladies had retired Charles said to me: "I'm sorry Lyle and I clashed over Charley like that, but as I warned you earlier at the chapel she's under great strain. What a pity it is that she and my mother don't get on! I'd feel much happier if Lyle could take a house in Epsom."

"I quite see it's the most difficult problem."

"To tell you the truth—and I didn't mention this earlier because I don't see how it can ever come to pass—I think the perfect solution would be for her to take a house near Starvale St. James. She likes Alan, and—"

"—and Dr. Romaine would be so pleased to look after her for you! What a splendid idea!"

"Yes, but you can imagine the difficulties—my parents would be angry—they'd feel slighted—there'd be jealousy, sulks, barbed remarks—"

I could endure his torment no longer, and taking a deep breath I prepared to plunge through his confusion to rescue him. "Charles," I said firmly, "your first duty is to your wife. Your parents must come second, and if they start to make a fuss you must be tough with them. I know how hard it is for you to be tough with your parents, but you should take the line that while you're fighting for your country you need their unqualified support. That's the kind of language your father at least will understand."

Charles actually sagged in his chair with relief. "You're right, of course," he said. "I can see you're right. Yes, that's the line to take." He began to look cheered. "I'll write to Alan tomorrow."

"Before you do that, follow the advice I gave you earlier at the chapel and have an honest conversation with Lyle about your mother. I can't stress to you how important it is that a husband and wife should feel able to confide in each other on even the most difficult subjects."

Immediately Father Darcy's voice exclaimed in my imagination: " 'Physician, heal thyself!' " but I pretended not to hear. Once again Charles had miraculously diverted me from my own problems, and besides . . .

I hardly wanted to think of Father Darcy on the night before my wedding.

7

AFTER the Ashworths had retired to bed Anne came outside to see me off. "I like Charles," she said. "I feel he's got great integrity underneath that glossy exterior, but I'm not so sure about Lyle. I think she could be a bit of a siren."

This astute remark prompted me to wonder how my body had ever judged Lyle worthy of an automatic sexual response. How disturbed I must have been! As I now compared Lyle's small, slim figure with Anne's generous, even queenly curves, I felt as if I were comparing a common garden sparrow with a golden eagle.

" . . . and what a way you have with children!" Anne was exclaiming. "You were amazing with that little boy!"

I opened my mouth to reply: "It was a parlour-trick. I did it to impress you," but the words which emerged were: "When I stroked him he reminded me of a cat."

"Funny little boy, what a pity he's so plain—but oh Jon, that baby! Isn't he adorable? I looked at him and thought . . . wondered . . . " She hesitated, but by the time I said: "Yes," she was already adding in a rush: "It's strange because I've never been particularly maternal. Perhaps I felt I didn't dare be maternal so long as I was unmarried—but now . . . Oh Jon, I do so hope—"

"Of course you do," I said, and a second later my tongue was dutifully wrapping itself around the words she wanted to hear. "So do I."

A prolonged embrace took place during which my mind was entirely occupied with picturing the consummation of our marriage. When I next spoke I only said: "You're not worried about tomorrow night, are you?" and she answered with a touching simplicity: "No, because you'll make everything come right."

For a brief moment I thought of Whitby, purring in absolute trust as he waited to be healed. Then the curtain came down over my memory, and giving Anne one last kiss I walked away down the drive to the village.

I HAD resolved to hold a service of Holy Communion the next morning, but I had asked Charles if he would be the celebrant in order that Anne and I might kneel together at the altar-rail. The three of us met at the chapel at eight. Lyle, to my relief, had chosen not to attend, although whether this was because she had no desire to communicate or because she was sensitive enough to realise that I wanted to be on my own with Anne before a priest at such a special time, I could not determine.

Charles performed his part with an unpretentious dignity which impressed me; I had never before seen him going about his work. Outside the sun was shining, and within the walls of the chapel I could sense in the extreme stillness the underlying unity of all things.

We were married at noon. In her desire that the occasion should be as unlike her ruined wedding day as possible Anne had wanted the minimum of witnesses, so the majority of her acquaintances had been excluded. However her aunt Miss Fielding came and so did the neighbouring Maitlands who had known Anne all her life. Mr. Musgrave the solicitor and Mr. Dawson, who helped Anne run the estate, completed the bride's guest-list. I had not heard from Martin and did not expect him to appear, so in the absence of my family I issued a handful of invitations to members of the local church. I invited Mrs. Wetherall, the wife of the absent vicar; I also invited the Bishop and his wife, although they were unable to attend, and finally I invited the Aysgarths. I felt Aysgarth could hardly trample on a second proffered olive branch, and when he accepted my invitation with civility I hoped that my peacemaking efforts would bear fruit in future.

There were also a number of other onlookers at the wedding; in accordance with Anne's wishes the indoor servants and the two gardeners trooped into the back pews with their spouses and offspring.

I wore my clerical suit. Anne, shying away from any costume which resembled a wedding gown, wore a bright blue frock. Colonel Maitland gave the bride away and Charles conducted the service as admirably as he had celebrated Mass. Although Anne had rejected most of the music traditionally associated with weddings, Mrs. Maitland played the piano (transferred from the house to replace the defunct organ) as we all sang the Twenty-third Psalm, and at that point the simplicity of the ceremony moved me. I was reminded of the services I had conducted in the Navy during the War when the well-worn phrases of the prayer book, recited in an unorthodox environment, had acquired a fresh meaning.

Finally the moment came, and glancing up at the north window I thought of the light I had seen in my vision. Then I put the ring on Anne's finger and became, after twenty-eight turbulent years as a widower, once more a married man.

PART THREE

THE FALSE
LIGHT

"We must beware of what the 'Theologia Germanica' calls the false light. 'The Devil hath his contemplatives as God hath his . . . ' "

" 'If a man seeks the good life for any reason outside itself,' says Plotinus, 'it is not the good life that he seeks.' "

W. R. INGE
MYSTICISM IN RELIGION

XIII

I

WE gave our guests as lavish a luncheon as war-time austerities permitted, and departed from the Manor at three o'clock when the chauffeur drove us to Starbridge. I was determined not to travel far on the first night. I entirely disapprove of couples who begin their marriage drained by weeks of increasing tension, debilitated by gluttony at the reception and demolished by a long journey in the opening hours of the honeymoon.

I had booked a room with an adjoining bathroom at the Crusader, the most comfortable hotel in Starbridge. I still had no money of my own, but when I had recently opened a bank account in the city the bank manager had had no trouble persuading himself that he should be obliging to a priest who offered the Bishop's name as a reference. Anne had offered to contribute to the cost of the honeymoon but I had refused. Years of bringing up a family on a modest clerical stipend had taught me how to make a little money go a long way, and although I deemed it essential to spend lavishly on the all-important first night, I had made more modest arrangements for the remainder of the honeymoon.

As soon as we had been shown to our luxurious chamber I took Anne in my arms, kissed her and said: "I don't want to wait a moment longer."

She seemed to find this statement eminently reasonable.

We went to bed.

AT the risk of sounding calculating I must confess that I had spent much time plotting the opening manoeuvres of my honeymoon, and I had come to the practical if unromantic conclusion that my first task was to attend not to Anne's nerves but to my own. To put the matter bluntly, one cannot rescue the maiden in distress unless one's rescue equipment is in working order, and although the evidence suggested that advancing years and a celibate life had not resulted in a fatal atrophy, I was still haunted by the knowledge that I was a sixty-year-old man who had not been intimate with a woman for seventeen years. Impotence, that dread state, is so often born not in the body but in the mind, and my mind, chaotic with passion and anxiety as soon as the blind was drawn, was at that moment hardly an example of masterly self-control.

I tried to concentrate on essential matters. I let her keep on her petticoat, first because she made no move to take it off and second because I thought she might be more inclined to relax behind some camouflage; her nakedness was a non-essential delight which could be saved for later. I myself took off all my clothes but that was for utilitarian purposes. I wanted nothing to obstruct my movements or mar my concentration.

It was essential, I considered, that we should be in a sensual environment, so I was relieved to discover that the double bed was wickedly soft while the linen sheets were voluptuously smooth. So far so good. It was also good that Anne was willing—shy, anxious but willing; I had been afraid of a last-minute panic. I wondered whether I should murmur something soothing in order to encourage the willingness and damp down the anxiety, but I was too afraid that words could only be banal in such circumstances so I remained silent.

As I began to kiss her I became aware that I was sweating. That worried me. Honest sweat has its place in the human condition but that place is not, I fear, between the sumptuous sheets of a double bed on the first night of a honeymoon. I started to wonder feverishly about strokes and heart attacks, but managed to convince myself that hypochondria, like Anne's nakedness, was merely a non-essential refinement which could be saved for later.

By this time I had obtained the only physical reaction which was of any importance, but before I could savour my relief I found myself plunged into the anxiety that I might be incompetent. The anxiety was heightened by the fact that I was now confronting the difficulty of consummating the marriage without causing pain; Anne's virginity might be non-existent but I was sure her bad memories were doubling by the second. I tried to stroke her soothingly but the next moment I realised I was dicing with disaster by attempting a postponement, and after seventeen years of celibacy I was in no position to dice with anything. I pressed on. My psyche was reeling as if it were punch-drunk. Emotion roared through my body like a tidal wave.

To my relief Anne continued to cling to me but she was so tense that I knew I must be hurting her. Deeply troubled, I paused, trying to decide how I might best help her relax, but when she moved, unnerved by my stillness and wanting, I knew, only to please me by an active response, the moment came and the wave broke. I had been inside her for no more than a dozen seconds.

I kissed her, rolled onto my back, stared up at the ceiling, thanked God that the marriage was at least consummated, and realised I was exhausted. I would have felt happy but I was too worried about Anne. Rolling over towards her again, I gathered her in my arms and told her how much she was loved.

She said in a small voice: "But I wasn't much good, was I?"

"Don't steal my lines—and don't talk as if you're a performing seal at a circus! We're here to love each other, not to bring an audience cheering to its feet."

She smiled. Using my last particle of strength I smiled back, kissed her again and sank like a stone into oblivion.

3

I AWOKE when the scars on my back began to tingle. For one confused moment I thought I was back in the London punishment cell, and shouting: "No!" at the top of my voice, I sat bolt upright in bed.

Anne, who had been caressing the scars with her forefinger, gasped in fright and at once I pulled her into my arms. Then I waited for her to ask about the scars. Betty would have asked. Hilda would have asked. Every other woman I had ever known except my mother would have asked, but Anne was silent and suddenly my good fortune overwhelmed me. I had waited sixty years for the right woman and finally I had found her. It seemed almost too good to be true. Perhaps it was indeed too good to be true. Perhaps it would all end in disaster. Perhaps—

"Anne, don't leave me."

"Don't *what?*" Anne was justifiably astounded by this idiocy, but although I struggled to pull myself together I could only tighten my clasp and remain silent.

"Silly man!" said Anne at last, wisely deciding to gloss over my insanity by adopting a brisk practical manner. "What an extraordinary thing to say!" And when she stroked my hair to soothe me I belatedly remembered that I was supposed to be soothing her.

Propping myself on one elbow I said firmly: "Don't worry about anything. What happened just now was a mere handshake. The real dialogue has yet to begin, but there's no rush. We'll let it develop at its own pace."

I saw her relax. No threatening demands were being made; our marital relationship would evolve steadily; there was plenty of time.

"I'll be all right in the end, won't I?" she said, touching in her vulnerability.

"We'll both be all right," I said with all the confidence at my command, and when she smiled at me in relief I felt sure I could ring down the curtain on her past as successfully as I had rung down the curtain on my own.

4

AFTER this bout of arrogance had lured me into underestimating the problem, some time elapsed before I realised that Anne's liberation from her past was going to prove more difficult than I had anticipated. Perhaps I was too busy weaving my new experiences into the fabric of my life; I found myself thinking often of the Order, of the difficult days which had resulted in spiritual growth, and I felt glad that I could still recall my years as a monk without any sense of time wasted. My monastic experience had made me the man I was and that man was the man Anne loved. I wondered if she would have loved the unhappy priest who had jilted Hilda, and thought not.

I remembered my past with Betty too and wondered if the scars on my psyche would be finally cauterised by my new marriage or whether they would always remain, like the scars on my back, to remind me of past suffering. However such speculation was difficult, reminding me that I had not been honest with Anne about my children, and soon I gave way to the urge to consign all thought of my first marriage to the very back of my mind.

On the morning after our wedding we departed by train for Dorset, where we were received at our small, modest but not uncomfortable inn (recommended by Charles) with a very civil hospitality. To our pleasure we found that our room faced across the low cliffs to the sea and was marred only by the presence on one wall of a sentimental canine portrait which, much to Anne's amusement, I immediately incarcerated in the wardrobe. Despite the existence of indoor plumbing I did suffer a pang of anxiety that Anne might find the inn too primitive, but to my relief she insisted that the simplicity delighted her.

The October weather was dry, enabling us to take long walks along the cliffs above the shingle beach, and the sight of the sea affected me deeply; I forgot the horror of the Battle of Jutland and thought only of the good times I had enjoyed in the Navy when the sea had represented freedom and the chance to draw closer to God. I began to talk in more detail to Anne about my years in the Navy, and when I told her I had decided to be a sailor at the age of eight after my mother had taken me on an excursion to the seaside, she began to talk not only about her own mother, whom she had already described in loving detail, but about her adored dead brother as well. Then gradually as she talked a third figure began to permeate the conversation, until suddenly I saw that here at last stood my true adversary as I struggled to sever Anne from her unhappy past. The fiancé had certainly been a disaster for her, but the seeds of his destructive behaviour had fallen on ground well-cultivated to receive them. Beyond the fiancé, beyond the broken engagement, lurked the household idol called DADDY whose influence lingered on malignly so many years after his death.

That was when I realised that healing Anne was going to be more difficult than I had anticipated. The straightforward ravages of the fiancé could be erased by a sustained diet of patience and gentleness, but the subtle, sinister crippling wrought by DADDY was far more difficult to obliterate, and as the picture emerged of an arrogant autocrat who had given her such a poor sense of her own worth as a woman, a terrible truth began to crawl out of the darkest corner of my mind into the light. I realised that DADDY was not unfamiliar to me; in fact he was a man I knew all too well.

"Daddy did love me," said Anne, "but he loved my brother better because Gerald was the boy and more like him than I was. I tried so hard to please him, but no matter how hard I tried I never felt I was succeeding and that made me feel so sad and upset. It was as if he never saw *me* at all—he just saw a girl who wasn't the sort of child he wanted, and then I'd feel so humiliated, so second-rate, such a failure. Of course he pretended I was wonderful, but I knew it was just a pretence; it was as if he couldn't accept me as I was so he had to pretend I was someone quite different, and looking back I can see he made the same mistake with Gerald when he set him up on a pedestal and idolised him . . .

"I'm glad Gerald wasn't younger than I was. If he'd been younger I'd have hated him for being the favourite, but as he was five years my senior

I grew up hero-worshipping him and the hero-worship elbowed all jealousy aside. It took me a long time to see how flawed he was. He was so athletic, so good-looking, so charming—and I was so plain, so shy, so hopeless at games and so useless with animals that I couldn't even learn to ride properly. Poor Daddy! I was such a disappointment to him. No wonder he preferred Gerald . . .

"The situation got even worse when I was an adolescent. It was so awful when Mummy died—well, I don't have to tell *you,* do I, what hell it is to lose one's mother when one's fourteen—but it was awful for me in all sorts of stupid ways which used to depress me so dreadfully and make me feel more inferior than ever. For instance, there was no one to advise me about clothes and I'm sure I always looked a fright and I never knew how to endure parties. Ugh! How I hated them! Poor Daddy was quite mortified by my lack of social success, and I felt so miserable because I knew I was letting him down.

"Gerald was a great social success, but although his girlfriends thought he was a story-book hero, all glamour and courage, he wasn't. He wasn't like that at all. Underneath the glamour he was frightened, frightened of not being the sort of man Daddy wanted him to be, frightened of being a failure and a disappointment . . .

"I thought he'd be better once Daddy was dead—I thought we'd both be better—but I was wrong. We still felt guilty, I because I hadn't been the kind of daughter Daddy had wanted and Gerald because he knew he couldn't live up to this idealised image which Daddy had created. So we both tried in different ways to escape from our guilt. I fell in love with Hugo; I think I knew from the start that there was something off-colour about the romance, but I just thought how pleased Daddy would have been that I'd got off the shelf. Then Gerald tried to escape by abandoning the estate and leading a wild life in London. He got in a mess in the end, of course—some woman or other, and I knew he was drinking too much—and when my engagement was broken off he was relieved to have a good excuse to turn his back on his problems in order to take me on holiday.

"When he was drowned I—no, I never thought it was suicide and the verdict was accidental death, but sometimes I think it was as if he subconsciously preferred death to life. That's a terrible thing to say, isn't it? But I think that sometimes the truth is very terrible and there's nothing one can do but stare it straight in the face in order to master it and go on.

"And I did go on after Gerald's death. The estate was in the red and I knew I had to save it because it was all I had left, but after a while I became aware that I wasn't acting through self-interest or even on account of a pious family feeling. I was saving the estate in order to show Daddy that I wasn't the second-rate creature he'd always thought I was; I was saving it to show him that in the end it was the despised daughter, not the idolised son, who was following so successfully in his footsteps. Isn't that odd? I was behaving as if he were still alive to see me, and sometimes I feel almost as if he *can* see me, although I don't truly believe he's a disembodied spirit perpetually looking over my shoulder . . . Jon, what does happen to the dead? What do Heaven and Hell really mean? What do you think really goes on?"

Overcoming my revulsion towards the appalling DADDY who might so easily have been described by Ruth, I slipped with relief into the role of priest and began to talk confidently about the hereafter.

5

"IT'S exceedingly difficult to talk intelligibly about life after death," I said, "because we're so pitifully limited by being trapped in time and space, but if you keep firmly in mind the fact that we're really incapable of thinking in anything but spatial and temporal terms, you'll see that Heaven and Hell are spatial symbols while eternal life is a temporal symbol. All religious language is symbolic in that it attempts to bridge the gap between the describable and the inexpressible, but that doesn't mean it's untrue. Quite the reverse. Just as poetry and myth can sometimes express truth better than prose or scientific aphorisms, so religious language can convey truth by symbols. The symbols point the way to reality, and reality is a kingdom of values. Insofar as we partake of the three absolute values—Truth, Goodness and Beauty—we can never die because those values are eternal. Plotinus, who was probably the greatest religious philosopher who ever lived—and a pagan, incidentally—said: 'Nothing that really *is* can ever perish.' "

"Yes, I see. Or I think I see. But—"

"You're wondering if we survive as individuals after death. Christianity says we do. On the other hand, the Indian mystics claim that we don't; we merely become absorbed in the Absolute. However Plotinus holds that although there's a merging with other spirits, individuality is retained; each soul is as individual as a face or a body. So the question then becomes: what is the relation of this 'soul' to the 'I' of personality? Or in other words, who is it who survives after death? Is it the ego, the demanding self of our daily lives whom we know all too well? Or is the real self not the ego at all but the spiritual presence which we share with all other human beings, the ennobled self which often prompts men to sacrifice their lives for others and share the burden of another's suffering? It's worth remembering, I think, that in classical times there was no word corresponding to our own 'personality' and that the cult of the individual, glorifying the ego, is a fairly modern phenomenon. I suspect that the doctrine of survival which has come down to us means not the survival of the ego but the survival of the true self, the spiritual self, which after death joins other spirits in everlasting life—although everlasting life, of course, being outside finite time, is quite beyond our power to imagine." I smiled at her. "But you're thinking I still haven't answered your question about whether your father can see you following in his footsteps."

"Yes, you have—he's not in space and he's not in time so it's ridiculous for me to picture him hovering on a cloud and watching me through a pair of binoculars!"

I laughed before saying: "Nevertheless it's possible that your father's essence, his spiritual self, can penetrate finite time and enfold your psyche in that eternal value, Love. If it's possible then your outward behaviour would reflect his love, like a mirror, and you'd be at peace, but what seems to have happened here is that his spiritual self is blocked from communicating with you because his ego is lingering on in your consciousness in the form of sad, difficult memories. That often happens when someone dies leaving unhealed wounds and unresolved conflicts. The dead ego leaves a stain on the psyche which has to be wiped clean." I was careful not to use the word "exorcism" with all its dubious and discredited connotations.

By this time several days of the honeymoon had elapsed and intimacy had become easier for her. As practice made me more adroit I was at least able to ensure she felt no acute discomfort, but her response remained maimed, reflecting the damage in her psyche, and soon I realised that her fear lay not in the possibility that I might hurt her but in the belief that she would disappoint me, just as she had disappointed DADDY, by failing to display an unflawed femininity. She seemed to be telling herself—unconsciously, of course—that if she refused to compete in this particular race she would run no risk of the ignominious failure she feared so much, and this psychological withdrawal manifested itself in a refusal to let me touch her where it mattered most.

As our honeymoon entered its second week I became more determined than ever to set matters right but I knew I had to employ some radical new strategy. Although I was doing my best to demonstrate in a multitude of ways that I found her very far from being second-rate, it seemed she could never quite believe that my attitude did not spring merely from a desire to be kind. The hallmark of psychological damage is irrationality.

One wet afternoon when we were in bed together she said suddenly: "Do you promise me you're not secretly wishing I were thin like all the first-rate women?" and when I retorted: "What's so first-rate about being thin? I like my women to be women, not effeminate boys!" she laughed. This pleased me. Laughter in bed represented progress. As a priest I am certainly in favour of treating the intimate side of marriage with a proper reverence, but I would argue with any puritan who insists that laughter has no place in the bedroom. Sexual intercourse should be a pleasure, not a penance, and laughter can lead to that vital relaxation without which the deepest pleasure can remain unobtainable.

I said: "I like to hear you laugh!" and when she kissed me I saw with my inner eye a psyche which was ready to be healed.

In my memory Father Darcy began to drone that I should exercise the charism of healing only with men and only when they became emotionally disturbed during the course of spiritual counselling, but I ceased to listen. Father Darcy had merely regarded women as a man on a diet might regard a box of chocolates: pretty to look at, delicious to taste but quite irrelevant to sensible nourishment, and certainly he had never known what it was like to be in bed with a wife who was so painfully longing to express her love in the fullest possible way.

However Father Darcy's training was less easy to slough off than his views on my suitability for the ministry of healing, and automatically I found myself struggling to perceive my motives. I knew I wanted to heal Anne for her own sake so that she could be completely happy in the physical expression of our marriage, but beyond this truth were other less edifying truths, and lurking in their dark shadow was my old enemy, the demon pride. The demon was making me unwilling to accept that I could not wholly satisfy my wife; he was demanding incontrovertible evidence of sexual success in order to blot out my fear of old age, and he was whispering that after seventeen years of celibacy I was entitled to the best possible marital pleasure in compensation.

Yet although I could perceive the demon's machinations so clearly, I told myself that Anne's need remained genuine, no matter how murky my motives were, and the next moment I had begun to pray.

I prayed in words, although the silence in the room remained unbroken, and offering my powers to God I prayed that He might use me as a channel for His Holy Spirit. In an attempt to override all my unsavoury motives by an expression of selflessness I also prayed: Let thy will, not mine, be done. But the prayer was a mere formality, no better than the magic incantation of the sorcerer, and the next moment it was *my* will which drove me to take Anne in my arms, *my* will which determined that I should now have what I wanted and *my* will which egged me on to embrace the solution I could no longer withstand.

6

HAVING taken Anne in my arms I said to her: "I'd like to try an experiment, but don't be intimidated; if it doesn't work it'll be my fault, not yours."

Despite my reassurance she immediately became nervous. "What sort of experiment?"

"An exercise in telepathy. Now"—I moved until I was astride her in such a manner that I could place my hands comfortably on her breasts—"don't protest that you're incapable of it! Imagine that I've switched on a wireless. All you've got to do is listen as I slowly turn up the volume knob—and listening will be easier if you now close your eyes and think of William."

"*William?* My cat?"

"I wasn't aware that you knew anyone else called William."

Anne laughed, and as she thought of the safe, comforting image of her cat I was conscious of her muscles relaxing. Some seconds passed. Then I found I could distinguish her psyche clearly enough to reflect it in my mind as a visual symbol; I saw it as a bright ball with a clouded patch deep in the centre. I was unable to see William but that was because she did not know how to project the image. As an experiment I projected the image of Whitby but there was no response. I was still too far away. Moving to the edge of the bright ball I began to press into it towards the central darkness.

"Imagine William washing his paws."

"I was! How clever of you!"

I thought this success was probably a coincidence; I was still unable to see William. "Is he in a basket?" I said, thinking of Whitby.

"No, William hates baskets. He's sitting on his special blanket in my room. No, wait a minute, it's not William at all! His hair's too long. I'm sorry, my mind's wandering, I must have been thinking of your description of Whitby—"

"You're doing splendidly. Now imagine that the voice on the wireless is becoming audible and that it's finally possible for you to hear the message." As I pressed on through the brightness I was aware of a change in the visual image; I now saw a patch of rapids on a swift-flowing river, and I was swimming steadily upstream towards the white water.

"I'm afraid I'm no good at this at all," said Anne. "I can't hear a thing."

"Say the first word that comes into your head."

"Love."

"Good. Now keep listening, listen to the voice, listen, listen, listen . . . " I had reached the rapids and there ahead of me in the centre of the white water lay the black rock which had to be crushed. I fought my way on.

"Trust," said Anne suddenly. "Hope. Faith."

The rapids died. The black rock lay unprotected before me and at once I began to draw my hands down over her breasts. Anne gasped, Whitby yelped and as the vertical line of time was fractured, past and present streamed side by side into the future.

"Jon, your hands—"

"Don't be frightened, just look at me, Anne, look and keep looking—" As I touched the rock the image of the river dissolved so that I found myself confronting the darkness at the centre of her psyche. The final visual image flashed in my mind; I saw the darkness as a cancer, and a second later my mind was stretching to encircle it.

"Jon—"

"Don't speak, just listen, *listen,* LISTEN—"

But Anne no longer needed to listen. She had heard the message of love which lay far beyond the power of mere words to express, and in a moment of direct communication her psyche lay open before mine. The cancer was encircled. For one long moment I focussed my entire psychic strength on it. Then as she herself placed my hand on her body the darkness exploded, her love expanded unhindered at last, and seconds later she was sobbing in my arms.

7

JUST as Whitby had expelled the fur-ball and all the matter which had been poisoning him, so Anne now expelled her anguish and pain on the subject of the opposite sex. She said she had hated her fiancé for calling her a sexual cripple. She had hated him for letting her down so cruelly. Men had always let her down, never asking her to dance, never taking any genuine interest in her, never realising she was just as much a human being as the girls who had the luck to be pretty. Sometimes she had even hated Gerald for treating her like an overgrown puppy; she had hated him because he had had access to the worlds which were closed to her, the worlds of freedom and independence where young men could chase the opposite sex and have a good time and escape from the clutches of DADDY.

"I hated Daddy too sometimes," said Anne. "He wouldn't let me do anything or go anywhere. I wanted to go up to Oxford, but he said higher education was pointless for women. I wanted to go to London and get a job but he said that was common and no girl of my class should consider it. All he wanted me to do was be a social success and get married, and when I failed it was awful—*awful*—I hated him just as much as I hated myself—but then I felt worse than ever, so guilty, because of course I did love him very much and he was so often perfectly sweet to me—" She broke off, unable to continue, but I picked up my counsellor's cue with the ease born of long practice and said firmly: "You didn't want someone being perfectly sweet. You wanted someone to understand the hell you were going through."

"But he couldn't help not understanding! It was just the way he was made!"

"My dear, no one should excuse their faults by saying smugly: 'I'm so sorry but this is just the way I was made.' "

"Well, he never actually did say that, but—"

"If he didn't you certainly shouldn't. I'm quite willing to believe your father was a remarkable and delightful man in many ways, but you should never forget that he was also human enough to make mistakes—and some of those mistakes may well have been so serious that you have every right to be angry with him."

"But that makes me feel so guilty—"

"Why? God made you as a unique individual in His own image. You wanted to be that individual and your father stopped you. This was not only a bad mistake; it was also morally wrong. You have a right to be angry, but you mustn't turn the anger in on yourself because that only compounds the damage which has already been done. You must turn the anger outwards. Hate him for hurting you! Be angry with him for rejecting your true self! And then when all that anger and hatred have been spent you'll be able to think: poor Daddy, never realising what a first-class daughter he had—poor Daddy, cut off from so much love and happiness by his lack of understanding—poor Daddy, how very, very sad! And when you see, as you will, that he was the loser while you've gone on to win the life you were denied, your old anger will dissolve, your new compassion will expand to take its place and then at long last forgiveness will become possible."

She was silent for a long time but eventually she said: "He must have been very unhappy. People always are, aren't they, when they can't face reality? He must have known Gerald was no good. He must have known I'd be better off up at Oxford. But he couldn't cope with the knowledge. Mummy would have helped him cope. She was a very sensible, down-to-earth person and she wouldn't have let him retreat into this fantasy world where Gerald was the faultless heir-apparent and I was the conventional heiress—she'd have helped him to put aside his dreams and face up to the way things really were, but without her he just didn't have the courage to do that. In fact," said Anne, speaking more rapidly as her insight deepened, "I can see now he must have been a frightened sort of person underneath that confident exterior. Insecure. Perhaps even a little weak. Isn't that strange? Maybe Gerald was far more like him than I ever realised . . . How eerie it is to think that families can spend years under the same roof yet know each other so imperfectly!"

"Eerie, but not unusual."

Another long silence elapsed. Then Anne said simply: "Poor Daddy. I suppose it was all a sort of tragedy, wasn't it?"

I took her in my arms to celebrate her first steps along the road to recovery.

8

LATER Anne said: "I feel as if I've climbed Mount Everest!" but I could only respond: "I'm wondering if I've sunk into a bottomless pit."

Anne looked astonished. "What on earth do you mean?"

I sighed and began to tell her how I had abused my powers during my days as an undergraduate up at Cambridge.

9

"I CAN quite see why you got into trouble when you were too young to know better," said Anne, exercising great charity after I had completed my confession, "but now that you're so wise and good why shouldn't you heal people if you want to?"

"Because I'm capable of being unwise and very bad."

"Oh, rubbish!" said Anne robustly. "You're setting yourself impossibly high standards!"

"Healing demands high standards. Father Darcy was always convinced I was temperamentally unsuited to any healing ministry which extended beyond the counselling of men."

She was baffled. "But why?"

"The humility required for such a ministry is so great that it really has to be inborn. I'm not naturally a humble person—I can attain humility, but I have to work hard to achieve it. My natural inclination is to be proud and arrogant."

"But why does healing require this great humility?"

"Because healing is really an exercise in power, and as everyone knows, all power corrupts. The humble man will be in a better position to withstand corruption because he doesn't find power attractive, but the proud, arrogant man is vulnerable because power provides the most delectable fodder for his hungry ego."

"But if you have the gift of healing," persisted Anne, "isn't it wrong not to use it?"

"Strictly speaking there *is* no gift of healing—all healing comes from God. A ministry of healing begins when an individual feels called to offer himself as a channel for the healing power of the Holy Spirit. The power comes from without, not from within."

"But surely you must have some inborn gift! What about the way you can make your hands tingle?"

"That's an interesting physical phenomenon but by itself it accomplishes nothing. You don't have to make your hands tingle in order to be a healer."

"Let's get this straight," said Anne in her most businesslike voice: "What exactly did you do just now?"

"I used my gifts as a psychic to perceive what was going on in your mind. Then I prayed for the charismatic power, the gift from God, to excise the blight from your psyche. This power was granted but the healing was accomplished not merely by the laying-on of hands but by the use of various hypnotic techniques and—most important—by the listening and counselling afterwards. Throughout the whole process the psychic power was used merely as a tool to buttress the charismatic power, and that's strictly orthodox, strictly as it should be."

"But if you followed the rule-book so conscientiously," said Anne mystified, "and the result was so successful, why are you so ambivalent?"

"Father Darcy said—"

"Yes, I know he said you were unsuited for a ministry of healing, but this wasn't a ministry, it was just one isolated act and I can't see any harm in it!"

"Father Darcy said I was never to heal women. If he'd ever dreamt that I'd again try to heal a woman under sexual circumstances, he'd have had apoplexy."

"But this was quite different from—"

"Yes. But it was a dangerous thing to do. Father Darcy said healing would always be dangerous for me. He wanted me to teach—that's a charism too, of course, and Father Darcy thought I was ideally suited to keep order, command my pupils' attention and cram knowledge into their heads with the maximum of efficiency. He said a touch of arrogance never did any harm in the classroom."

"But did you want to teach?"

"Not in the least, no, but I wanted to be a good monk so that meant I had to obey orders to the best of my ability. As a matter of fact I was a highly successful Master of Novices; nearly all my men went on to become priests. Father Darcy said—"

"Jon," said Anne, "have you any idea—any idea at all—how often you mention this man? And have you any idea—any idea at all—what a monster you make him seem?"

"He *was* a monster. I detested him all the while I was admiring him."

"How thoroughly creepy and peculiar!"

My psyche flinched. I said carefully in a voice devoid of emotion: "You speak, of course, from ignorance, so let me try to explain the relationship in terms you can understand. We were two mountaineers roped together and he was showing me the way up the mountain. That meant that the essence of our relationship consisted of neither love nor hate but trust. I trusted him to lead me to the top and he trusted in my ability to follow him there. As men we disliked each other but as psychics we found each other fascinating and as monks we were obliged to love each other as brothers."

"I've never heard anything quite so convoluted in all my life! Was he responsible for those scars on your back?"

"Yes, but—"

"What a sadistic brute! I simply don't understand how you could have borne to go on obeying him—he beat you up, forced you to do work you didn't want to do, *murdered your cat*—"

"He saved me." I used my harshest voice and saw her recoil. "He taught me how to live with myself. He showed me how to survive. Perhaps you think it's fun to be a psychic but it's not. It can be terrifying beyond belief. One spends most of one's time feeling either cut off from the rest of humanity or else invaded, battered and laid waste by forces beyond one's control. A lot of psychics either go mad or go to the Devil, but Father Darcy saved me from either of those fates—he made me the sane, healthy man you love today. What if he did beat me? What if he did kill that cat? Those were mere pinpricks compared with what I might have suffered if I hadn't met him! If you're drowning in the sea and someone comes along with a lifeboat, you don't care if he drags you aboard by your hair and slaps your face to revive you—oh no, quite the reverse! As soon as you're conscious you just go down on your knees and thank God that the lifeboat turned up in time!"

I stopped speaking. I was shaking. I opened my mouth again to apologise for shouting at her, but it was she who spoke first. She said in a small voice: "I'm terribly sorry. I didn't realise. Please forgive me for being so stupid and not understanding."

I groped for her hand and held it. Eventually I was able to say: "The fault's mine. I never explained my spiritual history. Anne, there's so much I haven't told you—"

"Well, at least I understand now about Father Darcy."

"Then you'll understand why I feel so ambivalent about the healing."

"Yes, but *I* don't feel ambivalent!" said Anne. "I think the healing was utterly wonderful and I want to make mad passionate love to you until we both pass out with exhaustion!"

Father Darcy's memory immediately receded. Indeed for the first time in seventeen years it occurred to me that I could survive remarkably well without him.

I 0

HOWEVER next morning Father Darcy had returned to his habitual corner of my memory and I became convinced that I was drifting into a most dubious spiritual state. Deciding that I should seek solitude in order to apply myself to some rigorous spiritual exercises, I wondered how to sever myself tactfully from Anne, but the problem was solved when she revealed she had encountered the onset of her monthly indisposition. With a clear conscience I left her to rest at the inn.

After walking some way into the hills I found a church set half a mile from an isolated hamlet and decided that I had reached the ideal place in which to smooth a bedraggled psyche. In fact by that time I could barely wait to sink myself in the austerities of meditation, prayer and *lectio divina,* and the hours passed in a healing silence as I read my missal, studied passages from *The Cloud of Unknowing* and prayed with all the concentration at my command.

After praying for Anne I prayed, as I did daily, that I might receive further enlightenment about my new call, and when I paused at last I found my mind dwelling idly on the ministry of healing. Was it possible that I now had the wisdom, the maturity and the spiritual strength to triumph consistently over my innate pride and thus attain the continuous humility which such a ministry required? Almost certainly not, and Father Darcy would have said the Devil had put this question into my mind. Nevertheless it was an interesting question. I saw no harm in allowing it to interest me, but of course I could hardly deduce I had received a call to be a healer just because my wife had been enrapt by a healing that would have given Father Darcy apoplexy.

"Stop whining that you've never felt called to teach!" said Father Darcy in my memory. "I want more priests at Ruydale. This house has been all brawn and no brains for too long."

The years continued to roll back and the next moment my father was saying: "If you want to be a clergyman I couldn't be more pleased—such a fine, respectable profession—and of course you could still teach eventually, couldn't you? With your ability you could have a most successful career at any of the leading Church of England public schools . . . "

My memory somersaulted away from him into my childhood until I heard myself say to my mother during our excursion to the seaside at Brighton: "I want to be a sailor when I grow up."

"I see you on a big ship," said my mother, gazing out to sea, "a grey ship with guns on it. But I don't think you're a sailor."

"Then what am I?"

"You're yourself, living in harmony with the universe," said my mother, much as she might have said: "Tomorro we'll have mutton chops for dinner," and added: "That's good. Most people don't."

"How will I know if I'm living in harmony with the universe?"

"You'll feel that your profession fits you as snugly as a bespoke suit from a very expensive tailor."

I recollected myself. My mind had wandered, and as I hauled it back from its travels I seemed to hear my mother wondering if the ill-fitting healer's clothes I had worn up at Cambridge had at long last been transformed into a bespoke suit from Savile Row. My mother would have been deeply interested in any career as a healer. But what would my father have thought? He would have seen a call to heal in professional medical terms, of course; in his view anyone practising medicine other than a qualified doctor was a quack. But in his own way he would have supported me. "If you want to be a doctor I couldn't be more pleased—such a fine, respectable profession—and you could still teach eventually, couldn't you? With your ability you could have a most successful career at any of the great London teaching hospitals . . . "

Again I recollected myself, this time with a shudder. What my parents would have thought of a call to heal was irrelevant. All that mattered was what God thought, and God was still silent, His opinion shrouded in a darkness which remained impenetrable.

Closing my missal I set off on the return journey to the inn.

I I

ANNE ran out to meet me as I approached the house, and to my alarm I saw she was thoroughly overwrought.

"Darling"—I held out my arms and she hurtled into them—"what is it? What's the matter?"

I sensed her relief receding as her anger gained the upper hand. "Where have you been?" she demanded in an unnerving echo of Ruth. "You've been gone for hours and hours! What on earth happened?"

"Nothing! I've just been praying, reading and meditating."

She stared at me. "All this time?"

I suddenly realised my premarital reticence was about to catch up with me yet again. "I'm sorry," I said rapidly. "I see now I should have warned you—"

"Yes, you damn well should!" stormed Anne. "How could you have been so thoroughly selfish and insensitive! Didn't you think of me at all?"

"Oh yes! I spent a long time praying for you—"

"I didn't mean that!" shouted Anne, and then stammering: "I thought you were dead," she collapsed sobbing against my chest.

12

"OBVIOUSLY I've been very much at fault," I said as we attained the sanctuary of our room.

"But you silly man, why didn't you tell me you liked lots of time for prayer and meditation?"

"I did tell you. When I was trying to explain about Betty, I—"

"You did drop a vague hint, yes, but you gave me no idea what you really meant. Now let's get this straight," said Anne, drying her eyes and taking refuge in her most businesslike manner. "How much time do you need and when do you need it?"

"Darling, you mustn't let it worry you—I'm prepared to compromise—I do realise that now I'm no longer in a monastery I can't expect to—"

"How much and when?"

"Well, I like to get up at five-thirty and pray, read and meditate for two hours before breakfast—"

"Why on earth didn't you say so? And why haven't you been doing this since the start of the honeymoon?"

I did not like to say I had needed the extra sleep after making love to her so frequently. That would have reminded her of my age. "Well, it was awkward—sharing a room—I didn't want to be a bore or a nuisance—"

"Now look here," said Anne, "I don't know why you felt you couldn't talk to me about this but I can't have you not being honest and tying us both up in some fantastic knot. You must take as much time for prayer and meditation as you need each day and I promise I shan't complain—I shall only complain if you starve yourself of solitude for my sake and then disappear into the blue for eight hours in order to make up for lost time."

"My darling Anne, I can't apologise enough—"

"Did you think I wouldn't understand about your need for solitude? But why? I like to spend time on my own too!"

"Do you? Truthfully?"

"Of course! After all, I've been on my own for six years; do you think I haven't learnt how to be happy with my own company?"

After a pause I said: "Betty never learnt."

"But I'm not Betty, am I?"

I merely embraced her, and as I did so the evening sunlight began to slant through the window into the room. In the distance the sea was a calm, soothing blue.

Suddenly Anne whispered: "Do you want to? You can if you like," but when she saw my astonished expression she was overcome with confusion. "Some men don't care about the curse, I know," I heard her mumble, and I knew the oaf of a fiancé had been wreaking havoc here too, trampling on her needs in order to satisfy his own. "But obviously if you find the idea repulsive—"

"It's not a question of repulsion. God made us as we are, bodily functions and all, but I do feel some private acts of the body aren't suitable for sharing, and my respect for privacy is such that I've always believed a man has a duty not to intrude on a woman at such times," I said, but although this speech reflected my feelings honestly enough, only some of my feelings were being revealed. I had been brought up amidst the peculiarly Victorian ethos which dictated that decent middle-class women, particularly the women of one's own family, should be set upon metaphorical pedestals, treated with reverence and protected from any sordid fact of life which might soil their carefully nurtured purity. When I had finally escaped from the monastic atmosphere of my public school and the extreme propriety of my home, I had been amazed to discover that women from other classes behaved as if this ethos had nothing to do with the facts of life and even regarded their middle-class sisters with pity. Betty in particular had had great fun puncturing any prim notions of femininity which remained to me after three years up at Cambridge, and part of her fun had derived from periodically seducing me during those times when any middle-class woman would have had the refined sensibility to withdraw into a self-imposed purdah. Thus Anne was now, without knowing it, seeking an intimacy which aroused both inhibiting memories of my middle-class upbringing and unsavoury memories of Betty's perverse exercise in power.

But there were other reasons why I had no desire for intimacy at that moment. The first was that after achieving intense spiritual satisfaction from an ascetic retreat I was reluctant to conclude the day by plunging into sensuality; such behaviour would have resembled following a glass of pure spring water with a slice of cream-cake. And the second reason why I wanted to abstain from intimacy was because I needed to; I had spent ten days living at a sexual pace more suitable for a man half my age, and the dread of impotence, never far from the surface of my mind, prompted an awareness that I should husband my resources more carefully.

"I'm sorry," Anne was saying in a rush. "You obviously think I'm behaving like a female sex maniac."

"Nonsense!" I said firmly. "A healthy desire for marital intimacy is entirely right and proper!"

"Even for a clergyman's wife?"

"Especially for a clergyman's wife. People entirely misunderstand Christianity when they think it's against sex. It's against the abuse of sex, which is quite different," I said, but as I spoke I was experiencing a revelation and it was not a pleasant one. I saw that by healing her I might have wrecked some hidden equilibrium which would have kept our relationship finely tuned not now, when I was an active sixty, but later when I was an aging septuagenarian. However that glimpse of the future was too disturbing to contemplate, and at once I scrabbled to scrub it from my mind.

"Let's go to bed."

"But you said—"

"Never mind what I said. I want you. If you want me—"

Victorian inhibitions, Betty's memory, ascetic inclinations and the dread of impotence—all were swept aside. I only knew I had a young wife who had to be satisfied; I only knew I had to fight with all my power to keep old age at bay.

13

AFTERWARDS, when Anne had slipped away for a quick bath before dinner, I crawled off the bed and limped to the basin to wash. Both my legs were aching, a pulled muscle was throbbing in my back and I felt stupefied by tiredness. Old age leered at me from the glass above the basin, and shuddering I looked away.

Anne eventually returned to the room. She seemed so young, so fresh, so brimful of vitality that I felt as if someone had plunged a knife into my psyche, and at once intense fear overwhelmed me again. As she wandered past I grabbed her so abruptly that she gasped, imprisoned her in the tightest of embraces and whispered: "Don't leave me."

"Jon!" She was shocked as well as astonished, and as I slackened my grip she reached up to cradle my face between her hands. "That's the second time you've said that. Why on earth should you think—"

"I'm so old. Supposing I have a stroke and become a vegetable. Supposing I can't make love to you any more. Supposing you get tired of me, turn to someone else, go away, never come back—"

Anne said violently: "I should never do such dreadful things. I shall always love you, even if you wind up a vegetable. Please stop being so silly this instant." She sounded shattered.

At once I struggled to pull myself together. To have an elderly husband was bad enough; to have a silly elderly husband would be intolerable. "I'm sorry," said my voice, "what an un-Christian panic! Of course I must face the future with hope and faith, not sink into an ignominious despair." The crucial word here was "ignominious." My pride had come to my rescue when hope and faith had failed.

"Dearest Jon," said Anne kissing me, "you don't have to apologise—I suppose we all have our irrational fears, even people like you who seem so wonderfully well-balanced, but I must say I do find it unnerving when you become so peculiar. It's as if you stop being the man I love and become someone else altogether."

There was a deep silence as I digested this speech and she tranquilly began to brush her hair. I saw so clearly then that in order to maintain her love I had to protect her from my irrational peculiarities. I had to be the kind of husband she wanted me to be: youthful, strong, sane, wise, authoritative, confident, fearless, sexually accomplished—and bewitchingly endowed with all manner of glamorous powers.

I began to think again of a ministry of healing.

XIV

*"[There exists] in the English Church an intense repugnance
against the priestcraft of the Roman hierarchy."*

W. R. INGE
OUTSPOKEN ESSAYS

I

THREE days later we returned to Starrington Magna and the regular
arrival of the newspapers which we had tried to avoid on our honeymoon. However even in the depths of Dorset without either a wireless
or a newspaper we had heard that the battering of London had been
continuing night after night: one hundred thousand books had been
destroyed in the University College Library and a bomb, crashing
through the roof of St. Paul's, had destroyed the High Altar. "Our ordeal
continues," wrote Francis. "Just as we were congratulating ourselves on
having survived the threat of a summer invasion, Anti-Christ plunges us
into hell again with his *Donner-und-Blitzen* tactics." And suddenly I saw
that I had been so busy congratulating myself on finding not only the
chapel of my vision but the woman of my dreams that I had overlooked
the fact that a new and possibly more demanding phase of my return to
the world was just about to begin.

My most immediate difficulty was that although I had to think of the
Manor as my home, I was still gripped by the desire to shun the main
reception rooms as much as possible in order to avoid the servants.
However I did realise I could hardly conduct my married life while
hiding in corners, and it occurred to me that if I were to acquire at least
one room where no servant would ever go, the knowledge that I had a
bolt-hole would give me the necessary mental stamina to survive the
intrusions of the servants elsewhere. Reluctantly I broached the subject
with Anne, but she was very sympathetic and suggested that I might like

to annex the large dressing-room next door to our bedchamber. This pleased me but trouble surfaced when I began to strip the room naked by hauling out all the wardrobes and tallboys. Apparently this ugly clutter had belonged to DADDY, and when Anne wanted to know why I was unable to be satisfied with the furniture of a country gentleman I felt exactly like the parlour-maid's son that I was.

"I'll choose another room," I said. "Perhaps I should be banished to an attic? Then you wouldn't have to worry about me not behaving like a country gentleman."

"Oh, shut up—stop being so prickly and proud!" cried Anne, much upset, and at once I panicked, apologised profusely and said it would be an honour to live with Mr. Barton-Woods's venerable wardrobes and tallboys.

"Now don't start being dishonest!" said Anne, becoming crosser than ever. "Why say it would be an honour when you've made it quite clear it would be a thundering bore? Chuck everything out and for goodness' sake make yourself thoroughly at home!"

When the bolt-hole was bare, I imported a small chest of drawers from one of the spare rooms and constructed a cupboard between the chimneypiece and the window so that I would have no need of a wardrobe. In the attics I found a table and chair, both broken, but they were easily mended and when I placed them by the window I thought they looked well. I put up a couple of shelves in the hope of increasing my book collection (I had already ordered the new edition of St. Augustine's *De Civitate Dei*) and built myself a small plain oratory in a corner. Before this refurbishment I had cast out the carpet and curtains and painted the room white; the black-out blind provided all the covering the window needed, and the revarnished floorboards were quite handsome enough to render any rug superfluous.

"Funny man!" said Anne when she was finally allowed to inspect the alterations. "You've created a monk's cell! But never mind—here's something which will soften the austerity," and she gave me the engraving of Starbridge Cathedral which I had admired when I had boarded in her spare room.

This gesture was without doubt both kind and generous, but I had been dreaming of a room where there would be no pictures to distract me, and although I admired the engraving I found I was still reluctant to abandon my dreams. Having accepted the gift with fulsome gratitude I hid the picture in the cupboard as soon as Anne left the room. Later, of course, she found out. Our consequent altercation could hardly be described as a row but it was definitely a tiff and afterwards I regret to record that I sulked. However eventually I remembered that I was a married man who should be prepared to compromise, not an abbot with a license to do as he pleased, so before I went to bed that night I hung the engraving over the fireplace. I always think St. Paul's admonition: "Let not the sun go down on thy wrath," should be permanently inscribed on the memories of all married couples.

I had barely succeeded in working myself into a position where I could regard at least a small corner of the Manor as "home" when the next problem loomed on the horizon: I had to revise my view that it was quite unnecessary for me to know anything about Anne's money. I had already made it clear that I did not want to take a penny of it for my own needs, that I wished to contribute, albeit in a modest way, to the cost of running the household, and that she was to continue to manage her financial affairs as if I did not exist, but in fact, as I now discovered, I had been insensitive. Anne wanted to share her money with me; she saw the sharing as a gesture of loving trust, and when I had repudiated it so peremptorily she had felt hurt. As soon as I realised my mistake I changed course. I agreed to be briefed on her financial affairs, but I still could not bring myself to accept her offer of a joint bank account, and when she tried to give me an absurdly large sum of money I was quite unable to conceal my horror of being "kept."

"You're being thoroughly pig-headed and proud again!" exclaimed Anne exasperated. "You know perfectly well you need some extra cash at the moment—take the money, pay off the loan from the Order and for goodness' sake buy some more clothes before the government starts to ration them! Daddy ordered all his clothes from a Starbridge tailor who used to work in Savile Row."

The word "Daddy" was like a red rag to a bull. Knowing I was being difficult but finding I was quite unable to stop myself I said obstinately: "Savile Row's not my sort of place. Unnecessary extravagance. I'll find a cheap tailor elsewhere."

"I don't want my husband dressed in cheap clothes!" exploded Anne, and at once the chasm of class yawned between us again, but this time it was she who made the effort to bridge it. Controlling her temper she said with a sympathy I hardly deserved: "Darling, don't think I don't understand what you're going through—I know how hard it must be for you to adjust to your new life and believe me, I spend a lot of time worrying in case you're secretly miserable."

That made me pull myself together with unprecedented speed. The last thing I wanted was to be such a tiresome burden to her that she spent her time worrying about me. "I'm fine!" I said firmly. "In fact I'm even beginning to feel comfortable with the servants." But I knew this statement still bore more resemblance to wishful thinking than to reality.

My extreme sensitivity on the subject of servants arose not merely because of my mother's background, although of course the fact that she had been a servant inevitably precluded me from adopting the comfortable upper-class assumption that servants were a race apart who welcomed being treated with an authority devoid of inhibitions. My own inhibitions, which I knew I now had to overcome, also arose from the fact that I had not been brought up in a house well-populated with servants. Priding herself on her housekeeping skills, my mother had preferred to do her own cooking, shopping, dusting, polishing and sweeping; a succession of raw young girls had been employed to shift coal, help with the laundry and toil over the heavy cleaning, but since these creatures had been mainly confined to the scullery I had seldom encountered them. Certainly I had never had to give them orders.

When I married, Betty had dealt with the inevitable female who had to be employed as the maid-of-all-work, and again my contact with the servant had been minimal. It was true that years later as an abbot I had been waited on hand and foot by numerous monks performing the work of servants, but since we had all been brothers, all doing our different work for God and for the community, my inhibitions had not been aroused. However my position at Starrington Manor was very different from my position at Grantchester, and I found it hard not to feel that a walk through the house was a walk through enemy territory where a housemaid lay waiting to ambush me around every corner. Ridiculous though I knew my inhibitions were, they still contrived to make me feel debilitatingly ill at ease in the early weeks of my marriage, but in fact the servants were very kind, possibly because they soon realised I had no intention of meddling in their routine, possibly because I treated them with consideration and never rang bells unnecessarily. When I sensed I had won their approval I did venture to hope that I would adjust to them in the end, just as I would eventually adjust to the fact that I should from time to time accept money gracefully from my rich wife, but the next obstacle in my path certainly seemed as if it might defy all my attempts to adjust to it. I found myself becoming increasingly troubled by Anne's social life.

I had already realised that Anne had a wide circle of acquaintances in the county but I had not imagined that she would have to see them so often. Doubtless I had been misled by my memories of the unsociable "Miss Fielding" at Allington, and I was surprised when she showed a pronounced inclination to be gregarious.

I am a sociable person in the sense that I find people interesting and am more than willing to devote myself to their spiritual needs, but I have a horror of vacuous conversation conducted amidst a surfeit of food and drink. Moreover after I had embarked on my curacy I found I was too tired in the evenings to regard dinner-parties as other than a senseless ordeal. I had been willing to be paraded at the estate office; indeed I had enjoyed my tour of the Home Farm. I had also been willing to be paraded before Anne's acquaintances; it seemed only polite that we should offer them hospitality to make amends for their exclusion from the wedding. But a lifetime of regular parading would have been unendurably tedious.

"I'm not suggesting we should give up our social activities entirely," I said, trying hard to be tactful, "but in future I must restrict myself to the engagements which are essential to my position as curate. And talking of my curacy"—I hesitated but felt impelled by the seriousness of the matter to continue—"have you thought yet about how you might best help me in the parish? I know I said I was willing to let your role evolve, but perhaps the time's come for you to give the evolution a helping hand. If you spent a little less time being a social butterfly and a little more time considering matters which are truly important—"

"How dare you call me a social butterfly!" cried Anne. "You know perfectly well I prefer to be curled up with a good book instead of talking to some old bore about hunting, shooting and fishing, but these are people I've known all my life and I can't cut them altogether just because I've married a clergyman! Some social obligations simply have to be honoured; it's a question of being polite and kind and decent—and if you can't see that I think you're being thoroughly un-Christian!"

Eventually we sorted ourselves out. I said that of course she must honour her social obligations and of course it was wrong of me to make additional demands on her time when she was already burdened with her vital war work on the estate and of course it would be sufficient if she did no parish work at all but merely came to church on Sundays. Anne said that of course she would do parish work and of course she would cut down ruthlessly on our social engagements and of course she understood my point of view. "I'm sorry I lost my temper," she added, "but I couldn't bear it when you started behaving like a Victorian autocrat bringing up a child bride."

I apologised again before saying tentatively: "I'm afraid I do tend to be very single-minded about my work, but I feel so deeply that when one's working for God every other activity is potentially a pointless distraction."

In the silence that followed I realised that at last Anne was seeing me not through a romantic haze but in the cold, clear light of reality, not as an alluring ex-monk but as a fanatical priest who thought nothing of carving up his wife's social life and dictating to her about how she should organise her spare time.

I panicked. "My darling Anne, you mustn't think I don't fight hard against fanaticism—of course balance and moderation are always essential in a religious life—"

"It's all right," said Anne abruptly. "I love you as you are, fanaticism and all, but I can see now that I've underestimated the importance of this curacy. I've been thinking of it as a hobby for you while you waited for your call to unfold. I didn't realise you'd take it so seriously."

"All work for God should be taken seriously."

"Of course. I've been stupid." Impulsively she gave me a kiss. "I'm sure you'll make a huge success of the parish!" she exclaimed with her warmest smile. "I shall feel so proud of you!"

And that was the moment when I knew I could never burden her with my rapidly expanding problems as the curate of Starrington Magna.

2

HOWEVER before my problems as a parish priest could unfold in their full magnitude I was busy repairing the rift with my children. On my return from the honeymoon I wrote again to Martin and this time, to my profound relief, my communication bore fruit. I received a letter which read:

Dear Dad:
Just collected your last two screeds—my old cow of a landlady hadn't forwarded them. Congratulations on the bride. That's fast work for an ex-monk. In fact that's fast work for anyone. But presumably at sixty one feels there's no time to lose, and why the hell shouldn't you have some fun while you still can? If that bitch Ruth is behaving as if you ought to be censored by the Lord Chamberlain, take no bloody notice.

MARTIN.

P.S. Despite my advancing years I got into the Army, first by persecuting the military father of an old school friend (long live the old school tie) and second by persuading the Army medical men in a triumph of acting that I'd never had a homosexual thought or too much to drink in my life. So now I'm busy learning how to kill people and I hope you're pleased.
P.P.S. New address enclosed but please don't write unless you can produce a letter which doesn't read as if it's come hot from the pen of a religious maniac.

I wrote the required careful reply, urging him to visit me as soon as he had leave, but no further word came. However at least I was able to assure Anne that I had been correct in assuming Martin's failure to attend the wedding was the result of ignorance, not ill-will. I could also tell her with pride that he was anxious to fight Hitler, but my pride was shadowed by the dread that in his desire to convince me of his masculinity he had picked a role he would never be able to sustain.

To distract myself from worrying about him I turned my attention to Ruth and wrote:

"I have been thinking so much of the difficulties which are keeping us apart, and I wonder if it would ease matters if you made your first visit to Starrington without the family? Much as I would like to see Roger and the children, I feel the need to give you my undivided attention." At this point I paused, remembering how DADDY, that repulsive specimen of masculine arrogance, had caused Anne so much unhappiness by treating her as if she were second-rate, and the next moment my guilt was driving me to add: "Please think of this invitation from my point of view as well as your own. I'm so anxious to show you off to Anne! You're my only daughter and *most important to me*. It's not enough for me to tell Anne how proud I am of you. I want her to see for herself how smart and attractive you are."

A week later Ruth and I were travelling from the station to the Manor in Anne's Rolls-Royce.

3

RUTH was looking exceedingly fetching in her over-dressed way but I knew she was nervous. Her nervousness unfortunately took the form of a manner refined to the point of caricature, but I told myself to suppress all critical thoughts and be grateful that she was on her best behaviour.

Anne was nervous too, and her nervousness took the form of abrupt remarks; I was reminded of "Miss Fielding" at Allington. But she tried hard to make Ruth feel welcome, and when she asked to see photographs of the children I could sense her guest becoming more relaxed.

Ruth appeared to admire the house, although to my annoyance I saw her testing the drawing-room mantelshelf for dust while Anne was looking the other way. Mindful of Ruth's interest in domestic matters I suggested that Anne might show her the kitchens, but Ruth at once became absurdly grand and declined. However after luncheon I made the right move and bore her off to the chapel, not merely because I wanted her to see it but because I knew she would welcome the chance to have me to herself. As she was wearing high-heeled shoes a walk through the woods posed difficulties, but fortunately Anne was able to lend her a pair of Wellington boots.

"Well, it's a lovely place, I must say," said Ruth, glancing back at the house as we crossed the lawn, "but isn't it funny that someone of her class could be content for her home to be so shabby and old-fashioned? I'd get a new three-piece suite for that sitting-room *and* I'd do something about the plumbing! That Victorian lavatory in the downstairs cloakroom is really very peculiar."

"Stop worrying about the lavatory and enjoy these beautiful woods."

"Yes, it's a nice garden, isn't it, and of course she's nice too, I can see that, although since she's got money I'm surprised she's not smarter. What a pity she doesn't do something about her hair! Still, never mind, the only important thing is that she's nice, although I must say you seem rather like a fish out of water in these 'county' surroundings. I shouldn't have thought it suited you in the least—a little flat over our garage would have been much more to your taste, but I do see that it'll be nice for you to have a young companion in your old age."

"Look to your left," I said, "and you'll see the chapel."

"Oh yes, how sweet. Of course the age difference doesn't matter now when you're an active sixty and she hasn't the dress-sense to look as young as she should, but in ten years' time—"

My patience snapped. I rounded on her. "Ruth—" I began, but I won the battle for self-control. All I said in the end was: "My dear, I do beg you not to be jealous."

"Jealous! What an obscene thing to say!"

I suddenly felt I could not bear her to enter the chapel. The thought of her polluting its serenity with her troubled psyche was repugnant to me. Still struggling not to lose my temper I said: "I'm sorry. Obviously I should make allowances for your profound unhappiness."

"I'm not unhappy!"

"I think you are—indeed how can you not be unhappy when you're cut off from God and adrift in such an unreal world?" I knew this was quite the wrong thing to say but as my patience finally expired I could conceal my true feelings no longer. "I can't tell you what a grief it is to me that you've stopped going to church and that your children are being brought up in an utterly secular environment—"

"Oh Daddy, please! *Please!*"

"I know it must be very difficult being married to an atheist who can think of nothing but unrealities such as possessions, but I feel so strongly that if only you could renew your links with the Church—"

"It wouldn't be any use. I'm just not a religious sort of person, and anyway in the end I came to feel that God wasn't interested in me, didn't care—"

"How can you say that when He's conferred such blessings on you? Of course I'm aware that there are difficulties. Life's never perfect, but by the grace of God even the most intractable problems can be—"

"Oh, for God's sake shut up about bloody religion and stop criticising me the whole damned time! You've got the sort of daughter you want now—although heaven only knows what you see in her—so why don't you just leave me alone?"

The scene ground remorselessly on into disaster.

4

"YOU both looked very white around the gills when you returned from your walk," said Anne after the chauffeur had borne Ruth away in the Rolls. "Was there some ghastly scene at the chapel?"

"No," I said, mindful that the scene had taken place in the woods.

"What did she think of the chapel?"

"Her exact word was 'sweet.' "

"What an extraordinary adjective to choose!" Anne said astonished but decided to press the matter no further. Instead she asked: "What did she think of me?"

"She said how nice you were."

"What a relief!"

There was a small but deadly pause as we both wondered what to say next. In the end I heard myself remark abruptly: "I dare say you were surprised by how common she was."

Anne's expression changed. I was acutely aware of her wondering how she could be kind without forfeiting her honesty, but to my relief she decided that to be honest was to be kind. "Well," she said, "to be absolutely frank, yes, I was."

"Betty was the daughter of a man who kept a tobacconist's shop," I said colourlessly, once more cursing the premarital reticence which had been regularly tripping me up, just as Francis had prophesied, ever since my journey to the altar. "Her mother was a cheap, vulgar, silly woman and when she took charge of the children some of that cheap, vulgar silliness inevitably rubbed off on Ruth. Martin escaped, of course; he went away to school." I hesitated but forced myself to add: "I'm sorry I didn't tell you all that earlier."

"Are you?" said Anne. "How curious. It's comparatively unimportant. What's much more important is that Martin's a homosexual alcoholic, and I'm very sorry indeed that you didn't see fit to tell me that earlier."

Here indeed was the day of reckoning for my premarital reticence. I felt as if all the breath had been battered from my body. "Ruth told you? She actually told you?"

"Well, of course she told me! She wanted to see how married we were and how far you'd confided in me, so as soon as you went to the lavatory after lunch—"

"But how dare she!" Panic and guilt were conveniently submerged beneath my rage. "How dare she behave like a spiteful little girl and humiliate you like that!"

"Don't be a damned fool!" said Anne in fury. "Do you think I let her get the better of me? Of course I said I knew everything there was to know about Martin!"

There was a long silence. Finally I found I had to sit down.

"It makes me wonder what else you haven't told me," said Anne, her voice shaking. "I thought we trusted each other. I feel very hurt. I'm sorry, I'm trying hard to be forgiving, but—"

"Oh Anne, Anne—"

"—it's pretty damn difficult. I felt so upset," said Anne on the verge of tears. "That horrid, glossy, manicured bitch hating me behind her ghastly facade of refinement—why didn't you warn me she was like that? The least you could have done was warn me, but no, you went on painting this utterly false picture of a charming housewife who disapproved of your quick marriage out of a saintly concern for your welfare! I was absolutely unprepared for her sheer vulgar awfulness, and then when she tried to trap me about Martin—oh, it was vile, *vile*—I hated every minute of her visit and I never want to see her again!"

She rushed out of the room. The door banged. In despair I covered my face with my hands.

5

"MY darling Anne, forgive me—I didn't mean to put you in such a humiliating position—"

"Well, you did. Look, I didn't mean to be so beastly about Ruth—she's probably not as bad as all that and I don't mind trying to be nice to her for your sake, but Jon, I just don't understand why you couldn't confide in me."

We were sitting on the edge of our bed. I was leaning forward with my elbows on my knees and clasping my hands so tightly that they ached. Anne was bolt upright, her fingers clutching the folds of the counterpane so hard that her knuckles shone white. At last with a great effort I managed to say: "My children show me in such an appalling light and I didn't want you to see me in any light which was appalling."

Anne stared. "That sounds as if you've tied yourself up in a most fantastic knot again. Why do you keep doing this? Why are you so frightened of being honest with me?"

"I have a horror of wearying you with my private burdens. I'm afraid of you losing patience, finding me an elderly bore—"

"Oh good heavens, I do believe you're worrying about being a deserted vegetable again! Now stop being so silly and let's sort this out. Why do you think your children show you in an appalling light?"

Very slowly I began to paint my painful portrait of the past.

6

SOME time later Anne said: "Plenty of people have to endure far less paternal attention than you gave your children, and most of them have no trouble turning out well. I think Ruth and Martin were very lucky to have a conscientious father who did his best for them in difficult circumstances, and if they now turn out to have ghastly problems why shouldn't they accept at least some of the blame?"

"That's a question Francis has asked. But letting them assume some of the responsibility for their fate does nothing to erase my guilt about my own share of the responsibility."

"But are you sure this guilt isn't misplaced? If you ask me, all that's really going on here is that you happened to father two children with whom you've no particular affinity—with the result that you can't dote on them quite as much as they'd like."

"That's a comforting theory because it exonerates me from blame, but—"

"—you can't believe in it. All right, supposing your guilt was justified; why is it still crucifying you? Didn't you atone for your guilt when you became a monk?"

"I went through the motions of atonement, certainly, but it was all based on the false premise of that superstitious bargain with God. I still can't feel that I'm forgiven for my sins."

"Well, I'm no theologian," said Anne, "but I thought that if one demonstrated a true repentance—"

"I always feel in my heart that my repentance isn't true. I always feel that if I were in the same position as I was in thirty-six years ago, I'd commit the same sins all over again because I'm incapable of being anything but an inadequate parent."

"But Jon, what about when *we* have a baby? You surely don't think—"

"Oh no, no, no!" I said rapidly, cursing myself for the fatal indiscretion. "Any child of yours would be quite different! My guilt about Ruth and Martin is all bound up with my guilt about Betty."

"But it must be such a crippling burden! If only you could feel you were forgiven—"

"Every time I see Ruth and Martin I always know the forgiveness has been withheld. I can't describe to you the sheer awfulness of the scenes which go on."

"Poor darling, but never mind," said Anne kissing me. "I'm sure that next time you'll be a huge success as a father—I've every confidence in you."

Before I could stop myself I was praying that we might remain childless.

7

THIS reaction shocked me so much, contrary as it was not only to a fundamental aim of Christian marriage but to Anne's hopes of happiness, that instead of celebrating Mass by myself the next morning in the chapel I confessed the sin before God, set myself a penance and spent an additional hour in spiritual exercises. I should, of course, have journeyed to Starwater to make my confession to Cyril—Father Darcy would certainly have thought this a more profound exercise in humility—but I told myself I was too busy grappling with parish matters; by that time I was very much aware that my major problem, the problem which overshadowed all others, was my ministry as a country priest.

Starrington Magna was a large village and the parish boundaries included not only the hamlet of Starrington Parva but an area of scattered farms and smallholdings. Altogether I had the care of some two thousand souls of whom about a hundred were Methodists who gathered weekly in a hall near the station. I was told there were no Roman Catholics in the parish, and this fact was declaimed in the manner of a virtuous housewife announcing that her home was free of mice. Of those who belonged to the Church of England, a minority never went to church and a majority entered it only for christenings, weddings and funerals but a respectable number turned up at Christmas and Easter. Allowing for the decline in regular church-going I thought the number of weekly worshippers was more than merely respectable, although of course I immediately found myself wondering how this loyal band of supporters could be increased. All this useful information about the parish had been recorded by Mr. Wetherall himself in an account which he had written for the benefit of those who had the care of his flock in his absence; he had also set out details of the various social clubs and the areas of the parish which required special visiting.

I had realised at once that transport presented a problem, for I could hardly go visiting the poor in Anne's chauffeur-driven motor, and although I was prepared to walk everywhere, long journeys on foot are time-consuming. As I had always worked in small areas I had never encountered this problem before, but fortunately Mrs. Wetherall, foreseeing my predicament, offered me her husband's bicycle and I soon accustomed myself to riding it. It had proved a pleasant surprise to discover how greatly the machines had improved in comfort and safety since my youth in the 1890s.

Mr. Wetherall had relied very much on his bicycle. He had been active among the rural poor in the remote areas of his parish, and his work in listening, helping and consoling had borne fruit; the congregation consisted not merely of the comfortable middle classes but of the humbler families as well. Obviously he had been an admirable pastor, and I found that thanks to his hard work I had inherited a parish that had been only minimally debilitated by eight months of caretaking.

From one point of view this was an asset, but from another it was a disadvantage. Mr. Wetherall had been popular. With his memory now glorified by his war service, the villagers tended to see him as a paragon with the result that I was continually being confronted with such fatal phrases as: "The vicar said . . . the vicar believed . . . the vicar did things *this* way." I could not even remove the most repulsive vase of dried flowers from a secluded alcove without a chorus of females telling me: "The vicar wanted the flowers to stay there because they came from old Mrs. Lacy who was so kind to him," and soon I realised that there existed an influential clique who believed any change whatsoever would be nothing short of stabbing Mr. Wetherall in the back. Of the two church-wardens one was Anne's friend Colonel Maitland who was anxious to be accommodating to me, but the other was a formidable bore called Pitkin, the local chemist, who talked as if he and Mr. Wetherall had run the parish unaided. I immediately realised that Mr. Wetherall, a man twenty years younger than this power-mad churchwarden, had allowed himself to be bullied far too often, and I saw that one of my first tasks was to teach Mr. Pitkin that his bullying days were over.

However a more serious problem lay neither with the potent memory of Mr. Wetherall nor with the troublesome male members of the congregation but with the females. As I have already made clear, I was unaccustomed to dealing with women on a pastoral level, but it is a notorious fact of parish life that middle-aged and elderly women form the nucleus of the congregation, representing the brigade of church-workers whom no clergyman can do without. I had to adjust to my brigade and adjust quickly, but I found it a strain which took a heavy toll on my spiritual stamina.

The women were mostly good women in their own way but soon I encountered bickering, backchat, gossip and a general level of pettiness sufficient to irritate any man beyond endurance. The problem was compounded, I am sorry to record, by the fact that as the male in the centre of their band I became an object of intense interest verging on obsession, and soon they were all vying in a most unedifying fashion for my favour.

It is easy to laugh at this problem, but the Whitby Affair had taught me that situations which start by being mildly amusing can quickly become dangerously bizarre. I knew I had to dampen the ardour of my ladies' hero-worship, but because of my inexperience as a pastor of women I was uncertain how this could be achieved. Being hero-worshipped by men is quite different; one can be firm to the point of brutality yet still put everything right by giving a brief smile at the end of the reproof. The result is that the men respect one's toughness, know they have to pull themselves together, yet know too that they remain unrejected. When I tried this approach with one of the women she merely dissolved into tears. I was both horrified and baffled. What was I to do? What had Mr. Wetherall done? But Mr. Wetherall was the same age as Charles and the prevalent feminine attitude to him had clearly been maternal. I was a man of their own generation and their attitude was predatory. It made no difference that I was married. They all appeared to like Anne, and besides probably none of them wanted me in any straightforward carnal way. They only desired endless carnal titillation from my presence. The situation was most perturbing, and the most perturbing part of all was that the more impeccably I behaved the worse the situation became. Impeccability evidently inflamed them. I began to suspect that short of transforming myself into a cross-eyed midget I was to have no escape from this absurd and potentially unhealthy situation.

I can never quite understand why women find me attractive, but since there is consistent evidence that they do I have been obliged to accept the attraction as a fact. And of course this fact is highly gratifying to my pride. (Small wonder that Father Darcy thought my ministry should be only to men.) But once pride is cast aside and the female attitude viewed dispassionately, the root of the attraction remains embedded in mystery. I am not in the least handsome in any conventional sense of the word. I have a bony, angular face which often looks positively ugly when I shave it in the harsh light of early morning. I also have a pallor which in a woman could be described as "interesting" but which in a man can only appear sinister. Apart from my unusual height the most striking detail of my appearance is that my hair and eyes are a matching shade of grey, but this is a recent development, and when I was a young man with mouse-coloured hair and pale eyes framed by spectacles I could only judge myself very plain indeed. However even in those days plenty of women appeared to disagree with me. I can only conclude that in some mysterious way my attraction lies in the powers, those "glamorous powers," which have so consistently embroiled me in trouble. Women sense them and respond. "You have such an unusual presence," a girl had said to me once, and another had added: "That air of authority's so striking." When I was in the cloister I had assumed that my grey hair would provide me with a new respectability, countering the unsuitable raciness exuded by the powers, but now I realised in dismay that instead I had acquired a touch of distinction which only enhanced my appeal to the opposite sex. The result was that I was probably less suited than I had ever been in my life to work in a pastoral capacity among women.

Even if I had been single I would have had no desire to misbehave with any of my attentive females, all of whom I found effortlessly resistible, and we were certainly a long way from an outbreak of hysteria at Matins, but the atmosphere of simmering sexuality was an intolerable distraction and very bad for everyone's spiritual health. Women should come to church to worship God, not to ogle at the priest. The priest should feel free to move without constraint among his flock, not smitten with the urge to groan when trapped in the vestry by a purposeful admirer.

I used the vestry as an office; I considered it my duty to be as accessible as possible to those who needed me, and my humbler parishioners might well have thought twice before knocking on the door of the Manor, but I was so often pestered by women who wanted to chat about nothing that I soon wound up well-nigh demented with exasperation. Most of my day seemed to be wasted on trivialities. I had little scope for my talents, and the work often appeared not only dull but unrewarding. I had struck an edifying pose to Aysgarth when I had insisted that the former Abbot of Grantchester should not be too proud to serve as a rural priest, but Aysgarth's argument that I had a duty to find a post commensurate with my abilities in order to serve God best had in fact been the sounder spiritual position. Deprived of the opportunity to exercise my special skill, the counselling of churchmen in varying degrees of distress, and unable to make use of my special experience acquired at Ruydale, the training of men for the priesthood, I found that my psyche was quickly invaded by boredom, frustration and restlessness.

My alienation from my new work was exacerbated by the fact that I still felt spiritually disorientated. Carefully I set aside a portion of each day for prayer and meditation, but I missed the framework of the monastic office and ever since my return to the world I had been depressed by the turgid level of worship in the churches. After seventeen years in a monastery, where worship is regarded as of the first importance, I could not help but be appalled by the poor singing, the lacklustre responses and the general air of genteel ennui. Possibly I was being too critical; probably I was setting an impossibly high standard for laymen; but the fact remained that my dissatisfaction increased my irritation with the curacy I had so unscrupulously managed to obtain.

Once or twice I started a frank letter to Francis but I tore my efforts up and sent a bland report instead. I was too proud to acknowledge the truth we both knew: that I had taken on the curacy for the wrong reasons. In addition although I was now paying the price for my self-aggrandisement, I was too proud to admit the cost was proving more expensive than I had anticipated. I did see Cyril at Starwater every two weeks to make my confession but Cyril, though a formidable priest in many ways, had neither Father Darcy's uncanny power of intuiting concealed truths nor the worldly scepticism combined with hard logic which made Francis so difficult to deceive. In other words, I found I could manipulate Cyril. However at least I was not too proud to recognise that this was a most unsatisfactory state of affairs, and finally I tried to face up to the mess by praying for the grace to improve my situation in the way which would prove most pleasing to God. It then occurred to me that instead of secretly moaning that the members of my flock were driving me mad with their trivial problems, banal activities and limp attitude to worship, I had to serve them with a verve that would rouse the entire parish from its languid mediocrity.

I had already dusted down the organist and shaken up the choirboys; the former had been playing at a funereal pace in keys which favoured alto-tenors, and the latter had become accustomed to stuffing themselves with sweets during the sermon. (The retired canon who had been taking the services had been too blind to see this disgusting exhibition of juvenile greed.) I now cultivated the organist by encouraging him to venture deeper into the rich pastures of English Church music, and I took a similar winning interest in the choirboys; I singled them out for special attention when I visited the village school once a week to take the obligatory Scripture classes. The choirboys' mothers also benefitted from my benign attention, with the result that all the little surplices were washed and starched, all the little heads possessed clean, parted hair and all the little feet were clad in shining shoes.

As I had proved at Grantchester, clean people in a clean environment perform their work better, and having polished the choirboys to a high lustre I turned my attention to the church by engaging a new cleaning woman who I judged would wage war on dirt with a zeal worthy of Ruth. I then organised my brigade of ladies into a flurry of flower-arranging and sent the altar-cloth to the cleaners.

More innovations followed. I changed the disagreeable brand of Communion wine despite howls of protest from the communicants who possessed a sweet tooth. Chopping verses ruthlessly from psalms and hymns I tried to make the conventional services brighter and brisker; it is a fallacy, as both the Low Church and the High Church parties have proved in their very different ways, that reverent worship can only be recognised by its dreary pace and somnolent content. Then I reduced the time of the sermon. It is a characteristic of Anglo-Catholic worship that less emphasis is placed on the sermon than on the liturgy, and rather than declaiming for half an hour in true Protestant fashion, I offered my congregation between ten and fifteen minutes of simple but I hoped not insignificant discourse. I am not one of those flamboyant oratorical preachers such as Dr. Jardine, the former Bishop of Starbridge, but nevertheless in my own austere way I have always been able to make an incisive impression on an audience. Preaching too is a charism, of course, and like all charisms it can be subject to abuse, but I was very careful, as I strove to rouse the parish from its apathy, not to give way to the temptation to resort to the shadier methods of evangelism.

I knew from the beginning that it would be unwise for me to introduce a form of worship that reflected my High Church inclinations into a parish where antipathy to Catholicism ran high, but when I embarked on my effort to stimulate my congregation I found I could not accept that the only Anglo-Catholic touch I was allowed to make was the reduced length of the sermon. Cautiously I introduced a few candles, and when no one objected I stealthily planted more. Still no one objected, and step by step I then began to incorporate further rich touches of Anglo-Catholic symbolism into my services. I took care to explain each innovation so that no one could accuse me of staging a mere pretty pageant, and for a while I thought I was encountering a miraculous conversion on all fronts to my belief that colourful ritual can aid devotion by making complex religious truths more accessible. But gradually rumours reached me of rebellion.

In the beginning no one made any pointed remarks except my bossy churchwarden Mr. Pitkin, who asked if it was true that I intended to install a statue of the Virgin and order my congregation to worship it. "The worship of statues constitutes idolatry, Mr. Pitkin," I said austerely, "and besides, although St. Mary must be regarded by us with the greatest reverence, worship should be confined to the Trinity." I added to reassure him: "This is the English, not the Roman Church!" and he retired satisfied, but I then made a fatal mistake. The following Sunday I announced during Matins that I intended to set aside a certain time each week for the hearing of confessions.

My purpose in making this move was not simply to gratify my longing to return to my work as a confessor; I still conducted a certain amount of spiritual direction by correspondence with men I had counselled as a monk so I was far from being wholly frustrated in this field. However I hoped that my gesture in offering myself as a confessor to my community might identify those who were in deep need of spiritual help yet had so far been too shy to come forward. Carefully I explained to the congregation that confession to a priest was not compulsory within the Church of England, but the very word "confession" reeks of Popery to a certain type of Protestant, and I found I had opened the floodgates to a tidal wave of complaints about my "Romish" practices.

In vain I insisted that the Anglo-Catholics did not recognise the Pope's jurisdiction and that the English Catholic Church had all the advantages of the Church of Rome (the heritage of the Early Church, the rich liturgical tradition, the distinctive spirituality) and none of the disadvantages (the accretion of superstition and myth, the chaotic history of the Papacy, the despotic power of a leader who purported to be infallible). To my Protestant congregation only the word "Catholic" was audible, and the fact that the Anglo-Catholics were within the Church of England merely provoked the response: "What can the Church be coming to?"

I was accused of genuflection as if it were adultery, of facing east at the crucial point of the Mass as if I were a Moslem praying to Mecca, of making the sign of the cross with the frequency of a magician performing a conjuring trick and of retaining my hold on the chalice as if I feared one of my communicants might run off with it. All my attempts at explanation—and naturally I was quite prepared to justify these alien practices—were brushed aside as the complaints thundered on. I had littered the church with "nasty Papist candles." I had a thoroughly objectionable habit of referring to the service of Holy Communion as Mass. (It was true that after seventeen years with the Fordites I did sometimes let slip the word "Mass" in public, but in fact the habits of one's early years die hard and I usually had no trouble remembering to say "Communion" instead.) Then I was accused of plotting to import a pyx, but fortunately I could deny this charge with a clear conscience since I had had the sense to realise that to introduce perpetual reservation at that stage would certainly have been to push my Anglo-Catholic luck too far. However I insisted that I would continue to reserve the sacrament for the sick, and my enemies, maddened by my firmness, roared back into the attack by accusing me of smuggling incense into the vestry; I had indeed planned to introduce incense into the services at Advent and had even gone so far as to order a censer, but when I saw that no one appeared able to pronounce the word "incense" without a shudder, my nerve failed and I protested that the incense was only for use in the village school's nativity play.

In the midst of all this nonsense my confession hour was overrun by my brigade of ladies, who saw it as a legitimate opportunity to talk to me alone, and the whole worthy experiment dissolved into futility.

I felt so enraged, so frustrated and so debilitated by these unedifying events that I actually sat down to pen a full confession to Francis, but the letter was never written.

The military police informed me that Martin had unsuccessfully attempted to commit suicide.

8

THE suicide attempt had been half-hearted, no more than a cry for help from an actor unable to sustain his role, but in the military hospital the extent of his alcoholism was discovered and he remained a patient there for some weeks before his inevitable discharge from the Army. Of course I visited him but since we still seemed to be incapable of meeting without upsetting each other, the psychiatrist in charge of his case deemed it wiser that I should temporarily keep my distance. I consoled myself with the thought that at least my son was being cared for in a safe place, but I was made very miserable by the incident and for a while all my other problems seemed trivial in comparison.

Anne was kindness itself to me throughout this agonising time but I remained haunted by the anxiety that I might try her patience too far; I was sure the last thing she wanted was to see me crucified by the legacy of my first marriage, and I was also afraid that in my distress I might betray my horror of begetting more children who might grow up profoundly unhappy. Accordingly I drew a veil over my suffering to protect her from it and renewed my efforts never to weary her with any self-centred display of grief.

I did write a brief letter about Martin to Francis, who replied with sympathy and urged me to visit him, but when out of a reluctance to discuss my other problems I declined to leave the parish at that time, I suspected Anne was relieved. London was still under heavy attack, and the Archbishop, bombed out of Lambeth Palace, had even withdrawn to Canterbury; I could not help but think critically of him for his retreat from the capital in such a time of crisis, but Dr. Lang was an old man now and perhaps it ill became me to criticise him when I myself was safe in the country. As all the reports made clear, London had become a nightmare, and soon the nightmare was extended when the Luftwaffe at last turned aside to bomb the provincial cities. In mid-November the great cathedral at Coventry was smashed to rubble, but no bomb could destroy the spirit that dwelt there. Immediately a cross was fashioned from the scorched beams and a month later the Christmas service was broadcast to the nation from the ruins.

Meanwhile the citizens of Starbridge were anxiously eying their famous spire but Starbridge, unlike Coventry, was not an industrial centre and its Cathedral remained intact, a symbol of the indestructible miraculously persisting in a world where destruction had become a way of life. I have always thought that one of the most demonic aspects of war is the way in which evil comes to be accepted as normal to such an extent that it is even woven into the mundane pattern of daily existence. I travelled around the parish with my regulation gas-mask and soon found I could sling it in my bicycle-basket with no more emotion than I expended in putting on my hat. I talked to the Home Guard, a jolly, friendly bunch of men, and found it easy to forget they had been licensed to commit murder. I spoke to air-raid wardens who enforced the black-out and never boggled at the possibility that a stray bomb could blow us all to smithereens. I embarked on a campaign to raise money for the victims of Coventry but soon ceased to be horrified by the revolting fact that these innocent civilians had been maimed by men deliberately pulling levers in machines travelling far above the earth. Insanity and normality went hand in hand, and as I approached the familiar Christmas festivities I saw my own private world reflecting the War in microcosm again, my dark stark problems flowing with a sinister invisibility alongside my comforting Christian routine.

With the help of Anne and the village schoolmistresses I staged a magnificent nativity play. A well-attended carol service, designed to cater to Protestant taste, followed the next day, and on Christmas Eve I decided I had earned the right to celebrate a midnight Mass in the best Anglo-Catholic tradition. My devoted ladies, all of whom had become Anglo-Catholics, praised me fulsomely afterwards, but the wretch Pitkin was outraged and before the end of the year I had a visit from the rural dean, a round, rubicund gentleman who supervised six parishes in my corner of the diocese and whom I found prowling around the altar one morning as if he were sniffing for incense. I gave him luncheon at the Manor, plied him liberally with vintage port and expected to hear no more from the authorities, but in the new year Aysgarth wrote to request an interview, and with a sinking heart I realised—too late—that my talent for disruption had landed me in the sort of trouble which any priest in his right mind would have been at pains to avoid.

9

I RECEIVED Aysgarth in the vestry. A small paraffin heater alleviated the chill in the room, but apart from this one touch of luxury my surroundings were impressively spartan. If Aysgarth had expected to see me languishing in luxurious vestments amidst a cloud of incense, he was doomed to disappointment.

"I'm sorry to trouble you like this," he said civilly when we were both seated. "After the rural dean reported that in his opinion the fuss was a storm in a teacup I was going to do no more than write you a letter, but since the Bishop himself has now received a complaint he's suggested that it might be helpful if we had an informal talk." He paused before adding blandly: "When a new clergyman takes charge of a parish it's important to iron out any initial difficulty as quickly as possible."

"I'm trying hard, I assure you, Archdeacon, to iron out my initial difficulty, but unfortunately Mr. Pitkin doesn't take kindly to being ironed."

Receiving this good-natured comment with a repellent absence of humour Aysgarth said stiffly: "I'm sorry to hear you've fallen out with Mr. Pitkin. It pays a parson to keep on good terms with his churchwardens."

I was well aware of this obvious fact of clerical life and I disliked being treated as a parish novice by a man who was young enough to be my son. Abruptly I demanded: "What's the exact charge against me?"

"It's said that you deviate frequently from the rubric."

"But everyone knows the rubric isn't strictly enforced nowadays!"

"Nevertheless it represents the rules governing worship in the Church, and if you deviate from orthodox practice your opponents have a legitimate grievance against you. For example, I'm told that you present the chalice to the lips of the communicants instead of "into their hands" as the rubric orders—"

"Would you like me to see the Bishop to reassure him that I've no intention of going over to Rome?"

Of course he hated being reminded that I had the Bishop under my thumb. I saw his hard mouth tighten but he kept his temper and merely continued to list the charges against me. One or two, like the example he had already cited, were justified. The rest were a tribute to Pitkin's anti-Papist paranoia.

"I can't urge you too strongly to stick to the rubric in future," concluded Aysgarth at last despite my vigorous defence of my rights as a Catholic within the Church of England, "and I'd also urge you to make your peace with the hostile minority by soft-pedalling the Anglo-Catholic touches for the time being. In a rural parish like this it's vital to acknowledge the strong conservative bias in your congregation by making changes slowly. Of course I'm willing to allow for the fact that you've no previous experience in a rural parish, but—"

"Thank you, Archdeacon, but there's no need for you to sweeten your reproof with a coating of sugar. I trust," I said, inwardly seething with rage, "that I'm capable of acknowledging my errors with a proper spirit of humility. I'm sorry you've been troubled by this matter. I shall do my best to see you're not troubled again."

That terminated the conversation but I could see I had once more annoyed Aysgarth by adopting a tone which would have been better suited to admonishing recalcitrant monks. I wished then that I had been less inflamed with angry pride, but the damage had been done and I knew we had wound up enemies again.

My career as a parish priest seemed to be going from bad to worse. I felt deeply depressed.

10

AFTER Aysgarth had departed I wanted only to return home to seek solace in the chapel, but instead I had to face a bunch of my ladies who arrived five minutes later for a committee meeting. We were due to discuss the arrangements for an evening of entertainment in the church hall to raise money for wounded airmen, but as usual at such committee meetings the conversation continually soared off at irrelevant tangents as my ladies fell increasingly in love with the sound of their own voices. I squeezed a couple of decisions out of them with a ruthlessness which I fear they enjoyed and then terminated the proceedings by announcing my obligation to visit the alms-houses.

The women drifted away, still gossiping, and I was just preparing to follow them when I heard a loud groan resounding in the nave. Hurrying from the vestry I found the new cleaner, Mrs. Purvis, doubled up over her mop and pail halfway down the central aisle. My ladies, clucking in sympathy, were anxious to help but the sufferer could only gasp that there was nothing they could do.

I strode down the aisle, the ranks parted and poor Mrs. Purvis, quite immobilised by pain, at once turned scarlet with embarrassment.

"It's my lumbago, Vicar." (I was often granted this title as a courtesy.) "I mean no disrespect but I can't move. I'm ever so sorry."

I felt as if someone had injected me with a drug which delivered instantaneous amnesia. I forgot the humiliating interview with Aysgarth, my unhappiness in my ministry and my misery over Martin. I was aware only that I was being offered the most alluring of challenges and beyond the challenge I sensed that an admiring audience was already poised to restore my self-esteem.

"Where exactly is the pain, Mrs. Purvis?" Kneeling beside her I put a reassuring hand on her arm.

"Low down in my back, sir—oooh, it's ever so awful, worse than childbirth—"

I touched her at the base of her spine. "Here?"

"That's it—oooh! I can't get up, truly I can't—"

"Never mind about getting up for the moment. Just keep in a position which gives you the least pain."

"I feel ever such a silly—"

"Never mind about that, either. Just concentrate on getting into the best position . . . That's it. Now try to relax as far as you possibly can. Relax your arms first . . . and let the relaxation spread up your arms to your neck . . . and slowly, very slowly, inch by inch down your back . . . Good . . . And breathe calmly . . . deeply . . . Excellent! Now Mrs. Purvis, I want you to concentrate very hard on that part of your body where the pain is and picture the pain as a big red glass ball which you want me to smash. Close your eyes and you'll be able to picture it better . . . Can you see it?"

"Oooh yes, sir—a beautiful red glass ball with air bubbles in it—"

"That's your pain. Concentrate very hard on it, very, very hard, so hard that your mind aches—and now picture me raising a hammer to smash the glass to pieces. Are you concentrating? Concentrating hard—as hard as you possibly can? Good. Now picture me raising the hammer. I'm going to count to five and when I say SMASH, the ball's going to shatter. Ready?" I prayed silently. "One . . . Two . . . Three . . ." I increased the intensity of the prayer, " . . . Four . . . Five—SMASH!"

"Oooh!" gasped Mrs. Purvis.

"Oooh!" gasped my ladies as I grasped Mrs. Purvis's shoulder with one hand and pressed hard on the base of her spine with the other.

"Oooh!" gasped Mrs. Purvis again, shocked into straightening her back. "That felt ever so funny, Vicar!"

"But you can move now."

Mrs. Purvis was stupefied. "So I can!" She turned her body gingerly from side to side. "Well, I never!" She was enrapt. Her honest country-woman's face was aglow with gratitude. "That's a miracle, that is!"

I made no comment but merely helped her to her feet before advising her to go home and rest.

"Yes, sir—thank you, sir—oh, just wait till I tell all my neighbours! Doctor can never do a thing for my lumbago, never, nothing he gives me for it ever does any good at all!"

I looked at my ladies. They were as breathless and shining-eyed as the monks who had witnessed the recovery of Whitby. Finally someone said in a hushed voice: "It *was* a miracle, wasn't it, Father?" and at once I answered: "Nonsense! Pain can often disappear spontaneously if the sufferer is relaxed and confident," but even as I spoke I could see that none of them believed me.

I shuddered at the memory of Father Darcy, but the terrible truth was, as I knew all too well, that for the first time since I had embarked on my curacy I felt genuinely happy as a country priest.

XV

"The line between a quack and a scientific healer is not always easy to draw."

W. R. INGE

A PACIFIST IN TROUBLE

I

"MIGHT this be a sign about your new call?" was Anne's immediate reaction that evening to the tale of Mrs. Purvis.

"Not necessarily."

Anne remained fascinated but I sensed her thoughts moving more cautiously. "*Was* it a miracle?"

"Good heavens, no! Of course there's a perfectly rational explanation. Mrs. Purvis was deeply embarrassed that she should have been caught in such a ridiculous position, and the pain would have been aggravated by her excessive tension. As soon as I had helped her to relax, the pain eased sufficiently to enable me to terminate the spasm by using a mild form of hypnosis. I need hardly add that I haven't cured her of the lumbago—she'll get another spasm sooner or later. All I did was alleviate the symptoms of a particularly unpleasant attack."

Anne said after careful consideration: "I don't see anything wrong with that."

"There's certainly nothing wrong *per se* in alleviating Mrs. Purvis's pain. The complications are going to set in when other people ask me to cure their aches and pains."

"Well, if the prospect troubles you—and it obviously does—why don't you go to Francis and ask his advice?"

"It's so hard to find the time to go to London."

"Surely you could find the time if you wanted to! I think it would do you good to unburden yourself to Francis about Martin and Pitkin and—oh good heavens, I nearly forgot to ask! What happened when Neville Aysgarth called on you today?"

I gave her a colourless account of the unpleasant scene in the vestry and she exclaimed angrily: "Of course Aysgarth follows his mentor Dr. Jardine who never had any sympathy with the Anglo-Catholics!"

I forced myself to say: "In a very real sense our conversation wasn't about Anglo-Catholicism. It was about my inexperience as a parish priest." With a superhuman effort I managed to add: "He had a point. I've probably introduced too many changes too quickly."

Seeing that Aysgarth had upset me, Anne became angrier than ever. "But think of all you've achieved! You've electrified the parish!"

"Yes—like a bolt of lightning which splits a tree in two," I said, but unfortunately this reply, intended as a light remark, emerged as a bitter comment and at once I was furious with myself. It would never do to bore her by moaning about my lot. "Isn't it an irony," I remarked, trying to dismiss the subject with good humour, "that the English, who pride themselves on maintaining the most elaborate ceremonial in so many areas of public life, have this extraordinary mass antipathy to any elaborate ceremonial in religion?"

Anne laughed but said with an unexpected earnestness: "Darling, I can see how depressed you are by all this bigotry, and I really do wish you'd cheer yourself up by slipping up to London for a couple of days' undiluted Anglo-Catholicism—"

"That sounds as if you want to have a holiday from me."

"Oh you silly man, don't talk such nonsense!"

"I'm not complaining about my work—please don't think I'm complaining—"

"I know you're not and sometimes I worry about that too. I don't think it's good for you to bottle everything up and pretend that everything in the garden's lovely—"

"Everything in the garden *is* lovely," I said firmly. "I just have one or two little difficulties at the moment, that's all."

But although Anne made no effort to argue further with me, I suspected that I had only partially alleviated her concern.

2

THAT night I was unable to consummate my marriage. It was not the first time such a failure had occurred after a long hard day's labour in the parish, but now in my depression I felt doubly humiliated, doubly angry and—worst of all—doubly frightened about the future.

"Don't say anything," I muttered to Anne, although she had given no indication that she was about to speak, and then before I could stop myself I was sliding into the most shameful tantrum. "How I hate being sixty!" I burst out. "I hate it, hate it, hate it!" But immediately I despised myself for being too exhausted to suppress the urge to complain.

After a while Anne said: "Am I allowed to speak now?"

"Yes, but don't tell me not to mind about being sixty." I was so miserable that I sounded like a thoroughly irascible old man.

Anne said gently: "I was going to remind you of our honeymoon. Do you remember when you said: 'Don't talk as if you're a performing seal in a circus'?"

"Maybe one day you'll decide you'd be better off with a performing seal."

"Oh, for heaven's sake, Jon!" Understandably she lost patience. "Stop being so damn ridiculous!"

Fear grabbed me by the throat and settled there in a lump. Burying my face in her breasts I tried to apologise but no words came. I was quite unable to speak.

"Silly man!" said Anne, somehow recapturing her patience and even lovingly stroking my hair. "What's one night? As if it mattered!"

But it mattered to me.

I lay awake worrying in the dark.

3

TWO days later at Matins every pew was occupied and afterwards a long queue of people formed to shake my hand as if they wanted to sample my "magic touch." A beaming Mrs. Purvis announced: "I told everyone how your hands gave off those funny electric shocks, Vicar!" and her husband, who was clearly enjoying his wife's new fame, declared admiringly: "Reckon we've got a magician for a parson!" I did say austerely that the practice of magic would hardly have been a fitting occupation for a priest, but nobody was listening. My parishioners were too busy asking me to call on aged relatives housebound by rheumatism, arthritis, lumbago, sciatica and a host of other debilitating complaints, and although I was careful to refer to the doctor anyone who had not received a professional diagnosis, I promised to call on the chronic cases which could no longer be helped by orthodox medicine.

I regret to say I found this deep interest in me immensely stimulating, and that afternoon when I should have been praying quietly in preparation for Evensong I was in such good spirits that I retired to bed with my wife and made amends in no uncertain fashion for my failure two days earlier.

"Thank goodness you got over that depression!" said Anne afterwards. "But after all the hordes in church this morning it's small wonder that you're in a good mood. Don't you think it's obvious now that you're being called to the ministry of healing?"

I knew the correct reply was: "I must continue to pray for guidance," but when I saw the passionate enthusiasm in her eyes, the words were never spoken. I could only bask in the warmth of her unstinted admiration and eventually I found myself reflecting that it did indeed seem as if my new call had begun to unfold.

4

I COULD do little for the housebound old people, although they all seemed determined to believe that I had relieved their pain to some degree. I suspected that they derived comfort principally from the fact that someone in authority was prepared to listen sympathetically to their troubles, but by this time the village was more than ready to believe their parson had miraculous powers, and I was just wondering how I should deal with the continuing stream of requests for help when I received a visit from the local doctor.

Dr. Garrison was a man in his fifties with a bluff, hearty manner and a resolute atheism courteously expressed. At our first meeting he had said: "I wish you well, Darrow, and if there's anything I can do for you let me know, but I'm afraid you won't see me in church because I'm a practical down-to-earth fellow who hasn't time for theories which can't be scientifically proved." In other words he acknowledged only five senses and was determined to justify this limitation by embracing logical positivism. However plenty of excellent people are logical positivists, and since he had tried in his own way to give me a friendly welcome to the parish, I had seen no reason to dislike him.

"Well, I won't beat about the bush," he said, bustling into the vestry and flinging himself down in the visitor's chair. "What's all this I hear about faith-healing? I wouldn't have thought a man of your distinction would dabble in quackery, Darrow!"

"You thought correctly."

Garrison at once became irritated, and beyond the irritation I sensed his fear of matters that defied conventional explanations. "Then perhaps you'd be good enough to explain the incident with Mrs. Purvis," he said abruptly. "How did you remove the symptoms of her lumbago?"

"I offered myself to God as a channel for the healing power of the Holy Spirit."

He went scarlet. "Don't joke about this, please. It's a serious matter."

"I don't joke about God. I'm a priest."

"You may be a clergyman—why do you have to use a damn Papist word like 'priest'?—but you're behaving like a witch-doctor! Don't you know that removing symptoms by hypnosis can lead to a serious illness remaining undiagnosed?"

"You diagnosed the lumbago in this case. I would never attempt to help anyone who hadn't first consulted a doctor, nor would I ever attempt to help anyone solely by using hypnotic techniques. The charism of healing can't be reduced to a parlour-trick."

"No? It looks damnably like a parlour-trick to me!"

"Dr. Garrison," I said, "you may choose to confine yourself within the narrow boundaries of medical science, but I fail to see why those you can't help should be similarly confined."

He was incensed. "That's a highly offensive remark!"

"Not half so offensive as your accusation that a gift from God is a man-made trick. Now may I suggest we conduct the conversation in a calmer, more rational manner? I'm not trying to steal your patients. I'm simply offering comfort to sick people by praying that the Holy Spirit will use me to ease their dis-ease, and if you're the sensible down-to-earth fellow you're always claiming to be you'll now ask yourself why we shouldn't work in harmony."

"I'm not lending my support to any goings-on which reek of superstitious quackery, and if I find you're wreaking havoc among my patients I'll bloody well lodge a complaint with your Bishop!"

"Why are you so upset, Garrison? What is it you're really afraid of here?"

"*Afraid?* Damn you, I'm not afraid of anything!"

"Then may I suggest you stop behaving as the Church behaved when the scientists first suggested the world wasn't quite so flat as everyone had always thought it was?"

He stormed out and slammed the door.

5

"*SILLY* old duffer!" said Anne that evening.

"He did indeed behave very stupidly, but I should have resisted the temptation to put him in his place."

"Nonsense!" said Anne. "It'll do him good! He's become much too bossy, and I've a good mind to transfer my allegiance to Charles's friend Dr. Romaine in Starvale St. James."

This certainly was a development I had not anticipated, and my instinctive response was one of alarm. Dr. Romaine "had a past," as we used to say so euphemistically in the 1890s, and although he had been living a life of flawless respectability with his third wife for some years I could not help but feel lukewarm about the prospect of him attending an attractive young woman of thirty-two who also—and here, of course, lay the rub—happened to be my wife. However since all my information about Romaine had come from confidential talks with Charles, I was unable to explain my feelings to Anne and had to content myself with remarking: "Romaine's in his late sixties. Wouldn't you prefer a younger man?"

"No," said Anne, responding in a way I might have predicted if I had been less absorbed in thoughts of Romaine's "past." "I like doctors to be fatherly."

"I'm sure Garrison will start behaving sensibly once he calms down—"

"I doubt that very much," said Anne frankly, and her doubt was soon justified. When my offer of peaceful co-existence was spurned a second time, I decided I should leave him to wrestle alone with his secret insecurity, and at that point Anne, exasperated by Garrison's pigheadedness, called on Dr. Romaine.

As I well knew from my conversations with Charles, Romaine was a man of considerable charm and guile. The result of the interview did not surprise me but I did not like to think of Anne being charmed and beguiled by a member of my own generation, and it cost me a great effort to retain a benign expression as she embarked on her paean of praise.

"He was absolutely delightful!" she exclaimed. "We talked for ages— he'd heard all about you from Charles, of course, and almost before I knew what was happening I was telling him about the healing. Darling, he was fascinated! He told me some amazing stories of healers in the East—apparently he lived for years in Hong-Kong, and his second wife was a Chinese Christian who firmly convinced him that all healing came from God—"

That was the moment when I bowed to the inevitable and acknowledged that Dr. Romaine, clever Dr. Romaine, had acquired another devoted patient. But I feared the rift with Garrison would become impossible to heal now that my wife had abandoned him, and my gloom increased the next day when I heard he had been invited to dine with Pitkin. The thought of a Pitkin-Garrison axis was most depressing.

By this time I was so frequently interrupted by parishioners in search of healing that it was becoming difficult for me to work in the vestry, and I was just toying with the idea that I might hold a special service in order to satisfy all the sick simultaneously when something happened that deflected me abruptly from any thought of my new calling.

Anne, returning from a second visit to Dr. Romaine, announced that she was having a baby.

6

THERE had been physical indications that conception had occurred but I had dismissed them as mere passing phenomena which were of no significance. I knew that part of Anne's interest in Romaine might have stemmed from his reputation as an obstetrician, but I had chosen not to dwell on this aspect of his practice. The truth was that by this time I had successfully hypnotised myself into believing I was sterile—once a man turned sixty surely fertility if not potency abruptly declined?—and fortified by this new-found faith I had regularly dismissed as impossible any hint that I might still be capable of begetting a second family. With this pathetic defence now brutally shattered, I found myself confronted by a truth I was unable to endure. Mechanically I tried to tell myself that God had seen fit to bless my marriage in the best possible way, but I found this statement represented a platitude that was beyond my power to believe. I could only reflect with horror that having bestowed on me the great blessing of a loving wife, God had now decided to crush us both by imposing a burden I was quite unfit to bear.

I panicked. My guilt about the past, laced now with a terror of the future, produced a lethal despair. I felt rebellious towards God—a disastrous state of mind for a priest—and my rebellion cut me off from Him. Hell is being cut off from God. I was in torment.

But of course I could disclose no hint of this torment to Anne.

"How very exciting!" I said as soon as she broke the news, and before my face could betray me I drew her into my arms for an embrace.

"Now look here," said Anne, giving me a jolt by disengaging herself and adopting her sternest voice, "it's going to be all right. You'll still have your peace and privacy—you won't be drowned this time beneath a tidal wave of disorder—and the baby will quite definitely be a good thing. It'll keep you young in outlook and soften the awfulness of being over sixty."

"My dear Anne, you're preaching to the converted! I'm absolutely delighted by the news, and it gives me the very greatest pleasure to see you so happy."

I retired to my cell. Prayer was impossible. I could only sit on my wooden chair and wrestle with the demon despair. My psyche was writhing like a flogged snake. I tried to stroke it with various meditation techniques but when it became more contorted than ever, I began to be afraid of uncontrolled bursts of kinetic energy. I tried to expel the energy by willing my pencil to fall off the table, but nothing happened. I was unable to channel the energy effectively, and rising to my feet I decided to go to Starwater to talk to Cyril.

But then I sat down again. What could a man who had never been a husband and father know of the terrible conflicts which were now grinding my psyche towards dementia? I thought how I enjoyed and needed marital intimacy yet often found it a physical strain and an emotional burden which interfered with my inner life; I thought how I wanted to give Anne a child yet recoiled from the prospect of fatherhood; I thought how my great longing for solitude was juxtaposed with my deep fear of losing Anne's companionship. How could I even begin to explain these tortuous paradoxes to either Cyril or Francis? No childless celibate, no matter how sophisticated, could possibly understand. Indeed so bizarre did the paradoxes seem that I began to doubt that anyone on earth was capable of understanding them. It was at this point that I automatically turned back to God, and overwhelmed by the compulsion to bridge the abyss which separated us, I decided to retreat to the chapel to make another desperate attempt at prayer.

But I never reached the chapel. In the garden the mild March sunshine was so pleasant that I sat down on one of the wooden seats by the lawn and sought to soothe my psyche by watching the daffodils nod tranquilly in the breeze. How long I sat there I have no idea, but just as I was trying to summon the energy to resume my journey, the daffodils began to change.

I watched them turn a brilliant yellow as the surrounding grass glittered into emerald-green, and all the while part of my brain was denying what was happening, declaring that this vision was arriving too soon after the last one to be genuine. As if to confirm my scepticism, the vision failed to develop. I found myself still sitting in the garden, still inhabiting my body, and at last the landscape reverted to its normal colouring. Having concluded that the alteration in my visual perception had been a freak generated by my beleaguered psyche, I then received a great shock. I saw that not only had the daffodils faded but the trees were in full leaf.

I gasped but before I could leap to my feet I became aware that I was no longer alone. The hair prickled at the nape of my neck but this sensation was experienced by the Jon of March 1941 because the other Jon, the Jon of the summer day around me, was tranquil. It was as if I were having an impaired vision with the result that I was in two times at once, neither of which seemed wholly real.

Very slowly I turned my head to the left.

A little boy was watching me. He was about ten yards away. He had fair hair, which I knew would darken later, and grave grey eyes set deep in a small serious face. Recalling a photograph taken when I was four years old I realised I was looking at my past self. I was sure of this because I could talk to him without words and I knew that at that moment he was longing for an invitation to sit beside me on the garden-seat. I signalled that I wanted his company, and as he understood he smiled serenely, reminding me of my mother. Obviously my psychic faculties had become addled because I was mixing up the past and present in the most chaotic way imaginable, seeing myself as a child in Anne's garden while telling myself all the time in the March of 1941 that my powers had gone beserk.

Then I became aware of a detail which stupefied me. The little boy was wearing dungarees and a pullover. I was just thinking dazed that I had projected my past self into modern times when I was further shattered by the revelation that the little boy was a stranger. Far away on the terrace I heard an unknown woman's voice call: "Nicholas! Nicholas!" and as the child turned his head in response, the darkness began to creep across my vision from the left.

I cried urgently: "Nicholas—don't go!" but I was in 1941 and he could not hear me. He ran off across the lawn but although I leapt to my feet in pursuit, the darkness blotted him out, the dizziness overcame me and sinking back on the seat I covered my eyes with my hands.

7

WHEN I opened my eyes the daffodils were nodding in the breeze and I was once more pinned firmly in time. I found I was in a profoundly emotional state. My hands were shaking. My cheeks were wet with tears. My voice was whispering: "Nicholas . . . Nicholas . . . " and suddenly I knew all would be well. I thought: "All shall be well and all manner of things shall be well . . . " And as the famous words of Julian of Norwich rang triumphantly in my mind I knew I had received another "showing." God in His infinite mercy had taken pity on me in my torment and had given me this assurance that I could go forward into the future with confidence. All would be well with the child, who had beyond doubt been revealed as the sort of son I had always wanted. All would be well with my marriage. All would be well with my ministry of healing. I felt as if a huge burden had been lifted from my psyche, and in a burst of joyous energy I rushed to the chapel to give thanks for yet another great deliverance from the demon of despair.

8

WHEN I returned to the house I recorded the vision and placed the account in an envelope which I sealed with wax. I was strongly tempted to tell Anne that I had seen our future son, but I had long since made it a rule that I should never discuss my visions with anyone who could be closely affected by them. There are many futures and not all of them come true, as I knew well enough from my previous psychic experiences. It was bad enough that I myself should occasionally wind up waiting for something which never happened; to impose such a burden on someone else, particularly someone I loved, would have been the height of irresponsibility.

It was only when the sealed envelope was safely tucked away in my cupboard that it occurred to me to wonder why I had chosen the name Nicholas for my new son. I liked the name but there were others I liked better. I could only conclude that it was Anne's favourite name and I had generously allowed her to have her own way.

That evening I was unable to resist saying to her: "What shall we call the baby if it's a boy?"

"Gerald after my brother," said Anne promptly, "and Jonathan after you."

Automatically I said: "I don't like my name." I was so taken aback that I was even tactless enough to add: "I don't like the name Gerald either."

"All right, what about Richard, Robert or Nigel?"

I was silent, trying to make sense of all these irrelevant suggestions, and the next moment Anne was exclaiming: "Why are we assuming it'll be a boy? Maybe it'll be a girl! I like the names Susan, Margaret, Penelope—" She paused expectantly, but still I was silent. "Come on, Jon! What are your favourite names?"

"Florence. Beatrice. Enid."

Anne laughed. "But no little girls are called Florence, Beatrice and Enid any more!"

"Aren't they?" I said vaguely, forgetting my bewilderment in the relief of seeing her so happy. Smiling back at her impulsively I clasped her hand in mine and added with regret: "No, I suppose they're not."

"Darling!" said Anne, tactfully avoiding any further comment on my old-fashioned Victorian taste. "I can't tell you what a relief it is to me that you're quite obviously in the best of spirits! It sounds silly, I know, but I had this terrible feeling that the baby would tie you up into one of your knots and I wouldn't be able to unravel you."

We laughed together at this absurd possibility. Then I said jubilantly: " 'All shall be well and all manner of things shall be well!' " But nevertheless as I spoke I again felt baffled that we should be so far from naming our future son after the perfect child who had visited me that afternoon.

9

AS I had anticipated, Dr. Romaine had advised Anne to abstain from marital intimacy until the most common time for miscarriages had passed, so without consulting her I set up a camp-bed in my cell; I had thought it obvious that if one is obliged to be chaste one should at least take the elementary precaution of sleeping alone, but to my dismay Anne was most upset and accused me of being "monstrously insensitive." At once I explained that my withdrawal would have been unnecessary if I had not still felt her to be intensely desirable, and when she saw my action had not sprung from sexual antipathy she calmed down, but afterwards I was angry with myself for not handling the matter with more tact.

I missed the intimacy, but I had to admit to myself that the solitary nights in my cell were exquisitely refreshing. Every night I would stay up late reading and meditating, sleep soundly for six hours and rise at five-thirty for prayer. Anne never woke before seven-thirty and as the pregnancy advanced she liked to be in bed each evening by ten. This meant that I had nine and a half hours entirely to myself, and my psyche, secretly undernourished after a diet of reduced solitude, began to thrive again. I found I had more energy for my work, and as this new energy developed, so my healing skills began to flourish.

I achieved a success which was even more dramatic than Mrs. Purvis's recovery: a child who had been immobilised for months after an attack of infantile paralysis was able to rise from his wheelchair and walk three steps. Word of the healing spread swiftly not only through the parish but through the surrounding villages, and soon a reporter from the *Starbridge Weekly News* was knocking on the vestry door. I declined to grant an interview on the grounds that it would be most unfitting for a priest to connive at publicity, but the reporter, undaunted, discovered several loquacious villagers who were only too ready to exaggerate my achievements. Less than twenty-four hours before my first service of healing I found myself confronting the highly unedifying front-page headline: MIRACLES IN STARRINGTON: EX-MONK'S MARVELS MESMERISE ALL.

I had thought and prayed a great deal about whether I should hold a service of healing. Certainly I judged it would meet the needs of the vast majority of those who called at the "surgery" which I now held twice a week at the vestry; these callers were far from being seriously ill but nevertheless they craved comfort for their minor ailments, and I was tempted to think that if I dealt with these lesser cases *en masse* I would have more time to devote to the chronic sick. These incurables needed my individual attention as I sought to improve the quality of their lives by renewing their spiritual strength, but although I did not think they were likely to be greatly helped by being treated *en masse,* I saw no reason why they should not derive at least some benefit from a service of healing.

I also favoured holding a service because I felt such a gesture would place the healing firmly in a respectable Christian setting. By this time Dr. Garrison was not the only person muttering about quackery, and I was aware of a growing desire to defend myself in the most dignified manner available against my enemies' uncharitable slanders.

However I knew I had to approach my task with care, and I realised that my first responsibility was to reduce the risk of any over-emotional behaviour by making the service as plain as possible; this was most definitely not the time to indulge in a riot of Anglo-Catholic ritual. Accordingly I drew up a service that included an opening hymn, a short address in which I exploded any misconceptions about the ministry of healing, an appropriate reading from the New Testament, three spoken prayers and a period of silent prayer. After this interval those wishing to be healed would assemble before the chancel where I could begin the laying-on of hands. I considered anointing but rejected it. I was too afraid my audience would associate the practice with Popery and I wanted no hostile feelings impeding the flow of the charism. Following the laying-on of hands we would sing a second hymn and then I would give a blessing to conclude the service.

These proceedings seemed harmless enough, but I knew I would still have to exercise great vigilance in order to beat back any demonic infiltration. Before I had entered the Order I had out of curiosity attended two services of healing in London and both in their different ways had appalled me. The first service, performed by a renegade priest, had been a spectacle centred on the glorifying of his own personality; the Devil had been hard at work there, cultivating the demon pride and calling forth an idolatrous response. The second service, performed by an individual who was clearly motivated by good intentions, had plunged into chaos because of his lack of authority; unable to control his congregation he had soon been presiding over a gathering where tears, groans, even shrieks were mingled with regular shouts of "Hallelujah!" Fortunately he had achieved no striking cures. If he had, the congregation would no doubt have tottered the last inch over the brink into the abyss of hysteria and some deluded victim would have insisted that the congregation was being visited by the Spirit.

From these descriptions it will be clear why the hierarchy of the Church of England tended to regard the public exercise of the charism of healing with a singular lack of enthusiasm, and having planned my service I knew my next step was to win my superior's approval. Accordingly, circumventing Aysgarth, I made a special journey to the Cathedral Close at Starbridge in order to call on the Bishop.

Dr. Ottershaw, once more displaying his endearing willingness to be wound, so to speak, around my little finger, confided that he had always been greatly interested in the charism of healing and declared that as I was such a distinguished churchman, he was sure that any service I conducted would be a model of propriety. He even mused what a pity it was that a prior engagement prevented him from attending the service himself.

I returned in triumph to Starrington.

Fortified by the Bishop's approval I then wrote to Aysgarth to inform him of my plan and received a chilly letter of acknowledgement. He told me that although he would not presume to criticise a plan which had had an episcopal blessing, he nevertheless feared that my scheme would only divide the parish more deeply than ever. Did I really feel that it was in the best interests of the Church to quarrel with such a pillar of the community as Dr. Garrison? Mr. Pitkin had said I was even giving interviews to journalists; surely such a move could only result in a publicity which would attract the wrong people to my service? In short, despite the Bishop's charitable response, should I not consider altering my course in order to pursue a policy of reconciliation with those who were so deeply opposed to this extension of my ministry?

After sparing a growl for the pest Pitkin who had so grossly misrepresented me, I was driven to the reluctant conclusion that Aysgarth had been right to worry about unseemly publicity. The headlines of the *Starbridge Weekly News* had certainly been unnerving, but at that stage I felt it was too late to cancel the service. Too many sick people would have been disappointed, and in addition I remained convinced that the service represented the logical next step as I advanced along the road of my new call.

On the appointed day I rose early in order to celebrate Mass by myself in the chapel. Then I fasted, prayed and meditated in absolute seclusion until two o'clock when I walked on my own to the village church. In the interests of austerity I was tempted to wear an unadorned black cassock, but I reluctantly concluded that this would make me look striking in a way that might stimulate quite the wrong response among the ladies, so on reaching the vestry I donned my white surplice in the hope that it would exude a suitably asexual aura.

Emerging from the vestry I noted that the pest Pitkin was conspicuous by his absence, but Colonel Maitland and his team of sidesmen were directing the assembling hordes into the pews with unruffled efficiency. My heart sank when I spotted four men exuding the insatiable curiosity of journalists, but I refused Maitland's suggestion that they should be asked to leave. Possibly these men were religious. Possibly as the result of the service they might become religious. Certainly they were entitled to charitable treatment, and I thought they should be given at least the chance to behave with decorum.

Anxious to be self-effacing in such special circumstances, Anne was sitting halfway down the nave instead of in her usual front pew, and beside her, I noticed with a disagreeable shock, were the Aysgarths. I had not expected Aysgarth to attend and I disliked the thought of him being present. My resolve to conduct a dignified service hardened; retreating once more to the vestry I said my final prayers and then, taking my courage in both hands, embarked on my new adventure.

I 0

AFTERWARDS I was so exhausted that it was impossible for me to talk to anyone, but I had anticipated this extreme debility after such a massive outpouring of my powers, and Anne had ensured that the motor was waiting beyond the back wall of the churchyard.

"Darling, you were utterly wonderful!" she exclaimed shining-eyed as I collapsed beside her in the back seat, but although I was immediately aware of a blissful security I was too exhausted to do more than grunt in gratitude. As soon as we arrived home I hauled myself upstairs to my cell, sank onto my camp-bed and slept for fourteen hours. The ban on intimacy had by this time been lifted, but I had kept the camp-bed in my cell to ensure chastity on the nights before I attempted any concentrated sessions of healing at my twice-weekly "surgery." The rock-bottom truth about sexual intercourse, a truth which it is becoming increasingly fashionable to forget, is that no matter how delightful the experience it only wastes energy which could be more profitably spent elsewhere.

However I had now had fourteen hours' sleep, my exertions as a healer lay for the moment behind me and I felt as exuberant as the most incorrigible hedonist. Waking promptly at half-past five I invaded the kitchens, and in the absence of the servants who never began work before six I made a great mess assembling an enormous breakfast for myself. Then much stimulated by this rare descent into gluttony I bounded back upstairs, bathed, shaved and slid naked into bed with Anne. I was feeling as frisky as a kitten and could hardly wait to prove that the humiliating weaknesses of old age were still a million light-years away.

"You were such a success yesterday!" sighed Anne when she finally had the chance to speak. "I was so proud of you!"

For ten seconds I luxuriated in the warmth of her approval. Then I remembered her companions at the service. "What did Aysgarth think?" I said with reluctance.

"It's hard to know what he thinks when he puts on his poker-face, but I'm sure he was impressed by your integrity—in fact I don't see how even your worst enemies could find fault with you this time!"

"Rest assured that they'll try," I said dryly, and sure enough a day later I received a letter from Aysgarth in which he invited me to Starbridge for a "frank and friendly" discussion of my ministry at Starrington Magna.

I I

"IT is my earnest wish," said Aysgarth with a pompous air which made me suspect he was nervous, "that this interview be conducted in a Christian spirit, Mr. Darrow, without the animosity which has characterised too many of our previous conversations."

"Such an aspiration strikes me as being entirely admirable," I said with a mannered politeness worthy of a character in Jane Austen's novels, "and I assure you I shall do my best to see that it's fulfilled." But as I spoke I was remembering Whitby, humouring a mouse by letting it think it could dictate the terms of the battle and then moving in with his paw for the big pounce.

We were seated in Aysgarth's study at his vicarage, a rambling townhouse adjacent to the church of St. Martin's-in-Cripplegate. The study, cosy and bookish, exuded an atmosphere of intellectual polish which pleased me despite the fact that the room was the antithesis of my uncluttered cell at the Manor. I was interested and not a little perturbed to see that Aysgarth's taste in reading was dangerously eclectic; below the works of theology, below the classics of English literature, below the tomes of history and biography, lurked a range of modern novels whose spiritual value was reputed to be questionable. I confess that even I, who had argued so fervently to Father Darcy that priests should not be too narrow in their reading, could only boggle at the sight of a volume with

D. H. LAWRENCE inscribed boldly on the spine. Aysgarth was not a monk and there was in fact no reason why he should not read widely to extend his knowledge of human nature, but I really did think that a man who was not only a priest but an archdeacon should take the trouble to encase the work of a writer like Lawrence in discreet brown paper before consigning it to a shelf in his library. However no doubt Aysgarth, being a member of the younger generation, would have judged this reaction to be a typical example of Victorian hypocrisy. I shall only add that there are times when I think "Victorian hypocrisy"—the younger generation's label for an attitude which values tact, discretion and good taste above boorishness, boastfulness and vulgarity—has been greatly maligned.

Since the books occupied most of the walls there were no paintings in the room, but the mantelshelf was adorned with framed photographs of his pretty, radiant wife and his bright-eyed, good-looking children. This flaunting of a successful family life irritated me, but I told myself all jealousy should be ruthlessly suppressed. I made a new resolution to be well-behaved.

Meanwhile Aysgarth, prim and proper in his archidiaconal uniform, was looking as if he had never heard of D. H. Lawrence, and this impression of a double-image, of a man with racy tastes living alongside a man who was the soul of propriety, intrigued me deeply. To some extent we all have our double-images, our public and private selves, but there are cases when the split between the two can widen into such an abyss that an intolerable strain is put on the psyche. I had encountered such cases during my work as a director of souls, and since all the men afflicted had wound up in a state of spiritual debility I now wondered anew about Aysgarth's inner life. However I was uncomfortably aware that such critical speculation ill became a priest who had shied away from his own spiritual director for some months while making only the most perfunctory confessions to the Abbot of Starwater.

"I was most interested in the service of healing," Aysgarth was saying as I recalled my wandering attention, "and I congratulate you on maintaining control of the congregation in such a charged emotional atmosphere."

I at once said: "Hysteria's actually very rare."

"Is it? In circumstances such as this when the clergyman attempts to assume extraordinary power over the congregation and stimulate the most primitive emotions? I had heard otherwise. However," said Aysgarth, giving me no chance to comment, "let's not dwell on the dangers you were skilful enough to avoid. How successful was the service in terms of healing?"

"Most of the sufferers have claimed improvement, but in some cases—

particularly the ones involving sight and hearing—it's still too early to look for marked results."

"You've had success with cases involving sight and hearing?"

"Certainly, but that's an area where healers are often effective."

"Dr. Garrison," said Aysgarth, speaking with great care, "has ventured the opinion that your successes are achieved entirely by a hypnosis which eventually wears off, leaving the sufferer's condition unchanged."

"Balls."

Aysgarth looked as shocked as if I had uttered a blasphemy and I began to feel exasperated. "Come, come, Archdeacon!" I said smiling at him. "There are no ladies present, and you can't tell me they don't use words like that up in Yorkshire!"

Aysgarth said with an insufferable priggishness: "I think a clergyman has a duty to avoid vulgar language even when there are no ladies present."

This of course was true but I was deeply annoyed that my attempt to lessen the stiffness of the atmosphere by injecting a casual masculine informality had been so ruthlessly rebuffed. Then I realised with fury that he had outmanoeuvred me. The word had not shocked him in the least but by pretending that it had, he had seized the chance to tilt the balance of power in his favour by administering a justifiable rebuke.

I tried to tilt the balance back. "May I suggest we dispense with the debate on clerical etiquette and stick to the subject under discussion? Let me state as firmly as possible that I'm not a quack performing tricks with hypnosis. I'm a priest offering myself to God as a channel for—"

"Do you deny you use hypnosis?"

I spared a second to reflect that this young man was wasted in the Church; he should have been sporting a barrister's wig and battering witnesses in a court of law.

"No," I said, trying to remain unruffled but aware that I was not entirely succeeding, "I don't deny I use hypnotic techniques occasionally as a tool, just as a surgeon would use a scalpel, but I tend to confine these techniques to situations where the patient is distraught. Certainly at the service of healing I made no use of hypnosis at all."

"What about the hypnotic power with which you controlled the congregation?"

"There was no hypnotic power. I was merely exercising the charism of leadership."

"You're saying the charism of leadership never involves hypnosis?"

"I'm saying the gift of leadership bestowed by God doesn't need hypnosis! It's the gift of leadership bestowed by the Devil that runs amok with hypnotic power—compare Hitler with Churchill!"

"You don't have to tell me that the gifts of the Spirit can be recognised by their fruits, sir, but since you admitted using hypnosis as a tool when you exercised the charism of healing, I thought you might also regard it as a tool when you exercised the charism of leadership."

He was relentlessly driving me into a corner and I knew I had to punch my way out. "Let's get this straight," I said. "Are you accusing me of abusing my powers? Because if you are, I'd like to assure you that I would never under any circumstances sink to manipulating people for shady purposes."

"No?" said Aysgarth blandly. "You seem to have been doing rather nicely with the Bishop."

I sprang to my feet. So did he. He was very pale and I sensed he was frightened of me, but I sensed too that he was determined not to let his fear stop him from speaking his mind and doing what he conceived to be his duty. I respected him for this admirable display of courage. But I was seething. I did not like this jumped-up pipsqueak of an archdeacon casting aspersions on my ministry of healing; I particularly disliked this jumped-up pipsqueak of an archdeacon implying that I, the famous spiritual director, was not as spiritually healthy as I should be, and I loathed this jumped-up pipsqueak of an archdeacon spotting the chink in my armour and moving in ruthlessly for the kill. I felt as Whitby would have felt if the mouse had stood up on its hind-legs and smartly bashed him on the nose.

"Enough of this skirmishing," I said tersely at last. "No more beating about the bush. I take it you hated the service."

"Yes, I thought it was thoroughly dangerous and should never have taken place, but in fact that's not the main issue at stake here. The main issue is that the service was just one more example of how you've torn that parish apart by your—I'm sorry but I must say this—by your arrogant, reckless and thoroughly insensitive behaviour. Please don't delude yourself that no one objected to this service except Pitkin and Garrison. There were many others who strongly resented their parish church being used to give a spurious air of respectability to practices which are generally held to be dubious in the extreme."

He stopped speaking. There was a silence while I mentally reeled under the impact of such monstrous insolence, but at last I was sufficiently recovered to say in my coolest voice: "Aren't you exceeding your authority? An archdeacon may be 'the Bishop's eye' but only the Bishop himself should deal with disciplinary matters. I'm not obliged to listen to your offensive lectures, Aysgarth, and I strongly object to being judged on the biased information provided by my enemies!"

"You shouldn't have enemies," said Aysgarth, cutting me down to size yet again with his ruthless forensic skill. "You pass judgement on yourself merely by using the word. As for Dr. Ottershaw, I shall now go to him and say that in my opinion an episcopal intervention is required. I regret that I've given you offence but I quite understand that you're far too proud to accept any criticism from a mere archdeacon."

I was so unused to being trounced in debate that for a moment I could only flounder speechlessly again, but then the instinct for survival asserted itself and I realised that the last thing I wanted was to be hauled before the Bishop. Anne would be upset and Anne had to be protected at all costs from any incident which showed me in an unattractive light. With a vast effort I pulled myself together.

"I'm sorry," I said in the special meek voice of the monk who concedes his recalcitrance. "I wouldn't like you to trouble the Bishop when I can see so plainly that I've been in error, giving way to anger and making this difficult interview so very much more unpleasant for you than it should have been. Let me now try to make your task easier by asking for your advice. I can't give up the healing; I believe it to be a call from God. But what can I do to stop it exacerbating the divisions in the community?"

Aysgarth said without hesitation: "Don't use the parish church for the healing in future—in fact try to keep the healing ministry as separate as possible from your parish duties. Is it possible, do you think, that you could confine all future healing to some quiet corner of the Manor?"

And then I knew I was face to face at last with the chapel of my vision.

XVI

*"I have long been interested in the claims of spiritual healers,
about which I am perhaps unduly sceptical."*

W.   R.   INGE

A PACIFIST IN TROUBLE

I

SO enrapt was I by the fact that the chapel was now poised to move to
the centre of my ministry that I found myself capable of penning my first
frank letter to Francis for some months.

"I confess I've found my life as a country priest difficult," I wrote, "and
no doubt this was only to be expected, since I took on the curacy for
the wrong reasons (yes, I admit it—better late than never!), but I'm
happy to report that at last events appear to be moving in a more
promising direction." And having given a detailed account of my new
ministry, I described the service of healing with an enthusiasm which I
was careful to temper with modesty.

"Unfortunately," I continued, my pen travelling with increasing flu-
ency over the paper,

the Archdeacon now informs me that the bigoted minority who have consistently opposed my efforts to improve the spiritual life of this parish have been
protesting about my use of the church for what they are pleased to call
quackery, and it's now been suggested to me by Aysgarth himself that I
should confine my healing to a "quiet corner of the Manor." Could there
be a clearer indication that I'm called to use the chapel? I think not. I also
see at last why the back pews must be removed: we'll be obliged to create
extra space for the wheelchairs. So bearing all these things in mind I have
no doubt now that this ministry of healing represents a true call from God,
and this confidence will give me the patience to tolerate the ill-natured

opposition. I admit I find the dissension in the parish tedious, but of course I see now that the parish is only of secondary importance here.

You will be wondering about my marriage so let me report that we're very happy with no problems whatsoever. No doubt you'll want to know what form Anne's parish work has finally taken, and I can tell you with pride that despite the heavy demands on her time made by her war work on the estate she has provided notable assistance at a number of special events held to raise money for charity. Certainly she gives me constant moral support and I couldn't wish for a better wife. Indeed I've quite overcome my fear that I'd be miserable as a married man—and I'm delighted to tell you that I've also quite overcome my fear of fatherhood. Anne is expecting a child in September.

I confess I could not immediately overcome this latter fear, but finally after a time of considerable emotional torment a miracle happened. Francis, I'm not a man who uses such language lightly, but in my opinion this incident was a gift from God. I experienced another "showing," and after that I was aware only of the kind of joy and comfort received by Julian of Norwich. I don't have to remind you of the quotation.

Having described the vision of Nicholas I added:

I feel God wouldn't have been so generous to me if I'd been on the wrong road, and that's why I believe this showing was not only a promise that I'm to have the sort of son I've always wanted but also a confirmation of my call to the ministry of healing. It's hard to describe how I felt afterwards, but it reminded me of how I feel when people ask me to heal them: all my problems fall away and none of my difficulties seem to matter any more. Isn't it wonderful that by the grace of God I can cast aside my self-centred preoccupations in order to serve others? I really believe that in this new ministry I shall both do good and find the most unique fulfilment at last.

I reread the letter carefully but could find no fault with it, and greatly relieved to have renewed an honest correspondence with my spiritual director, I waited in pleasant anticipation for a benign and laudatory reply.

2

"MY dear Jon," wrote Francis by return,

how very pleased I am that you have at last felt able to write to me at length. Of course you've been much in my thoughts during this silence, and now that we're in touch again I have the satisfaction of knowing that at least one of my prayers has been answered.

First of all may I congratulate you on your impending fatherhood and say that I'm extremely glad that you've been able to welcome the prospect. Your description of the new "showing" is certainly intriguing. Have you discussed it with Cyril? You will remember how adamant Father Darcy was that you should report any psychic experience immediately to your spiritual director and/or confessor so that the experience can be properly analysed. I'm not suggesting that this latest vision is a demonic delusion—your peace and joy afterwards are certainly more compatible with divine intervention—but it's always possible that such an experience isn't quite as you think it is and is in fact conveying a message which you've entirely failed to read.

I hesitate to conduct an analysis from a distance but I'd like to put two questions to you. (1) Did this child look *exactly* as you did according to the photograph taken when you were four? (Forget the difference in clothes.) I know a remarkable likeness can exist between fathers and sons, but an exact replica must be extremely rare, perhaps even impossible. (2) Who was the woman calling Nicholas from the terrace? Are you quite sure this voice was unknown to you? You're treating this experience as a glimpse of the future but in fact it could equally well be a bizarre distortion of the present and past.

I trust I'm not impertinent enough to discuss your marriage with you until I know a great deal more about it than the euphoric picture you painted in your letter. Suffice it to say that I'm delighted that you've been rendered so charmingly uxorious. I must confess, however, to a twinge of anxiety about your wife, who seems to be trying to be all things to all men: a farmer dedicated to producing more food for a nation at war, a wife dedicated to producing the ideal marital partner for a harassed country priest, and a woman dedicated to producing an infant. Dare I ask if you've actually had a frank conversation with her about the emotional, mental and physical stresses of her life at present? No, I daren't! Let me turn instead to your ministry of healing, a subject on which, unlike matrimony, I'm rather more qualified to speak candidly.

Of course I'm deeply interested by the turn your life has now taken, but I'm also deeply perturbed. I need not mention Father Darcy in this context; his opinion on your suitability for such a ministry is unlikely to have been forgotten by you, although you may well feel entitled to dismiss his opinion as irrelevant now that you believe you're responding to a call from God. However I feel bound to remind you that such a ministry poses great problems for those who undertake it, and as it's vital that you should be in first-class spiritual health in order to perform such work successfully, I urge you to see Cyril *at least* once a week to make your confession and discuss any difficulties which may arise. I'd also like you to come up to town for a couple of days to see me. I've no wish to cast any aspersion on Cyril, who's certainly more than capable of giving you the proper direction, but there's so much about you that Cyril doesn't know and something tells me—am I being excessively cynical?—that you haven't been too busy enlightening him.

There's more I could say but I shall hold my fire. I could ask, for instance, how the parish is going to fare now that you've dismissed it as being of only secondary importance. I could also ask whether the miraculous feeling of release from your problems, a phenomenon which you say accompanies your work as a healer, could not better be described as a psychological escape from reality. However I shan't ask either of those tiresome questions, my dear Jon, because I'm sure I've already irritated you quite beyond endurance, so all I shall now do is conclude this letter by begging you to let me know by return when I'm to have the pleasure of seeing you again.

This letter did indeed make me feel exceedingly irritated, and it occurred to me to wonder if Francis were jealous—subconsciously, of course—of my young wife and my new career in the world. Even a man who thrived on the cenobitic life was never immune from the desire to embrace the worldly blessings he had renounced, and deciding that Francis was being influenced by feelings which his jealous nature could not quite control I wrote severely but not (I hoped) unkindly:

My dear Francis,
I thank you for your letter but regret that I'm unable to accept your invitation. Much as I would like to see you I'm reluctant to leave Anne on her own at this time.

With regard to my new ministry, let me hasten to assure you that I'm well aware of the problems; I'm neither ignorant nor a fool. A very heavy responsibility has certainly been placed upon me, but since I have no doubt whatsoever that the call is genuine, I believe that by the grace of God I shall be granted the strength and wisdom to respond in the right way. The latest "showing," as I tried with apparent lack of success to explain, indicates that I can proceed into the future with confidence; I was unmistakably assured that all would be well. The fact that I'm being driven to use the chapel for my ministry—even driven to remove the back pews—also leaves me in no doubt that my call is unfolding in accordance with my vision.

What heavy weather you've made of the showing! The child was certainly very like me, but how can I say whether or not he was a replica? I had to compare this little boy with my memory of a sepia photograph which I haven't seen for many years. You're implying, I know, that he was not my future son but a mirror-image drummed up out of my subconscious mind, but although I myself thought this at first, I was convinced by the end of my vision that I was mistaken. If he was indeed my past self, why didn't the woman call him Jon? You're implying, of course, when you ask who the woman was, that at some time in the past I heard a woman call out: "Nicholas! Nicholas!" and that my memory has now tossed up this forgotten incident to complete my delusion. However a far more simple explanation is that the woman was the child's nurse; Anne is already talking of engaging a nanny for the baby.

As you say you don't intend to ask the questions which you nonetheless posed in your last paragraph, I really fail to see why I should answer them. But of course I must assure you that I shan't neglect my parish duties. Your suggestion that I'm in reality serving myself (by running away from my problems) instead of serving God (by responding to a genuine call) is worthy of Father Darcy at his most malign and I believe my most effective response is to preserve a dignified silence. I deeply regret that you should take such a suspicious, cynical view of my current activities.

Francis wrote in return:

My dear Jon,
I'm extremely sorry if I've given you offence. Remember that I write only with your spiritual welfare in mind and remember too that a morbid sensitivity to criticism is often a symptom of an unhealthily rampant pride.

Taking my courage in both hands I'll now point out a couple of distortions in your logic. (1) I see no evidence in your showing that the reassurance "all will be well" extends beyond your family life. If the showing be genuine it certainly has nothing to do with your ministry of healing and cannot be regarded as setting the seal of approval on it. (2) You mention the removal of the back pews as if this too were a confirmation of your call, but in fact all the removal proves is the remarkable degree of clairvoyance you achieved when you saw the interior of the chapel in your vision. You may now indeed feel you have a cogent reason for removing the pews, but this has no bearing whatsoever on whether or not your call is valid. You're like someone who sets a table and says: "Now that the table's laid I've proved that dinner's about to be served!" But in fact the larder's empty and no one's on duty in the kitchen.

I can't stress too strongly how careful you must be not to jump to convenient conclusions. Why have you really undertaken this ministry of healing? It may well be a call from God, but until you're completely honest with yourself about your motives, true discernment can only be displaced by wishful thinking, a self-deceiving frame of mind which will clog your psyche as you seek to open it to receive the Holy Spirit. Go and see Cyril, open your heart to him and let him help you put your current life under the necessary microscope.

If you're still reading this letter I shall now deliver my parting thrust which I've saved to the end in the hope that it'll ring the vital alarm bell resoundingly in your ears: REMEMBER WHITBY!

I laughed. Then I exclaimed: "What a blow below the belt!" and tearing up the letter I tossed the fragments abruptly into the wastepaper basket.

"*HAVE* you heard from Francis yet?" said Anne who knew I had finally written to him at length.

"Yes."

"What does he think of the healing?"

"He said he was deeply interested by the turn my life had taken."

"You mean he approved?"

I was silent.

"Jon, I do wish you'd confide in me! I've got this nasty feeling that you're busy tieing yourself into a knot again—"

"Nonsense!"

"Is it? If you think I can't see that Francis has upset you in some way—"

"He merely reminded me of the difficulties attached to my new work and advised me to discuss the situation with Cyril."

"Thank God. When are you going to Starwater?"

I was somewhat taken aback by this excessive display of relief but told myself allowances should be made for the emotional moods of pregnant women. "If you can spare the motor I'll go this afternoon," I said soothingly, "but my dearest, you really must try not to worry so much about me! If there's one thing I know beyond any shadow of doubt it's that all will eventually be well . . . "

"*I MUST* confess to anger," I said to Cyril five hours later. "I was furious with the Archdeacon and furious with Francis." And I told him not only about the interview with Aysgarth but about Francis's epistolary counselling.

Cyril was small and wiry with a curiously military presence; I always felt he ought to be sporting a moustache and wearing a khaki uniform. Twenty years of managing the boys' school at Starwater Abbey had made him brisk, bossy and a trifle too hearty. I found myself missing Aidan's subtle understatements and wily silences in the confessional at Ruydale.

"If you're so confident about the validity of this call," said Cyril, "why are you getting so rattled?"

"Am I getting rattled?" I said, smiling at him.

"Well, aren't you? No beating about the bush! Two people express disapproval, one in the world and one out of it, and immediately you're on fire with indignation! Why don't you just say compassionately: 'Poor chaps. They don't understand.' All this anger suggests something being covered up. You know your Shakespeare: one must be suspicious of people who protest too much!"

"Yes, Headmaster!" I said, still smiling at him.

"You're fencing with me, Jon," said Cyril severely. "Come along, roll up your sleeves and work harder."

I worked harder, which meant that I still fenced with him but disguised it. Cyril began to shift in his chair. His bushy eyebrows twitched. The Fordites use no confessional box, as the Roman Catholics do, and confessor and penitent sit facing each other across a table in a small plain room with an oratory in one corner. The difficulties are discussed first. Then the penitent makes the formal confession on his knees before the cross. Cyril and I were still facing each other across the table.

"I see no sign that you repent of this anger," said Cyril at last. "How do you expect me to absolve you?"

"How can you say you see no sign of repentance when I've had the insight to realise that my anger stems from injured pride in the face of justifiable criticism? I always repent of my pride!"

"Yes, yes, yes, don't we all, but what's really going on here, Jon? Since we seem to be going round and round the mulberry bush and getting nowhere, I suggest we now approach the problem from a different angle. Suppose you suddenly realised your new call was a delusion; what would you do next?"

"Continue with the curacy, pray for enlightenment and wait."

"Yes, but supposing the War ends, the vicar returns and you're out of a job. What then?"

"I'd have to find other work. I couldn't just sit back and live on my wife's money."

"Why not? Maybe God's provided you with a rich wife so that you can concentrate on your work as a spiritual director without having to worry about where the next penny's coming from!"

I stared at him. "But I've had no hint from God that I'm to continue with my work as a spiritual director beyond maintaining my correspondence with those I used to counsel."

"My dear Jon," said Cyril, "you're so busy being too proud to live on your wife's money that you wouldn't see a hint from God even if it were written in the sky in letters of fire! Now let's try to view this situation without pride—and without any preconceived opinions. If this call to heal is in fact a delusion, what would be the most likely work that God would wish you to do?"

"Spiritual direction. But—"

"Very well, supposing God allows for your weakness and realises that you'd die of shame rather than be supported entirely by your wife. What would be the next most likely work He'd call you to do, work which would earn you a salary?"

After a pause I said: "Teaching."

"Exactly!" said Cyril pleased. "Now supposing, just for the sake of argument, I were to tell you that I'm having a tough time here at present as so many of the lay teachers have left to serve in the War, and supposing I were to offer you a job. Would you construe that as a call from God?"

"No, I'd construe it as a call from you."

"I agree it wouldn't be suitable for you to come back to work among the Fordites—too disturbing both for you and for us—but there are other educational institutions in desperate need of teachers at the moment. The Theological College at Starbridge, for instance—"

"I'm not called to teach, Cyril."

"But you did wonders at Ruydale!"

I said nothing.

Suddenly Cyril said: "Why do you feel you're not called to teach?"

I still said nothing. If I were once to admit I disliked the idea of teaching, Cyril would say that I was putting my self-centred inclinations before the possible will of God.

"Do you know what I think?" said Cyril at last. "I think all this—the compulsion to heal, the reluctance to teach—is in reality a gigantic rebellion against your father."

The silence was absolute. I had stopped breathing. Perhaps Cyril had too. We stared at each other for a long moment before Cyril added as an afterthought: "Your spiritual father, I mean. Father Cuthbert. Father Darcy, as you always insist on calling him—correctly now, I suppose, since you've left the Order."

I said the first words which entered my head. They were: "Francis and I always thought Cuthbert was such an absurdly inappropriate name for him." I had started breathing again.

"I can't think why! St. Cuthbert," said Cyril, unable to resist the temptation to play the pedagogue, "was a most remarkable man, tough as old boots, who lived a Christian life of great power and acquired a band of followers so devoted that they even took his bones with them when the community had to flee from the Norsemen. And you're carrying your Cuthbert's bones with you, aren't you, Jon—except that they're not bones, they're memories. He forbade you to heal; he wanted you to teach, and now that he's dead and you've left the Order you're suffering from a compulsion to rebel against him, just as some of my pupils rebel against me when they leave school and start sowing their wild oats."

There was a pause. Cyril looked at me expectantly and at last I said: "You could be right."

Cyril looked relieved, as if an exceptionally dense pupil had finally comprehended the solution to a simple problem. "What you've got to do, Jon, is to sort out all these convoluted feelings of yours about Father Cuthbert, and then I'm sure the way ahead will become clear."

"Yes," I said. "Yes, I'm sure you're right." I assumed a humble, thoughtful, chastened expression, the expression of a man who understood his errors sufficiently to profess a valid repentance of his anger and pride.

"The truth is," said Cyril, "that in your heart you feel guilty that you're defying Father Cuthbert on the subject of healing, and this is why you reacted so strongly when you received criticism. You don't want to admit the guilt and you're too proud to concede the call could be mistaken. The road to repentance lies in summoning sufficient humility to reconsider your situation from a completely unbiased perspective."

"Yes, I understand. I'll try."

The penitent had professed a genuine repentance. Cyril was satisfied. Absolution was now inevitable. "Of course I'm not suggesting you don't need a lot more help here," he said, "and certainly I'm willing enough to try to give it to you, but ideally, I think, you should make a retreat under the direction of Father Abbot-General, who's so much better acquainted with you than I am."

"Unfortunately it's impossible for me to leave my wife at present."

"What a pity! Yes, I suppose it is." For a moment Cyril looked cross that I should be inconvenienced by such a distracting object as a pregnant wife but then he recollected himself sufficiently to say: "In that case you must come back and see me as soon as possible—in fact now that we've identified the source of your difficulties we should meet every week."

"I'd like nothing better, but there's a growing problem of obtaining petrol for the motor, and—"

"Leap on a train!" said Cyril briskly, as if he were addressing a slothful prefect. "Why not? You're surely not so old that you have to be carted everywhere in that delightful Rolls-Royce!"

"No, of course not, but the train journey is really most awkward—"

"Tolerate it. What's a little awkwardness once a week when your spiritual health is at stake?"

To keep him happy I smiled and pretended that I fully accepted his advice.

WHEN I arrived home I retired to my cell, knelt at the oratory and in Protestant fashion confessed my sins directly to God. I knew very well that my Anglo-Catholic confession before a priest had gone so seriously adrift that I could consider it a nullity. Cyril was the wrong confessor for me. I thought how Aidan, that wily old fox, would have said: "You were silent for a long time. There's something you'd like to tell me, perhaps, about that silence." And Francis would have said: "You're being wonderfully meek and contrite, but why is it that I always feel suspicious when you start behaving like a model monk?" And Father Darcy would have said as usual: "You're saying the words you want me to hear but I hear the words you can't bring yourself to say." Yet Cyril, springing energetically from conclusion to conclusion with the zest of a mountain goat leaping from crag to crag, had been too enchanted by his admirably plausible theory to realise he should have looked deeper and listened harder in order to extricate me from my difficulties.

However I felt it was unfair to condemn Cyril for a failure which sprang primarily from my inability to be honest with him, and in an effort to demonstrate my repentance I rose from my knees, sat down at the table and tried to approach my current situation with humility. There was, of course, no possibility that I might give up the healing—how could I when I knew beyond all doubt that my call was genuine?—but since I had embarked on such a difficult, dangerous ministry I might be wise to seek advice from someone who was far more experienced in the art of healing than I was.

This struck me as a pleasingly humble acknowledgement of my fallibility, and accordingly I wrote to Wilfred, the infirmarian at Ruydale, explained how I had been approaching my work as a healer and asked him not only for helpful hints but for stern criticism of any errors. This exercise in humility certainly soothed my conscience, and I then found I could face Francis's suggestion that the showing of Nicholas had been a delusion drummed up by my subconscious mind to allay my fear of parenthood.

Deciding that my most sensible course was to refresh my memory of the photograph, I wrote to Ruth, to whom I had given all the family memorabilia when I entered the Order, and asked her to send me the appropriate album. Fearful of tiresome questions I merely mentioned that I wanted to show Anne a photograph of my parents. My correspondence with Ruth had been sporadic since her disastrous visit to the Manor, and although we had formally patched up the quarrel I had made no effort to invite her to Starrington again.

I was still waiting to hear from Wilfred when the album arrived, and to my surprise I found I could hardly bring myself to open it; the thought of seeing my parents again aroused such powerful emotions, but eventually I managed to confront the picture taken on their wedding day. My father, tall, trim and bespectacled, looked dignified, decent and dull. My mother, her slender figure discreetly veiled in elaborate draperies, looked elegant, enigmatic and alluring. They were standing very close together but not touching each other at any point. Abruptly I turned the page and saw my mother holding an undistinguished bundle in a christening robe. She looked as if her thoughts were far away but she was holding the bundle with authority. More studio portraits followed—taken in the days before my father acquired his camera—and at last I found myself confronting the photograph I remembered, the picture of myself at the age of four.

I stared, trying to decide if Nicholas had been a hallucinatory mirror-image, but I was quite unable to make up my mind. The difference in clothes was distracting. Encased in a formal black suit with a frilly shirt I might have inhabited a different planet from the little boy in the dungarees, yet the eyes were the same and the bone structure was certainly similar. The hair should have been different but my mother had kept mine unfashionably short. I did think I appeared tougher than the child in my vision, but perhaps the unfamiliar camera had stimulated me to display the pugnacious side of my nature.

Later when I showed the album to Anne she was much intrigued. "You look like both your parents," she said. "How strange! I somehow got the impression you took entirely after your mother." And after studying the photographs again she remarked: "He's got a sad face. Was he happy as a schoolmaster?"

"Very. He had a gift for teaching."

"But you told me he was quiet and scholarly. Teachers like that often have trouble keeping order."

"Not my father. He had a commanding presence—that's something which doesn't come over in the photographs—and when he was before an audience he projected complete confidence and authority."

"You saw him in action? I assumed that as you hadn't attended the grammar school where he taught—"

"He used to lecture sometimes at the Working Men's Institute and he would take me with him if he thought the subject would be of interest. I was always enthralled. So was everyone else in the room. His gift was very remarkable."

"How sad that he didn't have a brilliant career at a leading public school!"

"He never complained." Abruptly closing both the album and the conversation I retired to my cell again to meditate on Nicholas; now that my attempt to distinguish him as a person other than my four-year-old self had neither succeeded nor failed I felt more confused than ever, and after rereading Francis's letter I directed my attention towards the unknown woman whom I had assumed to be Nicholas's nurse. Was I in fact entirely certain that I had not heard that voice before? Groping in my memory for a Nicholas whose mother I might have encountered long ago, I suddenly remembered the Nicholas who had lived three houses away on our sedate little street. We had met at Sunday school but he had been forbidden to play with the son of a parlour-maid, and on the one occasion when I had wandered into his garden to look for him, his mother, a very grand female who bedecked herself with lavish hats, had dismissed me so brutally that I had run home in tears.

I grimaced at the memory, rejected it as irrelevant and decided my careful re-examination of the showing should cease. In the absence of any evidence to the contrary I felt I could assume Nicholas was my future son, and I was still savouring my relief that I had repelled Francis's unpleasant insinuations when Wilfred's letter arrived from Ruydale.

6

WILFRED suggested tactfully that I was making various mistakes and his first concern was that I was being too indiscriminating.

"You can't heal everyone," he wrote firmly.

Nor should you try to. You're not a miracle-worker. You're an ordinary man with a special supply of energy, but this energy isn't inexhaustible and to squander it on all and sundry is unwise. You must be discerning. Learn how to say no, not only to those who suffer from a *maladie imaginaire* (and I fear they are legion) but also to those who are attracted to you as a source of "magic" which may succeed when doctors fail. You are quite right to refer everyone first to the doctor; this is good. But do not, whatever you do, succumb to the temptation to try to outdo the doctor by taking on every case he can't help. Accept that some cases really are beyond help. Learn to spot them and by all means offer sympathy, but don't waste your special energy when it could be put to more effective use elsewhere.

Now let me turn to the subject of services of healing. I'm opposed to such services for several reasons: (a) The Devil can so easily slip into the front pew and cause disruption. (b) A bunch of sick people tends to exude a melancholy aura which impedes the healing process. (c) The healthy members of the congregation are often present solely in the hope of seeing a miracle, and the aura they exude is thus essentially negative, creating quite the wrong psychic currents in the atmosphere. (d) The healer tends to exhaust himself before the end and this means that the last people he treats derive no benefit. This exhaustion is also bad for the healer physically, mentally, emotionally and psychically. *Never overstrain your powers.* If you do, you won't have the strength to fight the Devil.

This is how I suggest you should conduct your ministry: heal in small groups of no more than four patients but enlist the support of as many of their friends and relations as you can. This means that when you conduct the healing every person present will be there because he genuinely cares about at least one of the sick and is busy praying for his recovery. You'll have eliminated the seekers after vicarious thrills and the psychic atmosphere will be pure. Moreover you'll be in no danger of running out of energy and overstraining yourself, so your powers should be more effective.

The procedure should be as follows: (a) See the patient in a preliminary interview. (b) See him again with all the truly sympathetic supporters he can muster and explain to them how they should pray in order to be of maximum assistance. (c) Form a separate prayer group whose business it is to pray for the sick. This will give you extra support. (d) Hold the brief private service in the chapel when you feel everyone is ready. (e) During the service perform the laying-on of hands as before but in future administer unction as well. Oil has a very soothing effect and is not, as you seem to think, a mere sacramental gesture. If anyone objects to it as Roman Catholic ritual unfit for Protestants say: "Rubbish!" very firmly. Anointing goes back far beyond the founding of the Roman Church, as of course you know.

The above procedure is no good in emergencies, I admit, but then emergencies should always be referred to a doctor. Concentrate on the cases of chronic illness where you may well alleviate distress and thus induce remissions. Concentrate on the non-chronic but lengthy illnesses where the patient's recovery can be quickened by your power. But don't look for miracles. Never keep a tally of successes. Never make the patient feel he's to blame if the healing is ineffective. Never regard a death as a personal insult from God (I'm sure you wouldn't but healers do sometimes get unhealthily overwrought about their failures). If you do find yourself getting emotionally overstrained, *stop all healing at once* and seek spiritual direction. An overstrained psyche, burdened with undisciplined emotion, can be a very snug little nest for the Devil, so make sure your psyche is fit and rested. You should take the Holy Sacrament every day and make confession twice a week, but of course you're not in the Order now and such a regime may well not be possible. Nevertheless you should follow it as closely as you can and pray constantly. This all sounds very arduous, I know, but God can't use a channel which isn't kept clear for the passage of His Holy Spirit.

And after giving me his blessing and promising to pray for me, Wilfred added in a startling postscript:

I think it would be best, while you're adjusting to your new ministry, to avoid all exorcisms. They take a great deal of psychic energy and may debilitate you too much at this stage. Refer all requests to your Bishop, who doubtless has an exorcist at his disposal. I mention this subject because the ministries of healing and deliverance go hand in hand, and you may already have had requests to purge houses of unpleasant auras. This is a fairly simple procedure and a little prayer and holy water will usually do the trick (I never recommend celebrating the Eucharist unless a ghost has actually been seen), but nevertheless I think you should abstain even from simple exorcisms at the moment. Certainly avoid all exorcisms of people. Fortunately this type of possession is rare these days as such a large proportion of the population is baptised, but such cases can be *very dangerous* and exorcism should never be attempted without at least three strong men in attendance to give physical protection.

Forgive me if you already know all this. Perhaps you do. The late Father Abbot-General was the most gifted exorcist, of course, and may well have given you instruction. Certainly he and I had many interesting conversations on the subject during his visits to Ruydale. I miss him. He was a great man. The new Father Abbot-General is also a most gifted man, I saw that when he made his first visitation here last year, but his gifts are of a different order.

This communication interested me deeply, and because Wilfred had accepted my call without question, I showed his letter to Anne as evidence of support from someone within the Order. However this move proved to be a mistake since Anne was horrified by Wilfred's laconic references to the Devil. It is very difficult for a well-educated modern person to believe that the demonic force in our imperfect world does not cease to exist merely because a sophisticated civilisation has judged the Devil to be an unfashionable symbol. Even intelligent people are more influenced by fashion than they realise, and I sometimes think that it is only in the cloister, where every effort is made to exclude the ebb and flow of ephemeral fashions, that the fundamental forces of darkness and light can be clearly perceived.

"Are you going to follow his advice and give up the large services of healing?" demanded Anne.

"I must give one more because I've promised so many people that I would, but I can see the advantage of healing in small groups," I said, and indeed as soon as I tried implementing Wilfred's suggestions I found that his advice had been sound.

As the summer advanced I became so absorbed with this new approach to my ministry that I postponed the second large service of healing. The biggest advantage of a postponement was that it kept my ecclesiastical opponents quiet, for now that I was healing people so discreetly in my quiet corner of the Manor, Aysgarth had decided not to recommend an episcopal reproof; at the same time Cyril could be more easily manoeuvred to the conclusion that I was engaged in easing my way out of a mistaken ministry, and Francis, regularly dosed with the descriptions I sent him of my life as a dutiful parish priest, could be coaxed to believe the healing was an increasingly minor activity, undertaken solely to alleviate the lot of the chronic sick.

I did indeed try to be a dutiful parish priest, but I was very mindful that Wilfred had urged me to conserve my energies and soon I was reducing my parish work to a minimum. The reduction gave me a twinge of guilt but I countered it by reflecting that since I had done too much too soon to introduce my parishioners to more fruitful forms of worship, a touch of benign neglect would now do them no harm and might even help them to adjust to my less extreme innovations. Since Aysgarth had advised me to keep to the rubric I had eliminated some of my Catholic touches, but I found I could still practise a muted version of Anglo-Catholicism. It is one of the ironies of history that the Church of England emerged from the Reformation with Protestant Articles of Religion and a Catholic Prayer Book, and although my opponents might still grumble I had a perfect right to make the most Catholic use I could of the Book of Common Prayer.

I am uncertain even now, with the wisdom of hindsight, when my psyche began to slip into a serious dis-ease. Some would argue that it began when I tore up the last letter from Francis and manipulated the crucial confession to Cyril, but although I was without doubt gravely at fault I was still sufficiently aware of my errors to make my gesture of humility and seek advice from Wilfred. Indeed since my skill as a healer improved, thanks to Wilfred's counselling, my psyche must have been in tolerable working order for some time afterwards, but I can see now that my spiritual health was steadily degenerating. I was like a consumptive who, ruddy-cheeked and bright-eyed, looks the picture of health all the time the shadow is darkening across his lung, and like the consumptive I was in a position where any additional strain on powers already weakened could only accelerate my deterioration.

I suspect this acceleration began in June when I had to say goodbye to Charles. I had been seeing him regularly since my marriage but now his regiment was on the move and rumoured to be heading either for North Africa or the Far East. As soon as I heard this news I found myself tormented by the memory of my vision of the prison-camp, and when he came to see me for the last time before his departure I hardly knew how to conceal my dread.

At first he talked of his family. His wife and children had been installed in a rented house on the outskirts of Starvale St. James where Dr. Romaine, clever Dr. Romaine, continued to charm and beguile his way into Lyle's confidence. "Awful old villain!" said Charles, who was very fond of his elderly friend. "But I have absolute faith in his ability to look after her—and of course it's also a relief to know that you and Anne are so near." He then began to talk about his sons. There were various worries associated with the older one whose volatile temperament made him difficult to manage. "He needs a great deal of loving attention and Lyle is somehow inhibited about giving it to him . . . " I listened and thought how often a tragic streak ran through even the happiest of families.

"How far have you confided in Dr. Romaine?" I said at last.

"I said nothing for a long time. Then when I learnt I was going overseas I did tell him, but of course he'd already guessed. He thinks Lyle's secretly paralysed by guilt that she should have produced such a difficult child."

This struck me as a shrewd judgement. "If that's true," I said, "then you may find she'll be able to cope with Charley much better in your absence. She won't have to exhaust herself by worrying that you secretly find him a bore."

"But I've told her and told her—"

"Obviously your assurances aren't quite ringing true, and the most likely reason why this is happening is because you're not, in fact, telling the exact truth. After all, let's be honest; difficult children can indeed be a bore, so instead of protesting nobly to Lyle that you love him no matter what he does, might it not help her to relax if you were to say instead: 'Yes, he's a thorough nuisance sometimes, but never mind, I'm still absolutely committed to his welfare.' "

"I don't like to complain—"

"People make a great mistake when they never complain," said my professional persona, the accomplished spiritual director. "Whatever they gain by patience they lose in honesty. Conversations begin to ring false. Suspicions are aroused. Resentments multiply. Relationships are poisoned. I always look askance at a man who makes a virtue of never complaining no matter how great the provocation to do so."

"I agree martyrs can be thoroughly tiresome, but I'm just so afraid that if I complain, Lyle will immediately conclude I don't love her and sink fathoms deep into depression." He sighed before adding: "Sometimes I ask myself if I regret marrying her but I know at heart I don't. She presents an endlessly alluring challenge. A good, simple woman would have bored me in no time."

I smiled but said nothing and there followed a long silence which I gradually realised he did not know how to break. At last I said: "The time's come to talk of you, Charles. We've discussed your worries about your family; now tell me your worries about yourself." And as he responded with relief to my invitation to unburden himself of his darkest fears, I found myself slipping back twenty-five years to my days as a Naval chaplain before the great Battle of Jutland.

"I hate to admit it—well, I wouldn't admit it to anyone except you, but . . ."

I listened to him confessing his fear of death.

" . . . and I feel so ashamed. When I think of all those Christians bravely facing the lions—"

I recognised my cue and interposed effortlessly: "Do you honestly think the martyrs felt no fear as they marched into the amphitheatre? After all, it's only human to be nervous at the prospect of an unpleasant journey into the unknown, even if one has absolute confidence in the reality of one's final destination. And besides, why shouldn't you feel fear at the prospect of leaving Lyle a widow and your children fatherless? If you felt no fear I'd be exceedingly worried about you!" And I talked on, soothing him yet encouraging him to face his fears until the moment when he exclaimed: "How I admire your indestructible serenity—I can't tell you what confidence you give me!" Then I had to suppress a shudder of relief that I had managed to conceal my dread from him. I heard myself promise to pray daily for his welfare, and later when I had given him my blessing he said simply: "I'm ready for anything now."

We parted. I felt annihilated. After a while I was unable to stop myself trying to peer into the future but the fear closed my psychic eye, all possible futures were reflected in a blank mirror and I remained in a terrifying ignorance. Then it occurred to me that enlightenment might have been even more terrifying and that God was being merciful by keeping the mirror blank. In panic I retreated to the chapel, but my psyche was so lacerated by distress that I was incapable of achieving the quality of prayer needed to master such a profound anxiety. Instinctively I turned back to my work to keep my fear at bay, and it was then, when my spirits were at their lowest ebb, that I allowed myself to go too far with that proven panacea for all my troubles, my all-absorbing ministry of healing.

THE next day I had a visit from one of the farm labourers on Anne's estate, a man in his forties called John Higgins who lived with his wife and children in a tied-cottage and came to church every week. A simple soul, he had once told me that my services were as good as a visit to "the pictures," and knowing he had intended this dubious remark as a compliment I was well pleased; it confirmed my belief that Anglo-Catholic ritual is more successful in communicating religious truths to the working classes than the staid Protestant services patronised by the well-to-do. I took an interest in Higgins, and when I learnt that he had been neither confirmed nor even baptised, I offered to give him instruction so that he could be formally received into the Church, but the word "instruction" had intimidated Higgins, who was almost illiterate, and I was still trying to persuade him that membership of the Church did not depend on either one's education or one's mental ability.

On the morning of his visit I had been praying in the chapel, and it was when I left that I found him waiting patiently, cap in hand, on the steps of the porch.

"Pardon me for trespassing, sir," he said. "I did call several times at the church vestry but you were never there so finally I got desperate and came looking for you."

I suppressed the guilt that one of my parishioners should have had such difficulty in finding me, and doing my best to put him at ease I took him into the chapel. "Well, Higgins," I said as we sat down together in the nearest pew, "how may I help you?"

He twisted his cap and looked deeply embarrassed. I recognised an honest man in confusion, but beyond this elementary deduction which required no psychic skill whatever I was in ignorance.

"How's your wife?" I hazarded, offering a question that could pave the way to a discussion of marital difficulty.

"Very well, thank you, sir, but I haven't come about her. I've come about Him."

"Him?"

"Him who follows me about and gives me orders." More cap-twisting followed but finally he blurted out: "He's not a real person, he's a Thing in my head. He wants me to murder the cows and I'm afraid to go to work in case he forces me to obey him."

I made the diagnosis: paranoid schizophrenia. Aloud I said: "Does this person—this presence in your head—talk in words?"

"Yes, sir. He says: 'Take the scythe and cut the throats of the cows.'"

"How often has he done this?"

"Twice. I told him to go away each time and he did. But I'm afraid that one day he'll come back and won't go away when I tell him to."

"Exactly what words did you use when you ordered him off?"

"I said—excuse the language, sir—I said: 'For Christ's sake, fuck off, you bloody bugger.'"

I noted that Christ had been invoked, albeit with a blasphemous irreverence, but all I said was: "Had you been drinking?"

"I don't drink, sir. My father died of it and my mother made us all take the pledge."

"I see." I paused to consider the situation.

"Can you lay your hands on me, sir, and make me strong enough to keep him out?" said the poor man with a touching faith which was very hard to withstand, but I answered as kindly as I could: "I'd have to be sure that was the best way of dealing with the problem, Higgins, and I can't be sure until you've taken medical advice. Do you have the money for the doctor?" I added, for by this time I was accustomed to people who regarded me as a cheap alternative to Dr. Garrison, but Higgins said with admirable dignity that the money would be found.

I wondered what Garrison would make of the case, and the next day I was just debating whether I should call at Higgins's cottage when Anne returned greatly perturbed from the Home Farm. She had by this time reduced the number of hours she spent in the estate office, but she still liked to look in every day to talk to the agent. "What do you think's happened?" she exclaimed as soon as we met in the drawing-room. "Garrison's packed off Higgins the cowman to the lunatic asylum at Starbridge! Sane, stolid, respectable Higgins! I feel utterly shattered—do you suppose Garrison's finally gone off his head?"

"Much as I'd like to say yes, I'm afraid the answer's almost certainly no," I said reluctantly, and without disclosing any details of the case I told her that Higgins had visited me in a disturbed state of mind. "He certainly wasn't mad when I spoke to him," I added, "but possibly I caught him in a lucid interval. I did wonder if he was possessed, but there were no outward signs of possession and the most likely diagnosis is some form of schizophrenia."

Anne blanched. "But what's the difference? I thought possession was just the old-fashioned way of saying someone was mad!"

"In the old days when little was known about mental illness there was undoubtedly much confusion, but now it's easier to see that possession is quite distinct; for example, mental illness usually has an incapacitating effect on the sufferer, while the person who's possessed remains capable of holding a job, supporting a family and leading an ostensibly normal life. He's also sane enough to realise that he's being periodically invaded by an alien presence and he desperately wants to rid himself of the invader. Many victims of mental illness, on the other hand, have trouble admitting there's anything wrong with them.''

"But have you ever actually met someone you thought was possessed?''

"Good heavens, yes!'' I said surprised. "Cases of possession haven't ceased to exist just because doctors like Garrison fail to recognise them! I sought permission to perform exorcisms when I was a prison chaplain but the governor turned the request down and the victims were all transferred to hospitals for the criminally insane. However I dare say it was just as well my request wasn't granted. I actually knew very little about exorcisms before I met Father Darcy, and ignorance can be dangerous when you deal with the Devil.''

"How absolutely *foul,*'' said Anne vehemently, and to my consternation I saw she was profoundly upset. "Jon, I don't want you to have anything to do with Higgins's illness.''

"But, my dearest Anne, I've already said that Higgins showed none of the outward signs of possession—''

"What are they?''

Belatedly I decided that this was the most unsuitable conversation for a pregnant woman. "That's not important,'' I said firmly. "All that matters is that I don't think Higgins needs to be exorcised.''

That night Anne had a nightmare. "It's all this beastly talk of the Devil,'' she said, shuddering in my arms. "I'd never thought twice about the Devil until you turned up with all your talk of charismatic corruption and demonic infiltration and religious hysteria and drowned cats and sinister exorcisms and brutal old monks—''

"Anne, Anne—''

"All right! All right! I know I must calm down, but I hate all this talk of the Devil, *hate it*—that letter from Wilfred was thoroughly creepy and beastly—''

I was astounded as well as shocked. "But it was a model of down-to-earth common sense!''

"If you think that, you're mad. Or maybe I'm mad. I don't know, I don't know anything any more except that you've become much too peculiar—''

"Peculiar!'' I was horrified.

"You were all right before you took up the healing—you were unusual and eccentric, I know, but you were normally unusual and eccentric and I felt I could cope. But now I'm absolutely out of my depth and I've got an awful feeling something ghastly's going to happen and oh God, if only there was someone I could turn to but I can't think of anyone who could possibly understand—"

Although I was profoundly distressed I knew how important it was that I should remain calm, so I made no attempt to argue. I merely held her close, stroked her hair and repeated soothingly, using a mild hypnotic technique, that I had no intention of embarking on a ministry of deliverance. This reassurance comforted her, but when I had at last succeeded in coaxing her back to sleep I lay awake worrying for some time. Anne was not normally the sort of woman who tottered on the brink of hysteria, and I was driven to wonder if she had been overtaxing her strength as her pregnancy advanced. Perhaps now was the moment when she should retire completely from her work at the estate office. I toyed with the idea of seeking Dr. Romaine's advice, but as always I felt lukewarm towards this medical cynosure of so many admiring feminine eyes. I had not yet met him. I had been too busy shunning the social occasions where we might have encountered each other, and Starvale St. James, although nearer than Starwater Abbey, was still too far away to be visited quickly by bicycle.

However the next morning I found to my relief that Dr. Romaine's advice was not needed; Anne had even recovered sufficiently to be ashamed of her irrational outburst.

"I didn't mean what I said about the healing having a malign effect on you," she said. "After all, how could it? A call from God can only be benign."

"But if you're worried and unhappy—"

"I'm not! Pregnancy just makes me fanciful and silly sometimes, that's all. So long as you're happy in your work then I'm happy too."

A great load rolled off my mind and I found myself saying impulsively: "I won't hold another large service of healing after this next one in July, and I'll take on fewer small groups. Then you won't have to worry about me overstraining myself."

Anne looked relieved but said: "Do you really have to hold this service?"

"I don't see how I can cancel it—I've already postponed it once and disappointed numerous people."

"Can't you write and ask Francis if he thinks it's advisable to go ahead?"

"Well, I intend to write to him, certainly, but I'm rather busy at the moment and—"

"Quite," said Anne flatly, and turned away.

I suffered a sharp pang of anxiety. "I'll discuss the service with Cyril, of course—"

"Cyril doesn't have your respect as Francis does."

"Well, I concede there may be an element of truth in that, but nonetheless he's a very competent priest and—"

Anne suddenly seemed to lose interest in the conversation. "I'm being neurotic and stupid again, aren't I?" she exclaimed as if she were exasperated with herself. "For heaven's sake don't take any notice of me!" And having given me an affectionate kiss she added: "Don't worry, I do understand how busy you are and I quite accept that you haven't the time at present to write to Francis."

Some days later I was just reflecting in relief that Anne's moodiness had been entirely conquered when an event occurred which made me fear its revival: Higgins was discharged from the mental hospital. The doctors had been unable to find anything wrong with him.

8

WITHOUT telling Anne I called at Higgins's cottage and sat drinking tea with him in the front parlour.

"The hospital doctor said that after a rest I'd be as good as new," said Higgins placidly, "and I am."

"Why did he say you needed a rest from work?"

"Not from work, sir. From her."

I wondered confused if the presence had changed sex. "Her?"

"Mrs. Higgins, sir. My wife."

"Ah." I remained puzzled. "You didn't tell me there was a difficulty with your wife."

"No more there is, sir. She nags a bit, but I'm used to that. Her nagging's just water off a duck's back to me."

"Then why did the doctor think—"

"He was mad, sir, like all the poor souls in that place. He said that though I *think* I don't care about the nagging, deep down inside me I do, and when I want to kill the cows what I really want is to kill my wife."

"Ah."

"I did right not to tell Doctor what I thought of his idea, didn't I, sir? It wouldn't have been polite. But of course the truth is it's not *me* that wants to kill any living creature. It's Him."

"Did He visit you in hospital?"

"No, sir, not once. Maybe He's gone for good now."

"Let's hope so." I talked to him for a little longer but he did indeed seem the picture of bucolic health and his placid, sensible manner was very reassuring.

When I next saw Anne I said as casually as possible: "It seems Higgins had a mild nervous breakdown brought on by a marital difficulty."

"Marital difficulty?" said Anne astonished. "But they always seem so tranquil and well-suited!" Before I could attempt a comment she added: "Well, I suppose a lot of couples manage to cover up their troubles— thank goodness there's an explanation for his peculiar behaviour."

I thought no more of Higgins. I was too busy organising the service of healing, and as the appointed hour in July drew closer I became entirely absorbed in my preparations. Then on the very day of the service disaster struck. At ten o'clock that morning Anne's land-agent telephoned from the Home Farm to say that Higgins had butchered a cow, barricaded himself in the barn with a scythe and was bellowing that I alone had the power to deliver him from his nightmare.

XVII

"[Christ] unquestionably taught that unclean spirits, no less than the Holy Spirit, may make their abode within us."

W. R. INGE

CHRISTIAN ETHICS AND MODERN PROBLEMS

I

LUCKILY Anne was out, paying one of her regular visits to Dr. Romaine, so I did not have to endure another emotional outburst on the subject of exorcism. Responding at once to the urgency of the call, I mounted my bicycle and arrived five minutes later at the Home Farm to find that a large crowd had gathered outside the barn. The land-agent greeted me with the news that the village constable had already telephoned for reinforcements. Meanwhile the crowd of yokels, eyeing me with excitement, were all agog at the possibility of a supernatural intervention.

I dealt with this unedifying aura by telling them to keep well back. Then moving confidently in order to conceal my considerable trepidation, I announced myself at the door of the barn and promised Higgins that I would perform the laying-on of hands, just as he had originally requested, if he would abandon his scythe and come out.

The door creaked open an inch. When he saw I was alone the inch widened to a foot. He was still holding the scythe and his clothes were covered with blood. He looked frightened but sane.

"I'm not coming out," he said. "They'll overpower me. You must come in."

"Very well, but you must put the scythe outside the door—and I can't come in alone. I must have three people with me to pray while I perform the laying-on of hands."

"You promise they won't overpower me and tie me up?"

"Once you're delivered from this spirit who's tormenting you, there'll be no need to tie you up."

He considered the situation. I still saw no signs of possession. Finally he opened the door wider, dropped the scythe in the yard and said: "Come in."

A gasp rippled through the crowd as the scythe flashed in the light. Beckoning three of the burliest labourers, I said to Dawson the land-agent: "Keep everyone out, even the police." Then after instructing my bodyguards, I led the way into the building.

This particular barn was used for housing farm vehicles, and when I entered I saw that Higgins had retreated to a position behind the wheel of a tractor. However he made no attempt to retreat farther, and I was just concluding in relief that I had once more encountered the sufferer during a lucid interval when the nape of my neck prickled. I stopped dead, and suddenly I saw all the signs Father Darcy had described, the hidden look in the eyes, the tightening of the muscles at the side of the jaw and the abrupt unnecessary movements which were now manifested as the man sat down, drew up his knees in a foetal position, uncoiled himself again and finally leant back against the tractor. Sane, stolid, simple Higgins had vanished. Another presence occupied the shattered psyche. Automatically my hand reached for my pectoral cross.

Until that moment I had merely felt nervous but now I felt very frightened indeed. In preparation for the afternoon's service I had been spending hours in fasting and prayer, and my psyche, honed by this rigorous discipline, was at its most receptive, with the result that my confrontation with this demonic force formed the spiritual equivalent of being struck in the stomach with a battering ram. I had taken care to bring a small crucifix with me. Still holding my pectoral cross with my left hand I produced the crucifix from my pocket. The man flinched. Holding out the crucifix I ordered: "Repeat after me: Jesus Christ is Lord."

He tried to obey. Sweat stood out on his forehead. Then the fiend grabbed him again and as his fingers curled into his hands like claws— another symptom—he rushed forward shouting that he would tear my eyes out. Immediately my three bodyguards leapt to the rescue, but with the abnormal strength of the possessed he tossed them aside and rushed at me again. I shall never know how I stood my ground but I shoved the crucifix at the maniac and shouted: "In the name of JESUS CHRIST, depart from this man, you demon of violence, and trouble him no more!" Just in time I remembered that the spirit not only had to be named but directed elsewhere to avoid all risk of its merely moving from one body in the barn to another. "In the name of JESUS CHRIST," I shouted again, "depart and possess the body of a cow fifty miles away!" My choice of a cow indicated my extreme fright; as I confronted the shell of the cowman it was the only animal I could remember, and it is a curious, even astonishing fact that this bizarre command, far from sounding a note of bathos as any sane civilised person would expect, rang out with the lethal power of a bullet from a shotgun. Higgins had stopped dead in his tracks as soon as I had invoked the name of Christ, but now he was blasted backwards and the next moment he had slumped unconscious to the ground.

The evil miasma vanished from the atmosphere as abruptly as if someone had heaved it from the barn. For a second I thought I too would lose consciousness, but as the atmosphere lightened the dizziness ebbed. My three companions were shivering as if they were shell-shocked. At last I managed to say to them: "Thank you. You can leave now. Tell everyone to remain outside."

I prayed by the inert body until Higgins awoke ten minutes later. His first words were: "He's gone." Tears of relief sprang to his eyes. "He won't come back now, will He?" he said. "He'll never come back again."

I asked him to say: "Jesus Christ is Lord," and when he uttered the words without difficulty, I offered him the crucifix which he now had no trouble clasping. Before I laid my hands on him we prayed together, thanking God for the deliverance. Higgins cried soundlessly all the time and afterwards when I gave him my handkerchief he could only sob pathetically, "What's to become of me?" But unfortunately there was no easy answer to that question; I foresaw another visit to the mental hospital as the authorities went through the motions of closing the stable door after the horse had bolted, but at least I could promise that my wife would bring no charges against him for the slaughter of the cow.

"Poor Buttercup," said Higgins, shedding fresh tears. "She had such a lovely nature. Oh God, oh God, how terrible to think I killed her!"

I thought of my responsibility for Whitby's murder, and somehow found the strength to comfort him.

2

WHEN I returned home it was noon and I had exactly three hours to rebuild my strength before the service. The hours of fasting now combined with a delayed shock to render me disordered, even panic-stricken, as I realised how far I was from being prepared for the arduous afternoon ahead, and when Anne waylaid me in the hall I wanted only to escape from her.

"I've just got back and heard the news," she said, distressed. "Dawson phoned. Jon, how *could* you have been so utterly reckless and foolish! If you'd been killed by that maniac—"

"But I wasn't."

"No, and weren't you lucky! It just seems so appallingly irresponsible, tackling a lunatic when you were armed only with a crucifix, and anyway you promised me, you absolutely promised you wouldn't have anything to do with exorcisms—"

"How could I have ignored Higgins's cry for help when he was in such appalling torment? Look, Anne, I'm sorry but we'll have to talk about this later—I can't stop now." I spoke more sharply than I should have done but the increasing pressure on my lacerated psyche was fast becoming intolerable. However I had made a fatal mistake. The last shreds of Anne's patience deserted her as anger destroyed her self-control.

"Talk later?" she exclaimed. "You won't talk later! You'll sidestep any honest conversation as usual, but has it never occurred to you that I'm beginning to feel bloody well abandoned? I've tried and tried to be a good wife to you, never complaining about all the parish work even though I'm often worn out with the farm; I've stood by you in all your troubles, never offering one word of reproach when you alienate half the village, never uttering a word of complaint when you offend my friends by refusing to accept their invitations, never betraying a hint of what I really feel about this awful alien ritual which completely distorts all our cherished services—"

"Anne!" I was so dumbfounded, so wholly appalled that I could do no more than whisper her name.

"—never criticizing you as you go charging along hell-bent on getting what you want the whole damn time, but now I'm not standing any more of this monstrously selfish behaviour—it's time I told you how horribly unhappy you're making me! You seem to believe that so long as you can satisfy me in bed you can treat me like a doormat, but all I can say is that if you think you can go on trampling me underfoot like this, you've made a very big mistake. I need some respect, consideration and—yes, damn it—*love,* and I absolutely refuse to let you get away with treating me as I can now see you must have treated Betty!" And as I remained transfixed with horror she rushed away from me across the hall.

It took me several seconds to recover sufficiently to blunder after her. She had collapsed sobbing on the drawing-room sofa, but when I tried to put my arms around her she pushed me aside. "Go away."

"But, Anne, we must talk, we absolutely must—I insist—"

"There you go again. Always what *you* want the whole time—you're so arrogant, so self-centred—"

"But—"

"GO AWAY!" shouted Anne, and dashed out of the room. I tore after her but I was slow off the mark again and this time the door was locked as she took refuge in the library. "We'll talk later," I heard her say in a muffled voice, "after you've given your dazzling performance as the Wonder-Worker. Now just go away and leave me alone."

I was silenced. For one long moment I stared stricken at the closed door. Then I turned aside and crept away.

3

WORDS flickered in my consciousness, useless inadequate words reflecting my agonised state of mind, and the words were: pregnant, irrational, emotional, didn't mean it, couldn't mean it, just an overwrought mistake, she'll take every word back when she's calmer.

These words sustained me until I reached my cell. Then the overpowering sincerity of Anne's tirade blasted aside this feeble defence and annihilated my remaining strength so that for some time I could only sit numbly in a chair. Prayer was impossible, meditation quite beyond my power. All I could do was concentrate on recovering the will to move.

At length I managed to creep back downstairs. Anne had evidently recovered; I could hear her talking to someone in the drawing-room and I wondered who the visitor was, but I supposed the police might have arrived to talk to her about the cow. I had already made my statement to them and as I was in no mood to make another I took refuge in the dining-room. To my surprise I saw the table was set for two. That was odd. I had given instructions that I would need no food until after the service. Dismissing the extra place as a servant's vagary I moved to the sideboard, sniffed the decanters to identify the brandy and poured a hefty measure into a tumbler. I disliked brandy but I felt in desperate need of medicine to restore my equilibrium.

Having consumed the brandy as quickly as I could, I then found I had no idea what to do with the glass. I could hardly leave it on the sideboard. What would the servants think? I shuddered, but the brandy was giving me a new energy and moving swiftly from the room, the glass still in my hand, I escaped into the garden.

Halfway to the chapel I felt dizzy and knew the brandy had been a mistake. I sat down to wait until I felt better, and as I leant against a tree-trunk I thought how beautiful the sunlight was as it slanted through the beech leaves. I remembered teaching my novices about nature mysticism. "Excellent!" Father Darcy had exclaimed after eavesdropping in the scriptorium for half an hour during one of his annual visitations. "Now admit it, Jonathan—isn't imparting knowledge to an enrapt audience more satisfying than healing constipated cats?" And although I had wanted to hit him for this mocking reference to Whitby, I had been unable to resist a smile as I savoured such unprecedented approval.

Poor Whitby.

REMEMBER WHITBY, Francis had written, and I was remembering him, murdered martyred Whitby, lying stiff as a board on the Abbot's desk while Father Darcy pointed his finger at me and said: "*You* were the one who killed that animal with your disobedience, your vanity and your utterly intolerable pride."

I suddenly realised that I had to cancel the service. Father Darcy would be so angry if I held it. I shuddered, reminding myself that he was dead, but somehow his memory seemed to be hardening in my mind and feeding upon my psyche as it sought the strength to project itself upon the ether . . . But such a projection would have been a mere parlour-trick. Father Darcy was at peace, with God. I could hardly expect to be aware of him as a disturbed discarnate presence, and any ghost I succeeded in conjuring up would only have been a manifestation of my disordered psyche.

"I never recommend celebrating the Eucharist," Wilfred had written, "unless a ghost has actually been seen."

"That letter from Wilfred was thoroughly creepy and beastly . . . "

As Anne's voice echoed in my memory the brandy glass slipped from my hand and shattered on a stone. The sound had the same effect as the click of a hypnotist's fingers as he awoke his subject from a trance, and struggling to my feet I kicked the fragments of glass into the under-growth before I stumbled on down the path into the dell.

The chapel faced me at last, and suddenly as its serene atmosphere enfolded me I felt I could not possibly cancel the service. For the sake of the sick I had to cast all doubts aside.

In the chapel I knelt to pray but my mind was blank. Then slowly, very slowly, my battered psyche was bathed in a subtle alluring light until I could see the words of a prayer. It was inscribed on my consciousness in the most beautiful lettering and it read: "Grant me a spectacular cure today so that I can believe my call is right; grant me a spectacular cure so that Anne can admire me again; grant me a spectacular cure so that I can feel young and vital and successful, dazzling not only my wife but the world with my magnificent glamorous powers."

A second later I was recoiling in horror; I had recognised the Devil's presence in this travesty of a prayer, and automatically I grabbed my pectoral cross to beat him out of my psyche. Indeed so appalled was I by this spiritual deviation that it was some time before I could whisper to God: "Help me. Give me the strength I must have in order to comfort these sick people." But then I thought of Anne accusing me of being concerned only with my own wants and I realised that even this prayer was hopelessly self-centred. In despair I retreated to the vestry to change into my cassock and surplice.

When I had dressed I tried to pray for others. I prayed for Anne, whom I had wounded so deeply, and as soon as I remembered her I thought of the baby. I recalled my showing, its joyous aftermath, my absolute conviction that I was on the right road and that all would eventually be well.

The showing had sustained me in the past and now I knew it sustained me still. So long as I could believe in that showing I would survive, and rising from my knees at last with my faith restored I found I had sufficient strength to face the service.

4

THE congregation approached the chapel by passing through one of the side gates in the wall which encircled the grounds and proceeding for some two hundred yards along a track into the dell. By a quarter to three the chapel was packed and Colonel Maitland's sidesmen were being obliged to turn people away. However I gave permission for a number to stand at the back beyond the five patients in wheelchairs, and although the colonel expressed doubts about the wisdom of packing people into this confined space, I pointed out that if anyone should be overcome by claustrophobia the exit was conveniently close.

"The point is they're blocking the exit for the rest of the congregation," said Colonel Maitland, but unwilling to be distracted further by trivial details I dismissed him so that I could be alone again in the vestry. I had not ventured out of it to inspect the congregation because I was afraid Anne might have decided not to attend, and by then I felt it was vital that I did not risk becoming further distressed.

Three o'clock arrived. Colonel Maitland informed me that all was ready, and after a brief final prayer I moved from the vestry to the altar.

When I faced the congregation the first thing I saw was the hat in the fourth row.

It was a large hat elaborately bedecked with artificial flowers and it was being worn by one of my ladies, a widow named Mrs. Hetherington. But I barely saw Mrs. Hetherington. I was too busy staring at her hat, so like the hats worn long ago by our neighbour Mrs. Simmonds who had refused to let her child play with the son of a parlour-maid. But once little Nicholas had slipped out of the house when his mother was looking the other way; he had seen me passing down the road and he had wanted to say hullo to me, just as he always did at Sunday school. I could see him now in my memory, a small, thin boy with red hair, and in my memory too I could hear his mother calling: "Nicholas! Nicholas!" as she realised he was missing.

The showing shattered.

I knew then that I had gone horrifyingly astray, and as I stood paralysed with shock before the hushed congregation I felt the Devil himself gently stroke the hair at the nape of my neck.

The temperature in the chapel started to fall.

I stared around, wondering why no one was shivering. I felt deathly cold, and it was only with the greatest difficulty that I managed to speak. I said: "There's an enemy among us." I did not think before I spoke. The sentence arrived fully formed on my tongue. I had to let the Devil know that I was fully aware of his presence.

The congregation gaped, and when I realised in confusion that they had not understood I heard myself say to them loudly: "The forces of darkness are waging their eternal battle against the forces of light."

Still they stared, and shuddering with the cold I began to move forward to the first row of pews. "The forces of darkness," I said, speaking very distinctly, "are trying to destroy me."

A gasp finally rippled through the congregation, and at once it seemed as if the rows of faces were transformed into wooden blocks, dry and inanimate, waiting for the spark which would set them ablaze.

Meanwhile my glance was raking each row for the source of the evil that threatened me. I had realised that the Devil was no longer a climate, chilling the chapel. He had become incarnate, hiding from me behind a human mask, but I knew I dared not let him elude me. I had to hunt him down and force him into the open where he could be confronted, overpowered and vanquished.

"Stand up, Satan!" I shouted suddenly. "Stand up and show yourself!"

A second later I saw Anne's face, white with terror, but before I could yell at her to escape, the man beside her slowly rose to his feet and at once all trace of the rational world dissolved.

The man was Father Darcy.

5

I GASPED.

Then I tried to back away but something seemed to have happened to my legs; they were so heavy that I could hardly move them. I wanted to rub my eyes but my arms had become heavy too, so heavy that I could no longer raise my hands, and all I could do was stare at the figure in the Fordite habit. I knew I could not be seeing Father Darcy yet at the same time I knew it was Father Darcy I was seeing. Panic overwhelmed me. Dragging my arm upwards I scrabbled for my pectoral cross but found that in my disordered state I had forgotten to put the cross on again after donning my cassock.

My panic increased. I tried to say: "In the name of Jesus Christ . . . " but my tongue seemed to have disconnected itself with my brain so that I was unable to repel this manifestation of the Devil with the exorcist's most powerful weapon. Finally fear drove out the shock that had been inhibiting my movements. Backing away I bumped into the altar and swung round to grab the wooden cross, but I had forgotten its weight and the next moment it had slipped through my shaking hands. I bent to retrieve it; immediately it assumed the weight of lead and became impossible to shift. Unnerved by this malign displacement of the laws of physics I tried to say: "Jesus is Lord," and when nothing happened blind terror overwhelmed me for I had realised that *I* had become the Devil incarnate. The evil lay not among the congregation but in me. Having made a mockery of God's will by following my self-centred deluded desires, I had laid myself open to demonic infiltration and now the Devil himself had stepped forward to annex my soul.

This appalling truth flashed through my mind in a single second but I could not pause to dwell on it. There was no time. Looking back over my shoulder I saw Father Darcy not as the Devil incarnate but as God's servant the exorcist. He was as fit and active as he had been when we had first met, and all the jewels glittered in his well-remembered pectoral cross as he moved silently, eerily, purposefully up the aisle to annihilate me.

I whispered: "Keep away!" and edged around the altar-table, but I knew I would be powerless against him. In desperation I shouted: "No one must touch me! I'm the Devil—I'll kill anyone who touches me!" and at once the naked flame blazed in the tinder-box as someone screamed in terror.

Hysteria erupted. Screams, shouts, yells, cries, howls—we were all plunged straight into hell. A chaotic stampede broke out as everyone plunged towards the exit, but although I was aware of the noise increasing as the hideous wave of violence struck the packed crowd at the back of the chapel, I found I could not watch what was happening. I was mesmerised by Father Darcy. Oblivious of the pandemonium behind him he had reached the altar and was now facing me across the table. I sensed the power of his will as his concentration deepened, and when his psyche wrapped itself around mine I felt disorientated because it was not as I remembered it. Father Darcy's psyche had been muscular and powerful but subtle and sinuous. This new psyche was muscular and powerful but blunt and abrasive. Realising he was trying to disguise himself I thought: how clever! But I knew I had to let him know I was not deceived. Raising my voice above the chaotic noise I shouted: "I know who you are! You think you can destroy me just as you destroyed Whitby, but I'm going to put you back in your coffin, I'm going to burn you to ashes, I'm going to—"

Father Darcy suddenly moved with a speed which terminated my power of speech. He stooped. He grabbed the oak cross. He slammed it down on the table between us. Then he cried with a force which knocked the breath from my lungs: "In the name of JESUS CHRIST, I command thee, Satan, to depart from this man to a distant savage and never return!"

All the power drained from my body.

I lost consciousness.

6

WHEN I awoke I thought I was in the London punishment cell. Then I recognised the bare walls of the chapel's vestry. I was lying on the floor with an object that felt like a pillow beneath my head but which turned out to be my surplice, folded and bunched to make me comfortable. I was still wearing my cassock.

As I stirred, a chair scraped on the floor behind me and someone dressed as the Abbot-General of the Fordite monks quickly knelt at my side.

"Francis! Oh my God—" The return of memory and the return of sanity were equally horrifying.

"Here," said Francis, shoving his bejewelled cross into my hands, "hold this. You're all right."

I grabbed the cross, gabbled: "Jesus is Lord!" and collapsed back on the surplice, but fear soon elbowed my relief aside. "Francis, don't let them take me away—don't let them put me in an asylum—"

"No one's taking you anywhere. Calm down."

But I was in a frenzy. "Where's Anne?"

"She's not here at the moment."

"Has she left me?"

"Of course not!" Francis sounded scandalised.

"Francis, promise—swear—she hasn't left me—"

"I promise. Swearing's quite unnecessary."

"But Francis, Anne doesn't love me any more—"

"Nonsense! It's because she loves you that I'm here. She wrote to me."

This was very difficult to digest. "She wrote to you? Anne? But what on earth did she say?"

"What do you think? She said you needed help and she was desperately worried about you."

I said dazed: "You must have been the guest at luncheon. I saw the extra place laid in the dining-room but I never dreamed——"

"Cyril had also written to me, of course—he even sent me a blood-curdling cutting from the *Starbridge Weekly News,* and we'd just decided that one of us should intervene when I received the appeal from your wife and realised the intervention had to come from me."

I struggled for words but since I was now inundated with a shame which saturated the length, breadth and depth of my being, speech was quite impossible. I could only cover my face with my hands, abandon the last vestige of my pride and shudder with the most profound humiliation.

"There, there!" said Francis kindly in the manner of a nanny who had rescued a wilful child from a somewhat tiresome nursery prank. "It's not the end of the world! You took a wrong turn and wound up making a fool of yourself, that's all, but that's not an unusual thing to happen. Thousands of men wind up making fools of themselves every day but they soon recover and bounce back."

Anger restored my power of speech. "What a frivolous way to talk!" I exclaimed outraged. "How dare you toss aside a case of demonic possession so lightly!"

"There was no demonic possession."

I stared. Then I managed to stammer: "But I couldn't say 'Jesus is Lord'—I couldn't hold the cross——"

"My dear Jon, you were merely a magnificent example of someone self-hypnotised by guilt!"

I found myself becoming outraged again. "But if you didn't think I was possessed, why the deuce did you exorcise me?"

"Because I happen to have at least a rudimentary understanding of psychology. As soon as you revealed that you thought I was Father Darcy, I realised that the only way to deal with you was to behave as you expected—and wanted—the old man to behave."

"But the exorcism was so successful . . . " For the second time outrage was displaced by confusion.

"There was no exorcism," said Francis patiently. "How could there be when there was no possession? I simply defused your mental disturbance by a psychological trick. In fact this whole episode can be explained perfectly adequately in rational terms without resorting to the supernatural." He stood up. "Come into the chapel so that we can both sit down in comfort, and I'll do my best to help you understand what was really going on."

But I shrank back. "Not the chapel. I can't go in there, can't face it . . . How long was I unconscious?"

"Less than a minute at first. But then you opened your eyes, announced: 'I must sleep now,' and passed out for another three quarters of an hour. You'd obviously remembered that after an exorcism the person delivered always sleeps."

"I don't recall—"

"No, probably not. Well, if you won't go into the chapel, come and sit on the steps of the porch. A little fresh air certainly won't do you any harm."

I followed him unsteadily outside. The sun was still shining radiantly through the beech leaves. I felt battered, defeated, old.

"I know you'd much rather see yourself as a hero wrestling with the Devil instead of as an elderly priest floundering into an unholy mess," said Francis, speaking frankly but not unkindly as we sat down on the steps, "but I'm afraid this is the moment when you must cast aside illusion and face reality. Now let's start by considering how you've arrived in your present unfortunate state. First and most obvious of all, you've been under strain for some time with your divided parish, your demanding ministry and your unresolved private problems. Then during the past twelve hours you've been fasting, a procedure which in adverse circumstances can lead to physical debility. Have the circumstances been adverse? They have. You endured a horrific scene this morning when you overpowered a madman by mesmerising him into docility—"

"I exorcised him."

"Quite. But you must have realised by this time that I'm unable to utter the word 'exorcism' without a shudder of distaste—it's my own personal act of rebellion against our mentor. Why don't we just say you dealt with the cowman? You then had a row with your wife—"

"How do you know?"

"She told me. And that row, I venture to suggest, was the last straw. By the time the service began, your psyche needed the kind of control you were far too exhausted to provide, so is it any wonder that when you saw a man dressed as the Abbot-General you should start to hallucinate? Father Darcy always forbade you to exercise the charism of healing. I suspect that subconsciously you felt guilty all along that you were disobeying him, and because this guilt was never alleviated by an honest discussion with a spiritual director it was allowed to accumulate until eventually, in your severely weakened state, it broke into your conscious mind with disastrous results: the shock of the hallucination caused your psyche to reel around in panic and regurgitate the memory of this morning's nightmare."

After a long while I was able to say: "There was a trigger which sent me over the edge," and I told him how the showing had shattered.

Francis said simply: "I'm very sorry. But of course I couldn't help wondering if your psyche had cleverly devised a way in which you could live with your problems without facing up to them."

"He seemed so real," I said. "I was genuinely looking forward to him." To my shame my eyes filled with tears.

"You need food and drink," said Francis briskly, rising to his feet. "Come along, I'll take you back to the house in the motor."

I felt older and more battered than ever. "Motor?" I said blankly. "What motor?"

"*The* motor," said Francis, and when he had succeeded in steering me down the track to the road beyond the wall, I found not only Father Darcy's cherished Daimler but my friend Edward the master-carpenter who was sitting patiently behind the wheel.

We embarked on our short journey around the perimeter of the grounds but it was some minutes before the Daimler, swaying along at its customary stately pace, turned through the main gates of the Manor. Portman opened the front door before the motor had halted. I dared not look him in the eye for fear of what stories he had heard, but Francis said with his aristocrat's ease as we entered the hall: "I trust you received the message."

"Yes, sir. The sandwiches are in the drawing-room."

"Good. You can bring the tea now. Come along, Jon."

After I had been piloted to the drawing-room sofa I heard myself say anxiously: "Where's Anne?"

"She's not here at the moment." Once more Francis sat down at my side.

"But where is she?"

"She's gone to Starbridge with the Aysgarths."

"*Aysgarth was at the service?*" I nearly lost consciousness again. Then I said confused: "But why has Anne gone to Starbridge?"

"I'll explain later. Start eating those sandwiches, please," ordered Francis, and when out of habit I obeyed him, he embarked on a long, fluent monologue. At first I found it difficult to concentrate on what he was saying, but gradually I became aware that he was casting a sympathetic eye on my troubles in order to encourage me to beat back any incipient feelings of despair. I was duly grateful but after a while my gratitude was blurred by bewilderment as I realised he was repeating himself, albeit in a most elegant and skilful way, over and over again. What did this mean?

Was there perhaps a hidden reason for this interminable but stylish monologue? I tried to think coherently enough to answer these questions but was promptly distracted as he offered me yet another sandwich.

"Francis—"

"Well, yes, as I was saying . . . " He was off again, weaving his mysterious verbal patterns, and again my concentration ebbed and flowed as I grappled with my bewilderment. Isolated sentences caught my attention; isolated phrases surfaced and faded away. I felt as if I were listening to a wireless which possessed an erratic volume knob. " . . . so this doesn't mean that your original call to leave the Order was a delusion. I'm quite certain God has work for you to do in the world . . . equally certain the final revelation of His will is still to come . . . easy to see why you went astray . . . ministry centred on the chapel, everything seemed to fit . . . tempting to see the chapel as a stone siren luring you to disaster, but in fact it wasn't the chapel propelling you along, was it? Later we must discuss your motives, but meanwhile perhaps it's better to see the chapel as neutral, like money, something which can be used for good or for bad. . . . But let's forget the bad for the moment, let's dwell on the positive side . . . did a lot of good among the sick . . . genuine desire to serve God mixed up with your other motives . . . still humble enough to seek advice from Wilfred . . . picture by no means completely black . . . mistake to use the disaster as an excuse to wallow in guilt and self-pity . . . " On and on Francis continued in this soothing vein until I heard him say to the butler who had returned with more tea: "Thank you, Portman—and fetch the brandy decanter and one glass, please."

"No brandy for me," I said with a shudder, but Francis merely confirmed the order before he tried to embark on another ramble through the pastures of sympathy and consolation.

It was at this point I interrupted him by asking the question which had been bothering me for some time. "Why are you stuffing me with food and drink like this?"

"Because I want you to regain your strength as quickly as possible and since you're not interested in food and drink I know you've got to be force-fed. Do you remember Father Darcy saying—" And he launched into a reminiscence which lasted until Portman returned with the brandy decanter, the soda-siphon and a tumbler.

"Francis, I really don't want—"

"Nonsense, of course you do. Brandy's a splendid restorative."

"Yes, but"—I waited till Portman had left the room—"I had a brandy before I went down to the chapel and it nearly finished me off altogether. I don't see how I can possibly face alcohol for a second time today."

"Try a little will-power."

Since it seemed less trouble to give in than to protest I began to sip the brandy. In fact by this time I was feeling considerably stronger. Francis's utter sanity was very bracing.

"That's better," said Francis when my glass was empty. "Now we'll go upstairs. When I told your wife I wanted to wear my habit for the service, she kindly allowed me to change out of my clerical suit in a room which she referred to as your cell. I'll just change back now into my suit and you can shed that cassock. Then Edward will drive us to Starbridge."

I stared at him. "To Starbridge?" Dimly I realised I was about to grasp the scene's hidden dimension, and at that same moment the fear scythed through my psyche as I saw the darkness falling across the future. All I could manage to say was: "Something's happened."

"Yes, there was a crush in the chapel when everyone panicked." Francis spoke calmly but with increasing speed. "Several people were knocked over and one of them was your wife, but very fortunately her doctor was among the congregation and when he said she should go to Starbridge Hospital the Aysgarths volunteered to drive her there. I wasn't aware of all this at the time, of course. I was too busy dealing with you, but later a gentleman called Maitland came to the vestry while you were still asleep and—"

Terror finally untied my tongue. *"Why the hell didn't you tell me this straight away?"*

"Because you were in no fit state to be told! Of course I had to keep you here while I built up your strength—I couldn't have let you tear off to the hospital after an unbroken fast, paranoid hallucinations and a complete physical collapse!"

"But if Anne's dying—"

"My dear Jon, it's not even certain that she's miscarrying—she may be quite all right. She's only gone to the hospital because the doctor thought it best to take no chances."

But I was already visualising unutterable horrors, and without further delay I blundered from the room.

7

THE Aysgarths and the Maitlands were in the hospital waiting room. It was very hard for me to face them, particularly as I could sense their embarrassment mingling with their anxiety, but to my relief Francis took control of the situation. He said: "How kind of you all to wait, but after Jon's very public ordeal in the chapel he would prefer this ordeal to be entirely private. Would you care to give me your telephone numbers?

Then I can keep you informed of Mrs. Darrow's progress." Francis was hard to withstand when he was wielding authority with such ruthless tact; even Colonel Maitland hesitated for no more than three seconds before offering his telephone number and departing. Aysgarth, handing Francis his card, paused long enough to say to me: "I'm sorry. This is terrible for you. Please don't doubt that you have my sympathy," but the next moment he too was gone and I was alone with Francis and half a dozen strangers in that large room with the cream-coloured walls and the battered wooden chairs and the floor covered with olive-green linoleum which had cracked at the seams.

I said to Francis: "I'm sure you now want to withdraw to Starwater. All these hours in the world must be very tedious for you and I'd be selfish if I claimed your company a moment longer."

"My dear Jon," said Francis, "I'd be a poor sort of priest if I scuttled back to the cloister when a brother was in such desperate need."

I was still struggling to frame a grateful reply when a large figure in a white coat ambled into the waiting room, spotted the two men in clerical suits and padded swiftly in our direction. At once I recognised him from Charles's descriptions, and as he held out his hand I said before he could introduce himself: "You're Alan Romaine."

It is always curious to meet a person about whom one has heard so much for so long. I was at once aware that I knew him well yet at the same time had never grasped the essence of his personality. I recognised the stoutness of his tall frame, the shrewdness in his bright eyes, the way he moved gracefully, lightly, like an elderly cat accustomed to prowling all manner of alleys with insouciance. But his psyche, scarred with past pain and exuding a profound intuitive sympathy, was new to me. I had thought of Romaine as a failed doctor, prevented by his past mistakes from rising to the top of the medical tree in London. Now I realised that God, by cutting him off from the worldly success which would have inevitably destroyed someone of his sensual temperament, had in fact saved him so that his gift for healing had been able to develop to the full. I thought how in my arrogance I had judged him harshly, and I was ashamed.

Absorbed by these thoughts I at first forgot Francis's information that Romaine had witnessed my breakdown at the chapel, but even when I remembered I felt no embarrassment. Possibly this was because by then I could think of nothing except Anne's crisis, but possibly too it was because Romaine, unlike the Maitlands and the Aysgarths, showed no embarrassment himself. As a healer he was far too busy being concerned for my welfare.

"I'm sorry we should meet under such difficult circumstances," he was saying, "and I'm even sorrier to have to tell you that your wife's miscarrying. Let me say straight away that I don't anticipate unusual complications and I expect her to come through safely, but of course it's not a good situation and I'm afraid it'll be some time yet before it's over."

His quiet authority was so reassuring that for the first time I allowed myself to believe that Anne might survive. I heard myself say urgently: "Can I see her?"

"You could. But whether you should is a different matter. You're quite understandably very upset and it's important that she should be surrounded now by people who are very calm, people she doesn't have to worry about."

I saw the good sense of this. "I don't want her to worry about me. I'll wait here," I said, but as soon as the words had been spoken I was plunged into terror again. My voice said: "I've got to be told if she's dying. Supposing she died and I wasn't there?" I suddenly found I had to sit down. Sweat was trickling down my forehead and my heart was hammering in my chest.

Romaine said at once: "Of course you'd be summoned if things went wrong."

"You're just saying that to calm me down. You don't really mean it. You'd forget all about me and then only remember when it was too late." I was losing control of myself. In desperation I turned to Francis. "I can't find any more words. You tell him. Make it absolutely clear that *I've got to be there when she dies.*"

Francis immediately stepped forward. "My name's Ingram," he said to Romaine. "I'll look after him. I'm sure you want to get back to your patient."

But Romaine sat down beside me; Romaine took my hand in his as if we were old, old friends, and Romaine said to me in the gentlest possible voice: "You've lost someone before in tragic circumstances, haven't you? And you've never forgiven the person who failed to summon you to her bedside when she was dying."

There was a silence broken only by the visitors murmuring on the far side of the room. I was dimly aware that Francis was transfixed as if he had received some electrifying revelation, but my eyes could see only Romaine. I said: "So long as you understand, that's all right. I'll wait down here."

Francis said to Romaine: "Is there a place where I can sit quietly with him and drink some tea?"

"Go down to the end of the hall, turn right and keep going." Releasing my hand he stood up and patted me on the shoulder. "You'll be constantly in my mind," he said, "and I give you my word that no matter what happens I shan't forget."

Francis led me to the hospital canteen, an even larger, drearier, cream-painted room where we drank strong tea out of squat white cups at a secluded table. For a while he waited for me to talk but I was too absorbed in my anxiety, and eventually when he realised that I had failed to grasp the magnitude of my revelation he said: "It's curious, isn't it, how often we think we know the truth about a person and then suddenly we make a discovery which puts all the familiar facts in a different light. I remember you said to me once that exploring a personality is like peeling an onion. You have to strip off layer after layer of skin before you finally reach the core."

I nodded but I was still thinking only of Anne.

"I always did think it was strange," said Francis, "that a young man from your very respectable background should have sampled such a variety of women so speedily once he had escaped from both his home and his boarding school, but now for the first time I believe I understand what was happening. You weren't just flailing around in an unsuccessful attempt to find a woman who matched up to your mother, were you? You were trying to work out how you could relate to the opposite sex without laying yourself open to pain. Hence the brevity of your affairs; you knew you had to leave your girls before they could leave you."

It began to dawn on me that he was saying something important. My worry about Anne was temporarily displaced.

"And of course I see your marriage in quite a different light now," I heard Francis say. "You didn't just marry for sexual reasons. It was all far more complicated than that. You married a woman you didn't love because you knew that if she left you, you wouldn't care enough to suffer as you'd suffered once before."

Instinctively I clung to the last layer of the onion-skin. It was a reaction I had seen so often in those I had counselled. The thought of an unhealed wound being exposed to the cold air of truth is very threatening to a disturbed psyche.

"I don't understand you," I said, but he only answered: "I should have guessed earlier. Almost your first words when you awoke this afternoon were: 'Has she left me?' You're afraid that any woman you love will abandon you, and it was this irrational fear which lured you into cutting such a dash with your powers. You felt you had to keep your wife spellbound in order to ensure she didn't go away."

I said: "When I was healing, none of my fears mattered any more." Then I said: "I'm so old and she's so young," and rubbed my eyes. Finally I whispered: "I'm a dull sort of person really, not sociable in the accepted sense, absorbed in my work, obsessed by ideas which are unfashionable among the younger generation. Anne didn't know me when she married me. She just saw me as a mysterious, alluring ex-monk. I was so afraid she wouldn't want me any more if she found out I was just a dull, difficult, tiresome old man. That's why I had to go on being mysterious and alluring. That's why I took up the healing. It was so glamorous. I dazzled her. She loved it."

"At first, perhaps, but later? Why do you think she turned to me for help? Because she saw you not as an alluring ex-monk nor—heavens above, what unprecedented humility!—as a dull, difficult, tiresome old man but as a much-loved husband whom she intends to stand by 'till death do you part.' "

"Yes, but . . . one never quite knows. Someone may say: 'I shall never leave you,' and yet—"

"But she didn't mean to leave you, did she?" said Francis, and I knew we were no longer talking about Anne. "She didn't desert you voluntarily."

"No, but all that mattered was that she wasn't there. The pain was indescribable. There was no one else who understood, you see; no one else with whom I could communicate on a psychic level."

"I quite see it would have been a devastating bereavement." Francis allowed a pause to develop before adding: "You must have felt angry later."

"Eventually, yes." I thought carefully, viewing the extreme past from my remote position in the present, and was relieved when I felt no emotion. Emotion might have detached the last layer of the onion-skin. "I wanted to blame someone for the catastrophe," I said, "but don't misunderstand—I didn't wind up hating my mother and turning against all women. After all, as you pointed out, she didn't leave me voluntarily. And I couldn't wind up hating God either; even at the age of fourteen I was too much aware of His reality to believe He was just a cross old tyrant with a cruel streak, and in fact it was my awareness of God's reality which enabled me to survive that terrible time. I knew He understood me even if no one else did, and eventually I came to accept that the suffering was His way of making me the man he wanted me to become."

"So if you couldn't be angry with God," said Francis, "and you couldn't be angry with your mother—"

"It was all very awkward," I said, as if we were discussing some embarrassing breach of social etiquette. My psyche was still clinging fearfully to the last layer of onion-skin. "I wasn't allowed to be angry with anyone else. Nobody ever got angry in our house, you see. Nobody ever complained."

"Ah!" said Francis. "So I got it wrong. This story isn't about your mother after all."

And then at last after its long imprisonment in the darkest corner of my psyche my father's memory, complex and multi-faceted, began to move steadily forward into the light.

8

"MY father's name was Jonathan Darrow," I said, and as I spoke I knew Francis's understanding was generating the trust which would finally enable me to let go of the truth. "My mother called me Jon to distinguish me from him, but my father always called me by my full name. Jonathan. I hated it. It wasn't me. It wasn't me at all. It was him.

"My father wanted a replica. He wanted another Jonathan Darrow, just like him, to live the life he'd never managed to lead. That makes him sound like a monster, but he wasn't. He was . . . But how can I describe him? I realised just now when I met Romaine how hard it is to convey the essence of a personality in words. I told Anne my father was a good man with a gift for teaching, and that was true. I told you that he was quiet and scholarly and a little afraid of me when I was grown up, and that was true too. Yet those descriptions convey the impression that he was essentially a nonentity, and he wasn't. Not my father. He wasn't a nonentity at all.

"He was a *proud* man. That was the essence of his personality. He was very, very proud, far too proud to admit he'd made a mess of his life with that socially disastrous marriage which had blighted his career as a schoolmaster. My father never complained, not because he wanted to be saintly but because he wanted everyone to believe he had no regrets. His pride was such that even the most genuine compassion would have been intolerable to him.

"So there he was, good, kind and decent, never complaining, but as I grew up I realised that underneath all this sweetness and light there was a powerful, intimidating personality. It was his other self, his true self, the self that came alive whenever he taught. I was very much afraid of this hidden self when I was a child; all the pent-up emotion, the dense invisible ball of anger and frustration, generated a frightening psychic aura, and I lived in terror of displeasing him. Whenever he was displeased with me the kind gentle mask would slip to reveal the fierce stranger beneath, but as I grew up I realised that the way to keep the mask permanently in place was to be the replica, the son who would live his life over again for him and wind up the headmaster of a famous public school.

"At first it wasn't too difficult to be a replica. It simply meant getting good reports at school and taking a precocious interest in Shakespeare. Then the going got harder. He recognised the psychic affinity I shared with my mother and started to worry about me being 'odd.' For years she and I concealed my developing psychic gifts from him, but shortly before she died I had my first vision and then no concealment was possible.

"The mask slipped. He was outraged. First of all he thought I was lying. Then he thought I was going mad and it took a Harley Street specialist to convince him that there was nothing wrong with me. But all the time my mother and I knew that the real problem, the problem that bothered him most of all, was that I wasn't behaving like a replica. He worked himself into a frenzy, and I became so distressed by his inability to accept me as I was that my mother finally turned on him. 'Why should you assume everyone else is as limited as you are?' she said. 'You yourself may be obliged to wear spectacles, but you're hardly so stupid as to believe this means everyone has defective sight!' It was the only time I ever heard her speak harshly to him, and of course he was much too proud to answer back. He simply preserved a dignified silence, and with my psychic eye I saw him nailing the mask back in place. Later he just said: 'This incident is never to be referred to again and we'll treat Jonathan's aberration as if it had never happened.'

"I might have been seriously disturbed by this hostile attitude to my developing psychic powers, especially as I was at such a vulnerable age, but fortunately my mother was there to put everything right. She said to me: 'You mustn't be frightened by the vision. It's part of nature and nature is in the mind of God. The vision was God's thought, flashing in your soul.' Then she found a faith-healer who gave me lessons in controlling my psychic energy, but we never told my father about him because my father wouldn't have understood.

"After we found the faith-healer I said to my mother: 'I'm finding it more and more difficult to be Jonathan, but I can't tell Father because he'd be so disappointed.' Of course she understood exactly what I meant. She said firmly: 'You must be yourself. How else can you fulfil God's purpose for you?' And then to my great relief she added: 'When the right moment comes, I'll deal with your father.' I was so grateful that I exclaimed: 'What would I do without you?' and she answered with a smile: 'You'll never have to do without me. I'll always be here.'

"She died a month later. It was typhoid. I was away at school. Typhoid's a long illness and in her case the crisis didn't come until the third week. My father had ample time to send for me but he never did. He said he hadn't been able to believe she'd die. Then he said he hadn't wanted to upset me. Then he said he was sorry, he realised he'd made a mistake. I looked at him. I just looked at him. I was much too angry to speak. I could only hate him and wish he were the one who had died—but then I hated myself for thinking such an evil thought, and the guilt made me more miserable than ever.

"My father didn't understand how miserable I was, how desolate, how absolutely alone. He just said: 'You're being very brave, old chap. I'm so proud of you.' And I said sweetly: 'You're being very brave too, Father'—but all the time I was shouting in my head: 'You don't care she's dead! You don't care that I'm in hell!' And I hated him more deeply than ever. My poor father! Of course he cared in his own way, but I was too young then to understand that and I felt quite cut off from him.

"Later we repaired the relationship. He was so good, so kind, so decent, always writing to me so regularly when I was at school, always coming to see me whenever he could, always looking after me so conscientiously whenever I was home for the holidays. How could I have gone on hating someone who was such a model father? I couldn't have lived with my guilt—and indeed I began to think that my one hope of keeping the guilt at bay lay in playing the model son. So we went on living this fiction that I was growing up into a replica, but finally the day arrived when I had to confess I wanted to read theology, not English, up at Cambridge.

"Francis, I can't describe to you how frightened I was of telling him! I worried myself into a frenzy, I hardly slept for nights on end—but in fact he took the news wonderfully well. He still couldn't accept that I didn't want to teach, of course. He merely saw me teaching theology instead of English literature, and even later when I broke the news that I wanted to be ordained, he still couldn't accept that I wanted to be a priest doing pastoral work, not an academic clergyman teaching in a Church of England public school.

"However when I was ordained I was finally obliged to tell him that I'd made up my mind not to teach. What a terrible moment that was! I was waiting for him to discard his mask and roar with rage at last—in fact I was almost looking forward to it because I thought we could then have an honest conversation, but Francis, he kept that mask in place. I'll never know how he did it. He was so kind, so decent, so full of enthusiasm and admiration—ugh! How unreal it all was! I wanted to hit him, but of course I didn't; I smiled and shook his hand and said how grateful I was to him for understanding . . . and so it went on.

"Later when I was in my mid-twenties he remarried. That was when I realised that the boot was on the other foot at last and he was the one who was frightened. He hardly knew how to break the news, but Francis, you can't imagine how good and kind and decent I was, how magnificently Christian! I gave the performance of my life and I gave it because I was my father's son and I knew that this was how one had to behave when one was upset, yet all the time I was being so saintly I wanted to shout: 'You bastard, how dare you be so disloyal to my mother's memory!' But of course I said nothing and soon he had married this plump, frothy little widow, someone from his own class at last, and he was so happy that I hated visiting them, hated it, but I did visit them, I visited them regularly, had to, no choice, because I knew that was my Christian duty.

"I wondered if he was still hoping for a little replica but none arrived and perhaps now that he was so much happier he lost interest in the idea of living vicariously through a son. But I always knew I'd disappointed him by not being a replica, and I never forgave him for . . . for what? For refusing to accept me as I was? For trying to relive his life through me and thus putting me under an intolerable psychological strain? For failing to send for me when my mother was dying? For turning his back on her memory years later? Why can't I forgive him and exactly what is it I can't forgive?

"Sometimes I think it's the lack of honesty which I find so unforgivable, and then I blame that pride which drove him into such a destructive dissimulation. But sometimes too I think I can't forgive him because I know, in my heart of hearts, that he came to regret marrying my mother and I'm sure this would have made her unhappy. Outwardly they seemed a contented couple, but who really knows what goes on in any marriage? I could so often sense the emotion swirling around him like a tornado and now when I look back I can see how he must have felt. After all, he'd given up his most precious ambitions to marry this woman—and what was the result? My mother was an excellent housekeeper and made him very comfortable, but when all was said and done she was still the cat that walked by herself. Marrying her must have been like grasping shining water and seeing every drop slip through one's fingers. I know he always said he loved her, but how can I be sure he meant it? Of course he'd say he loved her! His pride wouldn't have permitted him to say anything else.

"Naturally he wanted me to marry well. I've often wondered if the main reason why I married Betty was to hit back at him—to be able to say: 'You wanted a replica. Well, here I am, marrying a working-class girl out of lust, just as you did! Aren't you pleased and proud?' He was always immaculately civil to Betty but my marriage must have been a horrible disappointment to him—which of course was exactly what I had in mind. I *wanted* to disappoint him. Teach? Good God, no, never! The idea of being a schoolmaster revolted me. That was what *he* wanted and he bloody well had to be disappointed. I felt that if I disappointed him I'd make him angry and if I made him angry the mask would slip and if the mask slipped I'd have a chance to communicate with him, *with him,* my real father, the true self he kept locked up, but no, he wouldn't share himself with me, he didn't love me enough because I wasn't a replica, and so everything was cheating, everything was lies, everything was false, *false,* FALSE from beginning to end."

I stopped speaking and gave a violent shudder. Around us in the sparsely populated canteen the low murmur of voices droned in my ears and I could hear the clink of cups as they were collected on a trolley nearby, but these were background sounds, unimportant, and only the silence which followed my monologue was meaningful. I felt numb. My psyche lay limp, stripped naked. There was a large hole where years of hidden grief had been gouged out, and gradually I became aware of Francis's own psyche padding around the gaping hole as delicately as a velvet-pawed cat and patting it gently at the edges to staunch the flow of blood. When he said: "Now at last I see what has to be done," I sensed the presence of the Spirit and knew that by the grace of God I would eventually be healed. Despite all my charismatic power and my psychic gifts, despite all my confidence and my pride in my ability to heal others, I had always been quite unable to heal myself.

I felt as if God had reached out with a long scythe and slashed my arrogance to shreds.

It was a moment of the profoundest humility.

9

AT nine o'clock that night Anne was delivered of a son. Romaine came to tell me the news minutes afterwards. "She's all right," he said, "and I see no reason why she shouldn't continue to be all right, but I'm afraid the news isn't so good about the baby."

I was so overpowered by relief that Anne should be alive that I failed to comprehend the last part of the sentence.

"I'm afraid he's very premature," said Romaine.

I grappled first with the pronoun, then with the present tense but could register neither. "Of course it's dead," I said, "but I'd expected that."

"No, he's alive."

This information was very difficult to grasp. For months I had been expecting Nicholas and although this illusion had shattered I had had no time to develop a new mental image of the infant. Moreover Anne's miscarriage had led me to assume that no new image was necessary. I began to struggle with the idea that somewhere in the hospital was a small being quite unknown to me for whom I was now responsible.

Francis was saying to Romaine: "We'd better not delay the christening."

"The hospital chaplain's been sent for."

I roused myself. This was a detail I could understand. I myself had been a chaplain accustomed to spiritual emergencies. Firmly I said: "I'll christen it." Then I remembered the infant was a boy. "Christen him," I corrected and tried to imagine a son who was neither Nicholas nor Martin. The mystery of this unknown person began to intrigue me. I allowed myself to picture his future.

"I think that might be too much for you, Jon," Francis said as my imagination conjured up a fair-haired choirboy in a spotless surplice. "Why not leave it to the chaplain? I'm sure he'll be very competent."

"I'd be competent too!" I protested, but I was beginning to feel confused, aware that I had one foot on the shore of reality and one foot in the boat of illusion while the water widened inexorably between the two. Uncertainly I added: "All the same, perhaps you're right and I should leave it to the chaplain. The baby's not real to me yet."

"Let me take you upstairs," said Romaine as if he not only understood my confusion but wanted to help me grasp reality. "I'm sure you want to see both the baby and your wife."

I saw Anne first. She looked real, even surprisingly normal, deep in sleep after her anaesthetic, and I was reassured by her peaceful breathing. Then I was shown the infant, a little bundle of skin and bones in a blanket.

"Are you sure he's alive?" I said amazed to Romaine.

"Yes."

"But surely he must be dying!"

"Yes."

"Ah, I thought so," I said, but in fact I had no idea what I had been thinking. "I see," I added, but my psychic eye was confronting only the blankness of a future which would never happen. I felt increasingly distressed that he had no reality for me beyond the idealised dreams concocted by my imagination.

The chaplain arrived, an elderly man who spoke in a whisper, and on Romaine's recommendation the baby was christened not in the distant chapel but in the empty side ward next to Anne's room. Remembering Anne's wishes I chose the name Gerald. The baby never cried, not even on the application of the water. I still had difficulty in believing that he was not already dead.

"Of course I must stay here till he dies," I said afterwards to Francis, "and of course you must now set off for Starwater."

"Even if you told me you wanted to be alone with him, I'd simply wait in the motor."

"I doubt if there'll be long to wait," said Romaine before I could attempt to argue, and minutes later the baby's condition began to deteriorate.

I saw myself as if from a great distance as I stood up and I heard my voice as if from a long way away as I said: "He's almost there." I knew the moment had come because the walls of finite time had become fluid and now as I watched, they curved to form the mouth of the tunnel. There were gates but they were open and as I saw the great darkness which marked the start of the journey I knew at once I had to tell him there was no need to be afraid. "God is love," I said, "and love is stronger than death," but of course I was attempting to reach him with words, impotent inexact useless words, words which he had never had time to learn, and I knew that communication must lie elsewhere. Picking him up I held his minute hand firmly with my thumb and forefinger to tell him he was not alone, and suddenly I felt the flash of psychic recognition as the departing soul, perfectly formed, utterly individual, brushed mine lightly, gratefully, lovingly in the dark.

I cried: "He's alive!" For love is the great reality, and in that moment, the moment of death, he became real to me at last. Then the gates of finite time closed soundlessly after him as he began his journey through the darkness to the bright light at the end of the tunnel, and the moment I was alone I found myself finally face to face with the full horror of what had happened.

I laid the infant on the empty bed of the side ward, and suddenly I stood not in the hospital at Starbridge but in the Abbot's room at Ruydale. I was facing Father Darcy across Whitby's corpse and Father Darcy was saying: "*You* were the one who killed that animal with your disobedience, your vanity and your utterly intolerable pride."

I turned to Francis. I said as my son's lifeless body lay between us: "I killed him," and the next moment I had broken down completely beneath the weight of an unendurable grief.

PART FOUR

THE LIGHT FROM
THE NORTH

"The mystical experience seems to those who have it to transport them out of time and place and separate individuality. This, of course, brings us at once among the most formidable philosophical problems. Those mystics who are also philosophers generally hold that neither space nor time is ultimately real."

W. R. INGE

LAY THOUGHTS OF A DEAN

"If we believe that the world of time and space, which necessarily supplies the forms under which we picture reality, and the language in which we express our thoughts, is an image or reflection of the real or spiritual world, we must recognise that, except when we are concerned with the absolute values, and even then when we try to interpret them to ourselves, we cannot dispense with symbols."

W. R. INGE

MYSTICISM IN RELIGION

XVIII

"Truth is one of the absolute values, and those who seek it must follow the gleam, humbly but confidently."

W. R. INGE
MYSTICISM IN RELIGION

I

EVERYONE was very kind—Romaine, the sister on duty, even the chaplain who talked in such an irritating whisper—but they all seemed so far away, like figures glimpsed through the wrong end of a telescope, and Francis was the only one who was near. When someone in a white coat offered me two pills I said: "I never take drugs," but Francis exclaimed: "Why are you turning up your nose at conventional medicine? What arrogance!" and this language, so harsh yet so familiar, was the only language I could still understand. I took the pills. Francis bore me off to Starwater. I had expected to be housed in the guest-wing but Cyril took me to a little room off the infirmary where a very large monk offered me an evil-smelling concoction of herbs. I said: "Where's Wilfred?" but I was confused by the drugs and wanted only to sleep.

I slept for ten hours and when I awoke I found Francis was once more at my side.

"I'm staying on here for a few days," he said after I had remembered where I was and what had happened. "Cyril has some difficult war-time problems concerning the school and I need to study them carefully so that I can help him reach the right solutions. I suggest you stay on too until your wife comes out of hospital. It's very important that you should be properly looked after."

"But I must see Anne!"

"Edward will drive you to the hospital every day while I'm here, and after I return to London Cyril will arrange for one of the local people to provide the necessary transport."

"But Francis, you don't understand the difficulties of travelling at present—non-essential journeys are discouraged—"

"But of course it's essential that you should see your wife every day!"

"Yes, but what I'm saying is that you'll never be able to get the necessary petrol coupons—"

"Nonsense, these things can always be arranged," said Francis with a superb nonchalance. "Whenever I want extra coupons I simply ring up a most charming gentleman in Whitehall."

I boggled and then bowed to the inevitable.

2

MY first visit to Anne was very difficult. During the opening minute I was incoherent and the words of remorse were repeated in a feverish fashion until it dawned on me that Anne was much more concerned about my health than my guilt. Then I realised that I was much more concerned about her own health than about my self-centred need to indulge in an expression of penitence. Having at last sorted ourselves out and agreed we were both on the road to recovery, it was then Anne's turn to display remorse. She said in a small voice: "Can you ever forgive me for writing to Francis behind your back?"

"Don't be ridiculous—it was the wisest thing you could possibly have done!"

"I was very nervous before he arrived," said Anne, "because you said he looked like one of Shakespeare's wicked cardinals. How could you have misled me like that? He's not in the least like Beaufort or Wolsey— he's more like an avuncular Prospero! Anyway before I knew where I was I'd dissolved into tears and told him everything—I didn't mean to, I kept thinking how angry you'd be, but he was so kind and understanding that I just couldn't help myself. He held my hand and gave me the most beautiful handkerchief to cry into and—"

"This all sounds most improper!" I said, and when we laughed I felt we had passed a small but significant milestone along the road to recovery. Realising that we were now strong enough to discuss our loss I said gently: "Have you seen the baby yet?"

"No. I don't think I can. I don't think I could bear it. So long as I don't see him he's not quite real and I can beat back the pain, but if he were to become real—"

"He *was* real." I told her about my psychic experience at the moment of death, and when she began to cry I said: "Grief's nothing to be afraid of. Nor is it something to be swept under a rug and forgotten. Your grief is a symbol of your love for him, and why should you want to lock up your love like some monster which must never see the light of day?" I let her weep for a little longer before I added: "If you never see him then we can share him only through my memories, and in the long run will that really be good enough for you?"

She shook her head, but still she wept.

"I think that in days to come you'll want a memory which belongs to both of us," I said, but she was barely listening. Drying her eyes at last she whispered: "He mustn't feel that I'm rejecting him. He mustn't feel unloved," and then I knew she had already embraced his reality.

Leaning forward I rang the bell for the nurse.

3

LATER when she was holding him she said: "Are you aware of his spirit now?"

"No, he's too far away. It's only older people who have the psychic strength to imprint themselves on the atmosphere for a few days after death."

We were silent for a time before she said unsteadily: "Dr. Romaine said I might have miscarried anyway. Seven months is a very common time for miscarriages and the cause isn't always known."

"He told me that too when I broke down and blamed myself for what had happened."

Anne said fiercely: "You mustn't blame yourself. That makes it seem as if this were all a punishment, but I refuse to believe God kills babies to punish people."

"That would indeed be a very primitive view of God and not at all compatible with the teachings in the New Testament."

"Then why—" The ancient question was again hammering on the door of mystery, the great mystery of the imperfect world, the great mystery of a Creator who would permit the impermissible, the great mystery of human suffering. "Why did Gerald have to die?" said Anne. "Why did this have to happen? What's the point of putting him in the world only to take him away again?"

Recognising the call of a soul drowning in the sea of mystery, I set off at once to the rescue in the lifeboat of mysticism. "Those hard, painful questions only seem unanswerable," I said, "because you're viewing them from the wrong position: you're in the world and looking out. But now step outside the world and look in. The first thing you'll notice is that it's a world of change. There's this huge dynamic force, life, which is constantly banging against the walls of time and space as it contracts, expands and develops. Now step closer and you'll see that this continual change can't be represented by a vertical line, only by a circle. Half the circle is dark and half is light. The dark side of change is suffering, the light side is growth, development, flowering, and the dark and the light follow each other endlessly in the great cycle of birth, death and resurrection. Now this means that the light and the dark sides of the circle aren't merely related to each other; they're interdependent, and this interdependence means that without suffering there can be no growth, no development, no flowering. Without suffering, in fact, there would be no life as we know it; we'd all be wooden images, utterly static, in a world where nothing ever happened and where God's love would fall on barren soil."

"That's all very well, but—"

"Now step back and look at the world from yet another angle. Look at it as an idea in the mind of God, a brilliant dynamic idea which we ourselves can't fully grasp except that its dynamism ties us to the change we can't escape. But beyond the idea, beyond the mind of God, is God Himself, the unchanging perfection of ultimate reality. In other words, this cage we live in, this prison of time and space, isn't ultimately real. Gerald may have slipped out of the cage ahead of us, but that doesn't mean he's ceased to exist. As part of the ultimate reality his existence is reflected back into the world of time and space in the form of the absolute values, the values which can never die, and the value in which we can most clearly see him reflected is Love."

"Yes, but—"

"Love transcends suffering, and it's Love that gives Gerald's life meaning. What we have to do is to weave our love for him into the fabric of our marriage so that our love for each other becomes richer, stronger and more complex. The truth is the wheel of change is still turning—and beyond the suffering the new growth, the new development and the new flowering are all waiting to begin. What we have to do now to make Gerald's life meaningful is to scramble up onto the back of the darkness and then use it as a springboard to leap into the light."

I paused for breath but I had not spoken in vain. Amidst the profusion of symbols which I had thrown out to her in the manner of a sailor heaving a succession of lifebelts to a drowning man, one had been gratefully clutched and embraced.

"I like the idea of our love weaving Gerald into the fabric of our marriage," she said. "I can see our marriage as a Persian carpet, very unusual and interesting, and he'll be a small, beautiful pattern which recurs in unexpected places."

I relaxed. Then I said to conclude my rescue as I hauled the victim into the lifeboat: "You see how important his reality is for us? Plotinus the pagan summed it all up in that single famous sentence: 'Nothing that really *is* can ever perish'—or as St. Bernard wrote from a Christian viewpoint: 'Love is the great reality.' And for both of them, Christian and pagan, that great reality is eternal."

Anne was crying again, hugging the baby tightly, but when I stopped speaking she dashed away her tears, kissed him and pulled the little blanket back over his face. "I'm glad we've both seen him," she said. "It'll make it easier to weave him into the fabric. I feel better now."

Leaning forward I took her in my arms.

4

GERALD was buried three days later next to Anne's brother in the church-yard at Starrington Magna, and I conducted the service myself. I sensed this shocked some people who felt I should be bowed down by grief or even bowed down by shame after my very public spiritual collapse, but I had done my grieving, and since I was still a priest I saw no reason why I should crawl into a corner like a defrocked villain when my son required burial. I also felt that conducting the funeral would be an act of love, similar to the holding of the infant's hand as he approached death, and since I knew his individuality would remain distinct as his soul merged with others in the stream of eternity, I could not regard the funeral as a gloomy acknowledgement of his extinction. As Plotinus wrote, at death the actors merely change their masks.

Since I had announced the time of the funeral to only a handful of people, I was not required to drum up the courage to face a crowd. Anne was still recovering in hospital, but the Maitlands came with the land-agent and his wife, and Aysgarth's wife surprised me by travelling all the way from Starbridge to attend the service. But my biggest surprise came when Romaine slipped belatedly into a back pew, and as I allowed him a moment's prayer before I began the service, I remembered Charles telling me that Romaine was a churchwarden in his parish of Starvale St. James.

Afterwards I said to him: "How very good of you to come," but he only answered: "It's hard when a child is lost."

On an impulse I invited him back to the Manor where I had planned to spend the day before returning to resume my convalescence at Starwa-ter. The invitation astonished me for I had thought I wanted to be alone, but when we sat down together in the drawing-room, I with my small glass of sherry, he with his cigarette and his whisky, I wondered if I had been instinctively seeking a healing presence. I found he had a soothing effect on me; he was calm and relaxed and seemed quite untroubled by my long silences.

"Does Father Ingram's absence mean he's gone home?" he inquired idly after a while.

"No, he's still at Starwater but I wouldn't let him come to the funeral. Monks in an enclosed Order shouldn't be required to leave their cloister unless it's absolutely necessary."

"I rather thought Father Ingram was taking absolute necessity in his stride! Incidentally, how does he get the petrol for that fantastic machine of his?"

"I think it's probably wiser not to ask."

Romaine laughed but said nothing else and suddenly I realised that his silence was the silence adopted by doctors and priests when they want to encourage confessions, the sympathetic, deeply intuitive silence of the listener who signals that he has all the time in the world to hear whatever needs to be said. Then I realised that there were indeed questions which I wanted to ask a medical man with a wide experience of the world, but even though my pride had been so severely chastened there were some fears which I was still reluctant to air. In confusion I said tentatively: "I'm glad you're here."

At once Romaine recognised that I wanted to communicate with him. "How are you feeling?" he said casually. "You look better than I thought you would, but after so much distress I dare say you still feel considerably shaken."

With relief I grasped the chance he was offering me to be honest. "Well, to tell the truth," I said, "I do feel much older than usual."

"Disturbing."

"Very."

"Worried about staying in good working order?"

As soon as I heard this peculiarly apt phrase I realised that no detailed explanations would be required; he had already guessed the cause of my anxiety. Gratefully I said: "I'm not too keen on being over sixty. In fact sometimes I feel thoroughly depressed about it."

"Very natural," said Romaine comfortably, puffing away at his cigarette. "When I turned sixty I was so depressed I nearly ordered my coffin."

"Really?" I was deeply interested.

"Ate, drank and smoked too much. Couldn't even cheer myself up in bed any more."

"Really! But how did you—"

"My wife took me in hand. Put me on a diet, rationed my cigarettes, locked up the drink and packed me off to the golf club twice a week for exercise. Wonderful! Within six months I was a new man."

"Ah! So now—"

"—so now my wife makes sure I stay that way. But you don't need a fierce wife to keep you in order, do you? You're naturally strong-minded."

"Well, I don't smoke, certainly, and I'm not much of a drinker and I take a fair amount of exercise on my bicycle—"

"My dear fellow, you're an example to us all! Keep going along those lines and I assure you that you stand an excellent chance of ticking over briskly for some time to come."

This was very encouraging but I still had trouble regarding the future with unvarnished optimism. "Nevertheless," I said, "I can't help worrying about Anne. If I get really old—"

"But she'll keep you young! Regular practice and moderate habits—that's the secret once you're past sixty."

"Even so I suppose one can't expect to go on for ever."

"Why not?" said Romaine. "I certainly intend to! I plan to die in bed after a glass of champagne in a haze of postcoital bliss."

It was impossible not to laugh and impossible too that my next words should be other than: "I'm glad we finally met." I felt infinitely cheered.

"You must come and see me," said Romaine, "and I don't mean merely for a physical examination, although I'd be happy to look you over if that would set your mind at rest. Drop in for a social visit one day soon and I'll dig out another glass like that thimble you've got in your hand and pour you the required soupçon of dry sherry."

"That's most kind of you," I said, not sure how far he spoke out of compassion and how far out of a genuine desire to be friendly, "but I know doctors always lead such busy lives."

"Not when they get to sixty-nine. I've got a new young partner who can hardly wait to put me out to grass so I have to take a lot of time off in order to keep him happy. Wonderful! I just see the patients I like and leave all the tiresome ones to him."

"Well, I suppose that must be rather pleasant—"

"Pleasant? It's sheer bliss! In fact I can't tell you how much I'm enjoying life now that I'm within gasping distance of seventy—how absurd to think I spent my sixtieth birthday wallowing in depression! The truth is I'm back in the mainstream of life now that I have a family to look after. I teach Charley card-tricks, I read stories to Michael, I hold Lyle's hand when she tells me how awful life is without Charles—oh, it's all such fun, I feel positively reborn! So the message is never despair, you see, no matter how old you are, because you never know what delights may be waiting for you around the next corner—but of course that's a message you must have preached a thousand times over, isn't it? Silly of me—and how impertinent too to lecture a clergyman on the Christian message of hope! Do forgive me for being so thoroughly *louche!*"

But I looked at him, that battered old doctor with his nicotine-stained fingers, and knew I was hearing the voice of the Spirit. A psychic impression formed of the intricate patterns we all made as we wove in and out of each other's lives, but all I said was: "It was the message I needed to hear," and I thanked him.

"You will visit me, won't you?" said Romaine as we parted, and I knew now he spoke out of friendship. "Perhaps we could even play chess together. My wife keeps a strict eye on all my friends and pastimes, but I'm sure she'd be tickled pink if I started playing chess with a clergyman."

It occurred to me that this was the first friend I had made since leaving the Order, and I began to wonder if a more comfortable phase in my long, difficult adjustment to the world was finally about to begin.

5

"HOW is your wife adjusting to the idea that you might want—even need—to accept some responsibility for this death?" said Francis that evening when I had returned to Starwater.

"So far I've only skirted that aspect of the tragedy with her because at first it was clear she wasn't ready to face it. Her initial reaction was to avoid blaming me by blaming God."

"Railing against the mystery of suffering?"

"Precisely. It's a very common response to bereavement, of course."

Francis sighed. "This is one of those times when I'm very conscious of the fact that I've never worked as a priest in the world. What on earth does one say to a bereaved mother who rails against the mystery of suffering?"

"Well, of course each bereaved mother is different, and provided that the priest is exuding a genuine sympathy some women may prefer the sentimental approach, but I'm always reluctant to respond to the death of a child with some banality such as: 'Don't worry, he's safe with Jesus.' The mother doesn't want the child to be safe with Jesus; she wants him to be safe with her. In my opinion it's best to confront the mystery of suffering as just that—a mystery—and then try to illuminate it by the use of mystical symbols. The sufferer may only understand one word in ten, but at least she knows the priest is talking about matters which he's studied deeply and at least she knows he's treating her suffering with the utmost seriousness. If the priest can then set the suffering in the context of the absolute values and somehow relate it to the redemptive and creative power of love—"

"This is obviously the voice of a pastoral miracle-worker. I'd still be stammering: 'Don't worry, he's safe with Jesus.'"

"No, you wouldn't! You'd be unleashing that peculiarly theatrical charm of yours as you held the sufferer's hand and offered her your best handkerchief to cry into!"

"Ah, so your wife's been revealing my rusty pastoral skills with the opposite sex!"

"I thought they sounded rather well-oiled. Anyway, to return to the subject under discussion—"

"Yes, how successful has your mystical approach been with Mrs. Darrow?"

"I think we've made a little progress; she's accepted the idea that the suffering can be used creatively to strengthen our marriage, but of course the loss is very difficult for her and there's still anger beneath the grief. It would be better if she could acknowledge the anger by directing it against me for holding the service, but she won't and now that she's no longer blaming God there's a real danger that she'll turn the anger in on herself and lapse into a profound melancholy."

Francis looked concerned but did not immediately reply; I sensed he was pausing to consider the situation. "I agree it might well be better for her if you took some of the blame for the disaster," he said at last, "but do you in fact feel you're to blame? It would be wrong to manifest a synthetic guilt."

"Well, of course I'm to blame!"

"What about Romaine's suggestion that the tragedy might have happened anyway?"

"Romaine was right to remind me that we never know all the circumstances of a tragedy," I said, "and from there one can certainly argue that all the judgements should be left to God, who alone knows exactly what happened, but personally I find it very difficult to believe the miscarriage wasn't caused by the events in the chapel—the events for which I must assume full responsibility."

Francis ventured no opinion of his own but merely asked: "You see the tragedy as a punishment?"

"Yes, I do—I allowed my pride to cut me off from God, with the result that I'm now grieving for a lost child and consumed with misery that I should have brought such suffering on my wife. That's a punishment. But the punishment didn't come from God. It came from my wrong actions."

I saw Francis make the counsellor's decision that this verdict was worth underlining. "In other words, you're saying that we create our own punishments when we cut ourselves off from God, just as we create our own repentance when we try to understand our errors sufficiently to renounce them and turn back to Him."

"Yes, but how can that best be explained to Anne? If I could only show her that guilt, like suffering, can be used constructively to redeem a tragedy and rebuild a life, then perhaps she wouldn't fight shy of expressing her anger and the process of healing would be unimpeded . . . But these are difficult concepts to grasp when one's distracted by grief."

Francis said cautiously: "Mightn't this be a case where actions speak louder than words? If you let her know you accept some degree of responsibility for the death and then go on to rebuild your life in the most positive way possible, you'll be spelling out your message in unmistakable terms. And if that's so—"

"If that's so then my most immediate task is to get on with rebuilding my life—which at present means sorting out all my private problems not only to ensure such a disaster never happens again but to ensure my ears are wide open to receive the real call from God which is still to come."

"Precisely."

There was a silence while I groped my way forward through my confused emotions, but at last I managed to say: "Thanks to our recent conversations I do feel I've travelled a long way towards sorting out my private problems."

"Hm."

Immediately I experienced a pang of alarm. "You don't agree?"

"I think our conversations—particularly the one which included your long confession in the canteen—have certainly helped you to take a major step forward. The problems have now been identified. But have they been resolved? I think not."

I automatically opened my mouth to argue with him but he allowed me no chance to speak. "There seem to be two major problems which are closely but not inextricably linked," he said. "The first is your mother's death and the second is your father's life. The first I regard with optimism; I believe that with your wife's help you'll finally be able to master this irrational terror that every woman you love is going to leave you. But the second problem is much more complex and intractable. It's a question of forgiving your father, isn't it? And to be quite frank I don't think you're anywhere near a genuine forgiveness at present."

I was both astonished and appalled. "But I told you in my confession—

or at least I implied—surely you didn't think I was entirely without the understanding necessary to generate forgiveness?"

" 'Why can't I forgive him?' you said in the canteen—"

"That was really a rhetorical question. I then went on to analyse the situation and I made it clear that I could at last regard him sympathetically. Don't you remember me saying how difficult it must have been for him to be married to a woman who was so detached?"

"Yes, but I suggest to you that this sympathy is purely intellectual. At an emotional level you're still angry and bitter, unable to sympathise with him at all."

"That's not true!" I was deeply upset.

"Isn't it?" I saw the scepticism join forces with logic again in that combination which made Francis such a hard man to deceive. Leaning forward across the table, he said abruptly: "Supposing I were to say to you as Father Darcy once said: 'Jonathan, you must teach.' "

I recoiled.

"You see?" said Francis. "You haven't forgiven him. You're still paying him back for trying to make you into a replica." He stood up. "Go to bed and think about it," he said, not unkindly, "and we'll talk again tomorrow."

6

THE next morning we went for a walk together by the lake in the grounds of the Abbey. The school term had recently ended and the boys had dispersed, leaving Horatio Ford's country mansion shadowed and still. I thought of the teaching monks sinking back with relief into the enclosed section of the house and savouring the prospect of eight weeks' peace as they renewed their spiritual strength. Teaching was hard work. I could remember not only my bouts of mental exhaustion at Ruydale but my father relaxing quietly with his books as he recuperated from his day at the grammar school.

"Well?" said Francis as we sat down on a seat overlooking the lake.

With extreme reluctance I forced myself to confess: "You were right. I'm still angry. There's been no forgiveness."

"Congratulations! If you can acknowledge that, then you've taken another major step forward."

"The only trouble is that I don't see where to go next. I feel as if I'm now confronting a brick wall."

But for Francis the way ahead was clear. "You need to discover a genuine sympathy for your father in order to discard this synthetic pity you've created," he said. "If you could set aside the distorting effect your anger must inevitably produce and reconstruct his memory accurately, you might stumble across something which would help you to identify yourself with him."

"I think not. The estrangement ran too deep."

Francis remained patient. "You say that because your anger's creating a distortion as usual, but just try to suspend your anger for a moment and cast your mind back to the days before the anger began. Surely you don't deny love existed once between you?"

"He killed my love for him by not loving me as I was. He was only capable of loving the replica."

"That reply seems to indicate you're incapable of suspending your anger," said Francis, still immaculately patient. "Very well, let's tackle the anger directly and try to explode it with logic. Now consider for a moment: aren't you painting this picture in somewhat crude dark primary colours? And wouldn't you come closer to reality if you stroked in a few subtle pastel shades? After all, what actually happened all those years ago? Your father had a dream: he wanted you to follow him in his profession. A lot of fathers have this dream. It's very common. Inevitably there's disappointment if the cherished dream fails to come true, but in most cases the dreamer picks up the pieces and goes on—as indeed your father tried to do in the only way he knew, by never complaining, by putting up a brave front. If he hadn't loved you—loved *you,* not the replica—would he have bothered to go to all that trouble? Of course not! He'd have turned his back on you and refused to speak to you again. Obviously he loved you in his own way but for some reason he couldn't express that love in a manner which you would have found acceptable. Perhaps you reminded him too much of your mother and his relationship with her was so convoluted that it inhibited his ability to communicate his feelings to you. Perhaps he was paralysed by guilt that he'd failed to summon you to her deathbed and this effectively prevented him from revealing his emotions. Perhaps he was terrified he'd failed you by behaving so unsympathetically about your visions. Perhaps . . . But there are any number of explanations. All I'm trying to point out is that his desire for a replica doesn't necessarily mean that he didn't also love you as you were. It's a failure of logic to believe here that paternal love and paternal ambition can only be mutually exclusive."

"You can invoke the deity of logic as ardently as you please, Francis, but the fact remains that you're merely speculating. You never met my father. You've no idea what he was really like—"

"But have you any more idea than I have? You've just admitted the estrangement ran very deep."

"Of course I know what he was really like! Didn't I live under the same roof as him for years and years?"

"That's no guarantee of intimate knowledge, particularly if the parties are hopelessly estranged!"

"I don't deny the estrangement, but if you think I didn't know him inside out—"

"Prove it. Sum him up in a single sentence."

"He was a failure."

"A failure?"

"He failed me, he failed my mother, he failed himself. A wasted life. Pathetic."

In the silence which followed I suddenly became aware that Francis was engaged in a fierce struggle to control his temper. On the one hand he was telling himself sternly that a clever, well-trained monk, acting as a counsellor, should never lose his grip on his self-control, but on the other hand he was mentally shouting that I deserved a punch on the jaw. So startled was I by this cerebral battle which flashed before my psychic eye that for one long moment I could only stare at him speechlessly. Then I managed to say a feeble "Francis?" in an effort to express my bewilderment.

"Oh, don't mind me!" said Francis. "You just took my breath away, that's all, but don't worry, you have that effect on me sometimes, it's not unprecedented, and fortunately it only takes me a few seconds to recover."

"I didn't mean to sound uncharitable—"

"Oh, splendid! I'm so glad!"

"Now listen to me, Francis—"

"No, you listen to me! That flash of arrogance was quite intolerable and I absolutely refuse to let you get away with it. By what standards are you judging that man? I hardly think they can be described as Christian! Your father stood by your mother; he stood by you; he accepted his lot—and day by day, all through his working life, he served God by exercising his gift for teaching. Thousands of boys must have benefitted from his skill and had their lives enriched—how dare you call him a failure!"

I shouted: "But what about all the pain I suffered when he rejected me?" Then I said violently: "He failed me. He couldn't accept me as I was. He failed me." And without waiting for a reply I walked away, stumbling the few yards downhill to the shore of the lake.

An interval followed as Francis allowed us both time to compose ourselves. I stared at the limpid water beneath the light sky and struggled to master my misery. In an effort to turn aside from self-pity I thought of Francis, now almost certainly battling with his own distress as he reflected on the ruined interview, and resolved not to hold his harsh words against him. All counsellors, even the most successful, have their disastrous sessions when for some reason they are unable to maintain their emotional detachment, and suddenly I was recalling with painful clarity my failure to help Martin when we had met in Ruth's garden shortly after my departure from the Order.

The pebbles crunched behind me on the little shingle beach. Francis's voice said: "Sorry. My fault. What a mess," but as I turned to face him I answered: "It's all right."

"That's very kind of you to say so, but I don't see how it can be. I lost my temper, behaved like an overbearing counsel for the prosecution and even tried to force-feed you ideas which you're at present psychologically unable to accept! How on earth could I have made such appalling mistakes?"

At once I said: "Because my case means a great deal to you. Because the ordeal we both endured when you had to examine my call to leave the Order has bound us together in such a way that you feel deeply involved with my new career. Because you're so anxious to help me overcome my troubles that you couldn't resist trying to wind up the case in double-quick time before you're obliged to return to London. Now do you understand why I said: 'It's all right'? The mess arose not because you didn't care but because you cared too much, and besides . . . the mess was hardly all your fault." I sighed as I offered him my hand in reconciliation. "I'm sorry too. Obviously I need much more help."

Francis gratefully clasped my hand. "The trouble is that since you're beyond the reach of logic I'm not sure which approach to adopt next. I wonder what the old man would have done? I suppose he'd have wiped your mind clean by some esoteric exercise of his will and then claimed to have exorcised you. Ugh—how repulsive!" And he shuddered.

"You're only repulsed because you're mentally defining exorcism in the modern sense and associating it with witchcraft and quackery. But exorcism in the classical sense could be just as respectable as psychiatry. After all, what are the two facts about Christ which no one but a fool would dispute? He was a healer and an exorcist in the best possible sense of both terms."

"True, but—"

"Father Darcy wasn't Christ but he certainly wasn't a witch-doctor either, and I'm sure that in the present situation he would have adopted a traditional mystical approach, employing the ancient symbol of the battle between the forces of darkness and the forces of light: he would have called on God for help and then embarked on the task of ejecting the demon which was burdening my psyche."

Francis was unable to resist another shudder. "You mean he'd have peeled away all your defences in order to expose the raw psyche to the light of truth. What a dangerous game to play!"

"For a quack, yes. But not for the gifted exorcist who always knows exactly what he's doing."

"Well, I agree you need to see your father in the light of truth, but if you think I'm going to resort to exorcism—"

"No, obviously you can't do that, not because you're incapable of healing me but because you couldn't heal me by a process in which you've no faith."

Francis meditated on this before saying tentatively: "I suppose it's a question of how the healer turns on the light. I'm still groping for the switch to turn the light on by hand but the old man would have turned it on by sheer will-power."

"The old man would have claimed he never turned on anything."

"Yes, I'm sorry my metaphor was too secular. Of course he would have said the light was the light of God bestowed by grace, not a source of power which he could flick on and off at will."

"Precisely. He would have seen the light as a miraculous gift which inevitably triggers a major revelation in the psyche."

"Like the light in your vision," said Francis, "the mysterious light from the north." Restlessly he stooped, picked up a pebble and threw it in such a way that it skipped across the surface of the water. "And that reminds me"—he straightened his back—"did you ever read the magazine *Country Life* in 1931?"

I was considerably startled. "What an extraordinary question! Why?"

"Your wife tells me that there was an article in it then about Starrington Manor, complete with photographs of the chapel both inside and out. I just wondered if perhaps during one of those unusual trips to London from Ruydale after the Whitby Affair you found a discarded copy of *Country Life* on the train and—"

"My dear Francis!"

"—and received, as it were, a preview of your vision—"

"You appall me!"

"Of course I'm not accusing you of lying—obviously you've forgotten you read the article and the memory was retained only in your subconscious mind—but it would explain the extraordinary degree of clairvoyance you achieved in your vision. Now I'm willing to concede," said Francis generously, "that every story should be allowed one big coincidence, and in this case the coincidence would be your meeting with Miss Barton-Woods, as she then was, at Allington, but as far as your vision's concerned—"

I decided to terminate this sad spectacle of an intelligent man struggling in the toils of his earthbound logic. "Your trouble, Francis," I said kindly, "is that you're an incorrigible sceptic. I shall preserve a dignified silence which I hope will be even more effective than an equally dignified denial."

"A little healthy scepticism never did an honest psychic any harm! However," said Francis, becoming serious again much to my relief, "I shall respect your dignified silence and merely conclude this somewhat unfortunate session by urging you to have faith in the future and be patient. Despite your recent disaster and your continuing difficulties I'm still convinced that light will shine from the north for you in the end . . ."

7

"FRANCIS visited me on his way home to London," said Anne on the following day when I called again at the hospital. "He brought me those gorgeous flowers over there from the garden at Starwater. Wasn't that nice of him? We talked a bit about the baby—and about you too, of course. He was very interesting. He said I must be sure to speak my mind to you about various things because otherwise you'd be continually imagining I was thinking thoughts I wasn't really thinking at all."

I said dryly: "I'm afraid Francis is incorrigibly sceptical about my psychic powers."

"Oh no, I'm sure he believes in them, but he has such a refreshingly down-to-earth approach! 'Don't rely on Jon to read your mind accurately,' he said, 'because for every genuine psychic insight he receives, he makes two wild guesses which have no relation to reality.' "

"That's quite the wrong percentage! Good heavens, what a slander—"

"So I said: 'That's a relief because I don't want to be married to a miracle-man—I'd much rather be married to an ordinary human being who sometimes gets things wrong and stumbles into messes, just as we all do now and then.' That pleased Francis very much. He said: 'I thought so! Now make sure you tell him that.' So here I am, telling you."

"What did he say about the baby?"

"He said I mustn't be afraid to be angry or to show you that I was angry; anger was all part of the process of grief which had to be worked through. However I told him I didn't feel angry any more, I'd got over it because I felt Gerald's life would have meaning, woven into the fabric of our marriage. Then Francis said a very peculiar thing. He said that nevertheless you might need a bit of anger; he said that if I were angry with you, you could regard it as part of a penance and use it to come to terms with your guilt. 'Well, I'm sorry,' I said, 'but I can't display anger where none exists, and no matter what you say I think it would be more helpful if I displayed love, not anger.' Then Francis laughed and said how lucky you were to be married to me. He really is the most charming man."

"Hm." I had my own views about Francis's charm but I decided to keep them to myself. Anne belonged to the other sex. They saw men differently there.

However I was grateful to Francis for extracting from Anne important facts which might have taken me a long time to uncover, and on my journey back to Starwater I mentally composed him a letter of thanks. Meanwhile, as I discovered when I reached the Abbey, an equally important letter had arrived for me in the afternoon post: the Bishop had written, expressing with exquisite simplicity his sorrow that I should have suffered such a time of anxiety and grief. The service of healing was never mentioned, and in a paroxysm of guilt I immediately wrote back offering my resignation. By that time Aysgarth had recalled the retired canon to conduct the Sunday services while I recovered from my disasters, so my life as the curate of Starrington Magna had already moved into abeyance, but I thought that the least I could do in response to Dr. Ottershaw's most Christian charity was to spare him the ordeal of sacking me.

But instead of accepting my resignation with relief Dr. Ottershaw invited me to the palace to discuss the future, and on the day before Anne's discharge from hospital I found myself journeying to Starbridge to see him.

Freed from the rigours of being wound around my little finger, the Bishop delivered an unexpectedly detached judgement. I saw then that I had underestimated him; he was at the mercy neither of Aysgarth, who would obviously be opposing the continuation of my curacy, nor of the Pitkin faction, who after the required amnesty following the death of the infant would now also be campaigning for my removal. He was quite capable of steering a sensible course of his own.

"I think I should abstain from any decision for six months," he said, "while you recuperate and receive regular direction from Father Ingram. It strikes me that what you need most of all at present is a breathing space—in fact I've always wondered if you were denying yourself the proper amount of time to settle down in the world after your long absence. Leaving the cloister's such a big step, isn't it, and in retrospect I confess I feel guilty that I allowed you to take on that curacy before, perhaps, you were ready for it. Yes," said Dr. Ottershaw, setting me an admirable example in humility, "there's no doubt I should share a large part of the responsibility for your present difficulties." And as he referred so tactfully to my spiritual breakdown I saw with a clear eye how erratically I had rocketed from one life to another without giving myself sufficient time to adjust to the world I had rejoined.

Much chastened I returned not to Starwater Abbey but to the Manor in order to resume my life at Starrington.

8

THE next morning I arose even earlier than usual and faced a task which I had been steadily postponing: my return to the scene of the catastrophe. I felt strongly that I had to perform a ritual purification, a symbolic act which would surmount my repulsion and heal the raw wound that memory was keeping open in my psyche.

It took a great effort of will to open the door but once I had crossed the threshold my tension eased. The chapel had been cleaned and tidied; the defilement was not visible to the eye, and although the atmosphere was clogged with an intangible grime I was confident that I had the power to cleanse it; I felt as if I were confronting an unwashed window and reminding myself that beneath the dirt the glass would still be clear.

I set to work. First I prayed. Then I filled a bowl from the tap in the vestry, blessed the water and used it in making the sign of the cross on every row of pews. I also made the sign on all the doors. Once this ritual had been accomplished I celebrated Mass. I knew no ghost had been seen; Father Darcy's image had merely been a projection of my disordered mind, but I thought Wilfred would have sanctioned a sacramental gesture to complete not the exorcism of the chapel but the neutralising of a painful memory.

The sun began to shine through the east window, and when I returned to the chapel after washing the chalice in the vestry I found that the atmosphere was once more pellucid and serene. Sinking down in the nearest pew I thanked God and savoured the peace.

Later when I had returned to the house I headed on an impulse to the conservatory and cut some of the lilies which Anne's grandmother had favoured long ago. Her handsome glass vase was still in the flower-room, and soon I was setting it in its old place beneath the brass memorial tablet. I thought I would take Anne to the chapel that afternoon so that she too might conquer her natural aversion to the scene of the catastrophe, and I hoped that the lilies, symbol of beauty, would help her to see that the chapel was no longer polluted.

Once again I returned to the house. Then as soon as I had breakfasted I summoned the motor and set off to Starbridge to bring Anne home from the hospital.

"JON, there are more things which Francis said I should tell you," said Anne as we sat hand in hand in the front pew during our visit to the chapel that afternoon. "I thought I wouldn't be able to just yet but the chapel's so soothing and you're so serene again that I no longer feel frightened."

"Frightened?" I was appalled. "But my dear Anne, what on earth do you mean?"

"Didn't you guess? That awful outburst of mine just before the service didn't spring from anger but from terror. I thought the reason why you were neglecting me to sink yourself so fanatically in the healing was because you were secretly miserable and dissatisfied."

"With the curacy, you mean? Well, I must confess—"

"No, not just with the curacy. With everything. I was absolutely tormented by the dread that you were bored to tears in quiet, dull little Starrington Magna and had come to regret your hasty marriage."

"Regret my—I'm sorry, obviously I've misheard you. Did you actually say—"

"That's why I encouraged you to take up the healing," said Anne, rushing on. "I wasn't easy in my mind about it, but I could see it kept you busy and happy and compensated you for being such a big fish in such a small pond. I thought that so long as you were happy being a healer you wouldn't get tired of me and go away."

"Go away? *Me?* But—"

"That's why I didn't speak up to you about all the Anglo-Catholic business—I knew you were making a mistake by introducing those changes so quickly, but I didn't dare say anything because I was afraid of making you upset. I thought: so long as he's happy, worshipping in the way he wants, he'll be able to overlook the fact that I haven't followed the example of his devoted ladies and become a fervent Anglo-Catholic—"

"But I don't want a wife who switches to Anglo-Catholicism for all the wrong reasons!"

"Yes, but I was so afraid you might be secretly regretting your marriage to someone you couldn't convert—"

"I could never regret our marriage. I don't care whether you're Low Church, Broad Church or High Church. All that matters is that we belong to One Church, *the* Church, Our Church, the English Church—"

"Darling!" said Anne, kissing me. "But you do see, don't you, why

I felt I couldn't be honest? I was so terrified that you'd become dissatisfied."

"But my dearest Anne, I spent my whole time fearing that *you* might become dissatisfied! I was so worried about being old, so anxious that I wouldn't be able to satisfy you in bed——"

"*You* were anxious about that? But Jon, I tortured myself with the terror that *I* wouldn't satisfy *you!*"

"I must be imagining this conversation," I said. "I'm hallucinating."

"I used to think to myself: it's all right now I'm young but supposing he gets tired of me when I'm middle-aged? That's why I got so upset when you set up the camp-bed in your cell as soon as I was pregnant. I thought you were already tired of me and were glad to have an excuse for a separate bedroom."

"My darling Anne, I . . ." Words temporarily failed me. However at last I managed to say in my firmest voice: "I shall never get tired of you, no matter how middle-aged you become. How on earth did we sink into this absolutely appalling muddle?"

"Francis said that since I'd had the painful experience of Hugo and you'd had the painful experience of Betty, it was inevitably going to take the two of us much longer to learn to trust each other than it would take the average couple."

I had a vivid memory of Francis saying: "Of course I'm just an ignorant old bachelor . . ." and I felt humbled. Here indeed was a case where the onlooker had seen most of the game.

I could only exclaim stupefied: "But this is unforgivable of me! I was so absorbed in my own fears that I completely forgot about your adverse experience with your fiancé—I just assumed that once the sexual difficulty had been overcome all would automatically be well, but how could I have ignored the possibility that not all the psychological scars would be healed?"

"We both have our scars. But all that matters now is that we're not hiding them from each other." She kissed me again before adding in her briskest, most businesslike voice: "Jon, there's one thing more I simply must say and it's about bed and it's this: sex is very nice but if it results in us perpetually worrying ourselves into a frenzy about whether we're satisfying each other then it's soon going to become very awful. Please try not to worry about me too much. As far as I'm concerned love's more important than sex, and there you'll always satisfy me, even if you wind up bald, bedridden and toothless. You see, to be quite frank"—she took a deep breath—"I like you being old. I could never trust any man of my own age again, but an older man . . . Well, the older you get the more secure I shall feel. The last thing I'd ever want is a young husband. I'd never have a moment's peace of mind."

And then for the first time since my mother's death I found I could love without fear of the future.

I O

LATER that afternoon when Anne was resting I retired to my cell, removed from the album the best photograph of my mother and propped it up on the mantelshelf. I found I could look at her without pain; it was as if I could at last see her death in perspective. Now it seemed so obvious that the unhealed bereavement, damaging my trust of the opposite sex, had been one of the factors which had driven me into the fatal marriage with a woman I had not loved, the marriage which in turn was to drive me towards those seventeen years of celibacy in the Order. I could see clearly too the power of my Maker, that ultimate force, as He had quite literally created me, casting me into the crucible of suffering so that I could be moulded into the man He wanted me to become. Out of the pain had come the growth and the development; after the darkness had come the light. And as I saw my life illuminated by these mystical symbols I could look at my mother's photograph and think: yes, it was a terrible bereavement. But I lived through it, I endured it and now at last I know I've survived.

"How lucky you were to have the perfect mother for fourteen years!" Francis had said during one of our healing conversations as he had shifted the emphasis from the pain I had suffered to the love I had enjoyed. "But what would it really have been like if she'd lived? Could you ever have looked seriously for a wife with this remarkable woman always hovering in the background? Even the most heterosexual of men can have problems with remarkable mothers, particularly if the remarkable mother falls into the notorious maternal trap of being too possessive, and although your mother might have been perfect for you when you were a child, would she in fact have been quite so perfect later? Even if you'd managed to detach yourself for long enough to reach the altar, how would she have got on with your wife? These are difficult questions, and perhaps it's just as well that you've never been obliged to answer them."

Remembering these disturbing questions which it had never occurred to me to ask during all the decades of my long bereavement, I wondered for the first time what my mother would have thought of Anne, but they were so far apart in time that it was hard to picture them together. My mother would have been eighty-four if she had lived. I tried to imagine her as an old woman, perhaps a little querulous and demanding, not in good health, maybe even verging on senility, and I shuddered. My mother would have hated old age. She would have wanted me to remember her as she was in the prime of life, bewitching in her silence as she glided across the daisy-studded lawn and idly stooped to stroke her cat by the peach tree. Then remembering Chelsea I found I knew exactly what my mother would have thought of Anne. I could hear her saying as she picked up William: "This is a most intelligent, interesting little creature, not only sensitive but sensible too—a good companion, always loyal and affectionate and never a yowling nuisance. Chelsea was always very partial to tabby-cats."

I smiled, left the photograph on the mantelshelf and strolled downstairs into the garden.

The weather had changed. The sky was now heavy with unbroken cloud and the sultry air hinted that a storm was approaching. Halfway across the lawn I almost turned back to fetch an umbrella but in the end I decided not to bother; the humid heat was conducive to laziness. Drifting on across the lawn I entered the woods, which were verdant with the summer foliage, and wandered in the dim green light down the path which led to the chapel.

I was thinking of nothing in particular. I had already decided that concentrated thought should wait until I reached the chapel, so I strolled on like a somnambulist, my mind restfully inactive as I listened to the distant call of a wood-pigeon. I had just become irritated by his persistence when I glanced below me into the dell and realised in a single electrifying second that I was finally duplicating the walk I had taken in my vision.

I never stopped. On I moved, my brain blank with shock until at last, scarcely able to breathe in case some wrong movement should shatter this bizarre replication in time, I crossed the floor of the dell. As I walked I glanced to the right but although the suitcase stood beneath the trees I saw it only in my memory, and on reaching the porch I ran up the steps without a backward glance.

The latch clicked. The right-hand door swung wide, and there before me was the chapel of my vision, the wide space at the back where the pews had been removed, the wooden cross on the plain altar-table, the lilies which I had placed that morning beneath the brass tablet. For one long moment I stood staring at them all. Then closing the door I crossed the open space and began to move down the aisle.

No light shone through the north window.

At the front pew I stopped and waited. Sweat trickled down my temple; I had to make an effort to breathe evenly. Then I told myself that the light in the vision had been symbolic. Had I really expected a light to shine from the north? Yes. How unrealistic! I now had to stop thinking like a befuddled romantic and behave like an intelligent priest. Reminding myself that the hallmark of genuine mysticism is a practical no-nonsense outlook, I knelt in the front pew, closed my eyes and applied myself with a workmanlike efficiency to the task of communicating with God.

To liberate the full power of my psyche I had to phase out all distractions; it was as if my mind were a brilliantly illuminated house and I were engaged in moving from room to room to extinguish every lamp. Only in the darkness, as I knew from past experience, would I have the light to see with the eye of the soul.

The process of darkening took some time and required an intense concentration which I found almost impossible to sustain because of my spiritual debility. I was like an athlete who had fallen out of training, but I prayed for grace and persisted. More time passed, although in such states of altered consciousness time tends to fragment into a succession of timeless moments. I prayed again for grace but that was my last prayer in words. The river of consciousness became darker and deeper. I tried to see but my psychic eye was still myopic; closing it again I waited in the dark. God was there, but it was the God of the Neo-Platonists, the God of the Pseudo-Dionysius, the God of John Scotus, above everything, beyond everything, indefinable because any definition would only render Him finite. I knew Him by His absence and by His very absence He was there.

Then I felt His warmth. It was like the sun coming up over the horizon, but although the warmth was very bright it was a brightness which no eye could perceive so I still saw only darkness. The warmth was as paradoxical as the brightness, bracing not ennervating, clear and pure as ice in the radiant heat. Yet even as I saw the image of ice I recognised the warmth of life and in the heart of that life was the flame of love. God was here, too, not the God of the Neo-Platonists but the God of Julian of Norwich and Walter Hylton and the unknown author of *The Cloud of Unknowing,* the God of the joyful English mystics, personal, loving, immanent, real.

I opened my eye again, the psychic eye, and in the warmth I was able to relax without consciousness of the self. I could see clearly then; I saw all kinds of people, both the people who had sought my spiritual direction when I had been a monk and the people whom I had yet to meet. I saw not their faces but their psychic entities; they formed a continuous strand so that I knew my work in the world would be similar to the work which I had undertaken as a monk, but the exact nature and context of that work remained hidden from me. I was aware that all the burdens and constraints of my monastic life had been rolled away so that I could concentrate on my work with a new freedom; I was aware that so much past sorrow had been smoothed away, slotted into place at last in the jigsaw of my life, but immediately I saw the image of the jigsaw I realised one piece was still missing and that this piece was somehow blocking the light of the revelation. I could only grasp the knowledge that I had been sent back into the world to be neither a parish priest nor an unqualified doctor but to reflect Father Darcy's training on some broad stage which at present lay beyond my power to define. Contrary to what I had always supposed, the end of my monastic career did not mark a complete break with the past; in a very real sense there was no new life beginning, only the old one continuing, but now God had responded to my deepest needs by giving me the right wife so that with both body and soul in harmony at last I could reach the height of those powers which I had long since dedicated to His service.

I had a sudden awareness of God's generosity, and the next moment I was overwhelmed by the boundless and indescribable nature of the divine love. I opened my eyes—my physical eyes—and for a split second the psychic and material visions collided so that my oak cross on the altar vibrated with light. I saw Christ crucified, Christ redeemed—and at that moment it was imprinted on my mind that I was finally liberated from all my past guilt. The tide of forgiveness was too strong; no anguish and self-hatred could face it and survive.

I heard Julian of Norwich call across the centuries: "He is Love!" and the darkness blazed with fire. I could not look at the light pouring through the north window but I knew it was there and as I stretched out my hands towards it I felt the brilliant darkness enfold my psyche. For one radiant second my fingertips touched eternity, and then as I slipped back through the levels of consciousness into the prison of time and space I knew that the missing piece of the jigsaw lay with Martin and that I had to write to him without delay.

XIX

"The mystics all speak the same language. But there is something singularly impressive in reading [Plotinus'] testimony, vibrating with restrained emotion, not in some ascetic of the cloister, but in one of the great thinkers of all time, a Greek and a loyal disciple of Plato, the last deep organ-voice in that long series of lovers of wisdom, which begins with the cosmic speculations of the Ionians, and ends, as we have seen, in a profoundly religious philosophy. . . ."

W. R. INGE
MYSTICISM IN RELIGION

I

I AM unsure how long I remained in the chapel while I recovered from the immediate effects of such a profound experience, but as soon as I was strong enough to put one foot in front of the other I struggled back to the house.

On reaching my cell I sank down at the table and picked up my pen to embark on the vital letter. "My dear Martin," I wrote and stopped. I had belatedly realised I had no idea what I was supposed to say. Had I really thought that God would write the letter for me as soon as I held my pen over a blank sheet of paper? I was behaving like a befuddled romantic again. Conscientiously I roused my intellect and began to frame in my mind the conventional enquiries about Martin's health and activities, but almost at once I realised that conventional enquiries were now irrelevant; they had been no more than meaningless platitudes offered by a father bowed down by guilt. Again I was overwhelmed by the tide of forgiveness I had experienced in the chapel and suddenly I saw what I had to write. Instead of cowering behind the wall which my guilt had built around me and shooting polite arrows of enquiry over the ramparts, I had to abandon my bow and arrow and walk out of my refuge to meet him.

Without further hesitation I wrote:

I've recently wound up in the most humiliating mess: I had a spiritual breakdown before a large congregation when I thought I was possessed by the Devil. I'm better now but Anne had a miscarriage as the result of this catastrophe and the baby was born prematurely, dying within an hour. We called him Gerald. I should have written to you and Ruth but I was in such an agonised state of mind that I didn't. I'm sorry. The notice did go in *The Times* but I don't suppose either of you saw it. Anne is home now and I'd so much like you to meet her. Please come and see us. I feel very old and battered at the moment and I need you to cheer me up with some of your amusing theatrical stories.

Yours, etc.,
J.D.

This letter, so painfully honest, so utterly unlike any letter which I had ever written to either of my children, seemed so strange to me as I reread it that I even wondered if I had finally lost my mind. But I knew the letter had to be sent. Cramming it in an envelope I printed the address in capital letters to make sure there was no misdirection, slapped on the stamp and bicycled straight to the village to drop the letter safely in the pillar-box.

2

"*DEAR* Dad," wrote Martin by return of post,

You poor old sod! I do sympathise—making a balls-up before an audience is the actor's permanent nightmare. I remember I was playing Jack Worthing once in *The Importance of Being Earnest* when Lady Bracknell went over the top. You've no idea how powerful that line about the handbag can sound when screeched out with the volume of four express trains about to dive into a particularly nasty tunnel. We had to carry the poor thing off the stage in the end, but six months later, believe it or not, she was hamming it up in some ghastly farce and saying she felt positively reborn—so the whole story had a happy ending.

I shall arrive on Saturday at lunchtime unless I hear from you to say this doesn't suit. Please lock up all drink and offer me fizzy lemonade very firmly.

Yours,
MARTIN.

P.S. Sorry the new little Darrow was so short-lived. You don't have much luck with your replicas, do you?

I stared at this sentence for a long, long time. Then I wrote a brief line to say how much I was looking forward to seeing him.

"IT'S good to escape into the country for a few hours," said Martin. "London's hell at the moment. Maybe I should chuck up my dreary clerical job, abandon all my efforts to get into ENSA or the BBC and volunteer to work on the land, but the trouble is I'm most definitely not the bucolic type. And talking of farming, that reminds me: what a secretive old devil you've been about your farmer-wife! I thought you'd married some upper-class nitwit who was incapable of reading anything but *The Tatler!* Why didn't you tell me you were married to this charming business woman who possesses not only the entire works of Noel Coward but a cat called William after Shakespeare?"

"I'm afraid I haven't been very good at communicating vital information to you, Martin—"

"Well, never mind, better late than never . . . My God, what's that down there? It looks like Inigo Jones's pipe-dream of the Eighth Wonder of the World!"

I showed him around the chapel and was pleased by the genuine admiration which lay beneath his actor's hyperbole. "I love beautiful things," he said. "The world's so foul and ugly but a glimpse of something beautiful makes one forget for a moment how bloody awful life is."

I cleared my throat. "That sounds as if you've succumbed to the Manichaean heresy, but it's a mistake, in fact, to see the world as—"

"Oh my God, he's going to play the Priest with a capital P! Don't do it, Dad, don't do it! I can't stand it when you start playing your favourite roles. I like you so much better as you are now with all the greasepaint stripped off by your experience of going over the top as a miracle-worker—I feel I'm seeing your true self at last. You're *such an actor,* Dad! In fact sometimes when I see you acting I wonder if against all the odds I did wind up after all as that replica you always wanted."

From the moment I had read the postscript of his letter I had known this moment would arrive. I was aware of the urge to retreat, take cover, hide, even bury my head in the sand and pretend I had not heard him, but I conquered the temptation to be a coward; I stood my ground. I heard myself say: "I've been thinking about that a lot lately. I must have made life very difficult for you when you were growing up. Perhaps now's the moment when you should finally tell me exactly how difficult it was."

And then at last I knew I no longer saw my father in the dark glass of estrangement but with blinding clarity, face to face.

"*I'M* not sure when I first realised I was meant to be a replica," said Martin, "but I remember the sheer awfulness of my panic. I thought: I can't possibly grow up because once I'm grown up he'll discover I'm not a replica. And I couldn't bear the thought of disappointing you. I mean, there you were, always so good, so kind, so decent, never complaining no matter how naughty Ruth and I were—and you were such a hero too, fighting in the War, winning that medal at Jutland . . . what an act to follow! I remember lying awake at night and shuddering at the terrible task which lay ahead of me.

"At first it wasn't too difficult to be a replica; I just worked hard at school and took a precocious interest in religion. Then gradually it dawned on me that you wanted me to be not just any priest but the sort of priest who would go right to the top of the Church of England tree—it dawned on me that I was supposed to live your life again for you without making the mistakes you made when you married a woman of the wrong class and wound up in a dead-end chaplaincy. *My* life (so you thought) was going to be quite different. I was going to marry well and glide effortlessly upwards from vicar to canon to archdeacon to dean to bishop, redeeming your past and keeping you perpetually drenched in paternal pride. What a dream! But I knew it hadn't a hope of coming true. God knows what I think about religion—I'm still too mixed up about it all to know—but I've never deluded myself that I could succeed as a churchman. I'd have died of boredom while I was still a curate—it just wasn't 'me' at all. But you didn't want to know 'me,' did you? I wasn't allowed to be 'me.' I was only allowed to be the replica. My God, I used to feel so angry and miserable, trapped in the cage you'd created for me and worrying myself to death about where it would all end . . .

"Then when I was eighteen the end came and I told you I was going to be an actor—but lo and behold! I dropped the bomb and there was no explosion. No shouts of horror, no shrieks of rage—only a saintly resignation. In fact you were so kind, so good, so sympathetic, so understanding, so noble and so heroic that you bloody nearly killed me with guilt! But after I'd recovered from my relief that I'd survived I began to feel angry. At first I didn't know why. Then I realised it was because none of the emotions you were projecting were real. You *hated* me being an actor! You *hated* me not going into the Church! And most of all you *hated* me smashing your cherished dream that I'd be a replica! Oh, if only you could have shouted: 'You silly little bastard, how dare you do this to me!' Then we could at least have had an honest conversation, but no, our relationship had been dishonest for years and that scene just put the final nail in the coffin of our dishonesty. After that no matter how often I yelled at you all I got was this mask of saintly resignation studded with Christian platitudes.

"After I had my breakdown I said to the psychiatrist: 'The most ghastly thing about my father is that *he never complains.* He just smiles and says whatever I do he still loves me, but can't he see that's all rubbish? Can't he see that if he really loved me he wouldn't wall himself off from me with all this acting? Can't he see that he's absolutely destroying me by maintaining this relationship which is false from beginning to end?

"The psychiatrist was a maddening old bird who often pretended to be stupid in order to needle me into talking. He put on his stupid look and said: 'But why can't you believe your father when he says he loves you whatever you do?' I told him you couldn't love any son who wasn't a replica, but he just said: 'Why should the fact that he wanted a replica mean he didn't also love you as you were?' God, how he irritated me! I said: 'My father rejected my true self by wanting a replica. If you reject something you don't love it,' but the stupid man couldn't accept that. 'If he's rejected you,' he said, 'why didn't he wash his hands of you as soon as you told him you were going to be an actor?' 'Because he's an actor himself!' I shouted. 'And he felt he had to put on this fantastic act for me!' And do you know what this madman said next? 'What an exhausting thing to do!' he said. 'If he cared nothing for your true self, why should he go to all that trouble?'

"Well, of course one can't argue with doctors who think they know everything so I said: 'Okay, perhaps he does care about me in his own peculiar way, but he shouldn't have wanted me to be a replica.' I thought that if I made that concession the conversation would come to an end, but no, back came the madman with the question: 'Why do you think he wanted a replica? If you understood this desire better perhaps you wouldn't be so angry with him.' 'I understand it perfectly,' I said coldly, and trotted out my theory that you secretly wanted to compensate yourself for the career you never had. Then the moron exclaimed, pretending to be enlightened: 'Ah! So what you're saying is that your father is a deeply frustrated and unhappy man! How sad! Why don't you stop being angry with him and feel sorry for him instead?' Silly old fool! Of course I then told him in no uncertain terms that you'd always been happy as a lark ever since your ordination—except when Mother died and your happy marriage came to an end.

"At that point the madman pretended to be puzzled. 'Funny!' he said.

'If your father was so happy, why should he have wanted a replica? I don't think your theory can be correct. There must be some other reason. Is your father perhaps very proud and arrogant, the sort of man who desires a replica of himself to fuel his self-esteem?' That made me laugh. 'You couldn't be more wrong!' I told him. 'My father has very simple, modest tastes, he's devoted his whole life to helping others and he couldn't possibly be described as proud and arrogant!' And do you know what the madman said next? He said: 'Well, if he doesn't want a replica because he's miserable and he doesn't want a replica because he's proud, why on earth should he want one at all? I'm beginning to think that he's both miserable *and* proud but you've never realised it. How well do you really know your father? Is it possible that you've never really known him at all?'

" 'Of course I bloody well know my father!' I shouted, finally losing patience. 'He's the war-hero, the crusader, the brilliant priest, the devoted husband and parent!' 'Now isn't that interesting!' said the madman. 'I'd formed the impression from you earlier that he was an actor, a religious fanatic and the very opposite of a family man—in fact I was reminded of Kipling's cat that always preferred to walk by himself.'

"Well, of course he was deliberately twisting what I'd said earlier in order to make me think more deeply about you, and although I was so exasperated that I stormed out of his office I did in fact begin to ponder later on your resemblance to Kipling's cat . . .

"You really do prefer to walk by yourself, don't you? Or are times changing now that you're again stalking along with the right companion at last? I wonder. I can't forget that Kipling also wrote about the leopard who couldn't change his spots, and I suppose you'll always tend to be aloof, but I shan't mind that so long as you stop this interminable purring at all the wrong moments and hiss occasionally like any normal feline . . . Funny the way you always had with cats. I'll never forget that tigerish masterpiece you introduced me to up in Yorkshire, the one who almost talked to you—and think of Pussy-Boots long ago in Starmouth! He used to shiver in ecstasy whenever you entered the room. I remember Mother saying how spooky that was . . . Incidentally, talking of Mother . . . Dad, I know you were devoted to her, but did she ever drive you crazy occasionally? I mean, I can see how luscious she was and of course I adored her, but somehow every time Ruth drives me mad with her tempestuous stupidity I look at her and remember Mother and wonder if your devotion ever got a little frayed at the edges . . ."

Very slowly, often faltering in my quest for the right words, I embarked on the task of introducing myself to the son who had known me only as a stranger.

THAT evening after Martin had gone I opened the album and took out the photograph of my parents on their wedding day. My father no longer looked dignified, decent and dull. He looked dignified, decent and dedicated. I could see the dedication clearly now, the dedication to a son who baffled him, the dedication to a wife whose spirit had eluded him, the dedication to the career which had gone in the wrong direction, the dedication to the present which meant that no word of regret could ever be uttered about the past. I felt I knew at last how much all that dedication must have cost him, and suddenly in the light of my new knowledge I saw his refusal to complain not as hypocrisy but as heroism. I realised how lonely he must have been, isolated by his marriage, struggling to come to terms with his broken dreams, eking out whatever happiness he could find with his mysterious wife and son while all the time he poured his whole soul into his teaching, the one part of his life where he could escape from his troubles and express his true self.

Propping the photograph on the mantelshelf alongside the photograph of my mother, I continued to stare at both my parents as they stood so close together without touching each other at any point. I felt as if I was inspecting their marriage from a perspective which I had never dreamed could exist, and I realised then that although they had loved each other enough to try hard to make the marriage a success they had remained fundamentally mismatched. No doubt my mother's death had been a release to my father, just as Betty's death had been a release to me, and no doubt he too had had to wrestle with the complex aftermath of guilt and grief which had followed his bereavement. As this insight dawned on me, I remembered again how I had felt in the chapel when Martin had opened my eyes and unstopped my ears; I felt I was seeing my father not as the alien stranger but as my mirror-image, my other self.

I knew now why Francis had become so angry with me by the lake at Starwater. What right had I to judge my father when I had not only never known him but had committed all the same errors, cutting myself off from my own son in my unhappiness and laying upon him a psychological burden which had crushed his spirit? Martin had been more vulnerable than I had been in childhood and adolescence; the damage had been greater there. Yet I had had the insufferable arrogance to judge my father a failure! I wondered how I could have been so blind for so long, and it was then that I realised how profoundly my mother's death had dislocated our relationship. If she had lived she would have acted as a bridge between us, but her death had sealed us off for ever in our private worlds. In my need to blame someone for the disaster I had tried to exorcise my grief by projecting the unbearable anger onto my father, yet despite my efforts the exorcism had failed; the anger had been projected but the wound had remained unhealed until the day of Gerald's birth and death when Francis had exposed the sore to begin the process of healing.

I could now see how the healing was evolving. Having accepted my mother's death at last, having come to believe myself secure with Anne, I had been ready to hear what Martin had to say and the last piece of the jigsaw had finally fallen into place in my psyche. The light from the north had been the light of revelation but the revelation had not, as I had always blithely supposed, been of my new call. The revelation had been of myself, of the dark corners of my soul, and now that this psychological landscape had been illuminated I was at last able to perceive the call which had always existed but which before I had always been too maimed to hear.

Instinctively I wished my father were alive so that I could beg his forgiveness for my part of the estrangement, for the eyes which had failed to see and the ears which had failed to hear, but I knew I was already forgiven. The light in the chapel had bleached my psyche clean and now, as I remembered that intersection of eternity with finite time, I knew that my father had returned to my life not as a malign memory but as a benign presence. In that world of values which represented the eternal reality, the quality which I had recognised as his dedication was reflected back at me as love, and in the light of that love I could see the way ahead fully revealed.

I sat down to write to Francis.

6

WHEN Francis received my letter he telephoned me. My first reaction was to be shocked that I should be offered spiritual direction through the medium of such an unpleasant modern instrument. Then I realised I was glad to have the chance to talk to him.

"I shall put all this in writing so that you have the chance to meditate on it properly," he said, displaying a reassuring self-consciousness about his latest effort to bring the Order into the twentieth century, "but I thought I should warn you immediately not to rush into any impulsive action while you're still in a euphoric state following this extraordinary catharsis. Remember your position. You're a curate subject to the authority of your Bishop who has wisely advised you to take six months off work so that you can rebuild your spiritual strength. Your duty to God at the moment is to get fit, not to rush off to the nearest educational institution and say: 'Here I am!' "

"But I feel so much stronger now! I'm sure I don't need six months to—"

"You need it. And remember that patience is the most difficult of all virtues but one which it would undoubtedly pay you to—"

"What an unsatisfactory instrument the telephone is!" I exclaimed. "Are you smiling or have you become genuinely pompous?"

Francis laughed, said neatly: "Of course I assumed you could see me as well as hear me," and hung up the receiver before he could hear my exasperated laugh in reply.

7

CYRIL had offered me the weekly guidance of his best counsellor, a younger man than myself but one who I soon realised was greatly gifted as a director of souls, and helped not only by this new acquaintance but also by Francis's regular letters I worked hard to regain my spiritual health. Later I made a week's retreat in London. I was saddened to see that a bomb had damaged the chapel, but the monks were already busy with the repairs. Meanwhile the War had entered a new phase. Hitler had attacked Russia, that graveyard of European dictatorial dreams, and I thought the tide would now turn for England, just as the tide had now turned in my own personal battle to find peace in a hazardous world.

In November as I studied the war news I suddenly said to Anne: "The Japanese are going to sink a lot of American ships in the Pacific and the United States will enter the War." But after Pearl Harbor I said to her: "For heaven's sake don't tell anyone I prophesied the attack or I'll be tempted to start a new career as a miracle-man!" I was very mindful of the danger in which I stood as I struggled to recover my spiritual health, but I had already made much progress and when at Christmas Anne lapsed into a depression at last I was able to use my new strength to help her overcome her grief. "I was so sure I didn't feel angry," she said in the new year. "I didn't want to be angry at all." But bereavement can take many unwelcome forms and often, as I knew all too well, cannot be mastered by a simple act of the will.

When Anne was better I then nerved myself to make a long-postponed visit to Ruth. I fully expected emotional scenes to erupt as usual as soon as I set foot in her house, but to my astonishment the atmosphere remained tranquil; it was as if some vital ingredient had disappeared from our explosive relationship, and when Ruth said marvelling: "You're different. Everything seems much calmer now," I realised what havoc had been wrought by my disturbed psyche, writhing beneath the burden of my guilt. Ruth even said: "I'm glad you married if it's made you happier. People get difficult when they're unhappy—I know that better than anyone," and the next moment she was telling me that Roger had recently ended a long affair with his secretary.

" . . . and she treated him so badly that he was shattered enough to suggest we should make a fresh start. At first I was proud and said no, but then when I started thinking about what I really wanted—"

I expressed admiration by telling her she was being exceptionally courageous, and at once the warmth of my sincerity had a radical effect: Ruth was at last able to relax in my presence.

"I'm sorry I was so awful when I visited the Manor," she said in a rush. "I expect you thought it was because I minded Anne being young, but it wasn't. It was because I minded her being a lady. I thought your choice of someone upper-class was an indirect criticism of me for not being quite . . . although I've tried so hard to better myself, truly I have—I even took elocution lessons once and I've read dozens of books on etiquette and I always try so hard to dress in the very best of taste—"

"My dearest Ruth!" I felt so shattered by this further evidence of my past blindness that I was at first unable to respond to her pathetic confession, but when she even whispered: "I always thought you might love me better if I was a lady," sheer horror enabled me to find my tongue. "Ruth," I said, "I married Anne not because of her class but in spite of it. I was the son of one working-class woman and the husband of another. The only question here is not whether you're a good enough daughter for me but whether I'm a good enough father for you, and I can only conclude, when I review my gross insensitivity towards you over the years, that I'm not. I seem to have been a quite unforgivably stupid and useless parent."

I might have wallowed in guilt for much longer but Ruth—fortunately, perhaps, for our emotional equilibrium—decided I was joking. I was called a silly-billy, given a kiss and patted on the head as if I were a naughty old duffer for whom allowances had to be perpetually made. Then she manifested her forgiveness in a more acceptable fashion by suggesting that she should visit the Manor again, this time with the children, during the Easter holidays.

I felt like a guilty man pardoned after a magnificent display of clemency, and feeling greatly chastened I travelled back to Starrington.

It was on the day after my return home that I journeyed to Starbridge in response to a summons from the Bishop. Dr. Ottershaw, welcoming me with his customary courtesy, soon said how delighted he was to see me looking so well after my six months' recuperation, and at once, somehow contriving to conceal my excitement, I declared myself ready to undertake whatever work he saw fit to assign to me.

"Well, I've been thinking and praying about this, of course," said Dr. Ottershaw, "and I've finally decided—after considerable deliberation—because of course there are many pros and cons—and indeed one can easily get into a state where one can't see the woods from the trees—or sift the wheat from the chaff—but I've finally decided," said Dr. Ottershaw, rescuing himself from this labyrinthine sentence, "that it would be best if you resumed your duties as curate."

There was a silence. This was not what I had expected. I was aware of my heart sinking.

"Unless, of course," said Dr. Ottershaw, ever courteous, "you have some very pressing reason to persist with your resignation."

I somehow resisted the urge to wind him around my little finger. "It must be absolutely as you wish, Bishop. If I hesitate it's because I'm so acutely aware of all my past mistakes."

"Well, that's just it," said Dr. Ottershaw, seizing the chance to explain his decision. "You're like a man who's fallen off a horse and the best possible thing to do after such a disaster, as any equestrian will tell you, is to get back on again as soon as you're fit to do so. In fact the way I see the situation is this: you're going to have to live in that parish, and as things stand you're living with the unhealed wound of all that dissension. So I feel I must give you the chance, for your own sake as well as for the sake of the parish, to attempt a ministry of reconciliation. Why don't you have a shot at it and we'll review the position in a further six months?"

"Very well, Bishop," I said, meek as a model monk, but I was bitterly disappointed and this time it was I who resorted to the telephone to talk to Francis.

8

"OTTERSHAW'S reached a difficult decision after much prayer," said Francis. "Who are you to say he's mad as a hatter? What arrogance! Do I really have to remind you that we're called to serve, not to run around whining: 'I want, I want, I want,' like some detestable spoilt child? Pull yourself together, stop thinking selfishly and start reuniting that parish which you've successfully split from end to end—and don't you dare try to tell me that's beyond the scope of your infamous glamorous powers!"

I rang off and slunk away.

THE resumption of my curacy was, I think, one of the most difficult tasks I have ever faced in my career as a priest, but once I had vowed to be flexible and unobtrusive instead of intractable and flamboyant, I found that after the first agonising Sunday my ordeal was not as humiliating as I had feared. Drawing on my experience in the Navy when war-time conditions had often demanded a flexible approach to worship, I re-examined my task with as much detachment as I could muster and faced the fact that this particular flock in this particular corner of England at this particular time could best be spiritually nourished by being allowed to graze in their cherished conventional pastures. In times of great stress people need rituals which are familiar, and the parishioners of Starrington Magna, conservative by nature after generations of living peacefully in such a pleasant, well-ordered corner of the world, had earned the right to draw strength from their traditions at this crucial moment in England's history.

I could never have sunk into the bibliolatry of the Low Church tradition; that would have been quite alien to my spiritual inclinations, but I thought I could descend to the moderate Protestant pastures from my Anglo-Catholic peaks without intolerably compromising my ideals. Those who grazed in such pastures formed the backbone of the Church of England. Professional churchmen might divide themselves into Evangelicals and Anglo-Catholics and engage in internecine strife, but most laymen were uninterested in the finer points of theology and merely wanted to worship God without fuss. It was my task to nurture this simple, entirely admirable ambition, not to distort it, thwart it or even snuff it out by pigheadedly imposing my liturgical tastes on theirs. Setting aside my Anglo-Catholic touches with a selfish reluctance but with a Christian resignation, I resumed my career at Starrington not as the village priest but as the local parson, and my reward came some weeks later when I overheard one formerly hostile lady say to another: "I think even dear Mr. Wetherall would have approved of that service if he had been here."

I had many requests for healing but I referred them to the Guild of St. Raphael, the body which had been set up some years before to deal with all aspects of this ministry. I also had requests for exorcism but I referred these to the Bishop. It remained of great interest to the community that the unfortunate Higgins had completely recovered from his aberration; Dr. Garrison continued to bluster that Higgins had killed the cow as a substitute for his wife during a psychotic episode brought on by family problems, but naturally I had the good sense to offer no comment.

Easter arrived. Martin came to see me again, and soon afterwards Ruth made her promised visit with the children. My grandson asked numerous intelligent questions about the Home Farm tractor, my granddaughter insisted on sketching the chapel and Ruth herself was charmed by the Manor's electrical carpet-sweeper, an instrument which was referred to as a "Hoover." At one point I opened my mouth to declare that such modern material items were quite unimportant, but I realised just in time that such a remark would brand me as a priggish narrow-minded old codger. Instead I said how right it was that we should all occasionally pause to admire the mechanical marvels of the age.

"There's nothing more tiresome," Romaine had said to me not long before, "than an elderly bore who looks down his nose at today's way of life. One of my friends said to me the other day: 'If only we could turn the clock back to the halcyon days of the nineteenth century!' And I said: "Oh yes—child prostitution, public hangings and women dying *en masse* in childbirth. Wonderful!' That shut him up pretty quickly, I can tell you."

I enjoyed seeing Romaine for our weekly games of chess not only because he amused me but because he had regular news of Charles who was now in North Africa. Charles also wrote to me, but tended to confine himself to spiritual matters; Romaine offered more diverse news. One day in that spring of 1942 he showed me a letter in which Charles had written: "Now that you know Darrow better perhaps you won't be surprised when I tell you that he's the reason why I can face the future with confidence. When I last saw him he was so serene, so absolutely untouched by any profound anxiety, that I knew I was going to be all right. I felt that he must have received some psychic foreknowledge that we would meet again; if he'd had any premonition of disaster he couldn't possibly have maintained that remarkable serenity of his."

I read the letter. I looked at Romaine. I heard his unspoken question, and at once I saw that Charles's mistaken belief would protect him no matter what ordeals lay ahead. Quite unwittingly, by the grace of God who had covered my terror with tranquillity, I had ensured that Charles had the psychological strength to cling to life in circumstances where other men would die. I said to Romaine: "He'll be all right."

"Well, one never really knows, does one?" said Romaine, tucking the precious letter carefully away in his breast-pocket again. "And the Middle East is hardly a garden-party nowadays."

I said no more. It would have been wrong to behave like an infallible prophet, but I remembered how I had predicted the attack on Pearl Harbor with such accuracy and suddenly I knew with the absolute certainty of a successful psychic that Hitler's General Rommel would never take Tobruk.

I was still savouring this reassuring foreknowledge when my life as a curate came abruptly to an end. An ecclesiastical plough in the form of Dr. Ottershaw plucked me from my monotonous parish furrow and once more I found myself travelling to Starbridge.

I O

"*MY* dear fellow!" said Dr. Ottershaw. "I had absolutely no idea! Do forgive me—what could you have thought? If I'd only known—I do so reproach myself—I said to my wife: 'How could I have got in such a muddle?' and she said: 'All too easily,' which was so true but I confess I felt more mortified than ever. I do hope I'm not going senile."

I was by this time accustomed to Dr. Ottershaw's elliptical conversation when he was flustered. I said mildly: "Do you feel you've offended me in some way, Bishop? I assure you I've been quite unaware of it."

"Dear me, what a relief! You see, I had no idea—*no idea*—what had happened at Ruydale. I thought you'd been the prior! How could I have made such a mistake? I remember when you first came here to dinner I asked you about your career as a monk and I could have sworn you said you were the prior—although perhaps you only said: 'I could go no higher,' meaning that the Abbot was bound to be succeeded eventually by a fellow-Yorkshireman—"

A ray of light dawned. Still adopting my mildest voice, I said: "Please don't worry about it, Bishop. It's not important."

"But my dear fellow, that's just it—it's vital! I've been informed not only that you were the Master of Novices but that a high proportion of your men went on to become priests! Well, of course as soon as I heard that, I telephoned Cyril Watson at Starwater Abbey and he said that in the opinion of the late Abbot-General you were one of the most gifted teachers in the Order. 'Why didn't you tell me before?' I cried and he said astonished: 'But I assumed you already knew!' Well! I nearly had apoplexy but when I'd recovered I saw at once that God Moves In Mysterious Ways and that no doubt this delay has been All For The Best." Dr. Ottershaw enunciated the crucial words in such a way that I knew he had mentally assigned them capital letters.

"Yes, of course," I murmured, not entirely sure what proposition I was confirming. "Of course."

"If I'd known then what I know now," said Dr. Ottershaw, rushing on, "I might have been tempted to throw your parish to the winds and scoop you over here straight away, but that wouldn't have been right. I had to give you the chance to pour oil on the troubled waters." He sighed happily before adding: "You will come, won't you?"

"Come where, Bishop?"

"Oh good heavens, I've omitted the crucial explanation! I really must be going senile, but perhaps I'm simply dazed by my unexpected good luck. My dear fellow, haven't you heard about our crisis at the Theological College here in the Close?"

"As a matter of fact Father Watson did mention—"

"As the result of the War the shortage of teachers has become so acute that the principal's now saying he'll have to close the college unless he has at least one more experienced priest who can not only shoulder the burden of teaching but also assist with the spiritual direction—"

"Spiritual direction!"

"Yes, just up your street, isn't it, but of course I didn't know you had the right teaching experience. Quite obviously you're heaven-sent! I must arrange an interview with the principal at once."

By this time my curiosity had triumphed over my elation. "Before you do that, Bishop," I said swiftly as he reached for the telephone, "may I ask who eventually told you that I'd been the Master of Novices at Ruydale?" I knew Francis was more than capable of intervening on my behalf, but I had expected no intervention until I had served the full six months allocated to my ministry of reconciliation at Starrington.

"It was the most remarkable coincidence," said Dr. Ottershaw cosily, forgetting the telephone and settling down to gossip. "My predecessor Dr. Jardine is visiting Starbridge at present and staying with the Aysgarths. Jardine always took a keen interest in the Theological College when he was Bishop so naturally he asked how it was faring and when Aysgarth told him about the crisis he said: 'The solution's sitting right here in your diocese,' and began to talk of your achievements at Ruydale. Oh, he knew all about you! Apparently he'd been obliged to search for a spiritual director once for a young clerical acquaintance of his who was in deep trouble, and you were recommended to him by—"

"Yes, I remember the case. So Dr. Jardine's back in Starbridge! I wonder why."

"He's been busy looking up some of the official papers relating to his episcopate—did you know he was writing his memoirs? They say the Archbishop—no, Lord Lang we must call him, mustn't we, now that he's retired with a peerage—they say Lord Lang can hardly sleep a wink at night for fear of what the book may contain! Jardine, as I'm sure you remember, had a very singular approach to the truth."

"Very singular."

"Not that I wish to criticise him in any way," said Dr. Ottershaw hastily, "and really how fortunate it is that he should have turned up in Starbridge at the exact moment when I needed his help! But I'm jumping the gun—here I am, talking as if I've already captured you and I haven't even given you the chance to decline the offer! How arrogant of me! But I do hope you don't feel God has other plans for you."

"Now that I've had the chance to pour oil on the Starrington waters I hope I can make some contribution, no matter how small, to the welfare of the Theological College," I said with a humility which would have satisfied even Father Darcy's exacting standards. "I'm happy to serve wherever you think I'm needed, Bishop."

"Splendid!" said Dr. Ottershaw. "What a load off my mind! You must see the principal without delay." And expelling a vast sigh of relief he once more reached happily for the telephone.

II

TWO hours later after my interview with the principal I walked from the Cathedral Close to the church of St. Martin's-in-Cripplegate and knocked on the door of the vicarage nearby.

"I've just been offered a post at the Theological College," I said as I entered Aysgarth's study, "and since I hear the offer stemmed from information provided by your guest, I thought I'd call to thank him. I also called to say, of course, that I hope you and I will find it easier to be civil to each other now that I'm not busy turning an exemplary parish into an archdeacon's nightmare."

Aysgarth gave the shy smile which was so much at odds with his brutal mouth. He said: "You'll have noticed that I've had no complaints since you resumed your curacy. But I'm glad you've finally accepted work commensurate with your gifts." He turned aside adding: "I'll call Dr. Jardine," but the summons proved unnecessary. The next moment the door opened and in walked the former Bishop of Starbridge, flaunting his premature retirement by wearing an immaculately cut grey lounge suit, a daring tie, an elegant fob-watch and—horror of horrors—a carnation in his buttonhole.

It would of course be possible to write a long description of such a celebrated controversial figure as Dr. Alexander Jardine, but I shall leave his daring Modernist views to the theologians, his nouveau-riche episco-

pal extravagances to the social historians, his combative fiery personality
to the psychologists, his personal attractions to the ladies and his career
as a priest to God. My own brief description of his apparel, so monstrously inappropriate even for a retired churchman, will, I trust, convey
both the essence of his debonair attitude to life and my own opinion of
a priest who feels called to court all the publicity which unfortunately
the press are only too happy to provide.

"So we meet again!" he exclaimed as if we were in the habit of
bumping into each other, but in fact I had only met him once before.
After he had retired from his bishopric in 1937 he had come to Grantchester to seek advice about his future from someone who by chance knew
rather more about him than most people did, but since he was the kind
of man who seeks advice but seldom takes it, our meeting had hardly been
fruitful. During our interview I had done my best to overcome my
antipathy sufficiently to treat him with charity; nevertheless when I heard
no more from him afterwards I had assumed my charity had failed to ring
true, and the news that morning of his benign intervention on my behalf
had come as a considerable surprise to me.

"Well!" said Jardine, as I reflected on Dr. Ottershaw's reminder that
sometimes God did indeed move in mysterious ways. "Do we shake
hands?"

"I can't imagine why not."

"No? Back in 1937 I received the distinct impression that you disapproved of me!"

I saw then that my disapproval had rankled with him and that his
present intervention represented a desire to prove to me that he was not
such a bad fellow after all. I regarded this as an indication of a disturbed
psyche. We should not spend our time worrying obsessively about what
others may think of us; this shows an unhealthy preoccupation with the
self.

"If I gave you the impression of disapproval," I said, "then I must take
the blame for the unsatisfactory nature of our meeting. I'm glad to see
you well, Jardine, and I'm greatly in your debt for enlightening Dr.
Ottershaw about my career at Ruydale."

"That old scatterbrain! I assure you that if *I'd* still been occupying the
palace, you wouldn't have been left to moulder for months in a rural
backwater!"

Seeing my expression as I mentally reeled in the face of such bump-
tious discourtesy to Dr. Ottershaw, Aysgarth said in a rapid attempt
to change the subject: "Have you heard that Dr. Jardine's writing his
memoirs?"

"Yes," I said, "I understand that's the reason for his visit to Starbridge."

I turned to Jardine. "Or are the memoirs merely providing an excuse to look up old friends?"

"Now why should you make me feel as if even looking up old friends is a sin? What a very formidable fellow you are when you radiate that chilling austerity!" said Jardine lightly, and added amused: "You should warm up a little by writing your own memoirs—I'm sure they'd make fascinating reading!"

"On the contrary," I said, "you know as well as I do that when one's a priest all the best stories can never be told." I turned to take my leave of Aysgarth but Jardine remained determined to engage me in conversation, and suddenly beneath the mask of levity I sensed the complex, restless priest who was lonely enough to resent my lack of warmth. With a sinking heart I realised that I had to make a new effort to be charitable, and reminding myself of Jardine's recent important intervention in my life, I began to wonder if God had propelled me into this meeting for some special purpose. As far as I could see I had merely called at the vicarage of my own free will in order to be polite.

"Before you rush off," Jardine was saying, "you must let me congratulate you belatedly on your marriage. A wife who I'm told is charming and intelligent as well as good and devout is indeed one of the ultimate prizes . . . Have you ever talked to Father Darrow, Neville, about your quest for the ultimate prizes?"

Aysgarth at once said: "No," and looked wary, but his mentor ignored this hint that the subject should not be pursued. "Neville grew up in adverse circumstances," he explained to me, "and in order to inspire himself into surmounting them, he saw life as a quest for prizes—not just the commonplace prizes which were available to people from more comfortable backgrounds, but the ultimate prizes—the common prizes glorified. What this means in practical terms, of course, is that Neville's always chasing perfection."

Aysgarth cleared his throat. "Before Mr. Darrow reminds me that perfection is unattainable in this world, may I make it clear that I'm not a monster of worldly ambition? My one desire is to serve God to the best of my ability—"

"—and what's wrong with worldly ambition if it helps you fulfill that exceedingly laudable aim? For example, you're surely not ashamed of your Balliol scholarship which led you into a world where you could at last approach Christianity intellectually!"

"Well, I do agree, certainly, that the ultimate prize of a place at Oxford represents worldly ambition in its most acceptable form, but I'm sure Mr. Darrow's thinking—"

"Darrow's wound up with the perfect wife, the perfect home and the perfect new career—all ultimate prizes—so don't start imagining that he's too holy to know what ambition means! Why, I'll wager that at this very moment he's savouring his prospects at the Theological College and calculating his chances of becoming the principal!"

Aysgarth looked so acutely embarrassed that I decided it was time to ride to his rescue. "Come now, Jardine!" I said in the voice of an abbot addressing a boisterous monk who was continually smitten by the urge to show off. "You're just being provocative because you want to puncture what you've mistakenly diagnosed as hypocrisy on Aysgarth's part and priggishness on mine. In actual fact Aysgarth's very properly modifying your cavalier attitude to worldly ambition, and my expression of amazement which no doubt greeted your remarks springs not from priggishness but from concern. Surely a priest of your eminence should be declaring that true perfection lies only in the absolute values and that the ultimate prize for any soul can only be union with God?"

I had thought that this shaft would put the Bishop firmly in his place but I was mistaken. "My dear Darrow," he said exasperated, "have you entirely lost your sense of humour? I sincerely hope you didn't leave it behind with your habit when you left the cloister!"

"I haven't lost my sense of humour—I've merely retained my good taste. Good-day to you both and God bless you," I said in a tone which would have silenced even the most recalcitrant monk, and strode from the room without looking back.

I 2

ON the train to Starrington I conceded that I had responded too severely to Jardine's remarks and regretted that I had not been more patient with a man who was obviously unhappy. His bitter comment about my wife, home and new career indicated jealousy; his jibe about my ambition to run the Theological College suggested that his desire for my approval had declined into a resentful dislike when that approval had failed to appear. I had never thought Jardine spiritually gifted. Now, with his career cut short and his time devoted to the dubious art of autobiography, a form of writing in which both honesty and humility are famous for their absence, he seemed to be drifting deeper into a spiritual dead-end.

Remembering my speculation that God might have propelled me into the interview, I wondered if I was supposed to assist Jardine in some way, but I remained convinced that he was beyond my help, particularly now that our antipathy had hardened. Then I wondered if I was supposed to help Aysgarth; I was in fact deeply concerned that a young priest of such promise should have such a questionable mentor, but I could hardly offer my services as a counsellor unless I were invited to do so, and it seemed highly unlikely that Aysgarth, mindful of our past antagonism, would ever turn to me for help.

I thought of him, clever efficient Aysgarth, running his private and public lives with such conspicuous success, and I wondered what went on in his head when he talked to God. However one of the commonest errors a counsellor can make is to assume everyone is secretly writhing beneath the weight of intractable problems. Perhaps Aysgarth was one of those fortunate people who sail through life without encountering any major difficulties. Perhaps after surmounting his troubled background his path through life had been enviably smooth.

I might have continued to speculate for some time in this idle and unprofitable fashion, but I was too excited about my new career to ponder on Aysgarth for long. When I arrived home I found that Anne was out, visiting Romaine to discover whether she had succeeded in embarking on a second pregnancy, so I hurried straight to my cell to write to Francis. By this time my room was a cell no more; it had become a study, a silent witness to my final adjustment to the world. I had possessions. The room now boasted four shelves of books, a modern lamp, an easy-chair with a footstool (had I finally come to terms with old age?) and a pretty water-colour of the chapel which my granddaughter had painted from the sketch drawn on her Easter visit. On the shelf above the fireplace stood the photographs of my family, including my grandson in his new Naval uniform. I felt very pleased that Colin had chosen to serve in the Navy; I thought it would give us something to talk about at last. For a second I prayed, as I did every day, for his safety, but then I turned aside from all thoughts of the War and fingered the plain wooden frame which I had made to hold the photograph of my parents on their wedding day.

I pictured my father's reaction to my appointment. "The Theological College at Starbridge? Very distinguished! And how suited to your gifts—what scope for a rewarding career!" he would have said with genuine pleasure, and as his words echoed in my imagination I found myself wondering if I would indeed wind up running the Theological College. But of course that sort of idle thought, reeking of worldly ambition, came straight from the Devil and had to be ruthlessly suppressed. My task was to serve God, not to serve myself by pursuing the road to self-aggrandisement, and suddenly I was thinking of Aysgarth again, Aysgarth and his ultimate prizes.

It occurred to me then that God in His subtle way had propelled me into that interview at the vicarage not so that I could help either Jardine or Aysgarth (how arrogant that I should have automatically assumed I was being called in to play the wonder-worker!) but so that I should be prompted to meditate deeply, before I began my new career in the world, on the nature of ambition and its often ambivalent fruits. Of course one should regard any expression of ambition with suspicion, even if it appeared not to be centred on the self, but had I perhaps defined ambition's ultimate prize too narrowly when I had declared it could only consist of the soul's union with God? Perhaps Jardine had not after all been so wildly astray in taking a broader view and Aysgarth's chase for the prizes should not be automatically condemned. If perfection lay in the absolute values, that bridge between our world and ultimate reality, then perfection could be grasped by embracing those absolute values and trying to incorporate them into one's daily life. Naturally one's success would be limited, since the human race could never fully achieve perfection on this earth, but the absolute values could indeed be seen as ultimate prizes, something for man to aim at, a target for his innate acquisitive streak, a symbol luring him to stretch upwards to a better life when he might otherwise sink downwards into an animal existence which was unworthy of his unique power of reason and self-awareness.

I saw then in a moment of revelation that I too had gone chasing the prizes, the ultimate prizes of Truth, Beauty and Love, and now at last my quest had borne recognisable fruit: I had grasped the Truth about my past, an achievement which had set me free to serve God in a new way; I had found the chapel, that symbol of Beauty, which would forever stand at the centre of my life, and I had in Anne received the Love that made me whole and would eventually transform me, so I hoped, into a better man.

As I thought of those absolute values which reflected the spiritual world I suddenly saw them as Plotinus would have seen them, overflowing from the fountainhead past tier after tier of existence, the waters of ultimate reality bathing the world in light. Then I thought how the Christians had adapted Platonism, centring the absolute values in the person of Christ and the presence of the Holy Spirit which poured forth through the world into the minds and hearts of men. Why had not Plotinus become a Christian? I had often asked myself that question but Plotinus had left no answer. Perhaps he had disliked the organisation of the Early Church; mystics are notoriously antipathetic to organisations. Or perhaps he had merely felt that Christianity was a bastard religion, half-Hellenic, half-Semitic, just another syncretistic approach to the One, an approach which could only fall short of the glories of Greek philosophy. Or perhaps he had even felt that to be Christian in those days was to limit oneself to one sect, a prospect which would not have interested him as he strove to address all mankind. "The mystical faculty," Plotinus had declared encouragingly, "is one which all possess but few use." Could he conceivably have felt that those who used it could dispense with organised religion and that organised religion itself was only an aid to enlightenment for those whose mystical faculty would have remained otherwise undeveloped? This was the age-old trap which had ensnared so many mystics, but it was hard to imagine Plotinus, described by his disciple Porphyry as a man of great goodness and humility, ever being arrogant enough to divorce his mysticism from a formal religious context. Plotinus had been a deeply religious philosopher, and in his formal Hellenism mysticism and religion were inextricably entwined.

As I had discovered in my younger days, a mystic who dispenses with a religious framework lays himself open to corruption. But on the other hand a religious who tries to discard mysticism lays a dead hand on his spiritual life. Mysticism is the raw material of religion, as I had once said to Janet; without raw materials building is impossible, and without a structure designed by architects raw materials remain raw materials. However although the raw materials of mysticism can be found worldwide as they permeate all the great religions, the architecture which springs from them is as varied as the human race itself. The mystics may all speak the same language but the language has many dialects, and for me, if not for Plotinus, there was one voice which spoke that language more finely than any other, the voice of Christ as recreated by the Fourth Evangelist in one of the greatest mystical tracts ever written, the voice of St. John proclaiming the eternal values of ultimate reality as he unveiled the great mystery of the Incarnation.

I was still meditating on the Fourth Gospel and thinking what a model of clarity it was when compared with Plotinus' obscure, tortuous prose when Anne returned home with good news from Romaine.

"The baby's coming for Christmas!" she said, kissing me. "Alan said he hoped it wouldn't disrupt Matins!" And without giving me time to respond she asked me what had happened in Starbridge.

Sensing her fear that I might still be lukewarm about fatherhood, I took care to reassure her by postponing a full account of my own news and returning at once to the subject of the baby. "Now that I've got over my arrogant, self-centred desire for a replica by conquering my past unhappiness," I declared, "I shall look forward to this infant's arrival in the hope that we'll have a daughter who'll take after you. Then I'm sure I shall find parenthood very pleasant."

Anne was sufficiently relieved to exclaim generously: "I think a replica of you would be rather fun!"

"Oh no, it wouldn't!" I said with a shudder. "In fact I can see now what hell it would be to have a son who was as proud, arrogant, wilful and obstinate as I am—what would happen to my dreams of a peaceful old age? Life would be one long battle!"

"Nonsense!" said Anne firmly. "Anyway we can't have a girl because I've just had the most brilliant idea for a boy's name. Darling, as the baby will always be able to claim he was brought by the reindeer instead of by the boring old stork, why don't we call him after Father Christmas?"

"Father Christmas?"

"St. Nicholas!" said Anne happily, enrapt by her cleverness. "Don't you think that's the perfect solution?"

Utterly speechless I pulled her into my arms and wondered when I had last felt so ambivalent.

Author's Note

THE character of Jon Darrow is fictitious.

Darrow's religious thought is derived from the writings of William Ralph Inge (1860–1954), one of the leading intellectuals in the Church of England in the late nineteenth and early twentieth century. Educated at Eton and at King's College, Cambridge, where he obtained a first in classics, he then taught at Eton before being ordained in 1888. Following his ordination he became a fellow of Hertford College, Oxford, where Idealist philosophy was in the ascendant, and it was there that he turned from pure scholarship towards metaphysics.

In 1895 he began to read the work of Plotinus, first of the philosophers now called Neo-Platonists, and his encounter with Neo-Platonism led him to make a special study of Christian Mysticism, the subject of his famous Bampton Lectures in 1899. Inge played a leading role in the twentieth-century revival of interest in mysticism. He believed that this human experience of the presence of God provided an indestructible religious truth which the current attacks on the institutional churches and the authority of the Bible could not touch; in his view the mystical experience of God, vouched for in a similar manner amidst different religions at different times and in different places, represented a timeless witness to a reality that was not subject to passing fashions in theological or philosophical thought. Inge saw reality as the spiritual world, a kingdom of values which he equated with the Platonic doctrine of Ideas. When accused of being more of a Platonist than a Christian, his response was that in his opinion the Christian doctrine of the Incarnation perfected and completed the philosophical system of his much-admired Plotinus.

Inge was a successful, though strikingly individual churchman; using modern terminology one could say that although he operated "within the system" he was not "an organisation man." In 1904 his great friend Herbert Hensley Henson, then Rector of St. Margaret's, Westminster, and later to be Bishop of

Durham, offered him the living of All Saints', Ennismore Gardens, and in accepting the offer Inge at last moved from Oxford to the capital (and from bachelorhood to matrimony). However in 1907 he returned to academic life; he became Lady Margaret Professor of Divinity at Cambridge where he remained until 1911. At that point he received his famous preferment: he was appointed Dean of St. Paul's Cathedral, a post he held for twenty-three years. After his retirement he continued his writing, both scholarly and journalistic, and the fruits of a lifetime's study of mysticism were displayed in his last book, *Mysticism in Religion,* published when he was eighty-eight.

Inge was brought up in the High Church tradition but gradually he detached himself not only from the Anglo-Catholics but from the Evangelicals, the two powerful opposing wings of the Church. He claimed to represent a third party within the Church; he saw his "religion of the spirit" as not only embodying the highest wisdom of the past but offering a profound spiritual relevance to the world of today and tomorrow. In *The Platonic Tradition in English Religious Thought,* he wrote:

> My contention is that besides the combative Catholic and Protestant elements in the Churches, there has always been a third element, with very honourable traditions, which came to life again at the Renaissance, but really reaches back to the Greek fathers, to St. Paul and St. John, and further back still. The characteristics of this type of Christianity are—a spiritual religion based on a firm belief in absolute and eternal values as the most real things in the universe—a confidence that these values are knowable by man—a belief that they can nevertheless be known only by wholehearted consecration of the intellect, will and affections to the great quest—an entirely open mind towards the discoveries of science—a reverent and receptive attitude to the beauty, sublimity and wisdom of the creation, as a revelation of the mind and character of the Creator—a complete indifference to the current valuations of the worldling.

It is this religion of the spirit which I have tried to reflect in the character of Jon Darrow.

GLAMOROUS POWERS is the second of a series of novels about the Church of England in the twentieth century. The first novel, *Glittering Images,* was narrated by Charles Ashworth and set in 1937. The third novel, *Ultimate Prizes,* will focus on Neville Aysgarth after the War.

A NOTE ON THE TYPE

THE TEXT of this book was set in Bembo, a facsimile
of a typeface cut by one of the most celebrated
goldsmiths of his time, Francesco Griffo, for Aldus
Manutius, the Venetian printer, in 1495. The face was
named for Pietro Bembo, the author of the small treatise
entitled De Aetna in which it first appeared. Through
the research of Stanley Morison, it is now acknowledged
that all old-face type designs up to the time of William
Caslon can be traced to the Bembo cut.

THE present-day version of Bembo was introduced by
the Monotype Corporation, London, in 1929. Sturdy,
well balanced, and finely proportioned, Bembo is a face
of rare beauty and great legibility in all of its sizes.

Composed by The Haddon Craftsmen, Inc.,
Scranton, Pennsylvania
Printed and bound by Fairfield Graphics,
Fairfield, Pennsylvania
Book and ornament designed by
Margaret Wagner